CHANGE IN

Library of Congress Control Number:		2007903846
ISBN:	Hardcover	978-1-4257-6966-6
	Softcover	978-1-4257-6954-3

To order additional copies of this book, contact:
Xlibris Corporation
1-888-795-4274
www.Xlibris.com
Orders@Xlibris.com
37712

To Tommy,
My best friend and soulmate.

CHAPTER 1

I t was a typical fall day. The temperature held only a slight coolness, the leaves on the verge of bursting into their brilliant magnificence of colors. Unchangeable leaves blew in the wind, creating wayward patterns in the air. A crispness was on the edge of every breath inhaled, causing Amanda to smile up at the sun. Adjusting the strap of her bag on her shoulder, she closed her sweater a little tighter around her waist.

The college campus was set in the New York countryside. Beautiful historical buildings covered in century-old ivy. The search for knowledge by students of the past and the present echoed in the hallways. Academically driven herself, Amanda felt honored every day to be a part of this campus. Pulling open the large oak door leading into the academic building that loomed before her, she greeted several friends. Continuing upstairs, she walked to the second floor to her advisor's office. Hesitating before the door, she read the bold black letters painted on the frosted glass: *Maureen Williams, Ph.D.*

She knocked lightly and then stuck her head through the small opening she made.

"Mrs. Williams?" she called out and saw her talking on the telephone. Mrs. Williams smiled and waved her into the room. With hand motions, she let her know she was almost done. Amanda settled herself in the seat across from her. Picking up a magazine that was sitting on Mrs. Williams's desk, she started to look through it as her advisor finished up her conversation. As Amanda flipped casually through the pages, she glanced up at her advisor. Maureen Williams was a force to be reckoned with. A mass of graying hair was always twisted at the top of her head in a pile of frizzy curls, held up only by a pencil, always on the verge of falling out yet never doing so. Her features were strong; her brown eyes were kind. As a professor, her standards were high; as an advisor, she was always encouraging.

Within moments, Mrs. Williams was hanging up the phone and smiling her greetings again to Amanda.

"Amanda, sorry about that." She smiled. "How are you?" she asked as she shifted some papers around, looking for something in particular.

Amanda set the magazine down, smiling in return, stating, "I'm doing good!"

"Good . . . good," Mrs. Williams said. Then she found the papers she was looking for. Looking up at Amanda, she once again realized what a beautiful girl she was. She had long blond hair, so blond that it appeared almost white. Her large blue eyes seemed to sparkle with the joy she seemed to find in the things around her. Her face was small, framed by her thick hair, and her lips always gave the impression of being slightly puffy. When she smiled, her whole face lit up. She was petite and in shape. There were numerous times she'd run into Amanda jogging around campus or playing volleyball in the quad. She was popular with her peers as well. She liked Amanda, yet her reasons for this had nothing to do with her sweet appearance. Her personality and character were what pleased her advisor. She was a disciplined student and very determined to make the best of her time here.

"Now," Mrs. Williams began, "I ran into Mr. Montgomery last week."

Nodding, Amanda folded her hands in her lap. Mr. Montgomery was her history professor, and the mention of his name sent anxiety coursing through her mind. Amanda had a lot of respect for him, though he didn't have the reputation of being the friendliest of men. *What did he have to say about me*, she wondered.

Smiling, Mrs. Williams said, "I see I caught your interest. We were talking about this team he's putting together for the Foundation Committee of the Historical Society." *Now this was interesting,* Amanda thought as she sat up straighter in her seat. "Well, your name came up." Amanda's eyes widened.

"My name?" she asked in surprise. Enjoying his class, she worked hard to keep up with his standard of performance, but she never realized he even noticed her. Mrs. Williams smiled.

"Yes. He seems very impressed with your dedication to your studies and your passion for history." After pausing, she then continued, "You do know how influential it would be to have the Foundation Committee on your college resume, do you not?"

Amanda nodded excitedly. "Yes, I do," she declared. "I've known about the Foundation since I was a child—my father was a member of the National Committee. It's always been of great interest to me."

"Good." Mrs. Williams smiled knowingly. "Well. This is an assignment from Professor Montgomery," she said, handing Amanda a packet of papers across the desk. Amanda took the packet with shaking hands. She eagerly began to review the contents. "He's informed me that if you complete this thesis, on the particular topic he has listed, twenty pages, all the specifics—and if it's as excellent as your past work", she paused intentionally, "you'll be guaranteed a place on his committee." Amanda's eyes were positively glowing as she stood up excitedly.

"I don't know what to say, Mrs. Williams!" she declared breathlessly. "I never imagined being a member as a sophomore. I'm . . . I'm honored." Mrs. Williams stood up as well.

"As you should be, Amanda. This is a great opportunity and you've worked very hard to be offered as such. Now." She smiled. "You have some research and writing to do, don't you?"

"Yes, ma'am," she said, shaking Mrs. Williams's hand. "Thank you so much, Mrs. Williams."

"Don't thank me, young lady. You've done all the work," she declared. "Good luck to you!" she called out to her as Amanda left her office, walking down the hall.

Amanda stepped back out into the sunshine, so excited she felt like she was going to burst. Glancing at her watch, she mentally calculated the time she had until her next class. Estimating it wasn't for another forty-five minutes, she decided to go to her apartment, which was off Main Street. She needed to call her parents to tell them her news.

She reviewed the paperwork more thoroughly as she walked, already knowing she was familiar with the material and the topic. This wouldn't even be work for her, she thought excitedly. As she continued to read on, she stopped, suddenly feeling a chill creep up her spine. Looking up from her papers, she almost had the feeling she was being watched. Her eyes squinted against the sun as she scanned her surroundings. A slight breeze lifted and teased her hair as she again noticed what a beautiful day it was. Seeing nothing out of the ordinary, she smiled and shook the silly feeling off.

Amanda continued walking, and as she turned the corner, she ran into her roommate, Shelby.

"Shelby!" she said with delight. "You're never going to believe what I just found out!" Shelby and Amanda had been roommates as freshmen and couldn't be more opposite in looks and personality. With as much energy Amanda put into her studying, Shelby put it into partying. A carefree, restless spirit was Shelby. But they were the best of friends. Shelby carried her tall curvaceous body with complete confidence. With one toss of her long dark curls, boys would gather. It both amazed and amused Amanda. Her dark eyes were shaded by long lashes, and her full lips curved perfectly into a seductive smile. She exuded a vibrant energy that easily allowed her to be the center of attention.

"What? *What?*" she asked, seeing how excited Amanda was.

"I've just been offered a spot on the Foundation Committee!" she announced. Shelby's eyes widened as she screamed, "No way!" She grabbed Amanda's arms, and they jumped around, screaming, being silly. When they stopped jumping, Shelby hugged Amanda.

"Okay, now what *is* the Foundation Committee?" she asked. Amanda laughed and gave her a playful slap.

"It's only the greatest honor I can receive as a history major!" she declared with feigned exasperation. Shaking her head, Amanda sobered. "This is like the best thing that's ever happened to me."

"Oh, Amanda, I'm so happy for you. It couldn't have happened to a better person." She touched her friend's arm lightly. "I know how hard you work. Whatever this foundation is, you deserve it."

"Thank you, I think." Amanda chuckled. "I'm on my way to call my parents. I can't wait to tell them."

"Okay, I have class—," she started to say, frowning as she looked at her watch, then smiled sheepishly. "Well, I *had* class. I guess I got up a little late this morning."

"I guess you got home a little late last night, or should I say this morning?" Shelby shrugged her shoulders. "A girl has to have some fun, doesn't she?" She beamed a smile at Amanda. "I'm going to head over to Eddie's for some coffee. Meet me over there after you make your call."

"Okay, I will. But I can only stay for a few minutes, I have class."

"All right, I'll see you in a few." With that, Shelby crossed the street, calling out a greeting to another friend.

Amanda entered their apartment building, walking up the stairs and digging for her keys in her bag at the same time. Dropping her bag onto the floor just inside the door, she breathlessly reached for the phone. Dialing the number for the law firm, she assumed both her parents would be there.

"Tanner, Albert, and Finney Law Offices, may I help you?" answered Sheila, the receptionist.

"Hi, Sheila!" she greeted cheerfully. "It's Amanda."

"Hi, honey? How are you?" she asked sincerely. "How's school going?"

"Great!" she declared. "Is my dad around?" She was barely able to keep her excitement contained.

"Yes, he is," she said. "He'll be so happy to hear from you. Just hold a minute, all right?"

"Sure." Moments later, she heard her father's voice over the line.

"Hi, love! What a nice surprise." he greeted her. "Is everything okay?"

"Hi, Daddy!" she practically squealed. "I'm fine. You'll never guess what happened today." He chuckled at the enthusiasm in her voice.

"You're right, I probably won't. What happened?"

"Mr. Montgomery is offering me a place on his Foundation Committee!" she exclaimed. "Can you believe it?"

"Amanda, that's wonderful!" he exclaimed. "When did this happen? When did you find out?"

"Just a little while ago," she laughed. "I need to write a thesis for him, and he said that if it's like my other work then I'm guaranteed a spot on his team."

"Oh, honey, I'm so proud of you! But not surprised." He added, "I knew you would be noticed there. Congratulations!"

"Thank you, Daddy!" She beamed into the phone. "I'm going to start my paper tonight. I can't believe that it's a topic I adore! Just imagine, Daddy, you'll soon see my name on the members list of the Foundation Committee."

"You'll be the light in the stuffy old crone's world." He smiled into the phone. She laughed.

"Is Mom there?" she asked.

"No, she's in court today," he said. "Do you want to wait to tell her yourself, or do you want me to tell her?"

"You can tell her," she said. "I have classes the rest of the day, then I'm going to the library to start working."

"Okay, honey. How are you otherwise? Do you need any money or anything?" he asked.

"No, I'm good," she said. Then, whispering breathlessly, she added, "Daddy, I'm so excited."

"I know you are. I am too. I want a copy of that thesis," he said softly. "You're going to do great!"

"Thank you. I love you, Dad," she said. "Tell Mom I love her too and I'll call her tomorrow."

"I love you too, sweetheart. I'll tell her."

After hanging up, Amanda sat quietly with her thoughts. Then she stood, gathered her belongings once again, and left to meet Shelby for coffee.

Amanda leaned her head back and closed her eyes. She was tired. Glancing at her watch, she saw that it was close to eleven. With the library closing in an hour, she contemplated staying until then.

"Don't even think about it," said a masculine voice. Startled, she looked up into the beautiful brown eyes of Jared Evans. "I know that look, and you've worked long enough!"

She smiled tiredly. Jared worked at the library on a regular basis. With Amanda's determination and hard studying, she spent most of her time in the old building, and they had become fast friends. He had dark brown hair that parted to the side and was a little long, only enhancing his adorable face. His smile was slightly crooked, one side of his mouth going up more than the other, which made him more endearing. He carried himself with a great deal of confidence and had a great sense of humor.

There had been many a night when they would have hours of conversation on topics that would probably seem boring to most, yet the two of them would be animated and intent in the discussion. Jared always went out of his way to visit with her even if it was just for a few minutes. When a group of her friends got together, she would invite him along, enjoying spending time with him when she wasn't buried in her work. She noticed his extra attention; she couldn't say she wasn't flattered, but she would be the first to admit she was a bit of an overachiever. Because of that, she didn't allow much time for relationships. On nights like tonight, when she was so tired, she contemplated letting her guard down and letting him in.

"I am tired," she admitted wearily. He sat down across from her and closed the books that lay in front of her.

"You've been here since five thirty," he teased, but he was concerned. "You can *not* stay until closing. You need some rest."

She nodded, sighing. "You're right. But then, you always are."

"Oh my, you *are* tired, aren't you?" He chuckled as he folded some more papers and stacked her books.

"I guess I did get a little overexcited about starting this," she said, covering her mouth as a yawn snuck up on her. "But I can't complete it in one night." He stood up and came around the back of her chair, resting his hands lightly on her shoulders, beginning to gently massage them. Sighing again, she leaned into his hands. "Oh, that feels wonderful."

"Yes, a little excited. Old Montgomery isn't expecting you to finish in it one night either. We both know how important this is to you. If you're rested, you'll do better work." As he continued to massage her shoulders, Amanda felt her body relax under his hands.

"Amanda?"

"Mmmmm?"

He leaned over and spoke softly in her ear, "Let me walk you home." His soft voice was sending tingles down her back.

"Can you?" she asked, just as softly, tipping her head back to see his face. He nodded, and she didn't miss the heated look he gave her. A warmth slowly spread through her body, and she was too tired to fight her feelings. Opening herself up caused a whirlwind of emotions to fill her tired mind. Rising to her feet, she put away her things in her bag. He held her sweater out for her, and, stepping closer, she slipped her arms into the sleeves. He held his hand out for her, and she smiled and slipped her hand through his. "Aren't you supposed to stay until closing?"

"I've covered plenty of hours for Emily," he said, giving her hand a light squeeze. "She won't mind." On their way out, he stopped at the desk to pick up his belongings, speaking with Emily before he left. Rejoining her, they stepped out into the crisp fall night.

"Mmmmm." Amanda breathed in deeply. "Isn't fall just the best?" Letting go of his hand, she wrapped her arm around his, snuggling closer to him.

Smiling, he agreed. "Yeah, it is." They walked in silence for a few minutes, the wind blowing dried leaves around their feet. Passing a dorm hall, they heard laughter and loud music in the dark night.

"Amanda?" he asked softly.

"Hmm?"

"When are you going to let me take you out?" She remained quiet but gently squeezed his arm. "There's an attraction between us, you can't deny that. You must know that I care for you." Still hesitating in her response, she continued walking with him through the quad. Reaching the edge of campus, Amanda began, "Jared—" Without notice, he turned to her and took her face gently between his hands and kissed her. She instantly warmed from her nose to her toes. Moving toward him, she felt desire shoot through her, and she suddenly needed to be closer. Feeling the same, he deepened the kiss, wrapping his one arm around her waist and pulling her up against him. Sensations exploded through her, overwhelming her enough to pull back.

"Jared, I . . . my gosh," she whispered breathlessly. "Wait a minute."

He smiled, his eyes soaking in her features. "Amanda, you care for me, like I do for you," he said huskily. "And I know you want to be with me, like I want to be with you."

"Jared, I *do* care for you," she admitted, her hands resting on his shoulders.

"It's just that I don't think I'm prepared . . ." Her words trailed off. Unable to explain herself, she averted her eyes.

"Amanda." He smiled patiently. "We're not some project you can prepare for. What's between us just is." His last words were spoken softly.

Bringing her eyes back to his, she said, "But, Jared, my time is so limited—"

"Amanda, how long have we known each other?"

Shaking her head, she answered, "You already know that answer." She was slightly confused.

"Do *you?*"

"Of course I do. Jared, what does this have to do with—"

Placing a finger on her lips, he smiled again. "Just answer the question."

"Jared." She sighed. "It was a year on October eighth."

Smiling, he nodded. "Right. A year. I know you're schedule and I know you're routines." He paused. "I know *you*, Amanda Tanner. All I'm asking is to share some of that time with you."

Anxious, her eyes rapidly searched his. "But I can get so busy, and the Foundation Committee—"

"Then I'll be here waiting for you."

She reached up and touched his cheek gently. Without taking his eyes from her own, he covered her hand with his.

"It's not just that." She swallowed, pulling her hand out from under his, and stepped out of his arms. Walking a few steps away, she turned back to him, her eyebrows knitted together in distress.

"Then what, Amanda? Tell me."

Shaking her head, she answered, "I've avoided relationships for more than one reason." *This was humiliating*, she thought to herself. "I made a vow to myself, Jared." Pressing her hand to her forehead, she continued, "A vow that I would save myself for my husband and to keep myself pure." He smiled patiently.

Chuckling softly, he took a couple of steps toward her. "Amanda, I already know that. It's one of the things I love about you," he said softly. She searched his face anxiously.

"But you make me feel things that make me want more," she whispered, her body still throbbing after making contact with his.

"Amanda, I would never want you to break your vow. I have too much respect for you," he said.

"It's not *you* that I'm worried about," she whispered. He groaned and pulled her into his arms, holding her close. After a few moments, he spoke, "We'll take it slow, Amanda. We'll go as slow as you want, but let's just see what happens." He loosened his hold on her so he could see her face. "What *do* you want, Amanda?" he asked softly. She searched his eyes.

"To be a part of your life," she said softly. He leaned down and kissed her tenderly. Eventually they began walking again, Amanda holding tightly to his arm. They walked up Main Street and started to turn the corner to her apartment building and almost ran into two men walking quickly by them.

"Oh, sorry!" exclaimed Jared. "Excuse us," exclaimed Amanda. The men just kept walking, not even acknowledging their existence. Amanda and Jared looked at each other.

"What was that all about?" she asked. He shrugged his shoulders and watched them walk away.

"I don't know," he said.

"Did you see how they were dressed the same?" she asked. "How weird!" He smiled at her.

"No, I didn't see that." He pulled her back to his side. "I'm just glad that I'm walking you home." Nodding, she was happy that he was too. He walked her up the stairs and to her door. Amanda found a note sticking to the doorknob. Her stomach twisted as she read it.

"What's that?" Jared asked.

"Oh, it's a note from Shelby. She went out with Jake for a few drinks." She sighed. Concern crossed his face.

"Do you want me to hang out for a little while until she gets back?" he asked. Part of her wanted him to. She still wasn't comfortable living off campus and being alone at night. At least at the dorm there was always someone around when Shelby wasn't.

"Um . . . no," she said. "I'll be fine." She smiled up at him.

"You don't sound very convincing," he said, kissing her lightly on the lips. She wrapped her arms around his neck and kissed him back.

"I know," she said after the kiss had ended. "But I won't be a scaredy-cat."

"I can stay, Amanda," he assured her.

"I know," she said softly, reaching up to touch his lips with the tips of her fingers. "But I think I'm already liking this relationship thing too much."

He chuckled and pulled her to him again, hugging her.

"Okay," he said. "Lock this door as soon as you close it," he said. "I'll be on the other side waiting to hear the lock." She smiled.

"Okay, Dad," she teased. He leaned over and kissed her sweetly.

"Bye," he whispered.

"Bye," she whispered back, closing the door slowly. She locked the door with as much noise as possible so Jared could hear, and she then heard him whistling as he walked down the stairs.

Turning, she leaned against the door, a smile on her face. *Today had turned out to be quite an interesting day*, she thought to herself. She touched her lips gently. Sighing, she pushed away from the door and went to the kitchen to make some tea. She knew she would not be able to sleep without Shelby here, so she would have to occupy herself with something.

Returning a few minutes later with her tea, she grabbed one of her research books to review again. It wasn't long before her eyes began to blur, her neck was sore again, and her tea was cold.

A nice hot bath, she thought. *Yes, that would be nice.*

Walking into the bathroom, she turned the bathwater on and left the room to go get some candles from her bedroom. Suddenly she froze, her heart jumped into her throat. The front door was ajar. She hesitated, her breath locked in her lungs. Did Shelby come in when she was in the bathroom?

"Shelby?" she called out. Silence. Her heart began pounding loudly in her chest.

Remembering that she was making a lot of noise when she locked the door for Jared, she thought she probably just shook it loose. She tried to smile to herself, shaking her head as she closed the door and latched the lock. An overly active imagination was something she had never lacked.

Continuing to her room, she retrieved her candles and her robe and walked back down the hall. She pushed the bathroom door open; her eyes widened as she froze in terror. In that very moment, time seemed to stop. A sense of fear that she had never experienced rapidly spread through her. The large man dressed in dark clothing, his presence filling the small room, looked at her with cold, calculating eyes. She never felt the candles drop to the floor, or her robe slipping out of her hands. She turned to run, but someone grabbed her from behind. The strong arms wrapped around her, but she struggled. Terror driven, she kicked with her feet, her nails scratched at the arms that trapped her. Her cries escalated to screams, but within seconds, her mouth was covered, and a revolting odor filled her nose. She strained against the strength of the man, her fight abating as she struggled to breathe. The room became fuzzy. And then darkness fell, and her hands fell away, dropping limp to her sides.

CHAPTER 2

Amanda awoke shivering. Swallowing, she began to cough, trying to get that awful taste out of her mouth. Her throat burned. Her stomach lurched as her body tried to reject the foreign substance. Turning to her side, she rested her head on the floor. Slowly she forced her eyes to open, blinking, straining to focus on her surroundings. As she waited for her eyes to adjust, she took inventory of her shaking body. She was bone cold, and her body ached, but she didn't think that she had any serious injuries. Struggling to sit up, she bit her lip against the pain that shot through her, with her body stiff from her awkward position.

Blinking her eyes, she realized that she was in a shack. Light was streaming through the cracks in the walls, casting a strange, eerie pattern across her and the floor. It was only then, as she tried to push her hair out of her eyes, that she realized that her hands were bound in front of her. Squinting, she examined the strawlike twine that harshly bit into her wrists, turning her fingers red and swollen from lack of circulation. She choked on a sob, bringing her bound hands to her face. *Oh God, where was she?* she thought desperately. She remembered the dark terrifying figure that had been in her bathroom . . . *Why was he in my apartment? Why?* she screamed silently. Tears trickled down her cheeks, making a path through the dirt on her face as horrifying thoughts raced through her mind. What was he going to do to her? Why did he take her?

Looking around her, she saw that the floor was hard-packed dirt and the small room was completely empty, except for herself. Twigs, dried grass, and small debris scattered around her as a light breeze blew in through the cracks in the walls. Wide-eyed, her senses heightened, Amanda shifted herself up on her knees. A musty, sour odor permeated the dirt beneath her, mixed with the smell of . . . sap? Yes, sap from pine trees. Scanning the room, she saw a door. Bracing her bound hands on the cold dirt, she pushed herself shakily to her feet. Her knees trembled as she took small steps toward the wooden door. She stood before it, her swollen fingers touching the rough wood tentatively as her eyes scanned, searching for the doorknob. A sob escaped her throat, and she quickly covered her mouth when she realized there wasn't one. Shaking uncontrollably with fear, she began to pound on the door with her hands, sobbing and screaming,

"Help me! Help me, please! Someone . . . *please!*"

Slumped against the door, Amanda felt as if hours had passed. Her eyes were closed, her breathing ragged, her throat raw; her voice had finally given out. She allowed her body to slowly slip to the floor, feeling the rough wood scrape her sensitive skin through her clothes as she slid down.

Totally exhausted, she slowly brought her knees to her chest, resting her head on them; her crying had turned to quiet whimpering. *Oh, Daddy . . . please find me.* Her hands stung from her incessant pounding, and she was numb with cold. The sun was beginning to set, and dark shadows were falling on the small shack.

Her thoughts returned to her apartment; Amanda opened her eyes, remembering that there had been two men. Someone had grabbed her from behind and held her. She lifted her head and squinted in the dimming light at her nails. Broken and dark with dried blood, she couldn't tell if they pained her. She fought. She fought them, she thought, nodding her head stubbornly, taking a shaky breath, hoping she had caused them some pain even if it wasn't much. She wiped her face on her dirty white cotton sleeve and looked down at her filthy khakis and then noticed her brown loafers on her feet. *They must have taken them from her apartment!* she thought incredulously. *Why would they care if she had her shoes on?*

She buried her face in her knees again, trying to get warm. Jared. She could see his smile as they had said their good-byes only hours before. Her heart ached just to feel his arms around her again. *Jared, do you know where I am? Help me . . . are you looking for me?*

Tears slowly trickled down her face. *Am I going to die?* she thought. *What are they going to do to me?* Again horrible thoughts accosted her, fear building so much bile in her throat she scrambled to her knees, vomiting. When there was nothing left in her stomach, she fell to her side, rolling onto her back.

Amanda lay on the floor, cold, still, and unconscious.

There was movement outside, voices disturbing the night air.

Amanda twitched, slowly coming awake. Voices . . . they seemed so far away. Forcing herself to wake up, blinking her eyes rapidly, she tried to adjust her sight to the darkness. Flashes of light were bouncing back and forth outside the cabin as fear washed over her once again. Whimpering, she scurried across the hard dirt floor to one of the corners, trying to hide. But there wasn't anywhere to go.

The door shook and then opened. Amanda buried her face in her knees, her body trembling violently. *Please, leave me alone*, she begged silently.

"It's time!" boomed a deep male voice from the doorway. "Let's go," he demanded. Amanda slowly looked up; his large frame filled the doorway. He flashed the light in her face, causing her to wince. She tried to block the light with her hand as she squinted around it to try to see him.

Fear held her tongue.

"I said let's go!" he ordered gruffly. "Stand up!" She was still too terrified to move.

"Is she all right?" asked another male voice from behind him.

"She's fine!" he called over his shoulder, disgusted. He took a couple of steps closer to her. "If you don't move, I will move you myself." That worked. She struggled to stand, weak from cold and hunger. Dizziness assaulted her, and she leaned on the wooden wall. Gathering her strength, she hesitantly stepped toward him. Standing in the doorway, trembling, she stepped out slowly from the shack. Once outside, her mind clouded with exhaustion, her body weak; she struggled to focus. The shack was surrounded by large looming pine trees, the sky was brilliantly lit with stars. In the distance a coyote howled a lonely call to his far-off companions. Another dark figure was standing outside, waiting. Amanda was pushed toward him. She cried out as she stumbled, trying to keep her balance.

"Go!" he ordered. The other man held a flashlight, but not toward her face. He didn't seem as intimidating as the other man, but she couldn't see his face.

"I'll trail behind," the man grunted harshly from behind her. Then she heard footsteps walking away.

Amanda was shaking violently as she tried to see her captor. He seemed to be waiting for something, and then, suddenly, he came toward her. Flinching, she cried out when he took her arm and roughly led her into the woods. He walked fast, and she struggled to keep up with him. After losing her footing, causing her to stumble a couple of times, he seemed to slow his pace. Tears streamed down her cheeks as she fought against the pain and numbing cold. And the fear. Fear that was so great she could hardly breathe.

They had walked for some time before Amanda found the courage to speak. Nervously she looked over her shoulder for the other man, but all she saw was darkness.

"Where are you taking me?" she asked hoarsely. His head never turned, making no response as if he never heard her. Examining his profile, she saw that he didn't seem much older than herself. "Please? Please tell me what's happening. If it's money you want, my father . . . my father will pay you!"

No response came. She began to cry softly as she was forced to continue walking. She was so tired and so weak. When she slipped again, he stopped, patiently helping her up. Turning her toward him, he shut off his flashlight. She watched him shrug out of his light jacket then helplessly stood while he slipped the jacket onto her shoulders. He seemed to watch her for a few moments, and she slowly lifted her tired eyes to his shadowed face.

"It's not much farther," he said quietly. Then he took her arm and continued walking. *What's not?* she wondered, too tired to ask.

Before long, Amanda started to see lights through the trees. As they emerged out of the woods, she was amazed to see small cabins, built side by side, neatly set off to the side. She looked around her in confusion. *Where are they bringing me?* she thought. They turned the bend in the small dirt road, and there sat a small white church where lights were glowing and smoke billowed from the chimney.

When they reached the church steps, he stopped. Confused, Amanda looked at the man at her side as he turned to her. From the windows of the church, a warm light was cast on their faces. Fearfully Amanda looked from the building to her captor's face. What she saw could not have surprised her more. He *was* about her age, she was sure of it. His face was boyish, yet his skin appeared weathered, as if he spent a lot of time outdoors. His hair appeared to be brown, but she couldn't tell in the poor lighting. His eyes shone, the reflection hiding his eye color, but not the kindness. He too seemed to be searching her face, which filled her with fear and disgust. She looked away from him.

"You need to be prayed over by the people," he informed her. "It's a tradition."

"What?" she asked, just above a whisper. Turning back to him, she could see the turbulence of emotions tense across his face. He clenched his jaw as he pulled gently on her arm to lead her up the stairs. She pulled back, surprising him. "What tradition? I want to go home," she pleaded, fear on her small features. "Please, let me go home."

"Look, don't fight this," he said, taking hold of both her arms. "Just go in here, let them pray, so you can go get some rest. If you fight them . . ." He hesitated, looking at the door then turning back to her. "If you fight them, it won't be good."

"I don't want to go in there." She started to cry, suddenly terrified to go through those doors. "I want to go home, please . . . I don't understand what's happening." He tightened his grip on her as she panicked in his hands. She tried to pull away, to run, but he twisted her in his arms so that her back was now squeezed against his chest. They were both breathing hard.

"You need to do this," he huffed. "Or they will have someone else bring you in."

"They? Who?" she asked, terrified. "What's going to happen?"

"All they are going to do is pray over you," he assured her softly. "Nothing more, Amanda." She froze in his arms.

"You know my name," she whispered. She began to twist to face him, but he picked her up and carried her the rest of the way and pushed open the doors with his leg.

Amanda watched in amazement at the spectacle before her. The lights were so bright it took her a moment to adjust her eyes. The church was set up like any other. There were pews lining both sides, a worn wooden floor under their feet, and a large wooden cross hung on the temple. Hundreds of eyes rested on her, and not a noise was heard in the building.

The room became fuzzy as dizziness assaulted her; the young man still held on to her, but she was at least standing on her own. He walked her gently to the front, where a man stood holding a Bible. Amanda stared at the parishioners that were all dressed in black. The women wore veils over their heads, and the men watched her with scornful expressions. *This was a nightmare*, she cried to herself, *and she would wake up soon. She just had to.* The only noise that could be heard was a small whimpering, and she didn't realize that it was coming from her.

They stopped before the man in the front. He was tall, broad, and wore a long gray wool robe. His face was scarred with large pockmarks, and his skin was discolored. Below his bushy eyebrows were black beady eyes. The sight of him made her shiver, and the man holding her tightened his grip to keep her steady.

"Is this our newly saved child?" the man with the Bible asked in a loud, authoritative, and booming voice, causing Amanda to jump.

"Yes, Pastor," the man replied. The pastor nodded.

"Thank you, Matthew," he said as his eyes trailed down her body. "Well done." Amanda's eyes widened; she was dumbfounded. Newly saved child? Confused and frightened, she looked at the man that held her.

"Child, you have been chosen. You should feel blessed," the pastor spoke to her. "You will be cleansed, and we will return here next week at this time . . . for your wedding." He continued to speak, but his words became muffled in her ears. *My wedding?* she thought frantically. *What is happening? What is he talking about?* The room began to spin, and she collapsed in Matthew's arms.

CHAPTER 3

"Amanda!" called her father. He opened her bedroom door and popped his head in. She lifted her head off her pillow, grunting. "Get up, lazy! We have a jogging date this morning!" She grunted again.

"I'm up," she mumbled groggily. He laughed.

"Okay, I'll meet you in five."

Within ten minutes she met him outside, and in another three minutes they were running companionably with one another. After several blocks, he asked as they ran, "You know what?"

"Hmm?" she asked.

"I miss this!" he stated. She looked at him and smiled.

"Me too," she said.

"Are you all packed for the ride back?" he asked.

"Mostly."

"You have a heavy workload this semester. Are you ready for it?"

"Absolutely," she said, without hesitation. "Bring it on."

Chuckling, "That's my girl." Then, he asked, "Do you know how proud I am of you?" She looked at him and smiled.

"Yes, Daddy."

"Well, good, good," he said, smiling back. "Did I happen to mention how much I love you?" She giggled.

"Yes, Daddy!" she said. "Every day!"

"Good, good."

"When did my baby go and grow up?" he asked soberly. She looked at him. Smiling, she said, "Daddy, I'll always be your baby!"

"I'll always be here for you, Amanda, you know that?"

"I know, Daddy."

"Okay, enough sappy talk!" He smiled. "I'll race you back to the house." He ducked across a neighbor's yard.

"Daddy, you cheat!" she laughed and ran after him.

Amanda smiled with the memory. Stirring slightly, feeling warm and comfortable, she pressed her face deeper into the soft pillow.

Not smelling the coffee, she realized that she must have forgotten to set the timer, which wasn't like her. Sighing, she lazily stretched out her limbs.

"Good morning, miss!" Amanda froze. She opened her eyes to see a strange woman with red hair and that strange black attire standing over her. Her eyes widened, her heart raced, she scurried up to the top of the bed, bringing the covers with her. Horror washed over her as she realized she'd been dreaming.

"Now don't be frightened," she assured her with a kind smile. "I'm Molly. I'm here to help you with your cleansing."

"My . . . my what?" Amanda whispered. She pulled the covers tighter to her chest. Her breath caught in her chest, her trembling returned.

"Preparation for your wedding." Amanda began to shake her head, her heart pounding so loud she could hear it. *No no no!* she screamed to herself as she squeezed her eyes closed. *This is just a nightmare . . . it's not real . . . it's not real!* But to her horror, when she opened her eyes, the woman still stood before her.

"I'm . . . I'm not having a wedding," Amanda whispered. Molly smiled.

"I understand this is difficult," she said, "but I need to help you cleanse. It is my job." She walked out of the room and then came back with a white terry cloth robe. "You can change into this. We need to remove your worldly clothes." Cleanse . . . worldly . . . what kind of talk was this?

Amanda shook her head fearfully, looking around the room. Panic rose within her so quickly it caused her to gasp. She was in a small cabin of some sort—rustic and simple but moderately decorated. The bed she was in was connected to the wall; ironically, in any other situation, she would have thought it quite charming. Her eyes came to rest on the door that was off to the right.

Molly followed her vision.

"There is someone on the other side of the door," she said quietly. She set the robe on the bed. Amanda turned back to her.

"Where am I?" she asked her. "Can you help me?" She searched Molly's face desperately. But the woman called Molly just shook her head, compassion in her eyes.

"The only thing I can help you with is your cleansing," she said softly. She felt bad for the girl. It had been so long since she had felt what she must be feeling. She liked her life now and no longer missed the sinful world. "You need to accept that this is your new home. You've been given a great honor by being chosen by our people. We are God's people, and you will find happiness here."

Amanda stared at her in disbelief, the blood draining from her face. *Where the hell was she?* she screamed to herself.

"I don't want to be here. I didn't ask to be *chosen!*" she practically spat out the words. Anger began to rise in her, a rare emotion for her. "I'm not cleansing . . . I'm not getting married . . . leave me alone!" She was close to shouting now. Molly continued on as if Amanda hadn't spoken.

"Your bath is ready, hon," she said softly. "Your fiancé will be here to visit you in an hour. So you'll want to be properly dressed."

"I don't have a fiancé!" she yelled, her face becoming red. "I'm not marrying anyone! I want to go home." A sob wracked her body.

The door opened, startling Amanda, and a large man, dressed in black, stepped into the room. His presence alone was intimidating enough, and without realizing it, she cringed back.

"Are we having problems, Molly?" he asked her, his voice low, sounding hoarse.

"No, Simon, we're doing fine," she answered, looking calmly at Amanda. "We'll call you if we need you. You wouldn't mind helping with a bath if I need you to, right?" Amanda's eyes widened with fear as they flew back to Molly's face. The man called Simon looked at Amanda intently.

"Not at all," he said, his eyes not leaving Amanda.

"Good, thank you." She smiled sweetly at him. "That will be all."

He stepped back outside, and Molly turned back to Amanda.

"As I was saying," she continued as if there was no interruption, "you need to make the best of this. All of this"—she waved her hand around the room—"will all fall into place soon enough. Your fiancé is a wonderful man, so you have nothing to worry about. Now let's take that bath, it will make you feel better. The beauty oils are homemade and they are wonderful, if I do say so myself."

Terrified and frustrated, Amanda buried her face in the blanket and sobbed. *I just don't understand! Why is this happening to me?* She felt Molly's hand touch her shoulder lightly. Amanda looked up with a swollen, tear-streaked face.

"It's just a bath," she coaxed softly. "It will make you feel better. Come . . ." She took her hand and helped her stand up. But Amanda didn't want to feel better, she just wanted to go home. Molly led her into the bathroom where a steaming bath awaited her.

Molly handed her a towel and the robe. "Now I'll let you wash and dress, and I'll be in, in fifteen minutes." And then she left the room.

Amanda undressed numbly and slipped into the tub. The hot water did feel good on her skin. She watched the dirt from the last couple of days start to wash off. Grabbing the scrub brush that was set aside for her, she began scrubbing her body furiously. Her skin red and raw, she threw the brush away from her in frustration. Tears filled her eyes as she submerged her head underwater, wetting her hair. *I could just stay under here*, she thought hopelessly. *Then this would all go away.* Images passed through her mind. *Daddy . . . Mom . . . Jared . . .* She grabbed the edges of the tub and came up sputtering out of the water. Her shoulders shook with silent sobs, her hand covering her wet face. Only days ago, she was at school, a free person . . . and now . . . now she didn't even know what! She was stuck in some strange village with these strange people talking about strange things!

When Molly returned, Amanda was sitting on the edge of the tub, wrapped in the robe she was given. Molly smiled at her and held out a plain white cotton nightgown.

Speaking softly, Molly said, "Here, you can change into this. You'll be bathing three times a day in these beauty oils until the day of your wedding. It's tradition." Taking a brush from a shelf, she walked over to Amanda.

"Tradition?" she inquired quietly.

"Yes. Before one of our men from our village marries a sinful woman, she must be cleansed from all the germs and filth from the outside world. She must be pure," Molly explained. "We'll give you a new Christian name, and you will become one of us on the outside, and eventually"—she paused, placing bottles in a cabinet—"in time you will be one of us on the inside."

Interjecting, Amanda said, "It's illegal to force me to marry anyone."

"Things are different here," Molly said as she continued brushing Amanda's hair. "So pretty," she said as she ran her fingers between the strands. "Angel hair." Amanda hoped Molly was talking to herself.

"I'm not marrying anyone," Amanda repeated dully. Molly set the brush down, turning Amanda firmly by the shoulders to look at her.

"Fighting this will only make it worse for you," she spoke softly but seriously. "I'm just warning you. You have a strong will—but they will break you, if you push them to." With that, she stood up and walked to the door. "Now get dressed. He'll be here any minute now."

Amanda stared at the closed door. *Please find me soon*, she pleaded to the empty room. *Oh God, please find me soon!* She pulled the gown over her head, the hem falling to the floor, and the sleeves covered her hands. Numbly she opened the door and walked out of the bathroom. Stopping right outside the door, she watched Molly setting out two cups at the small table, then walking over to the small stove, taking the steaming teakettle, and pouring the hot water into the cups. She looked up and smiled at Amanda.

"A nice hot cup of tea, and some breakfast," she said warmly. She motioned for Amanda to take a seat. Amanda hesitantly walked to the table, eyeing the bowl of oatmeal and steaming tea, then hesitantly sat down. Her stomach growled angrily, demanding food. Once Amanda was settled at the table, Molly picked up her shawl and wrapped it around her shoulders. Fear washing over Amanda, she quickly stood back up again.

"Where are you going?" she asked anxiously. Molly smiled reassuringly.

"I'll be back," she said. "You need to get to know your fiancé in private. When your visit ends, I'll return for your next bath." Without another word, she walked out.

True to Molly's word, moments later there was a knock at the door. Panicking, she scrambled away, backing up against the bathroom door. Hurriedly she slipped in the small room, falling to her knees; she cowered by the side of the cast-iron tub. Trembling with fear when she heard the door open, she crossed her arms protectively in front of her. At first she heard nothing, then his footsteps came closer, and she squeezed the tub until her knuckles were white.

When he stepped through the door, he searched the small room, finding her huddled on the floor, terrified. She gasped when she saw him; her eyes widened with surprise. Recognizing him immediately, she saw that his face wasn't as worn as she had thought when she first saw him in the dim light only the night before. His features were well proportioned, his hair was a light brown, but what was most striking about his face was his eyes. Large crystal blue, almost clear in color, and full of kindness? *No*, she denied to herself. She wanted to see that. He was the man who brought her here. *What was his name?* Matthew. Yes, they called him Matthew. He wore the same black clothing that seemed to be the uniform in this strange place.

Matthew clenched his jaw, looking at the frightened young woman cowering in the corner. The gown was slightly big on her, making her look delicate . . . more fragile. She was so beautiful, he thought but never imagining that this would be so difficult. Her dark blue eyes were wide with fear, and he could see the puffiness around her eyes from crying. Clenching his jaw, he stepped toward her. Startled, softly whimpering, she cringed back against the wall.

"Don't be afraid," he said softly, "I'm not going to hurt you." Squatting down where he stood, he was about two feet from her. Her eyes watched him, rapidly moving back and forth, fear shining in their depths. "My name is Matthew Ryan," he said softly. Amanda was trembling from head to toe.

"You . . . brought me here," she accused him quietly. "W-why?" she asked, tears filling her eyes.

"You wouldn't understand just yet," he said. He looked down at the floor, then back up, meeting her eyes solemnly. "A brief explanation—this is a tradition in our village. Within our family. We need to take a woman from the outside world and save her soul by making her one of us," he said, attempting to explain. Then he continued, "I know it must sound absurd to you, because you're a sinful person, but it will make sense in the end."

Amanda pushed herself farther against the wall, closing her eyes, still grasping the tub for support, feeling dizzy. "I don't believe this," she whispered. "It doesn't sound absurd . . . it's insane!" Looking at him directly, she gave him a glimpse of her true strength. "You can't just steal people—it's against the law! I mean, *do you realize what you've done?*"

"Yes, I do," he assured her firmly, averting his eyes and rising to his feet. "All the men in my family have done it. This is the way it has always been done." Shaking her head, she looked down at her feet. Was he insane? He had to be. In her despair, she rapidly searched her memory, bringing up images of her loved ones. Her father smiling, teasing her mother; her mother shaking her head trying to be serious; Shelby lying on the couch in her pink flannel pajamas with her pink fluffy slippers, painting Amanda's nails as they drank wine, giggling throughout the night. *Oh God, this just can't be real,* she thought, her heart aching with longing.

"But . . . it's wrong . . . it's just wrong," she said, her vision blurring as the tears fell. Desperate, she looked up at him, crawling slightly forward. "Please let me go home? I won't tell anyone about you . . . or . . . your traditions . . . *please,* just let me go?"

He shook his head sadly, and she covered her eyes with one hand, beginning to cry. Shaking her head, she cried, "Please . . . please, let me go home. Please." He came over and knelt in front of her.

"I can't. I'm sorry." Removing her hand from her eyes, she wiped away her tears and turned her tear-streaked face up to his.

"Why me?" she whispered, shaking her head. "I don't understand why. Why did you take *me*?" Her wet red eyes moved rapidly; her eyebrows came together in confusion. "Do I know you?" Racking her brain, she tried to remember him. Searching her eyes, he hesitated to answer.

"I was given three choices," he said. "I chose you." Staring at him, she asked, "Choices?" She swallowed. "I . . . was . . . a choice? I don't understand—how?" she asked. "How did you know me . . . or . . . find me? Out of anywhere . . . you found *me*. Why did you want *me*?"

"Each girl is researched and observed," he said quietly. "I liked everything about you." The thought that he liked everything about her made her stomach turn. She searched his face, shaking her head in disbelief.

"Researched and observed?" Her mind began to race. "Am I some sort of experiment?" Then a thought struck Amanda. "Researched and observed . . . oh my"—her eyes wide with disbelief—"god!" She fell back against the wall. Her eyes accusing, she said, "I have seen you before." Her voice was a whisper. "You were outside my apartment. When I walked by with . . . with Jared." Standing up yet not moving from his spot, she watched him.

"Yes," he said softly. "Yes, Jared. Jared became a problem. We'd been watching your relationship and realized that we had to move things along quickly to keep you from being contaminated. We had to take you that night." Her hand shakily brushed her hair out of her face. *Jared became a problem. Jared became important.* Her fingers fell to rest on her lips as he watched her intently.

"I see you understand," he spoke very quietly, remembering the kiss that Jared and Amanda exchanged in the street. It was a moment he wouldn't soon forget, and the first time he ever felt any violent tendencies. So violent that he had almost revealed himself before it was time—never had he lost his focus or reacted emotionally in any operation before. She was chosen to be his wife long ago, and he had watched her closely for several months. To say that he had grown fond of her within that time would be an understatement. He had observed her in her classes, during her meals, when she spent time with her friends, and when she went jogging around campus. He had followed her home and watched her interact with her family and at work. Matthew had memorized all of her expressions and gestures. Her carefree spirit was contagious, her serious nature adorable, and her beauty . . . was breathtaking. Matthew could still see Jared pulling Amanda against his body, and he clenched his jaw as he remembered. His gut burned then as it did now.

"Contaminated?" she asked, just above whisper, lowering her eyes. He was so strange. Contaminated . . . what the hell did that mean? "How could I be contam—" *She wasn't sick, what did he mean?* Then she stopped as a cold chill trickled down her back with sudden understanding. *Her virginity,* she realized, as her cheeks flushed pink. She turned away, embarrassed at her naivety. She leaned over and rested her burning cheek on the cold cast-iron, swallowing and taking deep, shaky breaths. This was insane.

He knelt down. "To find someone with your morals, your values and most importantly, your innocence, was very difficult," he declared earnestly. "I found you. I couldn't lose you."

"If I had been *contaminated* then you wouldn't have taken me?" she cried, struggling to grasp what he was telling her.

He was silent, and when no answer came, she lifted her head up to look at him. Her face wet with tears, he sucked in a sharp breath, overwhelmed by the misery in her eyes.

"No," he said quietly. "We would have had to abort the whole abduction, and would have found someone else."

"So," she whispered harshly, shaking her head and looking away. "A decision that I thought was the right one, I'm now being punished for?"

"No!" he exclaimed, leaning forward, resting his hand on the edge of the tub, inches from her own. "That decision has saved you!"

Anger contorting her face, she suddenly screamed at him, "You don't know anything about me!" He pulled back at her heated outburst. "You don't know if I'm still pure or not! How could you?" Matthew sighed heavily, rubbing his face with his hands then dropping them.

CHAPTER 4

"We have members of the village that became integrated in your campus life," he admitted regretfully. "We know everything about you, Amanda."

Somewhere deep inside her, something snapped; hysteria overcame her, and she lunged at him, swinging, scratching, and kicking. Surprised by the attack, he was almost knocked over by her; but as she threw her small body at him, he managed to move to the side, keeping his balance, but her fists managed a few good hits before he was able to grab her wrists. As they struggled, she wanting to hurt him and Matthew trying not to hurt her, their shoulders slammed against the bathroom door, which threw Amanda off balance as pain shot through her weakened body. Crying out, she refused to stop the struggle; but he was much stronger than she was, so it didn't take him long to restrain her. With a similar maneuver he had used the night before, he had her back against his chest, holding her arms tightly to her side. As he tightened his grip, he lost his balance and fell on his side, bringing her with him.

Holding them still for endless minutes, their breathing began to even out. She felt so small in his arms, and when he looked down at her, Amanda's head was bent, her long blond hair hanging down in front of her. The white gown had been pulled up to her thighs in the scuffle, and his breath caught as his eyes fell on her beautiful white skin. Clenching his jaw, he averted his eyes.

He struggled to an upright position, still holding her in his arms. He could feel every rise and fall of her chest as she tried to regain her breath. The fight left her as she felt his strong arms around her and realized that this was very real. This wasn't some horrible nightmare that she was going to wake up from, but it was really happening. This stranger held her, in a very intimate way, and as Amanda's adrenaline decreased, her fear returned. Trembling, she just wanted him to let her go.

"They'll find me," she said quietly, more to herself, not willing to give up. He shifted his position until he was able to get his footing, then pulled them both up, bracing them against the wall. She winced, biting her bottom lip as she felt the bruises she had inflicted on herself.

"Amanda," he said softly in her ear. "My people have done this for generations. There's no trace of where you are." He paused then continued, "We've covered ourselves very well, and they won't find you because you've simply . . . disappeared."

Amanda closed her eyes as she absorbed his words. *They won't find you, you've simply disappeared.* There weren't any more signs of struggle from her, so he slowly set her upright on her own feet. She stood up, shakily at first, and the white material of her gown fell down at her feet.

"How long have I been gone?" she asked quietly, silently wringing her hands, something he recognized as a nervous habit of hers.

"Four days."

"Four?" she asked, her eyes whipped to his, surprised. "But, how?"

Meeting her eyes directly, he told her, "You were unconscious the first two days."

She stared at him, trying to see him for what he really was. He was a psychopath . . . they all were! Light stubble showed subtly on his tanned face, his shoulders broad on his lean body. After letting her go, he had shoved his hands into the back pockets of his jeans. He looked so normal.

"Matthew?" she said his name quietly. He met her eyes as she was shaking her head, her lips trembling. *Maybe, just maybe.* "I can't be here. I don't belong here. I'm not one of you." Her voice was shaking. "Please, *please just let me go home!*"

He shook his head, his expression somber, and stepped toward her. Her eyes pleaded with his.

"You'll be my wife," he said softly. "There's no going back."

She backed away from him, stumbling out of the small bathroom, not willing to accept this insanity.

"No!" she said shakily. "I won't marry you! I won't! *You can't make me marry you!*" His expression hardened; clenching his jaw, he turned away from her. When he turned back, the anger she saw frightened her. Seeing him walking toward her suddenly, she backed up until she reached the bed; scrambling onto it, she quickly reached the wall. Her fear of him frustrated him even more.

"You don't understand!" he growled at her. "You're here for good! You don't want to marry me? Fine! But my pastor *will* marry you to someone else here! You won't be set free! This is it, Amanda! Last stop! Is that what you want? To marry someone else?" he demanded. "I'll go arrange it right now because I don't like this anymore than you do!" He was standing at the edge of the bed, leaning toward her. "*Is that what you want?* I'm sure that there are a few men here that would like you for a wife . . . or as a second wife!" Amanda's heart raced, color draining from her face, and he didn't miss the panicked look in her eyes. *Other men . . . second wife*, she thought, horrified. Turning away, he stormed toward the door.

"No!" she called. "No . . . wait." Her voice was pleading, but then she wasn't sure what to do. She was cornered, and he knew it as he watched the emotions play across her face. "I . . . um . . . wait," she said, wringing her hands again, tears in her eyes. He walked slowly back to the bedside, and his heart lurched at the sight of her trembling lips and the desperation on her face—nothing could have prepared him for this experience. She put her fingers to her lips. "I . . . I . . ." She struggled, so afraid, looking down at her hands.

"Amanda?" he called her name softly. She looked up, tears streaming down her face. *What was she going to do? She was trapped!*

She shook her head as she whispered, "I don't know what to do."

"I have to go," he said abruptly; his voice was quiet, but his eyes still shone with his frustration. "I'll return for dinner." Turning to walk away again, she scurried to the edge of the bed, on her knees, her hand reaching out to the air in front of her.

"Don't," she cried out as he turned back. *"Don't give me away."* The tortured look in her eyes was almost his undoing. Never had he seen her like this, but what did he expect? For her to be happy about her abduction? She didn't understand that he saved her from living in an absolutely sinful world. He was giving her a chance to get right with God. Until he could explain this to her so that she would understand, this was going to be very difficult. He walked to the door, grabbing the handle roughly out of frustration.

"Please," she called out desperately. Swallowing, she forced herself to say, "M-matthew . . . please?"

"I won't, Amanda." he said without looking at her, then slammed the door behind him.

She sat back on the bed, staring at the door, numb with shock, her body still. Bringing her trembling hand to her forehead, she closed her eyes, trying to think. "Okay," she whispered, speaking aloud to calm her nerves. "I've been kidnapped. Accept this, Amanda, it's real. This is really happening." She continued to talk to herself. "How did this happen?" She stood up and used the bed to support her legs. "How can people just be stolen?" Desperately she thought back to that night. When she and Jared had passed the men in the street, she remembered thinking that they were strange. A cold feeling seeped into her bones. *Why didn't she listen to her instincts? Why . . . why . . . why?* Tears filled her eyes, but she stubbornly shook her head, biting her bottom lip. It didn't matter anymore. "There was no way for me to know that this would happen," she said, her soft voice filling the empty room. Her hands pressed both sides of her head, attempting to ease the pain. An image of Jared sitting across from her in the library, smiling his adorable grin, flashed through her mind, causing her heart to ache. Beginning to pace, she realized that she would rather die than be forced to marry anyone!

She stopped in the middle of the room, looking around her. The sunlight through the two windows was magnificent—so bright she could see the dust particles float through the rays. Slowly she walked over to the window and looked out, squinting. Off to the right, she saw the man called Simon, standing with his back to her. A large formidable man, dressed in black, guarding her like she was a prisoner. Unconsciously her hand came up to rest on the window. The glass was cool under her fingers, and her chest constricted, longing to be out in the fresh air. The wind was blowing, moving the branches of the trees that surrounded her prison, ever so slightly. Leaves and pine needles floated effortlessly in the breeze. Up above her, Amanda watched two birds playing. They dove in and around the trees, landing precariously on one branch, only to fly to the next, chasing one another. Amanda couldn't hear them, only imagined she could, envying them. Only days ago, she was free, like they were. If she had known that her freedom would be ripped away from her, she would have done so many things. Her breath hitched on a sob. Looking beyond the trees, she could just make out the tops of the small cabins she had seen only shadows of the night before, surrounded by more trees. Obviously she was separated from *them*. Walking away, she stood in the center of the cabin, the long white nightgown brushing the tops of her feet. "What am I going to do?" she whispered, her fingertips resting on her lips. She couldn't stay here, but how could she escape? They were going to force her to marry this man! How could she get away if that happened?

Glancing down at her bare feet, Amanda was struck by an idea. Immediately she began searching the room. Where did they put her shoes? Quickly she searched the bathroom, under the bed as she glanced nervously at the door, waiting for someone to walk in. If she had her shoes, escaping would be much easier. She was a runner, had been most of her life. If she could just get a head start, she knew that she could get away. The woods didn't intimidate her; her parents had brought her camping all through her childhood. She could survive, at least for a little while. Amanda opened the cabinets in the small kitchenette, searching the small draws. Standing up, she nodded, accepting the inevitable. She would have to escape without her shoes. The question now was how she was going to get away. *It would have to be when Matthew is here*, she thought to herself. He had feelings. Matter of fact, she thought, her brows coming together, he seemed to be just as upset at this as she was, which didn't make any sense, since he was the one that *chose* her. She would have to catch him off guard somehow, then she would have to worry about that man outside the door. *One obstacle at a time*, she thought. *She had to escape because she didn't want to die.* But she would, she had already resolved in her mind, rather die than face the horror of marrying a stranger and becoming part of this insanity.

Voices outside the door jarred Amanda from her morbid thoughts. It was that woman Molly. Amanda quickly ran to the bed, arranging herself as if she had been there all along. Knowing Molly was coming in, Amanda still jumped, her heart pounding in her chest, when the door opened.

Matthew knocked on his pastor's door, trying to shake off the frustration from his meeting with Amanda. "Enter," came the pastor's voice. Straightening his stance, he entered the office.

"Sir." Matthew nodded his greeting. His pastor sat at his large mahogany desk, facing Matthew, his hands folded around his stomach as he leaned back in his leather chair.

"Matthew, good man, I'm glad you came to see me," he said, his smile not reaching his eyes. Matthew didn't notice, for he was used to his cold demeanor. They both knew that he was told to come to see him after his first visit with Amanda, but they both played their parts well. "Sit . . . sit." Matthew nodded and sat. His pastor searched the young man's face, satisfied with what he saw. "So, tell me how the meeting went." Matthew cleared his throat then met his pastor's eyes directly.

"It was . . . difficult," Matthew admitted. "But I am confident that she will submit in a short period of time." Actually he didn't think that at all, but he knew what to say, and what not to. The pastor nodded, pleased.

"Good, good," he said in his oily tone. "You know what you have to do. The shorter the period of time the better. Until she submits, she is a threat to the peaceful lifestyle of this community. As you well know." Matthew nodded.

"Yes, sir," he said as he remembered Amanda attacking him in the bathroom. Thankfully she hadn't managed to hit his face. His pastor was quiet for a few moments.

"You've chosen yourself a pretty little morsel, Matthew. I'm impressed," he said, his eyes lit with a strange light. "Control her or you will lose her."

Matthew's eyes widened in surprise, not missing his meaning. Rising to his feet, banking his anger, he said, "I will control her, sir." He added, "Am I dismissed?" The pastor smiled knowingly.

"Yes, yes, go back to work." Matthew gave a curt nod and left the room. As he walked through the empty church, he shook his head in disgust. Oh, she would submit because he would be damned if he lost her . . . to anyone!

"Well, hello, there!" she greeted the wide-eyed young girl. "Back in bed?" She walked directly into the bathroom and came out with the white bathrobe, handing it to Amanda. "Sorry, I'm a little late, but I thought your meeting with Matthew would last a little longer. We need to start your second cleansing for the day."

She continued to walk around, doing things—walking to the kitchenette, filling the teakettle with water, setting it on the small stove. Humming, she cleaned up the teacups and untouched breakfast dishes from the table. When she walked back into the bathroom, Amanda stood up, holding the robe tightly against her body. Molly came back out a few moments later. "The bath is all ready for you."

Amanda slowly walked to the doorway, stepping past Molly. "I'll give you fifteen minutes. Just like before. Then you can dress in a fresh gown." With that, Molly closed the door quietly behind her. Amanda quickly pulled the white gown over her head and stepped into the hot tub. Once again the hot water soothed her tense muscles and sensitive skin, and Amanda reluctantly admitted to herself that she liked the light lilac scent of the oils that Molly put in the water. What a strange custom, Amanda thought. Bathing three times a day to prepare for a wedding. She searched her mind, trying to recall from her studies, different cultural practices, wondering if she ever heard about this. Yet nothing came to mind. She dipped her head under the water then came up out of the steaming water. Taking the bath sponge, she began to lather it with soap, noticing the redness around her wrists from the twine had faded some. Pausing, she stared unseeing into the water. Amanda felt her sanity literally being stretched at that moment. She longed for her mother. Just to have her mom wrap her arms around her, telling her that it was just a bad dream. Then she would bring Amanda down to the kitchen and share a cup of hot cocoa, telling her silly stories about her father, like she had done when Amanda was little. Closing her eyes, she let the hot tears stream down her already cooling cheeks. This would end, she acknowledged, one way or another. And she prayed that she would see her parents again.

Dressed again in a fresh gown, Amanda stepped from the bathroom, with a feeling of deja vu. Molly was again pouring tea, but a sandwich now sat on the table. Molly turned and smiled at her.

"There," she said cheerfully, "that wasn't so bad, was it?" Amanda looked down, not answering her. "Come and eat something. You need to keep your strength up." Amanda slowly took a seat at the table. Her appetite had moved from starving into numbness. Eating was going to be difficult now, but Molly was right, though not for the same reasons. Amanda needed to keep her strength up because she planned on getting the hell out of there! She picked up the sandwich and took a small bite. Molly watched her, nodding with pleasure at seeing her eating, then went to clean the bathroom. Amanda managed to eat half the sandwich then pushed the plate aside and began sipping her tea. She wasn't normally a tea drinker, but this wasn't a normal situation. The tea warmed her chilled body, and she admitted that she felt better now that she had eaten.

Finished, Molly came out of the bathroom, carrying white sheets in her arms. Still humming what Amanda recognized as a church hymn, she began to strip the bed of linens as Amanda watched her curiously. She was really a beautiful woman. Her red hair was thick, seeming to be straining against the confinement of her bun. The black clothes did not flatter her fuller figure—the long skirt, a thick wool, the black shirt, a thick cotton. The shirt was buttoned up to her neck, to a point where Amanda knew it had to be suffocating, but Molly didn't seem to notice as she worked happily. Molly must have felt Amanda's eyes on her because she turned to smile at her as she opened the sheet with a snap. "There's color in your cheeks now. After you finish your tea, you may want to take a nap, before dinner with Matthew."

Strangely, Amanda was feeling drowsy. Her limbs felt heavier, but she didn't realize it until Molly said something. "Molly?" she asked her, her thoughts foggy, placing her elbow on the table, resting her chin in her hand. "Why do you steal people? Aren't there enough women among your own people?" Not answering right away, she finished making the bed. Then she walked over to the table, picking up the dishes in front of Amanda.

"I know for a woman of your upbringing, you can't understand this." Molly spoke softly to her, her expression kind. "But it is our tradition to save women from the outside world. Our women *do* marry within our village," she explained as she brought the dishes to the kitchenette, "but there are a selected group of men that must choose a wife from where you're from." After setting the dishes in the sink, Molly turned back to Amanda, smiling as she saw Amanda's eyes trying to close, pleased the herbal additive she placed in her tea was working. Walking over, she gently helped Amanda to her feet. "Come, my dear, I think it's time for a nap." Amanda, not understanding why she was so tired, did not argue. "And we don't steal people, Amanda, we save them." Amanda shook her head as she crawled under the crisp, cool sheets.

Looking up at Molly as she tucked her in, Amanda whispered, "No, you stole me." She closed her eyes as her breathing deepened. Molly smiled and touched her soft ivory cheek. She had such an angelic beauty, she thought, knowing why Matthew chose her. Liking Amanda, she decided that she would do what she could to make her adjustment easier. Finishing the cleaning, she slipped out of the cabin quietly, so as not to disturb her sleep.

CHAPTER 5

"Daddy, you're just being unreasonable!" Amanda stood against the kitchen counter, her arms crossed in front of her. Her father held the same stance on the opposite counter, holding a cup of coffee in one hand.

"Now, Amanda, I understand that you feel that way, but it doesn't change my answer." His voice was calm, but firm. Amanda shook her head, frustrated.

"All my friends are going," she declared. "It's not like I'm asking you for the money—you know I have it." Her father sighed and shook his head.

"It's not about the money, Amanda," he explained patiently, "it's about your safety."

"Safety?" she exclaimed, exasperated. "I'll be with my friends."

"Amanda, you're sixteen years old, and so are all your friends," he said, still ever so patient. "You're not going backpacking across Europe this summer. My answer is no, and it will not change."

Tears burned her eyes. "You just don't trust me, that's it, isn't it?"

Her father had pushed away from the counter, set his cup down, and walked over to his daughter; knowing better than to hug her, he tucked a wayward strand of hair behind her ear. "Amanda, I trust you. You've lived a protected life with your mom and me, and you don't understand that there are bad people in the world. It's them I don't trust."

"If I've lived a protected life, it's your fault!" she said heatedly. "You're still being overprotective!"

"Yes, you're right. I am," her father agreed. "That's my job as your parent, and I will continue to be so. I know you're angry, but it will pass. My decision is final." He stepped back, picked up his cup, and left the room.

"I know how to take care of myself!" she called after him. *I know how to take care of myself . . . I do . . .*

Amanda blinked her eyes open sleepily. Her face pressed against the now-familiar herb-scented sheets, a sadness weighing on her. *Oh, Daddy, now I believe you—how stupid I was*, she thought as tears burned her eyes. This time she remembered where she was. The room was cast in warm light from several lit lanterns; her eyes went to the window, only to see the blackness of the night. A familiar humming came from the bathroom, and she knew it was Molly. Sitting up, she smelled something wonderful cooking on the stove. Sleepily she pushed her hair out of her face. Becoming more alert, she heard the running water and cringed, not wanting to take another bath. *She was clean already!* As if sensing her thoughts, Molly came out of the bathroom carrying the white robe.

"Good evening." She smiled, setting the robe on the bed by Amanda's feet. "Looks like you needed that rest." Molly searched Amanda's eyes and saw they were still slightly glazed. She realized the herb hadn't entirely worn off. "It's time for your cleansing." Amanda bit her lip but nodded her head. *Not much longer, Amanda,* she thought to herself.

After bathing, she dressed and came out of the bathroom, braiding her long damp tresses as she walked. When she saw the table, she stopped dead in her tracks. Molly had two settings on the table, candles lit, and a steaming pot of that delicious-smelling food. *It looked . . . romantic,* she thought, her stomach churning, suddenly feeling nauseous. The warm color that had been in her cheeks drained.

Unaware of her reaction, Molly continued her preparations. Dropping her arms, her unfinished braid slowly falling out, Amanda wanted to hide. Anywhere. She was turning to go back in the bathroom when Molly spoke to her.

"Why don't you sit down, Amanda." She smiled. "Matthew will be here any minute." Swallowing, Amanda hesitated. Molly stopped what she was doing and watched her. "It's quite normal to be nervous, hon, it will get easier each time you're together."

"No, it won't," Amanda snapped, not able to look at Molly. Molly nodded, knowing that it was fear that Amanda was suffering from, and turned back to the kitchenette. Before Amanda could decide what to do, there was a light knock on the door, and Matthew stepped in. Amanda's heart pounded in her chest as she remembered their last conversation, and she was unsure of how Matthew was now going to treat her. After he had closed the door, he turned and instantly met Amanda's wide eyes. Fear and uncertainty were shining in their depths as Matthew nodded his greeting to her.

"Hello, Matthew," greeted Molly, looking over her shoulder with her usual smile. "Dinner is ready." Pulling his eyes from Amanda's, Matthew gave Molly a genuine smile, knowing that she made his favorite meal.

"Thank you, Molly." He smiled, his voice affectionate. "You've outdone yourself as usual."

Molly waved her hand at him. "Oh, stop the flattery, boy," she teased. "Now eat while it's hot." She glanced at Amanda with concern. Matthew followed her direction and shoved his hands into his jean pockets. Amanda listened to their interaction with curiosity, twisting her hands until they hurt, until they both turned to her. *She did not want to have dinner with him, and she did not want to be alone with him;* she screamed to herself as she looked away. Yet anticipation began to build, knowing what her plan was tonight. "All right then." Molly nodded and smiled at Matthew. "Enjoy your dinner." Matthew nodded.

"Thank you, Molly," he said quietly.

Molly went to the hook by the door and removed her shawl. "I will see you in the morning, Amanda. Good night." Amanda's eyebrows came together in confusion, but she said nothing as she watched Molly leave. Amanda was left alone with him. They both stood, the silence awkward and uncomfortable, until finally Matthew said, "Amanda," Matthew began, his voice soft, "About earlier. I just wanted to say . . ." But he didn't know what to say. He'd been angry and frustrated, but she didn't want to hear an apology. She only wanted her freedom, and that he couldn't give her.

Tentatively she looked up at him. Fear sharpened within her, when he didn't finish, wondering if he had given her away to someone else, like he had threatened. Crossing her arms in front of her, she licked her lips nervously. "D-did you give me away?" she whispered, trembling. Surprise splashed across his face, and he took a step closer to her.

"No," he declared. "No, Amanda. I didn't give you away." Closing her eyes, she was surprised at the tremendous relief she felt. Watching her, he wondered what she was thinking inside. "Will you sit with me?" She opened her eyes and looked nervously at the table then nodded hesitantly. He walked over to his seat and sat down. Much slower, she followed suit. Searching her face, he asked, "How do you feel?" Not able to look at him, she said softly, "Fine." He reached over and picked up her plate, serving her the stew that

Molly had made, then set it back in front of her. "Molly makes the best beef stew in the whole village," he said as he served himself his food. "How do you like her?" Amanda picked up her fork, her hand shaking lightly, and looked up at him.

"She's been . . . kind," was all she could say. Matthew nodded and began eating his dinner. How could he sit here and talk with her as if she weren't his prisoner? Did he actually think that *she* could sit here and pretend that everything was normal, when it was really twisted? Looking down at her food, she felt the cold metal of the fork in her hand and finally discovered how she was going to escape and get past the guard outside her door.

She was unable to eat, she was suddenly feeling nauseous, and her nerves were on edge. Noticing she wasn't eating, he asked, "Are you not hungry?" Her eyes snapped to his, alert and shining.

"I can't eat here with you," she informed him. "We're not some couple on a date and I can't pretend to be." Quietly Matthew set his fork down. Okay, he thought, round two.

"No, Amanda, we're not on a date," he stated. "But we are a couple. In a few days, you will be my wife." Amanda shook her head, her face twisting in disgust.

"I will not be your wife . . . ever!" she spat, getting to her feet, knocking her chair down. She put her hand at her side, hiding the fork in the folds of her nightgown as she walked toward the door.

Rising to his feet, he watched her carefully. There was a different light in her eyes—a light of defiance. Crossing his arms in front of him, he waited, alert. "Amanda, where do you think you're going?"

She turned to him. "I'm leaving!" she said, just above a whisper, and, without notice, she flung open the door, startling Simon.

"Amanda. Don't!" Matthew called out. Adrenaline mixed with desperation pulsed through her, and she became violent in a way that she never experienced before. Screaming as if she were an Indian going into battle, Amanda lifted her arm, fork in hand, and attacked Simon. The fork sank deep in his chest, and blood instantly flowed around her hand. Startled and shocked by the attack, Simon gasped, wide eyed, stepping backward. This gave her the time she needed. Almost with no hesitation, she let go of the fork, grabbed the edge of her nightgown, lifting it, and she began to run. She was around the corner of the cabin within seconds; a shocked Matthew hurried to Simon's side. Amanda didn't care about anything but escape, and as she ran, she tied the side of her gown in a knot, leaving her legs free to run. With her hands extended in front of her, she ran through the trees. Using the shadows and the light from the moon as guidance, she was able to avoid bumping into the trees but could feel the branches and leaves whipping against her face and body. There was no pain; her desperation was driving her to be free.

With a growl of pain, Simon pushed Matthew's hands away. "I'm fine!" He gritted his teeth as he yanked the fork out of his chest. "Go get her!" Hesitating, Matthew backed up a few steps; then, nodding, he turned and ran around the cabin. "Wait!" Simon yelled out. Matthew quickly returned, exasperated at the time he was losing. "Here." Simon held out a flashlight. "You'll need this." Grabbing the light from Simon's hand, he again ran around the cabin and into the trees. Matthew didn't have time to react to the shock and disbelief that filled him; it would only take quick thinking and sure footing that would bring him to Amanda. He knew her athletic ability, and he knew that she could outrun him, but he had the advantage. Having grown up in these woods, they were imprinted in his mind in a mental map, and she had no idea what she was doing!

The wind burned her lungs; her heart pounded in her chest. The night was cool, the air crisp, and Amanda could see her breath as she ran. Pushing through a small clump of trees, she stepped out to the edge of a stream. Losing her balance and waving her arms, she cried out, grasping one of the smaller trees to stop herself from falling in. She pushed her long hair out of her face and looked around her. The moonlight glistened over the top of the moving water, creating shining sparkles of light. *What was she going to do?* Looking over her shoulder, she couldn't see anyone coming, but she knew better. She had to cross. Nodding to herself, she accepted the inevitable. Her feet were sinking in the thick, ice-cold mud, and she pulled them out, feeling the suction as she set them free. She walked down the embankment a few feet then found an opening that she could slip down into the water. Rocks and pebbles slid down with her; she gasped as the cold water hit her body. The current pulled on her, but it wasn't strong enough to move her. Taking the first few steps, Amanda cried out as she stumbled over the slimy rocks that made up the creek bed. In the middle, she paused, looking upstream from where she exited the trees. *Was that a light?* She turned back to look at the other side of the embankment. *Not much farther,* she thought, *almost there.* Her white gown pressed against her body like a second skin, the light material feeling heavy, cold, and wet. A foot away from the embankment, her foot slipped between two rocks and got stuck; she cried out and fell to her side. The water rushed over her head unmercifully, but she came out quickly, gasping and choking. *God, please . . . please, help me!* She pulled on her foot, but it was painfully positioned and wouldn't budge. Standing to her full height, she looked behind her, seeing a bouncing light through the trees. Panic filled her . . . *no!* She didn't come this far to be caught. Reaching into the water, using all of her strength, she lifted one of the large stones and flipped it to the side. Laughing and crying with relief, she stumbled out onto the embankment. Gripping the tall grass, she scrambled to the top. Once there, she paused on her hands and knees, taking deep breaths as water dripped off her.

Matthew ran surefooted through the trees, turning with precision and speed. He knew the creek was up ahead, and he needed to catch her before she reached it. Adrenaline pumped through him, knowing that she had no idea what she was running into. If only they talked, if only he explained the reality of her situation!

Amanda rose to her feet; at the same time, a figure emerged from the trees, light moving rapidly back and forth, scanning the creek. Whimpering, she gathered up her wet gown and ran into the trees. Cold and wet, her perception was hindered, slowing her normally fast pace. Coming to a dip in the landscape, Amanda stumbled and fell into the dark void. Rolling a couple of feet, she finally came to a stop. Stunned, she didn't move for several precious moments. Too many. When she pulled herself out, the light was much closer.

A coyote howled into the night, not sounding very far away, but Amanda ran, knowing that meeting a coyote would be much better than going back there. Weakening, she stumbled again, but not losing her footing.

"Amanda!" the voice yelled. Amanda looked fearfully over her shoulder and cried out.

"No!" she screamed, picking up her speed, not paying attention to where she was going.

"Amanda, stop!" Matthew yelled at her. But Amanda kept running, tears falling from her eyes, blurring her vision. It didn't take long for her to fall again. Close to hysterics, she struggled up to her knees, dizzy. Matthew caught up with her just as she fell. Seeing her go still, he stopped then shook his head when she pushed herself up and began to crawl. "Amanda, stop."

"No!" she gasped, getting to her feet then falling again. Matthew reached out to help her, but she cried out and scrambled to her feet and began to run again. Matthew shook his head, knowing she was exhausted and injured, but she was getting too close. He picked up a jog after her, and she stumbled on, and then he saw the lights. Fear overcame consideration, and he picked up his pace. "Amanda, please stop. I don't want to hurt you!"

"Go away!" she cried out. "Leave me alone!" Knowing there wasn't any other way, Matthew grabbed hold of her arm and yanked her toward him. She struggled away, twisting in his arms. "Amanda, damn it, stop!" he said and pulled her down to the ground. Hitting the cold dirt with a painful thud, the wind knocked out of her lungs, and at the same time, she fought with sheer wildness. Matthew bit back a curse that wanted to escape when her nails dug into his skin, but within moments, he had her small arms pinned beneath his own. Overpowered, she went still in his arms, struggling to catch her breath. Matthew was breathing hard, his arms still tight around her. "Amanda, stop." During the struggle, he had dropped his flashlight, and it lay a couple of feet away from them, pointing in the opposite direction. As they lay in the dark, the night sounds moved around them. The insects swarmed around the beam of light that was shining from the flashlight. The single coyote must have caught up with his pack because they sang their songs in the distance. The cool wind blew through the trees, leaves rustling in the branches and blowing around them on the ground. Amanda could smell the dirt beneath her, her face only inches away. Finally catching her breath, she shifted in his arms, causing him to tighten his arms around her, causing her to gasp.

"I want you to look up, over to the left," he breathed into her ear. When she shook her head, he squeezed her tighter, causing her to cry out. Reluctantly she looked up, trying to focus. Then saw the red flashing light. "Do you see it?" When she nodded, he continued. "That's the electric fence that surrounds the outskirts of our village. A few more feet"—he paused, taking a deep breath—"and you would have been electrocuted." Matthew felt her shudder. Then so softly that he had to strain to hear her, she said, "That would be better than going back." Matthew closed his eyes, resting his forehead on the back of her cold damp hair. Amanda's eyes burned with tears, her chest ached in her despair. *She had failed, oh God, she had failed.*

"Oh, Amanda," he whispered, not knowing what to say. The adrenaline gone, exhausted and defeated, Amanda began to feel the cold temperature of the night and the injuries her body had endured. Feeling her shake, he shifted and brought them both up on their feet. "Promise you're not going to run." Violently trembling, she said quietly, "I pr-promise." He let go of her, and she wrapped her arms around her freezing wet body, her head down. Walking over to where the flashlight lay, he picked it up, coming back to her side.

"Amanda?" he said her name. She lifted her head to look at him. He didn't have to ask why she did what she did. He knew. Her wide, miserable, tear-filled eyes looked up at him, telling him everything. "Are you hurt?" She shrugged her shivering shoulders, her lips blue and trembling. Nodding, he walked to her side, putting his arm around her shoulders, but she pulled away.

"D-don't . . . touch me."

"Let's go," he said solemnly, instead reaching for her hand, "before you catch pneumonia." But when his hand took hers, she tried to pull her hand away. Clenching his jaw, he held on to her, squeezing her hand tightly, assuring her that he wasn't going to let her go and began the walk back. Tears trickled down her cheeks, and she swiped at them with her free hand.

Wet and shivering, she had no choice but to follow him. They didn't talk; Matthew kept them at a steady pace, knowing that she needed to get out of her wet clothing. When they came to the creek, he turned and led them upstream a good distance, finally coming to a small narrow bridge. Amanda blinked tired eyes at the wooden structure, numb to the knowledge of how she would have benefited from its use. Every step they took was more painful than the next; her feet stung and her body ached. As they neared the village, Amanda began to stumble, too weak and cold to go on. Matthew felt her start to fall and caught her just in time, only inches from the ground. "Amanda," he gasped, then lifted her effortlessly into his arms. She struggled weakly. "D-don't t-touch m-me," she cried softly. Then her head fell against his chest in her weakness, her eyes closing. He looked down at her, her wet gown clung to her body, her hair hung in thick strands. Her ivory skin glowed in the dark night, her lips blue; shaking his head in frustration, he quickened his pace.

When he rounded the corner of the cabin, he was relieved that Simon was not there. He was dealing with all he could at the moment. He walked up the steps; letting one hand go quickly, he opened the door. Stepping into the warm room, everything was left the way it was before she ran; and without stopping, he walked into the bathroom, laying her down as gently as he could in the large tub. Situating her the best he could, leaving her gown on, he reached over and turned the water on. She needed to get warm, he thought, and this was the quickest way. Making sure the temperature was right, he turned back to her. Her eyes still closed, he gently brushed the hair from her face. Her features were small and delicate; her full lips were still a dark shade of blue. She didn't look like the young woman he chose to be his bride, he thought to himself as he gazed at her, she was scratched and bruised, and her hair lay in thick, dirty clumps against the white cast-iron tub. In the dimly lit room, her wet gown revealed much more than in the darkness of the night. As he watched, her breasts moved ever so slightly with each breath she took, soft and round, they were exquisite in size and shape. Aching to feel them under his hands, he wrenched his gaze away, moving them down her small body. Her waist was small, her abdomen flat, her hips rounded. Clenching his jaw, he resisted the urge to feel her soft skin and dropped back on the floor, resting his back against the sink vanity. He pulled his knees up, resting his arms on them, then laid his head down. What was he going to do? Pastor would know by morning. His chances of keeping Amanda for his wife were lessening. His time was running out. What would he do if she was taken from him? The fierce anger that rose up surprised him. He wouldn't let that happen. She was his and only his; he didn't come this far to lose her.

Amanda blinked open heavy eyes, feeling the warm water pouring on her feet. Slightly disoriented, she moved her hands and could feel warm water all around her.

CHAPTER 6

L ooking down at herself, seeing the muddy, bloodstained nightgown, she lifted a wet shaking hand to her head, biting her lip at the pain she felt just to move. Turning her head, she saw Matthew sitting on the floor, his head resting in his arms, and tears burned the back of her eyes. He stole her all over again. *Why did he keep doing this? Why couldn't he just let her go? She didn't want to die. She didn't, but she would not marry him!*

Matthew, sensing her movement, looked up then, meeting her eyes. He saw the tears and the resentment, but he was relieved that she was awake. After a few moments of looking at one another, she looked away, her body trembling.

"How do you feel?" he asked softly, but loud enough to be heard over the running water. Not answering, Amanda pulled herself up, realizing how intimately the dirty gown clung to her. Color rushed to her cheeks as she quickly brought her knees to her chest, wrapping her arms around them, trying to cover herself, resting her head on her knees, her head turning toward the wall. She was so humiliated she just wanted to disappear. He wanted her. He wanted her body, her mind, and her . . . soul. A few more feet and Amanda would have been electrocuted, and in that moment, she wished she had made it because she meant what she said to him. She'd rather die than be here. She'd rather die than let him touch her. "Look, Amanda," He shifted his position to kneel in front of the tub, his hands resting on the edge. "I know that you don't want to speak to me, and that's fine. But you have scratches that need to be tended to, and your head—you cut it pretty good when you fell." When she still made no response, he rose to his feet, reaching through the steam that had filled the room, turning the water off. "Why don't you wash yourself up." He reached into a small cabinet behind the door and pulled out a clean white nightgown. Hanging it on a hook near the tub, he then shoved his hands in his jeans. "Here's a clean gown." Silence. Then he turned, stepping to the door. "I'll give you some privacy." Closing the door behind him, he closed his eyes and sighed. Shaking his head, he moved to the small kitchenette to make an herbal tonic for her that would warm her and help her to sleep.

Hearing the door close, Amanda began to cry. Silent sobs shook her small frame. *How can this be happening? Mommy, Daddy . . . help me . . . somebody.* Lifting her head, she looked around the small room. "What am I going to do?" she whispered as a sob escaped her. "Oh God, what am I going to do?" Shaking her head, she bit her lip hard until she tasted blood, tears streaming down her face. There was no way out. She couldn't escape; she was trapped.

Frustration filled her, and she looked down at herself, the dirty gown drenched by the bathwater. Abruptly getting to her knees, water splashed to the floor; she yanked the gown off over her head and threw it against the door. "I hate you!" she suddenly screamed at the top of her lungs. "I hate you, I hate you, I hate you!" she cried. Falling back into the water, her head came to rest on the cool side.

Matthew went still when he heard the thump against the door. Setting the kettle on the stove, he slowly turned toward the bathroom, only to hear her scream at him. Her words were filled with anguish and despair; he listened as she cried. Leaning back against the counter, he rubbed his hands over his face, his own heart feeling as though it had been replaced by a piece of lead, heavy and weighed down. How was this going to work? he wondered sadly. Pushing away from the counter, he walked to the window by the door. Sitting on the soft chair, he looked out into the dark night and waited. At nine o'clock, he was expected at the nightly men's meeting. If he didn't show, it would be obvious that he was having problems with her. He had to be there.

Amanda cried until her head pounded and her throat swelled. Having sat for too long, the water had cooled, and she was shivering again. Reluctantly, she knew she had to get out. Quickly dunking her head, she washed her long blond tresses. Trembling as she stepped out of the tub, she began to rapidly dry herself off. As she did, she caught her reflection in the mirror and gasped. On her forehead, a large ugly gash trailed along her hairline, small scratches surrounding it; a shadow on her right cheek hinted the beginning of a harsh bruise. Her large blue eyes were red and swollen from crying, with dark circles beneath them. Moving her towel, she saw several more scratches and bruises, and her feet were throbbing with pain. Closing her eyes, she looked away from the ugly image and finished drying. As she pulled the gown over her head, an idea came to her. Maybe if she made herself so ugly then no one would want her.

She quickly went to the mirror, and her small fingers reached up to touch her soft cheek then slowly moved to her hair. She had already done a good job on her face, but her hair. *Yes, I'll cut it*, she thought, *I'll cut my hair, and let's see if you're so interested after that.* Shakily she opened the mirror, searching the medicine cabinet for scissors. Nothing but small bottles of bath oils, a toothbrush for Amanda, and homemade toothpaste.

Closing the mirror, she knelt down and opened the sink vanity. Moving aside several thick white towels, she found a black vinyl pouch. Her breath caught in her throat as she pulled the pouch out, unzipping it slowly. Inside, she found a man's razor, not a modern one, but one her great grandfather insisted on using until he passed away. She loved to watch him shave when she was a little girl. He would turn to her and wink. "A real man shaves with a blade," he would tease, "not one of those girlie contraptions." Amanda would giggle, begging to shave too, and he always let her. Filling her small palm with shaving cream, she would pat it all over her face, and her Grandfather would hand her a small black comb, and Amanda would pretend to shave. The tears that hit her hand brought her back to what she was looking for. Moving things aside, nail clippers, several combs, and a brush, there were no scissors. Throwing the pouch into the sink, its contents fell into the small basin. She leaned on the sink, her head down, eyes closed.

The knock on the door startled her so much she jumped. "Amanda?" Matthew called softly. "Are you decent?" Her heart pounding, her breath stuck in her throat, making it difficult for her to speak. "Amanda?"

"No!" she gasped out. "I-I'm almost done." Stepping to the door, she prayed that he didn't just walk in. It wasn't until he spoke that she realized that she had been holding her breath.

"All right. Five minutes. That's it," he replied as she let the air out of her lungs. Quickly she stepped back to the sink and began gathering up the items that fell out. Picking up the razor, she began to put it back then hesitated, going still.

Staring at it, her hand trembled; her eyes lifted to the mirror so that she was staring at herself. *I would rather die than be here*, the familiar words echoed in her head. Swallowing, she looked down at the razor then back up to her reflection. Death was so final. She said these words to herself over and over throughout the day, did she really mean them? *Was there a chance that she could go home? That she could escape this psychotic place?* Tears shined in the blue depths of her eyes, and she shook her head. After tonight, it didn't seem possible. Closing her eyes, she could see her parents at their best, laughing and teasing one another, her chest constricting in pain. If she were dead, she really would never see them again, and the thought of that was almost too much to bear. But he was going to force her to marry him. *How would she bear it? Marriage to a psycho?* Opening her eyes, she set her jaw, determined. She wasn't ignorant. With marriage came . . . actions . . . that she cringed to think about. *Then what? She would be forced to live in this . . . place?* Thoughts and fear of the unknown had her doubling over, nauseousness overwhelming her; she squeezed the razor in her hand, then cried out in pain as the blade cut through her skin. Straightening, she opened her hand to see it fill up with blood. The pain was harsh and stinging, but she didn't try to stop it. Lifting the bloodstained razor in her uninjured hand, she raised her bloody hand and gently rested the blade on the inside of her wrist. There was no other way; her lip trembled as she looked one last time in the mirror, her eyes wide, shining with tears.

"I'm sorry, Mom . . . Dad," she whispered, "I don't know what else to do."

The kettle screamed, steam shooting from its spout. Matthew quickly removed it from the burner, turning the stove off. What was she doing in there? He poured the hot water into the mixture he had prepared. Hearing a thump, Matthew looked over his shoulder at the door and listened. Not hearing anything more, he turned back and began mixing the drink. A few moments later, when she still hadn't come out, he walked to the door, his patience ending. He knocked briskly.

"Amanda?" he called. "You've been in there long enough." Silence. "I'm coming in whether you want me to or not." Still nothing. Matthew's brows came together; a strange feeling filled him. Knocking again, he called, "Amanda?" When he again received no response, he turned the knob and pushed the door open.

Amanda sat on the floor, her back rested against the tub, head down. Her arms lay on her outstretched legs, blood poured down her wrists onto her clean white gown, seeping into the floor beneath her. "Amanda! My god!" There was a sickening amount of blood; Matthew dropped to his knees by her side. "Oh no . . ." He cupped her face in his hands; her eyes were opened, but glazed. "Amanda, can you hear me? Amanda?" Blinking slowly, she whispered, "I'm sorry." Then her eyes rolled back in her head, and she went limp. "Oh Amanda." Laying her down on her side, he clumsily opened the cabinet, grabbing at the towels, quickly wrapping her wrists. This time, he couldn't handle this alone. He needed help. "I'll be right back." He knew that she couldn't hear him, but saying it kept him calm. He rose to his feet, his hands and pants covered in blood. Leaving the room, he bolted out the door, only to run into Simon. Startled, Simon yelled. "What's the matter with you people?" he yelled then saw the blood on Matthew. "What's happened?"

"Simon," Matthew gasped, "she's . . . hurt herself. I need the doctor." Simon hesitated.

"Are you hurt?" he asked, and Matthew shook his head impatiently. "No no!" he yelled. "Hurry, man!" The large man began to run in the direction of the village. Matthew stumbled back into the cabin, back into the bathroom; he lifted her small bloody body, carrying her out of the mess, setting her on the bed. Sitting next to her, he checked the towels again, making sure they were wrapped tightly, then he adjusted her head, placing pillows under her. "Oh, Amanda, why?" But he knew why; rubbing his hand on his face, he stood up and began to pace. "My god," he whispered, "what have we done?"

Within minutes, the cabin was filled with people. The doctor returned with Simon; Molly was sent for along with several other village women. Matthew was asked to leave, and after a little argument, he was escorted to the door by Simon who stepped outside with him.

Once outside, Matthew stood still, resting his hands on his hips, tipping his head back, and looked up at the sky, where brilliant stars lit the night. He breathed deeply, the crisp air filling his lungs. His mind was still reeling, trying to comprehend everything that had happened in the last few hours. Simon stood silently by his side. After several moments, Matthew turned to him. "How is your, uh"—he paused, gesturing toward his chest—"your wound?"

Simon scowled good-naturedly at him. "It'll take a lot more than a fork to take me down." Matthew gave a small smile, looking away, only to look back at him. Was that a smile on Simon's face? To see him smile was a rarity indeed. Simon crossed his bulky arms across his chest. "I have to admit that she is a feisty little thing."

Matthew shook his head and looked away and sighed. "How could this have happened?"

"It's not your fault, Matthew," Simon said, in his gruff manner. "I sure didn't think she was capable of any of this." He waved his hand toward the cabin. "I'm sure no one did." They both knew who he was talking about. Pastor.

Nodding his head, Matthew ran his hand through his hair. "Right."

"Why don't you get cleaned up," Simon suggested, his tone slightly softer. "You won't be allowed in until we know how she is." Matthew looked down at his bloodstained hands.

"Yeah, I think I will," he said quietly, looking over his shoulder at the cabin door.

Following his gaze, Simon said, "I'll send for you when they're done." Matthew nodded again and walked into the dark night.

Hours later, he sat on the cabin steps, his head cradled in his arms as he dozed on and off. He couldn't wait at home and had returned soon after he had left. Thankfully, Simon just nodded his understanding when he saw him walking down the path toward him, and they now took their vigil together. Matthew just wanted some word, someone to tell him something about Amanda, but no one came out. It wasn't until the sun began to rise, the morning dew blanketing around them with cold dampness, that the door finally opened.

Startled out of his sleepy state, Matthew stood up to see the doctor closing the door behind him. "Doc . . ." Fear multiplied when he saw the doctor's expression. Swallowing, he asked, "How is she?" Sighing, the doctor came down the steps; standing before Matthew, he reached out and put his right hand on his left shoulder, in a comforting gesture.

"She's still alive," he spoke softly. "But she's lost a lot of blood." Matthew searched the doctor's eyes rapidly, trying to figure out what he was saying to him.

"What . . . what does that mean?" Matthew asked quietly.

"I've stitched her up," he explained, "and treated her abrasions from earlier." Then shaking his white head, he added, "She's in and out of consciousness. I just don't know at this point." Matthew nodded his head, trying to accept what the doctor was telling him.

"Will she die?" he asked, wanting to know, needing to know.

Doc met his eyes directly. "She could," he stated honestly. "There could be many complications. Fever, infection . . . she may have lost too much blood."

"Can't we give her more?" he asked, exasperated. "Wouldn't that help?" Simon had stepped up behind Matthew, listening. Doc shook his head sadly.

"I just don't have the means to do that here," he said. "You and I both know that I'm limited to homeopathy. If we could get her to a hospital-"

"Let's take her!" Matthew proclaimed, causing Simon to intervene.

"Whoa!" Simon interrupted, stepping forward. "That's not going to happen. You know that we can't do that, Matthew." Angry, Matthew looked at him.

"She may die if she doesn't receive more blood!" he said, his voice rising.

"I understand," Simon said quietly, understanding. "There will not be any more talk of a hospital."

"Son, if it's God's will, then let it done," the doctor spoke softly. His brows coming together, Matthew shrugged the doctor's hand off his shoulder and took a step back.

"God's will?" he snapped. "We took her. God didn't do this, *we* did!"

Matthew walked up the stairs.

"Matthew, tending to her is the women's job," Simon said firmly. "You may see her, then you will leave." Matthew halted at his words, his hand on the door handle. Turning back, the two men were watching him; he said quietly, "Then I guess you'll have to physically remove me, Simon. It's my fault that she could be dying in there, and I'll be damned if I don't see her through this." With that, Matthew walked in and closed the door. Simon and the doctor exchanged concerned glances. Matthew had never defied an order in his life, and now he was challenging his authority, and they both knew that this would not be overlooked.

The cabin was warm, lanterns lit, casting a yellow light throughout the room. The air permeated of herbs that two village women were preparing in the kitchenette. They nodded to him, sober expressions on their faces as they glanced at the bed. Matthew took slow steps toward Amanda. At the same time, Molly came out of the bathroom carrying an arm full of bloody linens.

"Matthew," Molly said his name just above a whisper. Turning to her, he noticed how exhausted she looked. Worry was etched around her eyes. "Matthew, I'm . . . I'm so sorry." Her kind words almost brought tears to his eyes, but he forced them back and just nodded his head. Men were not allowed to show emotion in the village. He had stopped midway in the room, looking toward the bed, then turned back to Molly.

"How is she?" he asked softly. Molly's eyes were shining with tears as she shook her head.

"We just don't know." Walking over to the sofa, she set the linens in an awaiting basket. Matthew turned back to Amanda and walked over to her side. She was covered with a warm quilt, her arms lay on top, her wrists and one hand were bound in white bandages. Her hair had been washed and braided, her ivory skin was pale beneath flushed cheeks. The ugly gash on her forehead was flaming red, and there were multiple scratches on her cheeks. She was so small and fragile, and Matthew fought the urge to hit something. Anything, to purge the anger, resentment, and frustration that was consuming him in that moment.

Instead, he pulled the chair that was by the bedside, went closer, and sat down in it. Taking her small soft hand gently into his own, he rested his cheek against her knuckles. "Oh, Amanda," he whispered, closing his eyes. The women that had been working on the herbs had stopped to watch the intimate exchange, compassion and envy filling their hearts. Molly's snapping fingers brought them back to attention quickly. With a nod of her head, she dismissed them, handing over the basket to one of them, and they left the cabin quietly. Molly watched Matthew silently.

She had known Matthew since he was a boy and understood him as well as his mother did. Katherine had done a wonderful job raising a son who was strong, compassionate, kind, and giving. Even as a child, he had been different from the other boys. Oh, he ran around and caused mischief like the rest of them, but he was constantly aware of others' feelings, never having a mean word for anyone. It was well known that the pastor had labeled Matthew. He began making life harder for him after his father had passed away, pushing him physically and mentally. The other villagers knew what a wonderful person he was and couldn't share their pastor's feelings, men and women alike. Yet Matthew bore his burden with a smile and a light spirit.

He carried traits that most women only dream of having in a spouse, but she knew, as everyone did, that these were characteristics of weakness in Pastor's eyes. She remembered several "lessons" that he was given throughout his childhood to teach him about manhood in the village, but none of them changed him, only made him stronger. It was common knowledge why he was one of the chosen men to take a worldly wife. He was weak in Pastor's eyes, and Pastor knew that this would torment him like nothing else would. He was forcing him to purposely hurt someone, thought Molly sadly. Though in the end Amanda was going to benefit in her new life, she knew how difficult this was for him.

She walked over to his side, resting her hand gently on his shoulder.

"Matthew?" she whispered his name. After a moment, he looked up at her. "Go home and get some rest. You can visit later on today." Clenching his jaw, he turned back to Amanda.

"I'm not going home, Molly," he replied with an edge to his voice. "I'm not leaving her side." Shocked at his intent, and immediately knowing the disapproval he was going to bring on himself, she tried to reason with him.

"Matthew, I know you're upset," she began, coming around to face him, squatting down so that she was eye level with him. Her tired eyes met his, and she saw something she had never seen before—defiance. "You know this isn't possible. Please, Matthew."

"Stop, Molly!" he protested, more loudly than he had wanted. Then softening his tone, he met Molly's eyes. "I know the rules, and this time I'm bending them. Amanda's going to be my wife, and I will *not* sit by and watch from a distance. I'm the best person to look after her. I'm responsible here—no one else." Molly closed her eyes then opened them.

"Matthew, this is not your fault," she assured him softly. His sharp eyes came back to hers.

"No?" he asked coldly. "Then whose is it?"

"Matthew . . ."

"Don't you see?" he spat out. "*I* chose her. *I* brought her here. I should have handled this better, I should have—"

"Matthew, you've handled this perfectly." Molly refused to let him do this to himself. "There was no way you could have known she would do this."

"Molly, why do we do this?" he asked. "This isn't biblical—why do we do it?" Molly looked at the door, then back to him.

"Matthew, you mustn't say things like that," she insisted. "Pastor knows what's best for all of us. We live blessed lives because of his leadership. This is something that has been done from the beginning of our existence, you know that. Promise me not to talk like that again." Matthew searched her pleading eyes, knowing that he was being irrational at the moment. This is what his people have always done, and who was he to question a generational tradition?

Sighing, he retreated. "I'm sorry, Molly. I'm just upset. I know our traditions have stood the test of time." Relieved, Molly gave him a small smile. "But I won't leave her side. I'll deal with the consequences." Nodding, she knew his mind was made up. She rose to her feet.

"All right then," she said, "I'm going to go home and make Peter some breakfast, then I'll return to help." Matthew stood as well,

"Molly, stay home and rest," he insisted. "I can handle everything here." She pressed her lips together.

"Matthew, this is so improper," she said, shaking her head. "I don't think—"

"Molly, she's injured and unconscious, what do you think is going to happen here?" he asked, exasperated. Hesitating, Molly walked to the door, wrapping her shawl around her shoulders.

"All right then. Pastor will not like this, but you know that, don't you?" she questioned. Matthew nodded again. "I'll come back at dinner time. To feed *you*." Matthew smiled at her.

"That sounds good," he said. "Thank you, Molly."

CHAPTER 7

With Molly gone, Matthew stood in the middle of the room, feeling helpless. He really didn't know what he was doing, but he knew he needed to be by her side. He would make an herbal salve for her wrists, he decided, an advantage being raised by his mother—his knowledge for remedies was vast. He turned off all the lanterns, now that the sun was shining brightly through the windows. Then he walked to the kitchenette and began his work.

Hours later, as he dozed in the chair by her bedside, a small whimpering noise woke him. Looking at Amanda, she was turning her head back and forth, and her face was covered with perspiration. Standing up, he quickly wet a cloth and was back at her side, wiping her face gently. She continued to whimper, not really saying anything. "It's all right, Amanda, it's all right." Matthew noticed her gown was damp, clinging to her chest and shoulders. Here was the fever the doctor had warned about. Matthew nodded his head, resigning himself to the long hours it was going to take for the fever to break. He would get her through this; there was no doubt in his mind. Eventually her whimpering ceased, and she seemed to go back to sleep. Her cheeks were burning red, her skin hot to the touch.

Matthew found a ceramic basin and filled it with cold water, placing it on the bedside table. Every few minutes he wiped her face and neck down, whispering words of comfort. Though she seemed to be sleeping peacefully, he was concerned. Her sleep was too deep. She tried to kill herself, would she fight to stay alive? Would all their efforts to save her be in vain? It didn't matter, he knew, because he would fight for her life.

She didn't realize she was surrounded in darkness until light threatened her peacefulness. Struggling inwardly, she fought the light, not wanting it, but not knowing why. As the light grew closer, a sad heaviness began to seep into her consciousness, and she choked out a cry. It was a familiar and oppressive pain. The light grew even closer, and an aching deep in her bones spread through her; desperate, she willed herself back to the dark void she had been in but failed. Finally the light was so painfully bright that she moaned in pain, startling her awake. Not yet opening her eyes, she was overwhelmed with painful and uncomfortable sensations. A strong herbal odor lingered in the air around her. "Shhh, Amanda, it's all right." His voice was a light whisper. Blinking, opening her eyes, she saw his face inches from her own. Her thoughts were fuzzy as she tried to remember who he was. "Hey." Moving slightly, she looked away, but as much as she tried, she couldn't put any thoughts together. Her eyes were heavy, and she tried to lift her arm, but it was too heavy. Helpless, she turned back to the man at her side, her brows coming together. She knew him, recognizing his face, but his name remained out of her reach. Exhaustion pulling at her again, she closed her eyes and willingly surrendered to the darkness once again.

Matthew watched as her eyes closed, listening as her breathing deepened. She hadn't been fully conscious, he could see that in her eyes. It was probably for the best, he thought, considering the condition she was in. Rising to his feet, he took the small basin to the sink, dumping the water, refilling it with fresh, cold water. Then he returned and repeated sponging her down.

The sun was setting when Molly returned. Entering the cabin, she could smell the fever. Matthew was in the middle of sponging her down again, and he didn't look up when she came in. She quickly came to his side.

"Matthew, how long has she been like this?" she asked, concerned, examining Amanda as she spoke. Her hair was wet and pushed back, from the water and perspiration; her cheeks were bright red, her lips dry and white. She was whispering unintelligibly.

Setting down the wet cloth, he sighed and rubbed a hand over his face. "Hours." Molly nodded and walked away. Minutes later, Matthew heard water running and turned to see Molly emerging from the bathroom.

"We have to get her fever down, Matthew," she announced, "or we're going to lose her." His eyes snapped to hers, seeing the seriousness there. He stood up.

"What do we have to do?"

"We need to submerge her in cold water," she stated. "Gather her up and bring her in here." Hesitating, Matthew looked down at Amanda, then back at Molly. "If you can't handle this, then I can get someone else," she said. He shook his head. "No," he said, "she's so warm, placing her in cold water—"

"Will bring her fever down," Molly finished softly. "We have no other choice, Matthew." Matthew nodded, resigned. Molly walked back in the bathroom, and he bent down, pulling the covers off her. Her nightgown was pulled up to her knees, and her ivory skin was flushed red. Slipping his arms under her, he gently lifted her. Closing his eyes, he couldn't believe how small and frail she was. She sighed and rested her head against his chest. Walking quickly into the bathroom, Molly was shutting off the water. He looked at her questioningly. Using hand motions, Molly motioned him toward her.

"Leave the gown on," she said softly. "I'll change her afterward." Clenching his jaw, he nodded and slowly set her in the water. As the water first hit her hot skin, Amanda's eyes flew open, her hands grabbing on to Matthew's shoulders tightly. Matthew hesitated midair, lowering his eyes to meet hers. There, still glazed over, the fever reflected in their depths, was painful surprise.

"Matthew," she gasped. "What—"

"Matthew, set her in the water." Molly's firm voice broke through to him. He forced himself to pull his eyes away and set her all the way in the water. She clung to him desperately as the cold water hit every part of her body. Pain surged through her, and she cried out.

"It hurts, please . . . ," she cried. Matthew was practically in the water with her, Molly trying to pry her hands away from him. "Please . . . Matthew . . ."

"I know, I know. Shhhh . . . ," he soothed, forcing his eyes back to hers. "It's only for a little while." She shook her head as tears filled her eyes.

"No . . . please . . . ," she begged. Molly was finally able to pry her away, and she splashed back into the ice-cold water. Matthew straightened, watching Molly hold Amanda in the cold water. Amanda was shaking uncontrollably, and her pleas were too much for him.

"Molly, isn't it enough?" he asked. She looked over at him, shaking her head.

"No, Matthew," she said. "Go change the bedding." Matthew clenched his jaw. "Go, now!" He reluctantly turned and walked out of the room. His body was tight with tension, frustrated at his helplessness. He walked to the closet off to the right of the kitchenette and pulled out fresh linens. He changed the linens, heated up some broth, and fluffed her pillows three separate times. Twenty minutes passed, and he was pacing the room, and he couldn't take it any longer. Walking over to the door, he came to a stop when it opened, and a disheveled Molly stood in the opening. She waved her hand toward her.

"Come," she said softly, "she's ready to be put back in bed." Swallowing, he only nodded and walked into the bathroom. Molly had managed to dress her, braid her wet hair, and rest her on the floor, propped up against the wall. Amanda's head was slumped forward, her breathing deep as she slept. He knelt down next to her, hesitating. "She's asleep, Matthew," Molly spoke. "She won't remember this, don't worry." Matthew clenched his jaw, nodded, and slipped his arms under her limp body. Her head fell against his chest, and he could feel her fevered skin through his clothes. Laying her gently on the bed, he pulled the covers up over her. Molly came up behind him, looking over his shoulder, down at her.

"Now what?" he asked, his voice just above a whisper.

"If you look at her flushed skin," Molly replied, her tone somber, "the cold water barely touched her fever." She paused. "It's going to be a long night."

Matthew turned slightly, concern etched on his features. "You mean she has to endure that again?" Molly nodded, looking at him quietly for several moments.

"I'm sending you home," she decided. Matthew's back stiffened as he stepped away from the bed, and from Molly.

"I'm not leaving her," he declared adamantly. Molly followed him, her hands on her hips.

"Do you think that you're helping her by feeling sorry for her?" she demanded in a harsh whisper. "Matthew, this is not your place!" He turned around, meeting her eyes directly.

"I made a mistake!" he admitted. "I apologize for my weak moment. I can only explain my behavior because I"—he looked away, rubbing a hand across his face—"care for her."

"I know you care for her," Molly said, her own tone softening. "But—"

"It won't happen again." Molly closed her eyes and pressed her stray hairs back against her hair. "Molly, I won't leave her." Acknowledging his decision with a nod, she opened her eyes again.

"Let's begin sponging her down again, and in another hour we'll submerge her in cold water again. It may take several times . . . ," she directed softly. Matthew clenched his jaw and nodded, resolving to do whatever he needed to, to save Amanda.

The warm colors of dawn began to shine through the small cabin windows. The air was warm and stifled inside, the remains of an exhausting night.

Matthew slept in the chair by Amanda's bedside, his body slumped, his head leaning back awkwardly. Molly had left, going home to tend to her family, feeling confident that the worst was over. Amanda would survive. Together they submerged her four more times during the night, sponged her scalding body with cold water, and forced her to drink water. Amanda's fever had reached its peak, finally breaking around four in the morning.

Amanda blinked open her eyes, the knots and flaws of the pine wall slowly came into focus. Taking inventory of herself, she felt a weakness settling over her. Struggling to turn over, her eyes settled on a sleeping Matthew, having no doubt where she was. Scanning his sleeping form, she noticed that he looked much rougher than he had before. His dark clothing was wrinkled and messed, a day's worth of growth on his face left him in need of a good shave. Shave . . . the razor . . . now things were becoming clearer. It was then she felt the burning pain in her wrists. Lifting her arms, she twisted them back and forth slightly, examining the bandages. Images of the bathroom and her horrible decision swamped her. Choking on a sob, she brought her hands to her face. *Oh God . . . what had she done?*

Her small noise woke Matthew. He grimaced as he moved his neck and sat up. Rubbing his face, he looked down to see Amanda with her hands covering her face. Using his fingers, he rubbed his eyes, ridding them of sleeping debris. "Amanda?" His was voice soft. She moved her hands, and they came to rest on her chest. Her blue eyes were wide and moist. She was so pale, her lips were chapped, but she was alive, and Matthew was so relieved. The haunted eyes searched his face. "How do you feel?" Amanda swallowed, shifting her eyes away. He looked exhausted, she thought; then she was angry with herself for even noticing.

When she made no reply, he stood up and walked toward the kitchenette. She watched him return with a glass of water, his eyes meeting hers directly, concerned. "Here." He slipped his hand beneath her hair, lifting her head gently. Bringing the water to her lips, she took a small sip. After he set her head down, she licked her dry lips. "Are you in any pain?"

She searched his face.

"What?" she asked groggily, her thoughts still so unclear.

"Do you feel any pain?" he asked again. Taking a quick inventory, her body felt weak, and her wrists were sore.

"A little," she whispered. His eyes were so kind, she thought, and he seemed genuinely concerned, but she despised him, didn't she?

"The doctor will be here soon," he said quietly, watching her closely. "He'll be able to make sure you're okay." She looked away, toward the wall, her heart heavy. His gut twisted because he could see the misery on her face, and he knew that he was the cause of that misery. She tried to kill herself; Matthew still couldn't believe what had happened. The last couple of days had been like a nightmare for her and himself. He was wise enough to know that the nightmare was far from being over. Somehow he had to lift Amanda's spirit, convince her that this was the place for her. But that wasn't going to be easy, he surmised, rubbing his face tiredly. During his observation of Amanda he'd been attracted to her contagious joy and the constant state of happiness that she radiated. He *chose* her and by doing so he was destroying what he loved most about her. Once her eyes were alive and bright, now they were dull and lightless. He did this to her. Looking at her now, her beautiful spirit was being crushed, and it had only been a matter of days. Gone was the joy that lit her face on a daily basis, the glow that everyone noticed about her.

His heart weighed heavy in his chest. He was the reason . . . the cause of such a loss. How can this tradition be right? How can God like this, he thought to himself as he rested his face in his hands. Everything he thought and believed in now seemed confusing.

Distant memories came rushing back. As a child, he had attended many weddings. He remembered attending one particular wedding when he was but twelve years old. It was the marriage of a man named Micah. Micah had been a friend of his father's, before his father had died. He was a strong, burly redheaded man, with a close-cut beard and the jolliest green eyes. After his father had passed away, Micah spent a lot of time with Matthew, helping him deal with his loss by just being with him, telling him humorous stories about his and his father's childhood.

When it was time for Micah to marry, he came around a lot less. This confused Matthew until his mother had explained to him that it took a lot of preparation for a man of the village to take a wife. As a twelve year old, it was difficult to understand, but he soon found other things to occupy his time. He didn't think too much about Micah and his search for his new wife until the day of the wedding. Matthew had not been at the group prayer for the "sinful" woman, so his first encounter with her was on the actual wedding day.

He remembered sitting in the pew next to his mother, watching her being brought in. She was moderately attractive, and she had flaming red hair—brighter than Micah's, but her appearance wasn't what he remembered most about her. It was the wild look she had in her eyes as she twisted and turned in the arms of the men that held her. Micah stood at the front of the church with a somber expression on his face.

When she had reached the front of the church, Micah had reached over and said something in her ear that seemed to calm her enough so that her escorts could let her go. Then Pastor had begun his sermon, his booming voice filling the church. But in moments, chaos had broken loose. Pastor began the "name ceremony," and this woman had become wild again, attacking Pastor, scratching, clawing, and screaming at him.

When she was finally restrained, and Pastor had regained his composure, he approached her. He said something quietly to her that the congregation couldn't hear, and she reacted by spitting in his face. Matthew remembers the fear he felt in that moment to be very real. Pastor's face had flushed red, and the church became so silent that all of the members could hear the beating of their own hearts. Pastor was never to be challenged, his temper was always unpredictable. Yet he restrained himself in that moment, and there had been a community sigh of relief. The sermon ended, and Micah was officially married.

The memory didn't strike him as any different than any other wedding, except that was the last time he ever saw the woman again. Normally, within a week, the new couple would join the community Sunday meal, but she never made an appearance.

As a twelve year old, he didn't really know what he thought. But when he saw Micah again, he looked so much older than he had the day of his wedding—his bright eyes dull and lifeless. Matthew had run up to him happily, but Micah couldn't even manage a smile for him. Walking away, hurt by his friend's aloofness, he brought this up to his mother. His mother had become very serious in her tone and demeanor; she warned him to not speak of Micah or his wedding again. He had learned at an early age when you were told not to speak of something, you didn't.

That had been the last time he ever saw Micah.

Why didn't I remember that, he wondered, lifting his head. They were never spoken of again, and deep down inside Matthew knew they just didn't disappear. Everyone knew. There were whispers and shared glances amongst the villagers, but no one dared voice any concerns out loud. The unspoken fate of Micah and his new wife only escalated the fear of Pastor and his disapproval.

Matthew's entire life, he had always worked hard for Pastor's approval and acceptance; all the young boys did. Knowing he disappointed the pastor with his "soft" heart, his fear of his pastor outweighed his love for him. For the first time in his life, he was angry. He was angry with himself for feeling the fear he did. Doubts again ebbed at his conscience.

True to his word, there was a light knock on the door, and it opened moments later, revealing the doctor. Matthew stood up, swallowing the bitter taste in his mouth, and pushed his chair out of the way. Amanda slowly turned her head to see the older man. He was short and more on the lean side with bushy white hair and bushy white eyebrows to match. He wore the strange attire that everyone else wore, except the clothes seemed to hang on his frame. Matthew filled his clothes perfectly. *Now where did that come from*, she thought absently.

She watched Matthew shake the doctor's hand, and they were talking softly to one another. The doctor turned and walked to her bedside, looking down at her, and smiled. A kind smile that made his face wrinkle as he took her hand gently in his own.

"How is my young patient?" he asked, in a soft, scruffy voice.

She just looked up at him, not answering, then noticed Matthew walking to the door. Instantly an overwhelming sense of panic filled her that she tried to sit up, surprising the doctor.

"Whoa . . . ," he said, gently holding her shoulders. Looking over his shoulder, seeing Matthew turning back to them, his expression was of concern. His hand rested on the doorknob, yet he hesitated when he heard the doctor speak. With his attention turning back on Amanda's wide eyes, the doctor asked, "Do you want Matthew to stay, young lady?" Searching his eyes, she swallowed, feeling confused. *Do I?* Amanda tried to sort her thoughts. *Yes . . . yes, I do*, her eyes pleaded silently with the doctor's as she nodded.

"That's fine. But I need you to relax, all right," he said gently, helping her settle back in. "Matthew, she would feel more comfortable if you stayed."

"All right," was his quiet response as he walked back toward the bed, her panicked look beginning to subside. He watched her curiously as her eyes followed him, not missing the relief that had crossed her features.

"Good. Now, let's check you over." He began to examine her. "You gave us quite a scare, little one." He pushed and prodded, asking questions that he found difficult to get an answer to. "Now let's check under these bandages," he said, beginning to gently unwrap the cloths. Amanda flinched as he got closer to the wounds, tugging her arm away from him. She suddenly spoke.

"No," she gasped roughly, her voice hoarse from lack of use. Matthew searched her face, as did the doctor.

"What's wrong?" the doctor asked patiently. "Am I hurting you?" Hesitating, she looked from Matthew back to him.

"Please . . . just leave them," she said quietly.

"I need to make sure there is no infection," the doctor said gently. "I will be more gentle, if I'm hurting you." He reached for her wrist again, but this time, she yanked her wrist away, startling both the doctor and Matthew.

"No! Leave me alone," she said desperately. The doctor got to his feet, confounded. She had been somewhat cooperative up to this point.

"Doc, I just changed the bandages this morning, and the stitches look good. There didn't seem to be any infection," Matthew spoke quietly. The doctor looked over at Matthew.

"Good . . . good," he stated, relieved not to have to go farther with this sudden obstacle she was giving him. "Okay, well, then I will wait to check on them." He turned back to Amanda. "You, young lady, need to rest. You've lost a lot of blood and the fever took more of your strength than you think. You'll be weak for a little while, but only a little while." He patted her hand and smiled.

Before he left, he spoke to Matthew.

"Toward the end of the day, you might want to try to take her for a walk," he recommended. "Not a long one, mind you, she won't have the strength to go far, but fresh air will be good for her."

Matthew began to speak, but the doctor put up his hand.

"I know the rules, Matthew," he said quietly, "but she needs this. I will inform Pastor myself." Relieved, Matthew nodded.

When the doctor left, he returned to Amanda's bedside. She watched him as he pulled the chair back over and sat down. He gently reached for her bandaged wrist, and she immediately flinched, pulling away.

"It's okay, Amanda," he said softly. "I just want to wrap up what the doctor started to undo." She hesitated but then let him wrap her wrist. "Do they hurt? Is that why you didn't want the doctor touching them?"

She nodded tearfully. Knowing that wasn't the whole reason. She was unwilling to see the damage she had done to herself.

"I can give you some herbs for the pain." Shaking her head, she looked toward the wall. "The doctor will be sending Molly over. She'll help you wash and change into a fresh gown. I'm sure it will make you feel better."

Startled, she turned back to him, panic fresh on her face.

"Where . . . where will you be?" she asked, her voice soft.

CHAPTER 8

"Oh, I won't be here, don't worry. You'll have complete privacy," he said, misinterpreting her anxiety. She struggled to push herself to her elbows.

"No . . . no . . . please . . . I . . . ," she pleaded. She didn't know why such fear had come over her. The thought of him leaving her caused such a tightness in her chest and fear to travel through her. *Why do I feel this way? I don't need anyone! He did this to you! He kidnapped you*, she screamed to herself. Emotionally incapacitated, she was helpless to how she felt. She wanted him to stay.

He placed his hand gently over hers.

"Amanda, it's okay," he said softly, searching her face. "I won't go if you don't want me to." The tightness eased some, and she shook her head.

"No," she said, "don't." Her eyes pleaded with his, shining with unshed tears.

"I won't, Amanda," he said quietly. "I'll stay here with you, all right?"

Relieved, she nodded, and this time she didn't turn away. After a few quiet moments, Amanda brought her eyes up to his. She watched him.

"Why didn't you just let me die?" she asked, just above a whisper. Taken aback by her question, he hesitated in his response. Leaning forward, he rested his elbows on his legs.

"I don't want you to die," he said seriously. "Why would you do that? Why would you try to kill yourself?" She blinked and looked away.

"I don't want to be here. I need to leave," she said in a small voice. Matthew leaned forward in his chair, resting his elbows on the bed.

"Amanda, I know that when we took you and brought you here, it was terrifying. I know that everything must seem scary, but you have nothing to be afraid of." He tried to comfort her. Shaking her head, she looked at him incredulously.

"You know . . . you know how scared I was?" she questioned. "You have no idea! Terrified does not even come close to how I felt and still feel. It's never been done to you, has it?" She continued, not expecting a response, "You *stole* me away from everything and everybody that I love! How could you possibly know?" Turning to the wall, her next words were quietly defeated. "You ask why I would try to kill myself? Because I would rather die than be here." He leaned back in his chair, crossing his arms, studying her silently. No, he didn't know how she felt; he could only imagine. He was never taught to care about how she would feel, but he knew the woman he had studied for months, and this wasn't her.

"You're stronger than that," he said quietly.

Her head whipped back. "No, I'm not!" she informed him heatedly, pushing herself up with the last bit of strength she had left. "Don't tell me what I am or what I'm not! You don't know me! You think you do because you watched me or whatever you did—but you don't know me—" Putting her hand on her chest, she continued, "You don't know *me!*" As she sat up, she had pulled her gown tight against her body, her breasts rising up and down with her exerted energy. Matthew tried not to notice, but he was a man for God's sake. How much willpower was he expected to have? He forced himself to look in her eyes.

"Amanda, I may not know you well, but I know you are much stronger than you think!" he insisted, leaning forward again. "I've watched you, yes. I know what I saw in you was not my imagination and I know that I took you away from your life. But is that enough to die for? Don't you care about your own life? Or have you been living your life for everyone around you?" he countered her.

"Of course I haven't!" she argued. "But . . . I'm scared!" she said, bursting into tears. "I don't know what's going to happen to me. What *is* going to happen to me?" Looking at him, her face was wet with her fresh tears.

He reached over and gently took her uninjured hand into his own.

"You'll marry me," he said softly. "And that is all." Her eyes rapidly searched his face. *Is he lying to me? I can't trust him*, she reminded herself. *But if not him, then who . . . was there anyone?*

"But what will happen after?" she asked, her eyes pleading for the truth. "Are you going to hurt me?" The question came out as a whisper.

"No," he stated. "No, Amanda. Lord, no! I would never want to hurt you."

"But how do I know?" she asked, her voice uncertain. "You're the one who took me," she added, pulling her hand slowly away from his. "You brought me here." He sat up straight.

"Yes. I did," he said soberly. "I explained the traditions of my people and I did what all the men do here. I'm expected to uphold the traditions for our future generations. It's my duty, to the village and to God." Listening to him, she realized that he believed what he was saying. *He had performed this tradition because he was raised believing that this was the only way,* she thought to herself. *Was he a victim too?* She quickly dismissed any compassionate thoughts that tried to surface. "I know you don't know me, but we will have our whole lives to get to know one another. Amanda, you can trust me. I am an honest man. I work hard and I will make you proud to have me for a husband."

Amanda was overwhelmed by so many emotions—anger, frustration, sadness, fear. She covered her eyes with her left arm.

"Ohhhhh!" she moaned. "This is so twisted . . . *I just want to go home!*"

Just then there was a knock on the door, and Molly let herself into the cabin. Amanda lifted her arm to see who it was, then moaned again.

"I came to help out," Molly said slowly, looking from Amanda to Matthew. He stood up, their eyes meeting; the tension in Matthew was evident.

"Thank you, Molly," he said and waved his hand toward the bed. "I think Amanda would feel much better if she washed up and had a clean gown."

"Certainly," she smiled. "Amanda, I was so happy to hear you finally woke up. We were so worried about you."

We, she thought bitterly, *you and your strange village people!* She wanted to tell her to go to hell. But years of good teaching and a moral upbringing stopped her from being so rude . . . even in these outrageous circumstances.

"Thank you," she spoke softly, keeping her eyes closed.

"Can I help you to the bathroom?" she asked. Amanda heard movement next to her and opened her eyes quickly. Matthew was walking toward the door.

"No!" she called, sitting back up, the tightness instantly returning to her chest. "Wait . . . where . . . where are you going?" Molly looked at Matthew curiously. Matthew turned back to Amanda.

"You're upset," he said. "I assumed you wanted some time alone."

"No," she said, ignoring Molly. "I mean . . . no . . . don't go."

"Now that I'm here," interjected Molly, "it's only right and proper for him to leave. It's been completely improper for him to be here nursing you.

Imagine him by your bedside all this time. He's been the talk of the village and he needs to return to his work."

Amanda's eyes slowly traveled up to meet his own. *Nursing her? What did Molly mean?* He saw the confusion in her expression as the two of them watched one another silently.

"Matthew, you can go now," insisted Molly. "Go get some rest of your own."

"No!" Amanda interrupted desperately. "Please . . . don't . . . leave." Matthew hesitated. She really didn't want him to go. What was going on with her? Why did she have this need to have him here, when she made it quite clear that she disliked him so?

Molly came over, laying her hand gently on Amanda's shoulder, saying, "It's all right, Amanda. I'll take good care of you."

Amanda shoved Molly's hand away from her and struggled to get out of bed.

"Leave me alone!" she said. Matthew rushed to her side.

"Whoa!" he said, grabbing her by her waist. "Amanda, stop, you'll hurt yourself." Grabbing on to his forearms, she squeezed tightly with her good hand, looking up into his face.

"Don't leave me," she pleaded, tears shining in her eyes, her face so pale.

"Okay," he said softly, staring into her eyes. "I won't go. I promise."

"Matthew—," Molly began disapprovingly.

"I'm staying, Molly," he said firmly without taking his eyes from Amanda's face. Relief washed over her, and she went limp in his arms as he helped her sit on the bed. *He wasn't leaving her,* she thought, and almost cried as emotion choked her. *What is wrong with me,* she thought. *What is happening to me?*

"Let Molly help you wash up," he said softly. "I'll be right here waiting for you." Amanda swallowed, looking around Matthew to see Molly standing patiently a few feet from them. She didn't want Molly to help her wash.

"I can do it myself," she muttered stubbornly. Matthew chuckled, seeing a glimpse of the Amanda he had observed for the past few months. "Amanda, you're too weak to even stand on your own," he said. "I definitely cannot help you." Her cheeks flushed as she thought of him helping her. He was hiding his small smile. "Come on. You know Molly. Let her help you."

Amanda eyed her warily, knowing that Molly had been kind to her. "All right," she reluctantly assented. Molly came to her side to help her walk into the bathroom. Within half an hour, Amanda was washed and wearing a fresh gown. She hurried Molly with cleaning up because she wanted to make sure that Matthew was still there and he was. He just finished replacing the sheets and blankets with fresh, clean linens. *Had he really taken care of her by himself?*

He sucked his breath in when she came out of the bathroom. Her hair had been washed and lay damp down her back. Her blue eyes looked a shade darker next to her pale skin. Losing weight since her arrival, the gown was larger on her now than it was a few days ago, but he thought she was beautiful! She had an anxious expression when she first stepped out of the bathroom, relaxing immediately when her eyes had rested on him, a quiet sigh escaping her lips.

Matthew had folded back the covers on the bed and patted the mattress.

"Come on, Amanda," he said. "You look exhausted."

She was. So much so she didn't think she could keep her eyes open another minute. Molly helped her to the bed, and Matthew tucked her in gently. Blinking up at him sleepily, she reached her bandaged hand out to him. He carefully slipped his hand into her small one.

"Don't go," she whispered then closed her eyes and instantly fell into a deep sleep. His heart tugged as he watched her sweet face. This vulnerable change in her was bringing out feelings in him he didn't know existed. Conflicting emotions raced through him, a mix of guilt and pleasure . . . and a protectiveness. He reached over and touched her cheek with his free hand, his fingertips skimming her soft skin. Closing his eyes, he had no idea that he would feel this way about her. Having her here, finally after all the preparation, being able to touch her, talk to her, was overwhelming to him. In that one moment, when she held on to his arms asking him not to leave her, a small glimpse of hope began to grow. Would she come to accept him after all? When he envisioned his life with Amanda, it was a simple dream. They would live in the cabin that he was in the process of building, they would have children, and grow old together. Thinking of it now, he found that it seemed ridiculous, even childish. Since the day of the abduction, he had a rude awakening that this wasn't going to be simple, and any kind of dream he had vanished immediately. This small glimpse of hope he saw was enough to get him through the next few hours, and he was contented with that.

After a few quiet moments, Molly spoke softly over his shoulder.

"Matthew," she said, "were you able to get any rest after I left?" He looked over his shoulder at her, and then back at Amanda.

"Some," he replied. "She was restful for at least four hours before she woke." Molly's hand rested on him.

"She almost didn't make it," she said softly, "but the Lord has chosen her to live. It is a blessing." Matthew closed his eyes, knowing how serious her fever had been.

"Amen to that," he responded quietly.

"Why don't you go home and get some rest," Molly said. He shook his head.

"No," he said, "I promised I would stay."

Molly sighed. Stubborn boy, she thought.

"All right," she said. "Then why don't you go home and get out of your smelly clothes, eat something and then you can come back." Pausing, she continued, "She won't even know you're gone, Matthew."

"Smelly clothes, huh?" Matthew chuckled softly. "Thanks a lot, Molly."

"Oh, honey, you know I love you." Resting her hands on his shoulders, she added, "She's completely exhausted. She was falling asleep when she was washing up and the only thing that kept her awake was her wanting to make sure you didn't leave."

"Really?" he asked, slowly slipping his hand out of Amanda's now-loose grip. He stood up and stepped away from the bed.

"Yes, really." She smiled, seeing his pleased expression. "I see that makes you happy."

"Yes, strangely enough, it does," he said, shaking his head. "I guess I will go wash up and get something to eat. But if she even starts to wake up, send for me." She smiled at him. He really cared for this girl, she thought to herself.

"I will," she promised. "Now go," she said, gently pushing him toward the door.

CHAPTER 9

Once outside, Matthew began walking down the small road that led to his mother's cabin, massaging his stiff neck as he walked. The air was crisp, and he could smell winter coming. Unconsciously, he began calculating all the work that needed to be done before winter arrived.

On his way, he passed several village women, nodding his greeting. They nodded and smiled in return. The women were not allowed to talk to any men unless they were accompanied by their husbands, brothers, or fathers. He didn't miss their curious glances, and he smiled to himself when they walked by. He knew that he broke a lot of rules this past week, and he knew Pastor was not pleased with him. Yet for the first time in his life, he didn't care. He laughed out loud at this realization, shoving his hands into his jean pockets. Amanda had come into his world and turned everything upside down. The perfect structured life he had always known no longer existed since the day of her abduction.

He reached his mother's cabin. As he entered, it reminded him that this was going to be his home for only a matter of days, and then he would share his own cabin with Amanda, his wife. The thought made him smile, and he actually felt things were looking a little brighter for the future.

"Well, that is a nice sight," greeted his mother, with a smile. "I haven't seen that smile in a long time." She opened her arms, and he stepped into her embrace.

She was a small framed woman. Her dark hair, beginning to go gray, was long and always pulled back in a bun high on her head. Her skin was still smooth and beautiful, with just a slight sign of wrinkles around her eyes when she smiled. She came across as having a quiet and sweet disposition but was known throughout the village for her strength and stubbornness. She was a well-respected member of the village—as much as a woman could be.

His mom meant the world to him and was all he had after his father's death when he was a child. She was always encouraging him, teaching him to be sensitive to others' feelings and also to have strength of character, which she felt she succeeded in doing.

"What has brought that smile back?" she asked.

Smiling, he said quietly, "She's awake." Her brows came together as she searched her son's expression. He was in love . . . he loved this girl.

"That's wonderful!" she exclaimed, a little a shocked from this realization. "Here, sit, and I will fix you some lunch." He sat, still smiling. "Now, how is she feeling? Did Doc come and see her?"

"Yes, he did. And she seems to be doing fine," he said. "She's in a little pain, yet she won't take anything for it. But, Mom, there's something different about her."

"What do you mean?" she asked curiously, turning away from the oven to look at him.

"Well, she doesn't want me to leave her," he said. "After she woke, I tried to leave a couple of times and she became, I don't know," shrugging his shoulders, he continued, "upset."

"Well, that is a change," she said thoughtfully, searching her son's face.

He smiled again as he lifted his hand and rubbed his hair. "We talked a little. She's really angry with me, judging by the things she says—she hates me. When we talk she gets visibly upset, but in the next instance she panics if I start to leave the cabin." His mom turned back to the stove.

"Hmm," she said, then she went quiet. Resting his arms across his chest, he watched his mom as she stirred the soup.

"Hmm?" he repeated. Then he asked, "What does that mean?"

"Well," she said as she ladled soup into a bowl, then placing the bowl in front of him; she sat down across from him. "It sounds as if she's in shock."

"Shock?" he asked, his surprise evident.

"Yes," she replied. "Matthew, she has every right to hate you. You've kidnapped her." He could only stare at his mother. "What she's feeling is normal, but it seems, by what your saying, that you've now become a kind of security to her. She knows now that her future is in your hands. You've been kind to her and it could be that she identifies you as her protection. Seeing only kindness from you, that would be enough for her to feel safe. What she needs *is* to feel safe right now, to have a connection with someone. Think of all that's happening to her."

"On the other hand, she recognizes that you have brought her into this situation and to her it's confusing. She may feel she needs you for protection, but also resents you for what you've done to her."

Matthew sat silently, staring into his soup. She continued, "Her mind and body are in shock. Her body, because it suffered such a major trauma, and her mind . . . well, that's obvious, isn't it?"

"Mom?" Looking up at her, he asked, "Did you hate Dad when he saved you?"

"Ahhh." She smiled and folded her hands on the table in front of her. "I knew when you brought your future wife here, that this question would arise. To answer honestly"—she paused, looking into her son's blue eyes, then—"yes, I did." His eyes widened.

"But I always remember you and Dad being so affectionate with one another," he proclaimed, confused.

"And we were," she assured him. "It was quite genuine, our love for one another. But in the beginning, before you were born, things were . . . difficult. Honey"—she reached across the table and placed her hands on his and continued—"you were born into this life. It's all you know of what is good and proper. You've been safe and protected, and I'm so pleased at the man you've become"—pausing again—"but the women that have been abducted have known another life other than this one. Most of the wives have come from different backgrounds and situations, and we've had to adapt to a completely different way of life than we were used to. We've had to put all of our memories in a secret place, not to share with a soul. Family, loved ones—"

"Why didn't you share these things with me before?" he interrupted, somewhat frustrated.

"Because you wouldn't have understood," she admitted softly. "You needed to see for yourself the devastation that it causes."

"Amanda's soul will be so much better off than it was," he defended. "We are people of the Lord, she's saved now."

"Yes, she is," she admitted, her voice slightly strained, "but that is your training speaking now, not your heart."

Matthew looked down again, then back up at his mother.

"But you came around," he said, looking hopeful. "You loved each other." She looked thoughtful for a moment then smiled.

"Yes, I grew to love your father," she acknowledged. "You have a lot of his qualities, Matthew. He had the same compassion and love for others as you do. He was kind and gentle, and most of all patient with me. It took me a long time to accept that I wasn't returning to my old life. I had hope for a long time but slowly, so slowly that I didn't even realize it, I began to accept this life. Before too long, I became pregnant for you. And you"—her eyes lit up, her face glowing, she then continued—"you gave me new meaning to my existence. Things that weren't bearable for me, soon became so. Your father and yourself became my life. I fulfilled my role as a woman here, and I have been . . . content."

"You don't ever think about going back to the sinful world, do you?" he asked anxiously. She pulled her hands back and sighed.

"After your father died, I considered it," she admitted quietly.

"But, Mom, the risk of getting caught . . . ," he began.

"Is death," she finished soberly. "Yes, I know. I was so lonely after your father died because he had become so important to me." Her eyes filling with tears, Matthew reached across the table, taking her hands into his own.

"Mom," he said softly. She reached into her apron pocket and retrieved a tissue, smiling as she dabbed her tears.

"I still miss him so much," she said then cleared her throat. "But I quickly pushed the whole idea out of my head because I couldn't risk your death, and there wasn't any way that I was going to leave you behind."

"Now listen to me," she continued, "I'm telling you this to help you. If you want to do this right, and really have Amanda return your affection, then you need to listen to me. The fact that she looks to you for protection is a very good sign and the bitterness she feels toward you will soon fade, but her memories of her old life will take much longer. Talk to her about her old life—"

"But Mom, the tradition."

She waved her hand impatiently in the air.

"Oh bosh!" she exclaimed impatiently. "I'm telling you what will work to make the two of you happy. If you want to do it the hard way and be miserable then let's stop the conversation now."

He had never been in such an intense conversation with his mother before and was a little taken back by her frankness.

"No, I want to hear what you have to say," he said quietly.

"Good," she said, continuing, "talk to her about her old life in private. I don't want you to be thrown into isolation but let her know that you care about her feelings and who she really is. Not just that she's going to be your wife, but that she's a real person. You believe that she lived in a sinful world, but that doesn't mean that she is a bad person, or you wouldn't have chosen her to be yours. Allow her to work through her feelings with you, and she will learn to trust and accept you much quicker than if you try to force her to be what you want her to be."

He sat back in his chair. "Wow," was all he could say.

"Son, I see you have feelings for her already," she spoke gently. "If you listen to what I say, it can save you both a lot of heartache. Trust me. I know from experience what it feels like to be in her shoes."

"I had no idea that you felt these things so deeply, Mom," he said seriously. "I've just been living my own life, not even considering what you've been through. How selfish have I been?"

She smiled.

"You're a man in this village," she stated. "You're not taught to consider a woman's thoughts or feelings and you were raised as you should have been here. If I had intervened too soon, then you would have felt even more different from the other men than you already do." Leaning forward slightly, she added, "Matthew, I want you to have the same happiness that your father and I shared." Nodding, he searched her face.

"Mom, I'm so sorry that I never considered your struggles," he apologized sincerely. She shook her head and looked down at her hands.

"This was my destiny. You and your father were my destiny," she said quietly, lifting her eyes to his again. "Just promise me that you'll consider what I've said to you. I will not repeat what I have told you again because it wouldn't be wise. Trust me, Matthew."

"Mom, of course I trust you," he stated with feeling. "I promise to do whatever it takes to make this easier for Amanda."

Amanda opened her eyes slowly. The cabin was dark; the shadows from a flickering candle danced along the wall. She blinked, and the wood came into focus. She must have slept all day and, it seemed, into the night.

Matthew. *Did he leave her,* she thought suddenly, turning over and struggling to sit up. He wasn't in the chair next to the bed like he was earlier, and her heart began to race as she scanned the room. Then she saw him on the small sofa that was situated against the wall on the opposite side of the cabin. There he lay, on his side, his arm cushioning his head, sleeping. She sighed in relief when she realized he hadn't left her.

She sat still for a few moments just watching him. He seemed to be sleeping peacefully. His other arm lay across his stomach, and he was covered waist down with a small blanket. *He was handsome,* she reluctantly admitted to herself, *in a rugged sort of way.* Matthew. Amanda didn't remember his last name. Not knowing anything about him, except that he brought her to this strange world, she felt like she had been picked up and placed in some twisted science fiction movie. If her wrists didn't pain her, and her heart didn't ache, she would still believe that she was having a nightmare. Unfortunately her pain was real, her aching heart kept beating, and she really *was* living a nightmare.

Lying back, she rested her head on the pillow, staring up at the ceiling. She had lost track of how long she had been here. *Was it days or weeks since I had been taken? Are my parents still looking for me? How are they? Do they have any idea of where I am?* Tears filled her eyes. Her heart hurt as she thought of them. *I didn't get a chance to talk to my mom . . . to tell her how much I love her.*

Jared entered her thoughts. The memory of the first and last night they had as a couple. She was finally ready to have the much-avoided relationship; closing her eyes, she remembered the way he looked at her, after he kissed her for the first time—a look so tender and full of emotion . . . and so intimate. He really cared for her, and she did him. *I could have eventually loved him*, she thought painfully. *Now I'll never have the chance to know. Oh, why did I put him off for so long? I didn't tell him how special he had become to me. I didn't get the chance to do so much. I just want to go home!* She squeezed her fist tightly at her side, ignoring the searing pain it caused in her wrists. She was a prisoner.

Matthew stirred slightly in his sleep, his movements interrupting her thoughts. She opened her eyes, suddenly realizing that Matthew was sleeping. *There's no one else here.* Questions filled her head. *Could there still be someone outside guarding her? How far was this village from civilization? There has to be a way out.*

Struggling to sit up, she threw the covers back, moving slowly until her legs dangled off the side of the bed. Dizziness almost overwhelmed her, but sheer will held it off. *I'm so weak*, she thought as she looked at the door, and then her eyes rested on Matthew. *If I could just get away from this place, maybe I can find some help*, she thought desperately. *How many chances will I have?*

Standing, allowing the dizziness to pass, she then took small silent steps toward the door. Her eyes barely left Matthew's sleeping body. One noise, and she knew he would wake up; seeing his jacket hanging on the chair, she picked it up, slipping it on. It was most definitely going to be cold, and she looked down at her bare feet. *Not having shoes didn't stop her the last time*, she thought. *I have to get out of here . . . I have to get home.* Reaching for the door, her hand hovered above the doorknob, and fear rose in her throat. Simon had to be on the other side of the door. Reluctantly she allowed herself to experience a twinge of guilt about the injury she gave him with the fork. *How would she get by him this time? She just had to take the chance!* As she turned the knob, it clicked loudly. Trembling, she turned wide eyed to see Matthew sit up, startled.

"Amanda?" he exclaimed. Throwing the blanket off him, he was instantly on his feet. Frozen with fear, her hesitation cost her precious seconds. Then he was by her side, covering her hand on the knob. Inches from her own face, he asked, "What do you think you're doing?" Refusing to look at him, she tried to pull her hand out from under his, but he wouldn't allow it. She winced in pain as the weight of his hand pressed her wound into the knob. Tears blurred her vision.

"I just want to go home," she cried then looked up meeting his eyes. "Please, Matthew, please let me go home." His eyes searched her own, and he saw her pain, and it hurt him. It hurt him to know that he was making her suffer. For the first time since he brought her to the village, he wanted, with everything that he was, to let her go. Reaching up with his free hand, he touched her cheek softly with the back of his fingers.

"I'm sorry, Amanda," he spoke softly, "I can't let you go." Biting her bottom lip, she nodded as tears trickled down her cheeks. Her shoulders slumped forward, and she swayed slightly on her feet.

"Can't or won't?" she cried, reaching out with her free hand to steady herself against the door. Matthew closed his eyes, dropping his hand away from her face, his voice quiet.

"Both." He stepped back and, without notice, picked her up off her feet, cradling her in his arms, and walked in the direction of the bed. She laid her head on his chest and cried. It was with heart-wrenching tears that she mourned the loss of her life as she once knew it. The loss of her family, her freedom, her friends . . . her future. Escaping a failure, she couldn't even kill herself without screwing up. *What awaited her? What horrors was she going to have to face?*

His assurance that nothing would happen to her didn't give her any comfort—*she couldn't trust him!* He set her down on the bed gently, slipping his coat off her; she turned away from him, burying her face in the pillow. Matthew pulled the covers over her and sat down on the chair next to the bed. For the moment, her fight was gone, and her heart ached. She would have given anything to have her mother with her at that moment. The thought of her made Amanda cry harder. How worried her parents had to be, how devastated. She was their only child, and now she was gone. Matthew had said she just disappeared. *How can that be? Was there no one that saw her being carried out of her apartment? How can someone just disappear? Jared. Maybe Jared remembered seeing the two men dressed in black. He knew she was bothered by them, or why else would he had offered to stay with her? Maybe he told the police, and they will find her. Maybe . . .*

Matthew cradled his face in his hands, at a complete loss of what to do. Amanda's crying began to subside, and he didn't think he could feel any worse than he did right at that moment. After a few more moments, he lifted his head.

"Amanda," he called her name softly. At first, she made no response.

"I miss my family," she admitted softly.

Moving from the chair, he sat on the edge of the bed, touching her shoulder gently, a serious expression on his face.

"I know you do," he said. "Amanda, I'm sorry this has been so difficult for you. If it helps at all, I had no idea that this would be so hard . . . so hurtful."

"I'm really never going to go home again?" she asked tearfully, turning slightly so that she could see his face.

He looked down at his hands, not answering. How could he answer that?

"No woman has ever returned to her home again," he said, his tone forbearing. "It's just not done."

The pain she felt in her heart was almost unbearable.

"I don't understand, why is this happening to me?" she asked, her eyes on the ceiling. "I don't understand any of this." Matthew looked at her battered face.

"Amanda," he said softly, "promise me. Promise me that you won't try what you tried tonight. Promise me that you're done hurting yourself." His urgency did not go unnoticed by her. "Amanda?"

"Don't you see how desperate I am to leave here?" she said, becoming upset again. "Have I not proven that? I don't belong here. I want you to bring me home!"

"Ughhhh," he grunted, rising to his feet; he walked away from the bed. "Amanda," he said, turning back, frustrated, "I can*not* bring you home. *This* is your new home. With me. The sooner you accept it, and stop fighting it, the easier it will be."

She sat up, wincing in pain as she did. "I don't know how to accept it. Isn't that obvious?"

"When we're married," he sighed.

"I don't want to get married," she persisted softly. "I don't want to marry *you*!" He stared at her, his eyes searching her face.

"Amanda, we've been through this already. You told me that you didn't want me to arrange you to marry someone else. So, you *are* going to marry me." Now he was becoming upset.

"But I don't want to marry anyone!" she declared angrily. "I don't know you!"

"We'll have our whole lives to get to know one another," he reiterated, trying to remain calm.

"I don't want to get to know *you* or anyone!" she spat. He looked at her in amazement. She had been so docile and quiet, only moments before, and now she was radiating so much anger toward him.

"I see your fight has returned," he said quietly. "I can't talk to you like this. There's no point—I'm stepping outside." Turning, he walked to the door, taking his coat with him.

Once outside, he began pacing back and forth in the dark.

What did she expect him to do? Go against everything he's ever believed in? Break decades of tradition? And what was that in there? She went from one extreme to another? They needed to marry soon, much sooner than anticipated. With her illness and injuries, Pastor had decided to allow her more time, but Matthew knew now how unwise that would be. She didn't need any more time to hurt herself or find some other scheme to put into action.

The door to the cabin creaked open slowly, and she appeared in the opening, the soft light from inside the cabin silhouetting her.

"Matthew?" she called out to him with a shaky voice. He stopped pacing and walked to the bottom of the small staircase.

"What is it, Amanda?" he asked.

"I thought you left," she said in a small, weak voice then stopped.

He rested his hands on his hips and looked down at his feet. Subdued and anxious, she would continue to surprise him.

"Amanda," he said softly as he looked back up at her. "I think maybe I should send for Molly. You definitely don't want to be in my company right now."

"No!" she cried out, stepping farther out the door. "Please don't! Don't send for her. I don't want you to leave." He shook his head, confused.

"Amanda, it's clear that you hate me," he stated evenly. "Why do you keep insisting that *I* stay with you?" Wrapping her arms around her small frame, she looked up at the night sky.

"I don't hate you," she admitted softly; then a few moments later, she continued, "I want to hate you. But I don't." Looking down at him, she added, "Please don't leave."

"Why, Amanda?" His voice was quiet as he looked up at her. Meeting his eyes, she opened her mouth to speak then hesitated. She couldn't explain her need to have him near; she couldn't explain any of her feelings anymore. Squeezing herself tighter, she averted her eyes.

"I don't know," she whispered. Watching her silently for several more seconds, he nodded then started up the stairs slowly. She backed through the doorway. Closing the door behind him, he turned to see her crawling back into the bed. Taking his coat off, he walked to the small kitchenette. She watched him as he made some sort of mixture then brought a glass full of the liquid to her.

"Here," he said, holding the glass out to her. She eyed it hesitantly. "It's an herbal tonic. It'll help you sleep and reduce some of your pain." Nodding, she took it from him, still apprehensive of its contents. "It doesn't look very good." A small smile played on his lips.

"I know," he said. She lowered her nose to the glass, made a face, and pulled the glass away from her face.

"It smells horrible!" she declared. Then lifting it to her lips, she drank it down quickly, making a face when she was done. "Ugh! That was awful!" she announced disgusted. He chuckled softly as he took the empty glass back.

"Yes, it is," he said, "but trust me, it will help."

She slid down deeper in the covers, snuggling into the warmth. He came back, sitting down in the chair by her bedside, and she turned toward him.

He stared into her eyes—they were shining with pain and fatigue.

"Amanda." They looked at one another silently. Amanda closed her eyes then slowly opened them again.

"I just don't know what to do," she whispered. "I don't belong here, Matthew." He leaned forward in the chair.

"Just try your best to accept this, the best that you can," he said quietly. "It *will* be okay." Saddened, she nodded, though she didn't believe him.

"Okay," she whispered, blinking her eyes sleepily. He leaned over, touching her cheek gently.

"Okay," he whispered back. She closed her eyes, and sleep came almost immediately.

When she awoke in the morning, Matthew was gone.

CHAPTER 10

"Not to mention the work that has been neglected around the village because of your attachment to this woman. It's clearly unhealthy and the marriage ceremony hasn't even taken place yet. The intimacy that you have had with this woman just does not happen before the marriage, Matthew! And the trouble she has been . . ."

Matthew stood in front of his pastor's desk, his hands clasped behind his back, his eyes fixed on a spot on the wall. The lecture had been going on now for several minutes.

"I'm sorry, sir," Matthew spoke firmly.

The pastor leaned back in his cushioned leather chair, folding his hands over his stomach. "I'm considering canceling the wedding completely," he disclosed quietly. Matthew's eyes immediately met his.

"Sir?" he asked, his body tensed.

"Ah." The pastor smiled. "Now I have your attention. As I was saying, if this woman is going to be such a distraction for you, then I do not wish to burden you with her. We can find other uses for her."

"Burden me?" Matthew scowled. "Pastor, I want Amanda to be my wife."

"Yes, I know," he conceded quietly, standing up; he walked around his desk to Matthew's side. "But I do not like troublesome women. She could inevitably be a problem."

"I will keep her under control," Matthew assured him confidently, clenching his jaw, turning to him. "She won't cause any more problems, sir."

"Mmmmm, we shall see," he said. "We shall see. All right, Matthew, if this is what you want, then the marriage shall be moved forward as you requested. Then I want you back to work, and back to church services."

"Yes, sir," Matthew replied.

"Instead of arranging a church wedding on short notice, we will have a small ceremony right here in my office. Then you will take her back to the Holding cabin, where you will spend your three days of seclusion. On the fourth day, you are to return to work. I expect the marriage to be consummated. The marriage traditions will continue to be upheld, even though I've allowed you some room to do what you felt you needed to do. But not anymore. Is that clear, Matthew?" he said, his tone quiet but serious. Matthew met his eyes directly.

"Yes, sir."

The pastor nodded, walking to his office door, opening it.

"Good," he said. "Now the cleansing process has been interrupted due to her 'accident,' correct?" Matthew nodded as he followed his pastor to the door. "One more day of cleansing, then we shall meet here tomorrow night for your wedding." Patting Matthew's shoulder, he added, "I want her controlled."

"Yes, sir."

"Oh, and you're not to see her again until then," he ordered. Matthew clenched his jaw. "Simon has been placed outside the cabin again, and he has strict orders not to let you in." Matthew stepped through the doorway. "You've had plenty of time to get to know one another. Some may think a sinful amount of time. Go now, I will see you tomorrow night." With that, the pastor closed his door, leaving Matthew to stare at the worn wood.

Frustrated, Matthew walked through the sanctuary and out of the church. He was just beginning to have a connection with Amanda, and now he didn't know how she was going to handle this. Unable to tell her of the wedding himself, he couldn't even see her. Pastor had sent Simon for him earlier this morning, and thankfully, Amanda had still been sleeping, so he was able to leave quietly. He had all intentions of returning right after his meeting. Now what would happen between them? She has been so upset when he tried to leave in the past couple of days, and now he wouldn't be able to explain his leaving her now.

What are you doing, he berated himself. She's a woman! It doesn't matter what she feels or thinks, his learned thinking snuck into his thoughts. But it does, his heart rebelled against his mind. Matthew ran his hand through his hair, a natural sign that he was upset, as he walked toward his unfinished cabin. He needed to think.

Amanda slowly opened her eyes; the sunlight was shining through the windows. It looks like a beautiful day, she thought naturally. Scanning the room from the same position she had awakened in, it was quiet, and at first she didn't see anyone. Then she heard a soft female humming coming from behind the bathroom door.

Where's Matthew, she thought as her heart began to pound. She slowly struggled to sit up, her body screaming in pain as she moved. It didn't occur to her to think she could hurt worse than yesterday, but she did. Biting her bottom lip, she pulled the covers off her.

Slowly standing, she winced as she put all her weight on her feet. Looking up, she watched a petite woman, with dark hair pulled back away from her face, come out of the bathroom. When the woman saw her, she flashed her a kind smile. When she did this, Amanda couldn't help but think that there was something familiar about her.

"Well, hello there," she greeted with a soft voice as Amanda searched her face, confused. Swallowing the lump in her throat, she stood with her hands at her side, gripping the soft material of her nightgown in her hands, causing her knuckles to whiten.

"Where . . . where's Matthew?" Amanda asked quietly, feeling the tightness return as she spoke his name.

"Ahhhh," she said, smiling again as she stopped a few feet from Amanda. "Matthew was called away by our pastor. He didn't want to leave you, but he really didn't have a choice."

"Who are you?" she questioned the stranger.

"I took Molly's place for now," she said softly. "My name is Katherine." Katherine allowed Amanda to digest this information.

Amanda was silent. She didn't want this woman. She wanted *Matthew*.

"I've started your bath because we need to continue on with the cleansing process," Katherine spoke softly. "I also need to put some salve on your face—to heal those scratches."

Amanda slowly shook her head. "No," she whispered. "I want Matthew here."

Katherine reached out her hand to console her, and Amanda flinched back, scowling at her. Understanding, Katherine didn't react to her anger. She was pleased to know that she was right about the security Amanda found in her son.

"I know you do, hon," she comforted her softly. "Let's do what we have to and then we'll talk, okay?"

"I'm sick of these baths!" Amanda expressed, frustrated. "I hate these stupid white gowns! I don't want to talk to you or anybody! I hate everything about this place."

"Even Matthew?" Katherine asked softly. Amanda stopped ranting and looked at this woman named Katherine. Refusing to answer, her questioning eyes searched Katherine's. Katherine came and stood in front of Amanda, taking her hands into her own. Wincing, Amanda pulled her injured hand away.

"Amanda, I know," she said. "I was taken, like you, from all that I loved. I *know* what you're feeling. Many of the women here do."

Amanda searched the woman's face, looking into her beautiful expressive blue eyes. Eyes so similar to . . . whose? Amanda squeezed Katherine's hand in return, hope springing anew.

"Can you help me?" she asked, a note of desperation in her voice. "Can you help me, *please?*"

"Amanda, all I can do is show you how to survive here. I don't know what the future holds for you—but there are things you should know," she said, looking over her shoulder at the door. "Now, you need to bathe, then we'll talk."

Amanda's shoulders slumped. *Accept this the best that I can.* Tears burned the back of her eyes, but she refused to let them fall. *Will I ever stop crying,* she screamed to herself.

Within the next hour, Amanda had bathed, had her bandages changed and her scrapes and bruises nursed, and had eaten some soup. She now sat across from Katherine on the small sofa.

"First there is something that you need to know," Katherine spoke softly. "Matthew is my son."

Amanda stared at her silently. *The eyes. Matthew's eyes.*

"I didn't know," Amanda said, shaking her head. "I should have."

"Of course you wouldn't," she said, searching Amanda's face. "Just spending some time with you allows me to see why my son has such an affection for you."

Amanda's cheeks turned pink.

"I wish he didn't. I wish he never picked me," she said, looking away. Katherine grabbed her hand.

"I know, child," she said reassuringly, "but this is all he knows. He was raised here and after his father died, I had no choice but to allow the other men of the village be surrogate fathers to him. Matthew was eight years old then. He was taught the marriage tradition at fifteen, and it has been all he has believed. Until he brought you here." She looked toward the door consciously. "I've seen a change in him since he brought you to us. He's beginning to question things he never questioned before and I have such hope." There was a light knock at the door, and Katherine quickly stood, straightening her skirt as Simon entered.

"Katherine, I need to speak to you for a moment," he said.

Katherine smiled reassuringly at Amanda then stepped out of the cabin. *Matthew's mother was nice*, she thought, then images of her own mother flashed before her, and she choked up. *Mom . . . God, she missed her mom. Would she ever see her again?*

Moments later, Katherine stepped back into the room. Amanda looked up and saw her serious expression. Sitting back on the sofa, she took Amanda's hand into her own.

"Simon just informed me of Pastor's order," she disclosed. "So much time has passed since you were taken"—she looked into Amanda's eyes—"but with your accident, things were postponed, and you haven't done the complete cleansing process and—"

"And what?" Amanda asked, panicking. "What are they going to do to me?"

"They've moved the wedding up," she revealed softly. "It's going to be tomorrow night."

Amanda pulled her hand away from Katherine. *The stupid wedding again! Couldn't all this just go away?* Amanda stood and started pacing.

"Now, Amanda, you knew this was coming." Katherine spoke softly but firmly. Amanda covered her face with her hands.

"I know," she exclaimed as if she were in pain. "I just wish . . ." Her voice trailed off. *What was the point of wishing*, she thought bitterly. No, there would be no wishes fulfilled for her.

Katherine stood and came to her side. "Escaping from what you view as 'hell' is not going to happen from spontaneous attempts to flee. It is better that the wedding is tomorrow. Once you are married, you will be protected." Amanda lowered her hands and opened her eyes.

"Protected?" she asked. Katherine looked straight into her eyes.

"Yes. Protected," she said staidly. "Amanda, things are very different here than they are out in the real world. It took me many years to accustom myself to the rules, but I didn't have another woman to help me. That is what I want to do for you. It won't be so difficult for you, if you have someone to help. Matthew will help you as your husband but he will not be able to be with you all the time. Women are able to spend as much time as we want with each other."

"There are many rules, but the most important, Amanda, is to listen to Matthew. He would never put you in any danger, or hurt you, but you must understand that there are people who will hurt you. Rebellious wives are severely punished, as well as the husbands. He will guide you and teach you things that I cannot because I am no longer married. You see, things have changed since I was. The rules change quite often because our pastor is the law here. Do *not* cross him, Amanda. Please promise me. I don't care how much you dislike him, promise me that you will not cross him."

Amanda searched her face.

"What have I been brought into?" she asked weakly. "I'm trapped in a horrible nightmare."

Katherine grabbed her shoulders firmly with her small hands.

"Amanda," she said, "listen to me! I know this is hard for you but you must survive. I know"—closing her eyes, then opening them again—"I know that my son is beginning to see a lot more now that he has you. He is so protective of you now, and you've been here such a short time. You are my salvation, Amanda."

"I don't understand," Amanda cried, wiping the tears away from her cheeks in frustration. Katherine pulled her over to the sofa, and they sat down again.

"Listen to me," she said anxiously looking toward the door. "I was kidnapped twenty years ago from Miami, Florida. I was taken just like you and unlike these other women, I can't forget my old life. Matthew's father and I had a rough go of it, right from the beginning. Who wouldn't after being taken from your loved ones?" Amanda nodded tearfully, agreeing with her. "Eventually things got easier, and I did fall in love with my husband, and he with me. Matthew was born a year later and I was thrilled with the distraction of my beautiful baby. Over the years, I tried to make my husband see the truth. The truth of real life and the truth of God's true word. At first, he was so stubborn—a trait my son has admirably inherited—but then he started to actually see different situations that I pointed out to him. We actually talked about leaving the village. Oh, Amanda, the hope that I had!" The emotions played so vividly on her face that Amanda could feel them too. "But it was not to be." She sat back slightly, her face turning sorrowful. "On the hunting trip," She looked into Amanda's eyes, tears shining in her own. "The men hunt once a month," she explained. "John, my husband, was killed. He was shot in the back."

Amanda gasped, her hand covering her mouth. "I'm so sorry, Katherine," she whispered.

"They claimed it was an accident, but I knew. I knew it wasn't," she continued softly. "Matthew was just a child. I had no choice but to stay and continue my life here. Or risk my own life, and leave Matthew an orphan. So, I submitted. Through the years, I've had to grit my teeth about how rigid my son was becoming because of the other men in this place. But now . . . now you've come into his life and suddenly he's starting to actually see things for what they are." Katherine grabbed her hand into her own. "Amanda, I know in my heart that you will leave here someday. I just know it. I don't know when or how, but I do. I'm so hopeful, and I know you must be too, but have faith, child, because I know my prayers will be answered. I want my son to know what the real world is like. Not everything in the world is sinful and I want him to live and to experience life to its fullest."

"I know you don't know my son well. But you *do* feel safe with him, do you not?" she asked her in earnest. Hesitating, Amanda nodded. "Yes, good. If the two of you have each other, then the chances are even better for you both to leave someday."

Amanda searched her face.

"Do you really think I could leave here?" she asked. "Please, Katherine, please tell me you're not just telling me this to make me feel better. I'll see my family again?" Renewed tears filled her eyes, but these were tears of joy.

"Amanda, it could take years," she admitted honestly, "but I truly believe that you will see your family again. You will *not* have the same fate as me."

Amanda hugged Katherine tightly, not caring about the pain it caused in her wrists. For the first time since she had been abducted, she could see some light of real hope. *She would go home someday!* Katherine returned the hug genuinely then pulled away.

"This means that you will have to become one of us, Amanda," she explained quietly. "You'll have to conform and stop fighting everything that is happening to you. Can you do that?"

"I don't know," Amanda said. "I *so* hate it here."

"If you and Matthew do not live peacefully, then you will be under constant scrutiny and will never have an opportunity to leave. You will be labeled a troublemaker and, trust me, life will be very difficult for you here."

Amanda was so confused. In her mind she wanted to accept what she was being told and do what she needed to do for the end result of her choice. It was the way she handled all of the problems that had come her way in the past. But her heart was telling her the complete opposite. *I don't want to become one of them! I don't want to live here with these people!*

"But why can't we leave now?" she asked desperately.

"Because you need to have Matthew with you. And he may care for you—but he's not at the place where he would leave his only home for you. You don't understand the seriousness of this, Amanda. If you were to be caught trying to escape . . . the punishment is death."

Amanda stared at Katherine, her eyes wide with disbelief.

"Death?" she whispered, then she swallowed. "You mean that I would be killed if I were caught trying to leave?" Thoughts of her attempted escape through the trees came to her mind.

"Yes," she stated. "Once you are married, you will become a member of our village. You'll then be subject to all the rules that apply and that is the consequence for trying to leave. That's why there has to be careful planning on our parts. But you must be careful, and you must accept this way of life, or it will never work."

"I'm afraid to," Amanda said. "I don't know what to do."

"I understand that this is difficult for you," Katherine said softly. "Think about what I have said. It is the only way."

Amanda leaned back into the sofa.

How would she bear it? Marriage to a complete stranger, living in this bizarre place? Did she really have a choice? Closing her eyes, she knew she didn't. A heaviness weighed on her heart as she asked herself the most obvious question. *What was she willing do to see her family again?* Without hesitation, she opened her eyes. *Anything*, she resolved.

CHAPTER 11

M atthew was sitting on the steps of his unfinished cabin when Jimmy walked up.

"Hey, Matthew!" Jimmy greeted him. "I thought I would find you here."

Matthew grunted as Jimmy joined him on the steps. They sat in silence for a long time, staring at the beautiful view of the mountains and valleys below them.

"I heard that Pastor let you have it," Jimmy said quietly. "Do you want to talk about it?"

Matthew shrugged and stood up, walking down the steps.

"Not really," he said. He stopped a few feet from the cabin and then turned to his friend. "Why didn't you tell me that this"—he waved his hand toward the village—"was going to be so hard? When we saved Sarah, you never told me how difficult it would be!"

Jimmy sighed and walked to his friend's side.

"If I had told you, then you wouldn't have wanted to do it," he stated. "You needed to take a wife, Matthew."

Matthew laughed haughtily, without humor.

"Yes, you're right. But not like this!" he declared passionately. "For the first time, Jimmy, I don't agree with a tradition! This . . . this way of taking women, it's wrong, Jimmy!"

Jimmy's eyes widened, and he nervously looked around them.

"Matthew, *shut your mouth*!" he declared angrily, and, grabbing Matthew's shoulders, he shook him. "You're just upset! Think man, *before* you speak!" Again Jimmy looked around them. Then he whispered harshly to Matthew, "You know Pastor has his cronies everywhere! *Watch your mouth*! I don't want to see you whipped or *worse*!"

Matthew pulled away from him and walked away, turning his back on his friend. Jimmy watched him silently for a few moments then said,

"Matthew, I know that you feel things more deeply than I do. You always have and you've always had this compassion about you. I'm not like you. This rough time, will pass. Sarah and I had a hard time at first, but she didn't and still doesn't have a strong will. She was more pliable than Amanda has been for you. It just happens that you chose a woman that can be difficult. Her will can be broken, and that is what you need to do!"

Matthew turned back to his friend.

"I don't want to break her will," he said quietly. "I've watched this last couple of weeks slowly crush her spirit. Jimmy, we've taken everything from these women and . . . and I don't want to take all that I admired about her and destroy it!"

"Matthew, I've questioned this whole tradition myself, once or twice," Jimmy admitted softly, "but it's what my father did, my grandfather, and my great grandfather. It's what your father and grandfather did too! Who are we to question something that seems to have worked for all these generations?"

"But, Jimmy, we've been taught to live by God's Word," Matthew argued. "Where in the Bible does it tell us that men should *steal* their wives?"

"Oh, Matthew!" Jimmy said, exasperated. "You know that a lot of our rules and traditions don't have anything to do with the Bible! It's never bothered you before. It works. Our village works and has for decades! You've accepted everything, just as I have. We've been trained since we were boys on the marriage tradition. Why didn't you question it before? Why now?"

"Because I can see what it actually does to them," he countered hotly. "I can see what it's doing to Amanda!" He began to pace. "I don't know why I've always accepted everything so willingly. I don't know."

"Because questions and willfulness are dealt with harshly," Jimmy said, his voice low. "We've seen it our whole lives. None of us boys wanted to displease Pastor and you know it as well as I do. But as boys we had room to make mistakes . . . as men, Matthew, I don't care how pleased Pastor may be with you . . . as men, we have no room. Now is not the time to go and make waves. You've already taken her, you know there's no going back!"

"I know!" he retorted. "Trust me, I know." Matthew walked back to the steps, sat, and placed his face in his hands.

Jimmy slowly walked over to the steps, standing by his friend.

"Matthew, if it makes you feel any better, things will be fine with you and Amanda. It just takes some time." Matthew looked up at him.

"Jimmy, do you and Sarah really love each other?" he asked.

"Love?" Jimmy asked, surprised by the question. "Love, well, yeah, I guess we do." He sat down next to him. "Sarah, well, she's special to me. But it didn't happen overnight. Like I said, Matthew, you've always felt things more deeply than I have. I know you already have feelings for Amanda." They were quiet for a few moments. "She'll come around, Matthew, and I have a feeling she'll always keep you on your toes," he chuckled. Matthew smiled.

"How is she feeling?" Jimmy asked seriously. Matthew shook his head.

"She's healing," he said. "She tried to run again last night."

"What?" Jimmy asked, surprised.

"Yep," Matthew sighed, rubbing his face, suddenly tired. "I just want her to stop hurting herself."

"She will, Matthew," Jimmy said, resting a hand on his friend's shoulder. "She will."

"Pastor has moved the wedding up. He's performing a private service in his office tomorrow night."

"Really?" he asked, again surprised. "I can't remember the last time he did that."

Matthew turned to his friend, a serious expression on his face.

"He also warned me to control her or—," Matthew began.

"That means Pastor is concerned," Jimmy interrupted, standing up and shoving his hands into his black jeans. "Matthew, you *have* to control her, I know that you don't want to, but I don't want anything to happen to you. You're my best friend. Promise me that you'll take care of it." Matthew stared forward.

"I really don't have a choice," he said softly. "She'll have to submit because I don't want anything to happen to *her*."

Amanda stared at herself in the mirror. Molly had twisted her hair up into a bun and placed tiny white flowers throughout her golden strands. Her scratches were still visible, but not flaming red as they had been yesterday. Amanda looked at her reflection, surprised that she hadn't changed. She looked the same, except for the scratches, but didn't feel like the same person.

Less than three weeks ago, she was a college student, she was preparing to be part of an elite historical group, and she was going to make Jared an intricate part of her life. Now she was about to be married. She was to be married to a stranger . . . married into a twisted and warped society.

Moving away from the mirror, she stepped into the white satin slipper-shoes. The long white gown had been the gown that Katherine had been forced to be married in. Katherine had altered it for her, and now it fit her perfectly. It was a long-sleeved satin, with fitted three-inch lace around her wrists. It was a full-length gown touching the floor, and embroidered white flowers were sewn precariously on the bodice and skirt. The bodice was slightly tighter fitting than the rest but was cut just below the neck. *It is a simple handmade gown but is still beautiful*, Amanda thought.

"You look lovely," Molly commented from behind her. "Here, let's put the veil on." Amanda consented and sat down so she could place it properly on her head.

Molly had returned to the cabin this morning. Amanda was sad to see Katherine leave, but she had winked to her reassuringly before she left. She had given Molly no troubles throughout the day, bathing when she was asked, eating when she was asked, and dressing for the wedding when she was asked. Molly was a little uneasy with the cooperative behavior, almost expecting something to happen, but nothing did.

During the night, Amanda had lay awake deciding that she would do what she had to in order to go home to her family again. She would marry Matthew and become a member of the village. With this difficult decision, many tears were shed, and she eventually cried herself to sleep.

"There," Molly said softly as she finished setting the veil. "You make a beautiful bride, Amanda."

Amanda stood up and turned. She was shaky and a little nauseous. She didn't know what to expect at this wedding. Matthew hadn't come to see her, and she was worried. *He didn't find someone else for her to marry, did he?* It wasn't the first time she asked this silent question. She didn't want to get married, but if she had to, she wanted it to be Matthew. He was kind to her. He was safe.

"Now Simon will walk you to the church," Molly spoke softly in the dimly lit room. The candlelight cast different patterns on the walls surrounding them. "The ceremony will be in Pastor's office and it will be a private service. Normally the whole village would attend, but Pastor ordered it to be so."

"You're not going to walk with me?" she asked nervously, and Molly smiled kindly.

"No," she said. "When you arrive, Matthew will be there waiting and he'll take care of you." Relief swept over her. Matthew would be there. "Once you are married, he will be responsible for your care."

There was a light knock on the door, and then Simon entered.

"It's time," he said, trying not to stare at the beautiful sight before him. Molly nodded and turned to Amanda.

"Well, this is it," she said, tears shining in her eyes. "I can't believe we almost lost you."

"I'm sorry," Amanda said sincerely. "It must have been awful."

"Yes, well," she said, "I'm glad that you're here, but you need to go now. Be blessed child, and I wish you the happiest of marriages."

Amanda nodded, not sure how to respond to the well-wish. She walked to the door, and Simon gripped her arm securely.

He led her through the dark, and then Amanda saw the church. She sucked in her breath. Instantly she remembered standing in the front with Matthew, begging him to let her go. Shivering as they neared the steps, Amanda looked nervously up at Simon's hulking figure. Swallowing, she said, "I'm . . . I'm sorry about stabbing you." It took a lot to surprise Simon, but she managed to do it. Without turning his head, he glanced at her out of the corner of his eye and gave a curt nod of his head. Looking away, Amanda hoped that was his acceptance of her apology, but she wasn't quite sure.

As Simon walked her through the empty church, she felt slightly dizzy. *How could this be happening?* They reached a tall dark oak door. Simon knocked, and then came the firm response. When the door opened, she was gently pushed into the room, and there stood Matthew in front of the large desk.

He stared at her in silence. She was stunning!

Amanda felt a warm rush through her body at seeing him and immediately went to his side. "Matthew!" she cried in relief, instantly feeling better. He opened his arms, and without thinking, she entered his embrace. Her cheek rested on his chest, and she could feel his quick heartbeat.

He felt her small frame in his arms, and it warmed his heart that she still found comfort in him.

Pastor cleared his throat from behind her. Matthew relaxed his grip slightly, allowing Amanda to turn and see the pastor. He looked the same, but smaller, not as intimidating as he had been the first night she had seen him in the church. He wore a small smile on his face, but Amanda didn't sense anything sincere about him. His beady black eyes examined her.

"Well, I'm glad to see that the two of you are so close," he said smoothly. "It shall make the wedding much more pleasurable."

Matthew felt Amanda stiffen slightly, but she stayed in his embrace.

"Shall we begin?" he asked, moving to stand in front of them. Amanda slowly pulled herself away from Matthew, keeping only his hand lightly in hers so as not to hurt her. Scanning the room, she was surprised at how modernly decorated it was, compared to the cabin she was staying in. The desk was a large cherry wood, with a leather chair. The pine board walls had framed paintings hanging on them, and under their feet was a beautifully designed Persian rug. A tall candle lamp in the corner was the only light in the room.

"Now," spoke the pastor, "before we start the vows. I would like to welcome you, saved child, to our community and our homes. I expect complete submission from you and I have chosen your new name." He spoke firmly, "It will be Rachel."

Matthew felt her tense, and knowing she would speak, he squeezed her hand tightly, causing her to flinch in pain. Looking up to him, her eyes were questioning him silently. *New name? What insanity was this?* Keeping his eyes forward, she slowly looked away. Amidst her confusion, she had to admit he looked good in the stylish black suit he wore. Lifting her eyes to his face again, his blue eyes met hers with a look of warning. Amanda clenched her jaw, turned away, but kept her mouth closed.

"We are gathered here today . . ." The pastor continued on with the ceremony. Soon Matthew was slipping a gold band on her finger, and she noticed he was already wearing his. She looked up at him to see him watching her. Searching his face, she didn't know what she was looking for. "Now you may kiss the bride."

Kiss the bride! Forgetting about the kiss, she felt dizzy. Her face paled when he lifted her veil, and he could see the fear in her eyes. Leaning over, he brushed her lips ever so softly. The kiss was so quick that Amanda didn't have time to get nervous. When they turned back to the pastor, Matthew held her hand reassuringly. The pastor wore his insincere smile.

"Good, I'm pleased," he said then reached over and tipped her chin upward, noticing the scratches. "What do we have here?"

Amanda cringed away from his touch, and the pastor's eyes became slits.

"They're scratches, sir," Matthew said tensely. He turned his annoyed gaze on Matthew.

"I *know* what they are!" he informed Matthew. "What I want to know, is how they got there?"

"She was lost in the woods," Matthew said, after some hesitation.

"Lost in the woods?" he repeated, looking between the two of them. He crossed his arms in front of him. "I see. Yes, I see perfectly. Remember what

I said, Matthew. And I will let you know too, Rachel." Stepping closer to her, he took her chin forcibly in his hand, causing her to gasp in pain. "I will not tolerate disobedience. Do not anger me, little one, you will regret it!" He then dropped his hand and walked behind his desk.

Matthew pulled her close to him, her eyes shining.

"You may go," he said in his authoritative voice. "Your three-day seclusion starts now. When it is over, I expect to see you, Matthew, continuing your work."

"Yes, sir," he said; placing his hand on her lower back, he led Amanda out of the office.

She clung tightly to his hand, and when they walked out of the church, he turned to face her. The night was dark, the only light was coming from the church itself. He searched her face, not saying anything.

Amanda returned his look, her eyes shining with her unshed tears. He gently lifted her chin and looked carefully at her face, where Pastor had grabbed her. Not seeing any real harm, he took her hand and led her toward the cabin.

Neither one of them spoke when they entered the familiar cabin. He led her to the small sofa and gently directed her to sit. She did. She watched him take off his suit jacket and loosen up his tie. He really did look nice all dressed up and out of those terribly plain black clothes, she thought, not understanding the warm feeling in the pit of her belly. He came back over to her and carefully removed the veil and set it on the nearby table. When he returned, he squatted down in front of her, looking her in the eyes.

"Are you all right?" he asked softly. She shook her head, blinking rapidly to stop fresh tears from falling down her cheeks. "Did he hurt you?"

"A little," she whispered. "He scares me." He took her hand into his own.

"I know," he said quietly. "I'm sorry about what he did. Thank you for coming to the wedding without a fight. I wasn't sure, I mean, I wasn't allowed to come see you, to tell you myself."

"You weren't allowed to come see me?" she asked, confused. Shaking his head, he sat down next to her.

"No. Pastor ordered me to stay away from you until tonight," he revealed. "I wanted to be the one to tell you, to make you understand."

"Why did he think he could change my name?" she asked shakily.

"Amanda, I know this is hard for you," he began, "but you really need to understand the way things work. When we bring in a sinful woman into the village, the tradition is to make everything new about her. Like a new beginning, a fresh start."

"I'm not that sinful," she interrupted, looking down at their hands that were entwined. "I'm a good person."

"I know you are, Amanda," he assured her. "It's just the way things are done. You'll be addressed as Rachel now, by everybody. You must listen to me. Now that we're married, everything you do will reflect on me." She remembered Katherine explaining this to her. "It's so important that you listen to me, Amanda."

Amanda hesitated. "I know," she spoke softly. "But I don't want to be Rachel. I want my real name. Why must you take everything away from me?"

Matthew sighed.

"I don't want to," he admitted. "When we're alone, you'll still be Amanda to me. But when we're around people, you must go by Rachel."

"This is so hard!" she cried out, frustrated. "How am I going to do this?"

He pulled her into his arms, and she freely accepted his affection. She didn't question or reprimand herself because it just felt good to be close to someone again. He was her only friend in this place.

"We'll just take it one day at a time, all right?" he whispered, rubbing her back gently.

After some time, she finally pulled away from him. Her face wet and puffy from crying, he stood, retrieving some tissues from the bathroom and handing them to her.

"Thank you," she said.

"Hey, Amanda, I have an idea," he said. "Your new wardrobe was delivered while we were gone. Let's change and go for a walk. I want to show you something."

"Can we? I mean, are we allowed?" she asked. *It would be nice to go for a walk*, she thought.

"Well," he looked a little sheepish and smiled. "Not usually at night. But let's go anyway. It'll make you feel better."

She smiled. "Okay," she agreed. "Where are the clothes?"

"Your clothes are hanging in the bathroom," he said. "You go and change in there, and I will change out here." They both stood, and he walked her to the bathroom doorway. "You let me know when you're done, and I'll let you know if I'm decent."

She closed the door behind her and then saw the horrible black dresses hanging on the small hooks attached to the wall. *You will have to conform and stop fighting,* Katherine's words rang in her ears. *Okay, Amanda, you can do this,* she said to herself. She swallowed and reached for one of the dresses. *It could be worse,* she said to herself, trying to look on the good side, *they could be fluorescent orange,* she smiled. *There, much better,* she encouraged herself.

She started to take her gown off and realized she couldn't reach to undo the small buttons on the back of the dress. Molly had helped her dress. *Oh dear*, she thought, rubbing her hand on her forehead. She was going to have to ask Matthew. He nursed her when she fell ill, took care of her battered body—*why should she feel weird about asking him to help her with a few buttons?* Sighing, she shook her head. *Because he was her husband now, that's why.*

She knocked on the door from inside the bathroom.

"Are you all right?" he asked.

"Um . . . yes . . . but I need . . . I need help with the . . . buttons," she said, feeling ridiculous. She heard him chuckle as he walked closer to the door. When he came in, she couldn't help but stare. His white dress shirt was completely unbuttoned, revealing his chest and stomach. His body was smooth and toned, and Amanda had to force her hands not to reach out and touch him. She turned away, immediately, embarrassed at her thoughts. *What was the matter with her? Why would she want to touch his chest?*

"Here, let me see," he said and began helping her. "They're so small." She was very conscious of his fingers near her neck. As he undid a few buttons, his fingers touched her bare skin once or twice, causing Amanda to shiver. "Are you cold?"

"Yes," she lied quickly, blushing.

"There you go," he said. "Let me know when you're ready." He closed the door behind him.

When he walked out, he had to grab hold of the back of the wooden kitchen chair. She was so beautiful! Her soft white neck, so warm and kissable, he thought to himself as he pulled his shirt off for the second time. He didn't miss her response to him, either, making his restraint all the more difficult. He knew it was too soon for her, and he knew he was going to have to go slow. But her attraction to him was definitely encouraging; he smiled to himself as he finished changing.

Moments later, Amanda emerged from the bathroom, brushing her long hair. It was soft and wavy from being up in the bun for the wedding ceremony. She wore the black dress and black laced-up boots. She felt like she was in an episode of *Little House on the Prairie*, but she didn't think he would understand her comparison, so she kept this to herself.

He was dressed back into his normal attire.

"Ready?" he asked, admiring her beautiful hair. She nodded.

He held out a black shawl to her; she took it, holding her tongue at the hideous-looking item.

"It's a little cool out," he explained. "Let's go."

CHAPTER 12

O nce outside, he grabbed her uninjured hand, and they headed down a small dirt road. It was so dark Amanda couldn't see anything. Matthew walked with sure footing, knowing where he was.

As they walked, Amanda took a deep breath. Winter was in the air, she thought wistfully. But strangely, it wasn't that cold. *I wonder what state we're in*, she asked herself. She could smell the sappy trees and could hear the nighttime animals moving about. It felt good to be walking outdoors again, not to be terrified or desperate. Thoughts of her abduction, the terrifying ordeal, began to creep in her mind, and she shoved them back. *It won't do any good*, she yelled at herself. *She had to survive.*

"You know where you're going, right?" she asked as they got farther from the cabin and were surrounded completely in the thick darkness. He heard the uneasiness in her voice.

"Don't tell me you're afraid of the dark," he teased. "You didn't seem to have a problem the other night when you were running through the woods."

"No. But I was temporarily insane." She took his teasing well and went along with him. She was relaxed for the first time since her abduction. *You will be protected.* Again, Katherine's words floated in her thoughts. She moved closer to him.

"We're almost there," he said, letting go of her hand and pulling her closer. Soon they stepped into a clearing, and Amanda could make out the shape of a cabin. "This is it." He had such pride in his voice, "Come on."

He led them up the stairs and into the cabin. She inhaled deeply, loving the scent of fresh-cut wood.

"Stay here." Pulling away from her, he disappeared into another dark room. She wrapped the black shawl around her tightly, feeling slightly vulnerable. But he emerged from the darkness immediately, holding a lit lantern. He moved it slowly around the room.

"This is what I wanted to show you," he exclaimed. "This is *our* cabin."

Amanda stared at him, realizing what he was saying. This was *really* happening. She looked around the cabin. It was bigger than the cabin she had been in from the start of her captivity, and it was set up differently. There wasn't just one large room, there were other rooms as well. She could just barely see the empty doorways in the shadows. It was unfinished in many areas, but it was a nice cabin. She knew he was waiting for her response.

"It's very nice," she said honestly.

"Do you like it?" he asked, glowing. "It's almost done. After our three-day isolation, I'm back to work on it. It shouldn't take more than a week to finish it up."

She looked nervously away. She walked around the cabin absently, touching the wood lightly with her fingertips, then stepped back outside onto the small porch. He followed her out, standing slightly behind her.

"Out there," he said as he leaned in, over her shoulder and closer to her ear, pointing in the distance ahead of them, "is the most incredible view of the mountains and valleys below us."

Amanda could only see darkened shadows. She strained her eyes to see more, but all she could focus on was his warm breath tickling her ear.

"It's beautiful?" she asked softly.

"Incredible!" he whispered. Suddenly feeling very warm, she quickly walked down the steps, knowing exactly what she was feeling. Attraction. Gulping in the fresh air, she trembled at her realization. She couldn't feel this way about him. Conforming was one thing. Fitting in? She was going to try. But having an attraction to Matthew was not part of the bargain. Yes, she married him, she had no choice, but care for him? *No*, she screamed at herself. *You need him*, her conscience argued. *No, I don't need him. Yes, yes, I do. Here, in this place, I do need him*, she finally admitted.

"Amanda?" He followed her. "Are you all right?"

She stopped just a few feet away.

"Matthew?" she asked, her back still to him. He gently pulled her shoulder, turning her to him. He held the lantern up and could see her forlorn expression.

"I've upset you more," he said regretfully.

"No," she said, holding her bandaged hand up. "No, you didn't." She dropped her hand.

"What is it?" he asked softly. She looked up at him.

"What is the three-day isolation?" she asked, dreading the answer. Matthew sighed and turned slightly, looking in the opposite direction.

"Well," he began. "What do I compare it with? It's like what the people out in the world call a honeymoon?" He thought another second then nodded. "Yes, that's it." Amanda swallowed the lump in her throat.

"That's what I thought," she said, wrapping the shawl tighter around her.

He watched her shiver as she looked away.

"You're cold," he said. "Let's go back. "

"No," she said suddenly, turning back to him. "No, it's been so long since I've been out. Please, I don't mind the cold."

"All right," he relented. "But let's go sit on the steps." He stepped aside, and she walked back to the cabin steps, sitting down. Matthew set the lantern in front of them. Amanda pulled her knees up and wrapped her arms around them.

After a few minutes, Matthew spoke,

"Amanda, do I frighten you?"

"No," she said without hesitation.

"Do you think that I would hurt you in some way?"

She turned and searched his face. *Where was he going with this?*

"No, I don't think so."

"I never would," he declared. "Never intentionally."

She searched his face for several moments. It was strange, bizarre even, but she believed him. "So, then what bothers you?" he asked softly. She turned and watched the flame's movement in the lantern.

"Everything else," she admitted. "Matthew, what happens in the three-day isolation?" She turned to him, and he gave her a long look.

"I'll explain it to you, but I know that you're not going to like what you hear," he said. She looked down, tucking her hair behind her ear and nodded hesitantly. "We'll spend the entire three days alone in the cabin. We can leave the cabin, but no one can speak to us until the isolation is over. Our food is provided for, clothes, everything that we would need," he hesitated as she watched him closely. "It's also the time where we need to consummate our marriage"—he paused—"and we need to prove this to the village that we've done so." Her eyes widened. "Prove to the village?" she started to say. Matthew hesitated again.

"Part of the tradition," he explained. "There will be three women that will come to the cabin tomorrow to gather our sheets to make sure we have been intimate."

"So we have to," she said, pointing her finger at him, then at herself. He nodded. "But, Matthew, I don't even know you."

"I know, Amanda," he said, seeing the panic fill her eyes. "If things were different, I would wait until you felt more comfortable. But they expect it."

She started to try and stand up, but he grabbed her arms, stopping her.

"Amanda, wait," he said.

"What if I say no?" she whispered fearfully.

"Most of the women from the world do. But they're made to." He tried to stress his point gently. She searched his face anxiously, understanding immediately.

"So, you'll force me?" He searched her face knowing that was the last thing he wanted to do.

"I don't want to," he said firmly. "I always swore that I would never do that. But there is a punishment for not proving yourself."

"Even if I don't want to?" she asked desperately. Watching as she became more upset as the conversation continued, he quietly said,

"Amanda, take my hands." This time she hesitated but slowly slipped her hands into his. "Look at me." She reluctantly looked up into his eyes. "You are my wife."

Those few words slammed into her with such a force she lost her breath and flinched slightly. *I am his wife, a wife is expected to . . . God, no!*

"You and your village people say I'm your wife." She grasped desperately at something. "But how do I know that it's binding? That it's legal?"

"It's legal, Amanda," he assured her calmly.

Shaking her head, she whispered, "This just keeps getting worse and worse." She then continued. "I can't, I won't," she declared firmly. He watched her carefully, not saying a word. "I made a promise to myself to stay pure, to save myself for my husband . . ." Her voice trailed off as she looked at him accusingly. "But I planned on being in love with my husband. I don't even know you, Matthew. All I know is that you stole me."

She tried to pull her hands free, but he tightened his grip.

"Amanda, listen to me," he ordered her firmly. She met his eyes. "I need you to listen to me. Pastor is going to look for the first mistake, the first rebellious act from you to punish us both. Tonight will be difficult for both of us, but if we don't," He left the rest unsaid.

She bit her bottom lip and met his eyes. "I can't, Matthew. Please, I just can't." She then lowered her head. *This was crazy.*

He reached out and touched her cheek gently.

"We'll get through tonight," he said quietly. "I'd never hurt you."

"I know, I know, but," she admitted, "I'm . . . afraid."

"I would be concerned if you weren't," he said softly.

"God, I can't do this," she whispered, covering her face with her hands.

"Is any part of your resistance have to do with Jared?" he asked, searching her face. She dropped her hands and looked at him, her eyes wide with surprise.

"Jared?" she asked, then felt guilty because he really had nothing to do with her reservations. "No, Jared's a friend." Her eyebrows came together in confusion.

"I was there, Amanda," he said quietly. She looked at him, her eyes questioning him. "I was there that night, on the campus. When he kissed you."

Memories of that night flooded through her. She had been very attracted to Jared that night. She remembered the kiss vividly. His sweet face came into her sight, his charming smile. Her chest ached with pain.

Matthew was there, watching her private moment with Jared.

"Jared cares for me," she said quietly, pulling away from him to stand up. "Yes, he did kiss me. We've been friends for a little over a year, and that was the first time I *let* him kiss me."

Matthew stood as well.

"And you care for him?" he asked reluctantly. Looking at Matthew, she was confused at where these questions were going.

"I, yes, I do care for him," she admitted.

"Do you love him?"

"Matthew, why . . . ," she started to say, and then it dawned on her that he might possibly be jealous of Jared. Not knowing why she cared, she slowly shook her head. "No. I don't think that I love him."

"Would you have broken your purity vow for him?" he asked, watching her intently. She shook her head again.

"No, Matthew," she said quietly, "but I was never given the opportunity to find out." She again wrapped the shawl tighter around her shoulders. "I don't want to talk about Jared anymore. I want to go back now."

He nodded and picked up the lantern, blowing out the flame.

Reaching for her hand, she grabbed it earnestly as the darkness engulfed them. The walk back to the cabin was much different. Tumultuous feelings were churning in Amanda, and Matthew was trying to figure out the best way to handle this awkward situation.

When they arrived, Matthew immediately lit several candles around the cabin. Amanda stood in the center of the small room. When he was done, he turned to her. She was wringing her hands, and he slowly walked over to her.

"Amanda?" he asked softly. She didn't want to look up. She would feel things for him that she shouldn't feel. Not even a month ago, she was kissing Jared, and now she was going to become intimate with another man she was married to. *But he kidnapped her! Could matters be any more bizarre? Was she betraying herself and her family by being attracted to him? Did she really have a choice?*

He slowly lifted her chin until she was forced to look at him.

Fear and confusion swam in her eyes.

"Amanda, why don't you change into your nightgown," he suggested softly. She nodded nervously and slowly pulled away from him. Not before he felt her trembling. She walked into the bathroom and closed the door slowly behind her.

He rubbed his hands over his face. She was so fragile right now, so close to accepting him that he didn't want to push her away. He walked toward the bed and pulled down the covers then walked across the room and returned with a lit candle, setting it on the small table near the bed. He knew that he was not mistaken about her reaction to him, but if she didn't recognize her feelings for what they were, that would make everything all the more difficult, he thought as he began to unbutton his shirt. Maybe they could talk for a few more hours, he considered but then realized the longer they waited, the harder it may be for her.

He turned when he heard the click of the door opening. He held his breath, waiting as she stepped out. When she looked up at him, her eyes went immediately to his bare chest; her heart began pounding in her chest. Warmth spread to her cheeks, and she pressed her cool hands to her face. She stopped midway across the room and looked away, wrapping her arms around herself.

"Matthew," she began, and he noticed that she was shaking.

"Yes?" he asked her. She shook her head, biting her bottom lip.

"Matthew, I can't do this. I can't be with you. It's wrong," she pleaded, looking back up at him, tears in her eyes. He walked closer to her, stopping a few feet from her.

"How can making love be wrong between a man and his wife?" he asked gently. "God blesses our union."

She turned and walked away from him to the other side of the room, turning her back to him.

"I never wanted to be married now," she exclaimed. "Now I'm married, to you. You, who kidnapped me. You've taken everything away from me and now I'm expected to—" She couldn't even bring herself to say the words. "This just can't be happening."

He met her across the room, her back to him; he rested his hands gently on her shoulders, feeling her go rigid with tension.

"Do I repulse you?" he asked softly as he began to massage her shoulders gently. She squeezed her eyes closed. *God, she wished he did repulse her. Then she knew that she would feel nothing for him.*

She shook her head silently, beginning to relax.

"Talk to me, Amanda," he whispered softly in her ear, and an uncontrollable shiver ran through her body. He pulled her back gently against him, and she allowed him to wrap his arms around her waist. She could feel the heat of his skin through the thin material of her nightgown, causing a chain reaction of tingles to shoot through her body as she rested against him.

"It's wrong, Matthew," she whispered, "I can't do this. You're the enemy." He gently turned her in his arms so that she was facing him.

"Amanda, is that what you really think?" he exclaimed softly. She searched his eyes.

"Yes," she acknowledged anxiously, "I *know* that you are. You did this to me!" Her blue eyes wide with indignation, she then looked down. "But what I *feel* . . . ," she whispered.

"What do you feel?" he asked, but she refused to look up at him.

"What I *feel* is wrong!" she said desperately. "I shouldn't feel anything for you." She tried to pull away, but he held on to her waist. He lifted her chin gently, and Amanda had no choice but to look in his eyes. The affection that burned in them caressed her face.

"Amanda," he whispered and bent down and gently put his lips to hers. Her body tensed as he held her securely with one arm. He deepened the kiss, and a wave of emotions ran through her as she responded. He pulled her closer, and she felt her body reacting to him. She lifted her hands and pushed against his chest, looking up at him, breathless. Her fingers touched her swollen lips. Jared had opened only a small door that led to the awakening passion she held within her. With Matthew, she felt like she was on fire.

"Matthew, no," she said, her voice shaking with emotion.

Matthew reached out and traced her jawline gently with his fingertips. "Don't be afraid of me, Amanda."

"Please, Matthew, I can't do this with you," she said, her eyes shining, her voice pleading as she tried to pull away from him. He held on to her arms.

"Amanda, we'll take it nice and slow. All right?" he asked quietly, not taking his eyes off her face. Her eyes were wide, her head shaking.

"I-I don't know," she whispered. He pulled her close, her cry of protest was cut off as his mouth again found her lips. He tenderly teased her lips until she allowed him to deepen the kiss, her body unconsciously relaxing. His kisses played havoc with her senses, threatening to overwhelm her. A strange sense of urgency began to build within her, a pleasurable sensation that she suddenly wanted to hold on to. She unconsciously wrapped her arms around his neck, oblivious to the pain this caused in her wrists; she returned his kiss. Tentatively at first, but then letting go of her mind, she allowed her body to respond naturally. He held her pressed to his body, and he struggled for restraint, forcing himself to slow the pace, not wanting to frighten her. In her innocence, she had no idea the sensations she was causing to shoot through him as she pressed her soft body into his own. He broke away. "Oh God, Amanda," he breathed huskily. "You're so beautiful." Amanda's whole body was shaking, but this time not with fear, but with an unknown passion. As he looked down at her, she couldn't take her eyes off his lips. He leaned down and tenderly kissed her nose and then her cheeks and slowly kissed his way down her neck. Again she began to melt in his arms, helpless to her own desires.

He couldn't help thinking that her skin was like velvet caressing his lips as he kissed her. He brought his lips back to her mouth, and she gasped out his name. His hands gently caressed small circles on her lower back, massaging her, bending her will. Amanda lowered her hands until her palms were resting on his chest. She could feel his heart beating rapidly under her hand and knew her own heart could match the pace. She felt his hands gently massaging her shoulders, his fingers slipping under the thin ribbons on her nightgown, but gasped when she felt the cool air on her breasts as the nightgown fell to her waist.

Suddenly she realized how far they had truly gone in a matter of moments. Whimpering, she pulled away from him, gathering her nightgown up to cover her nakedness. Holding her nightgown up with one hand, she held her other hand out in front of her as a barrier. Her breathing rapid, her body throbbing, she choked on a sob.

"No . . . no . . . no . . . ," she cried. "God, no."

Matthew stood still, struggling with his own emotions and against the slap of coldness he felt when she had pulled herself out of his arms. His hands rested on his hips as he tried to even his own breathing and tamper down his desire. "Amanda." His voice was soft, and she cringed, feeling her body respond to him. She shook her head and backed away from him.

He saw the pain and shock in her eyes, and he silently reprimanded himself for moving too fast. Her passionate response to him was completely unexpected, and he allowed himself to get carried away. "Amanda, I've frightened you." Shaking her head, her tears shining in the candlelight, she took several more steps away from him until her back rested against the wall. Still grasping her nightgown close to her, she slowly slipped down the wall to the floor. *Oh God, what was she going to do?* She cried. Closing her eyes tightly, she wished at that moment she had succeeded in her attempt at death. *How could she respond like that? She was weak, weak, weak! He was the enemy!*

Seeing the state she was in ripped at him painfully. He rubbed his hands over his face. Now what, he wondered helplessly. He walked over to the bed, pulling the quilt aside; he yanked off the soft blanket that lay beneath. He slowly walked over to where Amanda sat and quietly knelt down in front of her.

CHAPTER 13

"Amanda?" he said her name softly. Startled, she opened her eyes to see him at eye level. He held a blanket in his hands, his expression tender. "Can I wrap this around you?" Taking a shaky breath, unable to speak, she hesitantly nodded. Lifting the blanket around her, she leaned forward so he could wrap her in it. He overlapped the folds on the blanket in front of her, and his eyes searched her face in the shadows. She swallowed and slowly lifted her eyes to meet his. Her tears were fresh, her cheeks damp, but her crying had once again ceased. Silently their eyes held for several moments, and Amanda was sure he could hear the pounding of her heart as it beat in her chest.

"I'm sorry, Amanda," he finally said softly. Biting her lip, she shook her head.

"Oh, Matthew," she whispered, her brows coming together as she pulled the blanket tightly around her, "I'm so confused."

"I know," he said quietly, sighing as he rubbed his face again. "I know."

"This is just so wrong." She pleaded, "Please, Matthew, please, don't make me." His hand lowered slowly, and his eyes met hers.

"Amanda," he said softly, "I wasn't forcing you." Amanda closed her eyes at this, her cheeks burning. They both knew he was right.

"But you will," she declared softly, her eyes opening and meeting his. "If I refuse, you'll force me to be with you?"

"Yes, I will," he stated without hesitation. "I will, to protect you from the punishment." She pressed her lips together and silently nodded.

Then not being able to hold them in, tears began to fall. "I'm so angry! God, I want to hate you!"

Matthew could only nod his head, though inside it felt like she punched him in the stomach. They were back to this again, and Matthew felt his own frustration building. Why did it have to be this way? Why should a husband force his own wife if she wasn't ready to become intimate? His brows came together as doubt once again assaulted him.

"You did this to me!" she accused, without venom. "I should hate you, I should but"—she wiped angrily at her face—"I can't." Moments later Matthew got to his feet and walked over to the window. He rested his hands on the top of the window frame and leaned forward, his shoulders tense, realizing he couldn't make this any easier for her. It was foolish of him to think that he could.

Amanda's eyes followed him as he walked away. The candle flickered across his back, casting shadows. Taking a shaky breath, her eyes skimmed over his body. His arms and upper body were solid and strong—strong from hard labor. His black jeans molded his backside in a very flattering way; closing her eyes, she reluctantly admitted to herself, once again, that she was attracted to him. Another time, another place, and she knew that the things that he made her feel would intrigue and excite her. But here, now, it was frightening. *Could the punishment be worse than this?* Deep down, she knew that it had to be because she believed with all her heart that Matthew would not hurt her if he could help it. Struggling to her feet, the blanket wrapped tightly around her, she walked hesitantly over to him. He turned his head slightly when she reached his side. Her eyes were wide and searching.

"Matthew," she said softly and pulled the blanket tighter, "I," She looked away, her eyes going out into the dark night. "I don't know what to do." Matthew watched her struggle. Dropping his arms, he straightened; stepping closer, he lifted her chin.

"We don't have a choice," he stated softly. She nodded, biting her lip. "There's an attraction here, Amanda. Let's go with it." She closed her eyes for several moments then opened them.

"I can't help but think—" she started to say, her voice shaky.

"Amanda, try not to think," he interrupted softly. "What we're going to do doesn't require thinking, just feeling." He felt a shiver run through her as she looked up at him.

She could only shake her head, her eyes shining with unshed tears.

"I'd never hurt you," he whispered. She looked away toward the darkness.

"I know," she whispered back.

"Then what?" He rubbed her arms gently with his hands. She shook her head, not wanting to tell him. "Amanda."

She looked back up at him. "What you made me feel . . ." Her voice trailed off; embarrassed, she shook her head and walked away from him. She forced herself to go to the bed, knowing the inevitable would lead them both there. Keeping the blanket still wrapped around her, she climbed onto the soft mattress, seating herself against the wall. Matthew watched her for a few quiet moments and then slowly walked over to her. He sat down on the edge of the bed, his waist twisted so that he could see her.

"What did I make you feel?" he asked softly. Without notice, her eyes snapped to his, and her features contorted in anger.

"God, Matthew!" she spat. "I can't care for you! Don't you understand? I'm afraid"—her voice cracked, her head shaking—"and I don't want to care for you!" Matthew stared at her silently then looked down at his hands that rested on his legs.

"I see," was all he said. Silence filled the small cabin for what seemed like an eternity to Amanda, lasting long enough for her anger to recede as quickly as it had come. Part of her felt badly for snapping at him, but he did this to her. Knowing her words hurt him didn't lessen her frustration of being trapped here, and now being forced to do something that she knew would change her life forever. She was looking down at the quilt, following the pattern of colors with her eyes, when he finally spoke. "You're afraid that the way I make you feel, will make you care for me?" Her eyes slowly lifted to see him watching her closely. Hesitating, she sucked in a shaky breath before she nodded. "Amanda, you're my wife. Don't you think that it's all right for you to care for me now?"

"But not by choice," she stated softly, her eyes not wavering from his. "Don't you see? I didn't choose you!"

"We're back to that again," he said, sighing and rising to his feet. Her brows came together.

"We'll always come back to that," she declared, her voice filled with emotion. "This is my life and you're trying to take it away!" His hands shoved in his jean pockets, and he turned back to her.

"No, the only one trying to take your life away, Amanda, is you," he stated softly. His words sliced through her; understanding their meaning immediately, she sucked in her breath. "I'm only giving you a different life." Amanda lowered her eyes.

"I liked my life as it was," she said, raising her eyes back to him. "I want my *own* life back." She paused as he listened. "But you won't let me have it. I don't want the life you're offering me! Can't you understand? If I let myself . . ." Her voice trailed off again, unable to finish what she was saying.

"Care for me," he finished for her. "If you let yourself care for me, then what, Amanda?" She shook her head, frustrated. Under the blanket, she struggled back into the straps of her gown. Throwing the blanket off her, she scrambled off the bed and began to walk past him. Moving quickly, his arms came up and stopped her. Her eyes snapped to his; anger sparked in the blue depths, but he matched her anger with his own glare. "Then what?" She tried to pull away, but he wouldn't let go of his grip. Her eyes glanced down at his hands squeezing her arms, and then back up.

"You're hurting me!" she declared hotly. He shook his head, ignoring her.

"Answer me, Amanda!" he demanded. Suddenly Amanda wondered if this was it. He was angry—angry enough, she thought, to force her. She swallowed, heat creeping up her neck, reaching her cheeks. *Would he hurt her?* Suddenly she wasn't so sure anymore. Her anger was quickly replaced by fear, and a bitter taste filled her mouth. Unable to look at him, she kept her head lowered.

"Then I'll be betraying myself," she finally whispered.

"How so?" he demanded, his voice softer, but his grip remained the same. When she didn't answer, he squeezed her arms tighter, causing her to wince and look up at him. "Amanda?"

She swallowed nervously. "Because I'd be accepting what you've done to me!"

He let go of her so abruptly she stumbled back. She looked up to see him putting his jacket on without a shirt. He walked to the door, and she struggled against the panic that exploded in her. He opened the door and was about to step out when he looked over his shoulder at her. "Amanda, think about what life will be like if you don't accept me. This is your life now, like it or not." With that, he walked out and closed the door behind him. A sob escaped her, and she covered her mouth with the back of her hand.

"Matthew!" she called to the empty room. "Oh God!" Walking quickly to the door, she flung it open and gasped as the cool air whipped through the thin material of her nightgown. The night was dark, and she had no idea what direction he had gone. Fearing being found by another psychotic member of the village, she walked down the steps, her arms wrapped around herself, and called quietly, "Matthew . . . Matthew!" The dirt was cold under her feet, and she tentatively walked in the direction that he had taken her earlier. The blackness seemed to swallow her as she moved away from the cabin. Tears streamed down her face. "Oh, Matthew, where are you?" she whispered. Tripping over a root, she fell to her knees and cried out as pain shot up her leg. Her wrists burned as her muscles strained in her arms as they hit the ground to protect her. The wound in her hand split open; she felt the blood seep through the white bandage.

"Amanda?" Matthew's voice came out of the darkness.

"Matthew!" she cried, relief washing over her as she struggled to her feet. "What are you doing?" Helping her stand up, he felt her ice-cold bare arms. "Do you want to catch pneumonia?"

"Oh, Matthew," she cried again. In the dark she grasped at his jacket and pulled herself against him. She pressed her cheek against his chest, which was as cold as the night air, but she could feel him, and her panic ceased. Hesitating, he wrapped his arms around her.

"Oh, Amanda," he sighed, lifting her into his arms. She was shivering and crying as she clung to him. He walked the short distance back to the cabin and kicked the door closed behind him. Matthew walked over to the bed and tried to set her down, but she wouldn't release her grip, nor did her crying stop. He turned and sat down, resting her on his lap. "Shhhh. It's okay, Amanda. It's all right." He rubbed her back as he soothed her with gentle words.

"I'm sorry . . . Matthew," she cried, "I'm sorry . . . I'll do . . . what you want."

"Amanda, calm down, hon," he soothed her, closing his eyes. This was not how he wanted her acquiesce. "Amanda."

"Please don't leave me," she cried. When he walked out that door, she was devastated and experienced real desperation at that moment. "Please, Matthew, just don't leave me alone here, please."

"Oh, baby, I'm sorry," he said softly. "I was just so frustrated. I needed a minute to cool off, that's all. I wasn't going to leave you. I swear it." He felt her nod against his chest, and her grip eased some. He reached behind him and retrieved the blanket she had discarded not long ago and wrapped her back up, trying to relieve her shivering. "Amanda, please stop crying."

"Okay," she said softly, trying to calm herself. She had wrapped her arms around his middle, her small hands stretched across his taut back. It was at that moment that she realized she already cared for Matthew. She knew his familiar masculine scent and his gentle touch. When he left, not only did she feel fear, but she felt as if part of her was leaving with him. *How could that be?* she asked herself. In a matter of weeks, she managed to fall for her kidnapper. *Of all the twisted scenarios,* she thought bitterly. Then she pushed herself away from his chest and sat back to look up at him. She searched his face, a bit dazed at her revelation. He gave her a small smile, thinking she looked adorable with her red nose and damp eyes. He tugged at the corner of the blanket, gently wiping her cheeks dry with it.

Lifting her hand, she was about to rest her palm on his cheek when she noticed the bloody bandage. "Oh!" she cried out, and he gently took her hand in his.

"You must have done that when you fell," he said. "Let's clean that up." Walking to the bathroom, he gently unwrapped the bandage, discarding it in the trash. She winced when he washed it with warm water, but he was gentle when he began to rewrap it. "You split it open." Biting her lip, banking her pain, she only nodded.

After leading her back to the bed, she sat down. His eyes met hers. She licked her lips nervously. "I'm sorry, about before," she whispered. "About the things I said."

"Amanda, don't," he said quietly. "You have every right to be angry." She averted her eyes and nodded. Taking a shaky breath, she brought her eyes back to his. "I'll be with you, Matthew." He searched her face.

"Amanda."

"I will, Matthew," she said softly. "Tell me what to do." He saw fear, and something else in her eyes. He didn't want it to be like this; swallowing his frustration, he hesitantly nodded. They had no choice, he knew that.

"Just relax and don't think," he replied softly. "Was it so bad before?"

Instantly her cheeks turned pink. "No," she whispered. "I just"—pausing and averting her eyes again—"felt so many feelings at once, that I got scared."

"We'll go slower, all right?" he suggested tenderly. She nodded, her eyes wide. He pulled her up, setting her on her feet, and shrugged out of his jacket. The blanket that had been around Amanda's shoulder's had slipped to the floor where they stood. Pooled around her ankles, she looked from the blanket to Matthew. Then taking a deep breath, she slowly lifted her hand to her nightgown strap. Matthew clenched his jaw as he watched her innocent assertion and painfully wondered how he could keep his promise to go slow. Seconds later, her nightgown joined the blanket on the floor, and Matthew went still. As his eyes drank in every inch of her beautiful body, his heart pounded. At first Amanda was incredibly embarrassed, but then seeing Matthew look at her, she suddenly felt beautiful. The fire that burned in his eyes scattered her senses. Her arms nervously came up; unconsciously she wanted to cover herself, but Matthew reached out and gently touched her forearms, shaking his head.

"Amanda, you're so beautiful," he whispered. "God made you just for me." His voice was full of awe and wonder. He slid his hands down her arms, finding her hands, and pulled her onto the bed. He lay back and pulled her gently on top of him; his jeans rubbed roughly against her bare skin. Her breasts rubbed sensually on his chest, and she gasped at the sensation. Tensing at the intimacy of their position, Amanda's eyes widened, and Matthew could see the panic in her eyes. "Relax, Amanda." His voice was soft. "Look at me." She did. "That's right. Remember, no thinking." She sucked in her breath. "No thinking."

"All right," she whispered. *No thinking, no thinking, no thinking*, she repeated over and over to herself.

"Just get used to the feel of my body, Amanda," he said. His hands rested lightly on her waist and burned to touch more. But he held his own, wanting to make this right for her. It only took moments for her body to begin relaxing, and when she realized this, she met his eyes with a small smile on her lips.

"Not so scary," he lightly teased. She shook her head shyly.

"Not scary. Nice," she admitted to him. Closing his eyes, he took a deep breath, trying to control himself. Opening them, he gave her a shaky smile.

"I'm going to move you aside now. All right?" he said, his voice slightly strained. She nodded, and he slid her over onto her back and rolled his leg over both of hers. He was propped up on his elbow. "Amanda, I have to touch you." He brought his lips down to hers and engulfed her in a torrential storm of sensations. His lips teased and nipped; his tongue tasted and tormented. Amanda thought she was lost in the wonderful things he was doing with his mouth. Then his hand began to caress her breast. Without knowing why, she arched her back up, moaning, his touch searing her skin. Pulling his lips away, he whispered her name as he began trailing kisses down her neck. His hands moved over her smoothly, exploring and caressing. Amanda reached her arms out and pulled him closer, needing to be closer. At the same moment he captured her breast in his mouth, his hand slid down, touching her so intimately she cried out. Urgent sensations began building in her, almost painfully. As she gasped his name, his mouth covered hers, drowning her in intimate touches, and then . . . he was gone. Her body screamed in protest, her breathing came rapidly. Blinking open her eyes, she watched him shrug out of his jeans. Then he was back by her side.

Next to her once again, their heated breaths mingled. Bringing his lips not an inch from hers, his eyes searched hers questioningly. "Amanda?" His voice was rough with emotion. The passion between them was electrifying.

"I don't understand all these feelings," she whispered, her eyes wide with confusion and desire.

"I know," he whispered. Then he continued, "Your first time may hurt a little."

He kissed her gently on her lips before meeting her eyes again.

"Do you want me to stop?" he breathed, knowing how impossible it seemed to do, but he vowed to find the strength if he had to. Her body was burning from the inside out; stopping would be unbearable.

"No, God, no," she gasped.

"Trust me," he whispered, before he kissed her again.

"I do, Matthew," she whispered. "I do."

Matthew was gentle and loving during their lovemaking—sensitive to her innocence. He brought Amanda to a place she never knew existed, and when she felt she could take no more, they became one. His lips captured hers as her body shuddered under the waves of passion; at the same time, Matthew buried his face into her shoulder, moaning her name. As their bodies began to descend into relaxed fulfillment, they clung to one another, their breathing becoming deep as sleep consumed them.

Hours later, Matthew, propped up on his elbow, watched Amanda as she slept. She was his angel, he thought. Her long blond hair was spread beneath her; her face was tilted sideways, revealing her delicate profile. Her response to him had been such a surprise, and still he couldn't believe how incredible their first time together had been. With the way the night had been going, he didn't know how it would end. The edge of the sheet covering her body revealed just the swell of her breasts. Matthew slowly traced the line of the sheet with his finger.

She moved slightly then slowly blinked open her eyes. She awoke to Matthew watching her, a tender expression on his face.

They had made love, she remembered. *It was wonderful* was her first thought. Then she thought, *How could you? After everything he's done to you. How could you?*

"No, Amanda," he whispered, seeing the mixed emotions flash across her face. "Don't think about it. I don't want you to have any regret. It was too special."

She looked into his eyes, tears coming to her own.

"Matthew."

"No . . . shhhhhh," he said softly, placing his fingers on her lips. "Let's not talk. I just want to hold you." He pulled her into his arms, and she snuggled closer.

Was she wrong? Shame stood on the edge of her conscience. *But he's all that I have*, she cried silently. *Am I wrong for what I did, for what I felt? He's my husband, whether I chose him or not*, she argued with herself. What could have been a horrible end to her virginity turned out to be special. Matthew was right; it had been special. Her hand rested lightly on his smooth chest.

Just before sleep consumed her once again, she struggled with her feelings. She was thrown into this nightmare, and she was clinging to her sanity. Matthew cared for her; that much was obvious. She needed him to survive here, and she was unable to deny that she cared for him anymore. She did. Somehow he went from being her abductor to her protector. Right now she was wrapped in his arms, and it felt good. Safe. Sleep tugged at her as she continued wrestling between her doubts and her heart.

CHAPTER 14

As dawn began to show its first light, Amanda stirred. With the first light came the realization that she was still wrapped in Matthew's arms. She had never been this intimate with a man before. Their bodies were naked and entwined. Thoughts of the previous night caused her cheeks to burn, and she was mortified at her behavior. Slowly slipping out of the bed, she hurried to the bathroom. She quickly dressed, desperately trying not to cry. *It's okay . . . it's okay . . . it's okay . . .* she repeated over and over again. *But oh gosh, she enjoyed being with him last night.* The shame she felt was almost unbearable. Sliding to the bathroom floor, she hugged herself. *What did she do?*

She slowly raised her left hand and looked intently at the gold band on her ring finger. She was married. *I'm married,* she thought incredulously. *How can this be happening? People aren't just kidnapped and forced to get married. These things are only supposed to happen in the movies! Yet, here she was . . .* she thought as tears trickled down her face. She was so tired of crying!

Deep in her thoughts, she was startled when she heard the knock on the door.

"Amanda?" he called. "Are you all right?"

She quickly stood up. "Yes,"—swallowing—"I'll be right out." She wiped her tears away with her sleeve. Opening the door, she was surprised to see him still standing at the doorway, wearing his pants, but no shirt.

He could see that she had been crying. He reached out and touched her cheek gently. "You're sad." His words were soft. She looked down, not speaking. Lifting her chin gently with two fingers, he asked, "Amanda, what is it?"

She was forced to look at him, but she couldn't answer him.

"Talk to me," he said softly. She pulled her chin away and walked around him, going to the window and pushing the thin curtain aside. She felt him come up behind her. Wrapping his arms around her waist, she rested her back against his chest—a natural reaction that she didn't think about.

"I feel so ashamed," she whispered. He squeezed her tightly then released her, turning her around. He took her face into his hands and looked directly in her teary eyes.

"Amanda, you've done nothing to be ashamed of," he assured softly. "We are husband and wife."

"But I barely know you," she whispered, "and yet I wanted . . ." She couldn't bear to say the words out loud.

"Amanda," he said, "there's nothing wrong with being attracted to me, or I to you. It's the way God made us. It's called chemistry."

"I'm not stupid, Matthew!" she declared softly. "I may have been a virgin, but I'm not ignorant to the human body." She paused. He smiled at her reprimand. "It's just that I hardly know you, yet I wanted to be with you and you kidnapped me! It's just wrong. Don't you see? How could I?"

"Okay," he said, dropping his hands to his sides and stepping back. "If you want to beat yourself up over what I thought was an incredible moment, then, by all means, go ahead. But, Amanda, I *do* care for you, and you *are* my wife. We will continue on as such, and we *will* make love again." Turning, he walked back toward the bed. He found his shirt, picked it up, and shoved his arms into the sleeves.

She'd hurt him. After everything that he'd done to her, she shouldn't care about his feelings, but she did. Walking over to him slowly, she was so confused, and tired. Tired of the struggle.

"Matthew," she said, coming to stand next to him. He turned to her. "Don't be angry with me."

"Amanda, I'm not," he said, running his hand through his hair. "This is hard for me too. But last night could have been horrible, for both of us. But it wasn't, and you know it. We both wanted each other! Don't you see that? We are strangers in a way, but if we're attracted to each other, isn't that a pretty good start to the marriage?"

Averting her eyes, she whispered, "I'm so afraid to care for you. I feel like I'm betraying myself."

"Because I'm the enemy." He used her own words. Looking back up at him, she slowly nodded. "But I'm not, Amanda. Not here." She nodded again.

"I know that, here," she said, putting her hand over her heart, "but in my mind—" He pulled her into his arms and held her.

"You need to listen to your heart," he said; taking her face into his hands, he leaned down, kissing her tenderly on her lips. Arousing those wonderful feelings from the night before, her body betrayed her once again. She wrapped her arms around his waist and gasped when he finally tore away from the kiss; passion burned in both of their eyes.

"Tell me you don't need me as much as I need you," he whispered huskily. She looked up at him, her eyes afire, her lips pink and swollen from his kiss, and slowly shook her head.

"I can't," she whispered. He groaned, pulling her tightly against his body. She reached up and put her arms around his neck, clinging to him. She did want to be with him; her blood coursed through her veins hotly, her skin was on fire. He slid his hands under her shirt, his hands wrapping around her small waist. She felt tense with emotion and anxious for his touch.

"Matthew, please," she whispered. Not wasting another moment, he picked her up and brought her back to the bed. There he began to show her how much he treasured her. The gentle caresses and tenderness brought them again to the height of their passion. Tears trickled down Amanda's cheeks with the knowledge that Matthew had reached within her and touched her soul. She had given him everything, and she knew deep in her heart she would never be the same again.

Later he pushed himself up on his elbows and kissed Amanda's tears.

"Did I hurt you?" he whispered, his voice filled with concern. Her eyes fluttered open, her lashes moist.

"No," she whispered back. He searched her face, his expression tender.

"Why are you crying?" he asked. Reaching up, she traced his jawline with her fingers.

"It was so," she whispered shyly. Her cheeks were rosy; her hair was tousled and hanging down the front of her, covering her breasts. Her beautiful blue eyes were wide with confusion.

"What?" he gently encouraged her. She shook her head, biting her lip. "Tell me. What?"

"Beautiful," she whispered, closing her eyes, embarrassed by her admission.

"Oh, Amanda," he declared softly, then rolled over and pulled her with him so that she now rested on top of him. He smiled at her startled expression. "You were made for me." She hesitated, searching his face, then slowly nodded.

"I'm beginning to believe that," she whispered.

"God has blessed our union," he said seriously, "by allowing us to fit perfectly together."

Searching his eyes, she knew he truly believed that. "Matthew," she asked softly, "do you really believe that God approves of kidnapping and forced marriages?"

He stared at her. How was he to answer that?

"I truly don't know," he said honestly, looking away. "I believed everything until I brought you here, and now I just don't know." Amanda closed her eyes and lay her face down on his chest. He needed to come to conclusions on his own, or she knew he'd never leave.

"Matthew," she asked, again, "am I an awful person for wanting to be with you?" He pulled her up so that she could meet his eyes, but she kept hers averted.

"Amanda, look at me," he demanded softly. She slowly brought her eyes to his. "No, you're not."

"But I didn't know you a month ago," she was saying again.

"So much has happened since," he intervened.

The same doubts and guilt plagued her. "I'm so confused. I feel like I don't know who I am anymore," she whispered painfully, tears shining in her eyes. Matthew squeezed her tighter.

"I know," he said softly. "I'm sorry it had to be this way. I wish I could have met you and dated, like the rest of the world does. But I do truly care about you, Amanda. I would never hurt you or let anything happen to you. Do you believe that?" She was quiet for a moment.

"Yes," she whispered. Then she added, "It's just so hard."

"Is being right here, right now, so hard?" he asked. She shook her head.

"But being here with you means I have to live here!" she said, refusing to let her tears fall. "You'll have to leave me to go and work or whatever you do and that terrifies me. I don't want to be here, without you."

"Amanda," he said patiently, "I'll be with you a lot more than you think.

You'll meet the other women and it won't be bad, you'll see." She laid her head back onto his chest.

"I don't want to," she asserted stubbornly. His chest rumbled under her ear as he chuckled.

"If it were up to me, I'd spend all day, every day with you." He smiled.

Suddenly there was a knock at the door. Amanda bolted upright, holding the blanket tightly to her. "Who's that?" she exclaimed, her eyes wide. Matthew sat up, looking at the door, then back to her.

"It must be the women," he said quietly. "The sheet . . ."

Amanda instantly remembered and blushed furiously.

"Oh God, this is humiliating!" She slipped out of bed, the blanket wrapped around her, and ran into the bathroom.

As she waited in the bathroom, she could hear Matthew interacting with the women, his conversation as casual as if they were over for tea, and not to pick up the sheet they'd just made love on! *This was so twisted,* she thought.

Washing up, she quickly redressed herself. By the time she was done, the women had left. She opened the door slowly to find Matthew waiting for her. He was sitting on the bed that was made with fresh linens. *She loved the sight of him,* she thought. *Oh Lord, was she in trouble!*

"They're gone," he teased. She blushed again, her hands flying to cover her cheeks. "Let me wash up and then we'll eat something."

While Matthew was in the bathroom, she rummaged through the cupboards. She was surprised to see them filled with everyday groceries. For some reason, she expected to see homegrown jars and packages. *Who knew?* She opened the refrigerator, gathering ingredients. She pulled a heavy cast-iron pan from the cabinet below with her good hand and placed it on the stove. Never having cooked with one of these before, she wondered if there was a significant difference. Shrugging, she started to make the omelets.

When Matthew came out of the bathroom, his senses were assaulted with delicious smells. He stopped in the doorway and leaned against the frame. Amanda was humming as she worked over the stove. His throat tightened as he watched her, realizing that his dreams had come true. When he first decided on Amanda for his wife, he would try and imagine this day, when he would have her for his own. Now she was here, cooking them breakfast.

She looked over her shoulder at him, a sweet smile on her face.

"Hey." Her voice was soft, her eyes warm.

"Hey yourself," he said, pushing himself away from the door, walking over to her. Wrapping his arms around her small waist, he nuzzled his face into the side of her neck. "That smells incredible!" She smiled and leaned back into him.

"Yeah?" she smiled. "I can't promise it'll taste like it smells."

She giggled, and he closed his eyes at the wonderful sound. Pulling away, he opened a cabinet over her head.

"I'll set the table," he said. She watched him out of the corner of her eye, thinking how strangely intimate this was. Oddly enough, it was a scene she'd witnessed countless times at home, with her parents. Remembering, she could smell her house, the scent of pine candles her mother loved so much and tobacco from her father's pipes. Placing the omelets on the plates next to her, she was filled with such a feeling of despair that she went still, staring at the empty pan, but not really seeing it. Shaking her head, she gripped the stove handle with both hands to keep her balance. *Would she ever see them again? Oh God, it hurts.*

"Amanda, what is it?" Matthew had come to her side, when he saw her go still. A pained expression on her face, he became concerned. "Are you in pain?" Turning to him, her brows came together in confusion.

"What?" she asked, not having heard him. He searched her eyes, concerned.

"I asked if you were in pain," he replied softly. Amanda looked down at the plates in front of her and shook her head.

"No," she said softly. "I'm fine." Picking up the plates, she tried to walk by him. He took the plates from her hands and placed them back on the counter. "Matthew, they'll get cold." He placed his hands on her arms and rubbed lightly.

"What is it, Amanda?" he asked softly. "Tell me what's wrong." She closed her eyes briefly then opened them.

"It's nothing, really." She met his eyes, struggling to bank her heartache. Telling him of the memory would not change anything; this nightmare wasn't going to end any time soon. He shook his head.

"Something put that sadness back in your eyes," he said, knowing she wasn't being completely honest.

"Matthew, please, let's eat," she replied. Eating was the last thing she wanted to do at that moment, but things had been going so well between them that she didn't want to ruin it. He searched her face for several moments, before nodding and taking the food to the table. Matthew said grace, and then they began eating. He took a bite of his food, closed his eyes, and moaned. "Amanda, this is delicious!"

She gave him a small smile and nodded. "It's better than I thought it would be."

"How did you learn to cook so good?" he asked. "I thought college students ate out of cans and used microwaves to cook." Amanda looked over at him, thoughtful.

"How did you know that?" she asked then gave him a small smile. "For most students, that's true. But I started cooking when I was about"—she paused, thinking, then—"fifteen, I think." Matthew took another bite, chewed it, and swallowed.

"Your mother taught you?" he asked. Amanda made a comical face.

"No, definitely not!" she laughed softly. "No, my mom's a lawyer, and a very good one. But she does *not* belong in a kitchen unless she's making something simple. Like toast."

"Then who?" he asked.

"My mom hired a chef to teach me," she stated matter-of-factly. "Every Tuesday afternoon, for four years of high school, I learned how to cook everything from cookies to gourmet meals."

"Wow, that's great," he said, smiling. "Did you enjoy it?"

"No!" Amanda exclaimed, scowling good-naturedly. "I hated it! I was in high school. I wanted to hang out with my friends, go to games, and—" Stopping midsentence, she realized that he wouldn't understand. Her smile slipped. "Anyway, I hated it at the time. My mom just didn't want me to grow up illiterate in the kitchen like she did. When I got to college, I appreciated all the lessons. My roommate Shelby and I would cook these huge meals and have a bunch of friends over, and—" Her voice faded away, the light dimming in her eyes. She swallowed and lowered her head. "I don't mind it now."

He watched how animated she was as she talked about her old life, and it hurt him to know that he was responsible for hurting her. Seeing her go pale and quiet, and seeing the joy leave her face, he sat in his chair, helpless. Leaning over the table, he covered her hand with his own. "Amanda, I like hearing about your old life," he said quietly.

Amanda bit her lip as she looked at his hand that covered hers. Then her eyes met his. *Her old life,* she thought bitterly—*it was her only life!* "I don't like talking about it," she stated quietly, devoid of any emotion. "Excuse me." Pushing her chair back, she stood and walked into the bathroom. Closing the door quietly behind her, she sat on the edge of the bathtub. Covering her face, she sobbed quietly. *There was no way she could do this*; she cried, her heart aching. *How could she accept this way of life? How could she accept being a wife and live like this. It was too much!* Her chest ached. *Why is this happening to me!* She just couldn't make sense of any of it.

The door opened quietly, and Matthew stepped into the small room. She continued to cry, not looking up. He hated this, he thought, clenching his jaw; he hated what he was doing to her. He knelt down in front of her; reaching up, he took her hands into his own. When he gently pulled her hands away from her face, she shook her head, her eyes miserable.

"I'm sorry, Matthew," she cried. "I just don't"—she breathed—"know how I'm going to do this." Tears shined in his own eyes.

"Oh, baby, come here." He pulled her down into his arms. Wrapping her arms around his neck, she clung to him. "You'll get through this. I promise." Strangely, she felt better in his embrace. His arms felt protective, his words soothing, and he really wanted to take her hurt away. *How could she feel this way about him?* As he rubbed her back, holding her close, she realized that it really didn't matter anymore. Time. Katherine promised her freedom. Amanda swallowed her last sob and squeezed Matthew. It was frightening how much she had come to rely on him, but she didn't know what else to do.

She pulled back some so her face was inches from his. He reached up and wiped her tears with his fingers as his eyes searched hers.

"I'm sorry that I've hurt you so," he whispered, distressed.

"Oh, Matthew," she whispered his name and leaned her forehead against his. "I don't blame you. Not anymore." Knowing this was true, she suddenly understood that this was why she allowed herself to become close to him—to care for him. Because she didn't blame him. She knew where the blame lay. Matthew was just another innocent victim to the psychotic man who had power over these good people.

He closed his eyes, wanting to believe her, but he blamed himself too much.

"I'm just homesick," she said, her voice shaky.

"I know." Opening his eyes, he looked into hers, his affection evident. "Amanda,"—he hesitated—"I wish . . ."

She nodded, understanding his feelings exactly. "Me too." This admission warmed his heart and gave him the slightest hope. She had to care for him at least a little, making an admission like that, right? He reached up and touched her hair lightly with one hand. Unable to speak, he brought his lips to hers, kissing her tenderly. With a small moan, she melted against him, wrapping her arms back around his neck, pressing her body to his. His lips worked the wonderful magic that he seemed to have over her, and she was overwhelmed at the desire that pulsed through her.

Within moments they were lying on the bathroom floor. Matthew had her skirt pulled up, touching and exploring as Amanda gasped at the pleasure of his touch. Trying to unbutton his shirt, her hands yearning for his bare skin, she fumbled with the buttons. Whispering his name, he understood and reached between the seam, wrenching the shirt open, sending buttons flying to the floor around them. Her hands touched and kneaded his back and chest, her bandages lightly scratching his skin. Their passion burned and grew until they both reached the edge of the precipice, when Matthew joined them together as one.

It was several moments before either one could speak. Matthew lifted his head, kissing her lightly on the lips. They looked at one another, their expressions intent and intimate. Lifting her hand, she touched his cheek tenderly.

"Amanda?" he began, propping himself on his elbows; a small smile creased his face.

"Hmm?" she replied, watching him.

"Do you happen to know how to sew?" he asked sheepishly. Amanda hesitated, smiled, then giggled. He laughed softly, kissing her nose before sitting up.

Amanda straightened her clothes and sat up, smiling. "I think I can sew buttons."

"Good." Matthew chuckled. "It would be a little difficult explaining to my mother how that happened." Amanda covered her cheeks, as they burned red, and giggled again. Helping her to her feet, Amanda hid her flinch of pain from her wrists.

"Why don't we get washed up again." He smiled. "I'd like to take you for a walk and show you the village." Amanda smiled, nodding eagerly, longing to be in the fresh air again.

Matthew had cleaned the breakfast dishes while she washed up again, and he readied himself in a matter of minutes. Leaving the bathroom, he saw Amanda standing by the window, holding her injured hand in her good hand. Guilt assaulted him when he realized he hadn't asked her once how she was feeling.

"Amanda," he called her name. Smiling, she dropped her hand and walked toward him. In that moment, he saw the small bloodstain on the stark-white bandage.

"Hey"—she smiled—"are you ready?" Searching her eyes, he saw the pain reflected in their depths, and it hurt him to realize that she didn't tell him. When he didn't answer, her own smile slipped as she noted his serious expression. "Is something wrong?" Clenching his jaw, he took her wrists gently in his hands and then lifted his eyes up to meet hers.

"You're in pain," he stated soberly. Swallowing, she looked down at her wrists.

"I'm all right," she said quietly.

"You split your hand open last night, and it's bleeding again, and you're in pain." His brows came together in confusion. "Why didn't you say anything?"

"Matthew, I'm fine, real—," she began.

"No, you're not!" he declared angrily. Her eyes flew to his face in surprise. "Why are you lying to me?" She opened her mouth to speak, but no words came out. Letting go of her hands, he gestured to the couch. "Sit down," he ordered her.

"Matthew," she said, finally finding her voice.

"Sit!" he barked, causing her to flinch. Walking slowly to the couch, she sat down. He walked into the bathroom, coming out with the supplies he'd been using for her injuries. Dropping them on the couch, he sat down and took her left wrist into his lap. The color had left Amanda's face, and she was suddenly unsure of Matthew. Seeing him angry last night had surprised her, but that had been provoked. This, she just didn't understand. Though his movements were abrupt, his touch was gentle. Unwrapping the bandage, she flinched as he neared the wound. His eyes settled on her pale face for several moments before looking back down at her wrist. The wound was flaming red, and Amanda gasped when she saw it. Her eyes went to Matthew's face, and she watched him clench and unclench his jaw. Didn't she know that if she didn't tell him, he couldn't help her? Cleaning the area, he rubbed a thick, nasty-smelling ointment on it, rewrapping it. By this time, tears were trickling down Amanda's cheeks. Setting her left hand aside gently, he reached for the right. Cringing, when he reached for the bandage on her hand, he looked up to see her tears.

His hand went to her cheek. "Why didn't you tell me you were suffering?" he asked, his anger gone, only to be replaced by concern.

Shaking her head, her lips trembled. "I don't know," she cried. "I wanted to go for a walk and . . ." Searching her eyes, it dawned on him. She thought he'd keep her locked in here.

"Baby, we're still going for a walk," he said, "but you need to tell me if you're in pain so that I can help you. Do you understand?"

She was tearfully nodding. "Please don't be angry with me, Matthew," she whispered. "I'm sorry."

"Oh, honey." He leaned forward, kissing her reassuringly on the lips. "I'm not angry at you. Just don't hide your pain from me, all right?"

"All right," she whispered. As he reached for her hand again, she involuntarily flinched. "I'm sorry." Biting her lip, she looked up at him to see him watching her. "It does hurt some."

"Oh, Amanda." He sighed. "I have to look at it."

"I know," she whispered, placing her hand back in his. Instead of unwrapping the bandage on her hand, he unwrapped the bandage on her wrist. In a similar condition as her other one, he treated it the same. When he was done, he hesitantly began unwrapping the bandage on her hand. Struggling not to flinch, he pulled the last of the bandage off. The pain was so severe she cried silently as he worked. Seeing the condition it was in, he looked up at her.

"A couple of stitches ripped out," he explained softly. Reaching up, he wiped her tears away, again. "Doc should restitch them."

Swallowing, she took a shaky breath. "No, I don't want them to be. It'll heal."

"Amanda, stitches will—," he began.

"Only make it prettier. I don't care about that. It's on the palm of my hand, Matthew."

Patiently he said, "They will also help prevent infection."

"Please, Matthew," she pleaded, "I don't want them." Shaking his head, he finished cleaning the area some more, wiping the thick ointment on, then began to rewrap her hand. When he was done, his eyes met hers. She was pale, and the warmth of the morning was gone from her eyes.

"I'm going to make you an herbal tonic to help take the edge off the pain," he said. Pain throbbed through her in waves, and all she could do was nod her head. Glancing at her from where he stood, he began mixing the herbs. As concern filled him, he had to admit she'd been right. By her appearance, she was in no shape to be going for a walk. He fought his urge to make her lie down, knowing how important it was for her to get out in the fresh air. Finishing, he slowly walked over to her. Feeling him near, she blinked open her eyes as he sat down next to her. As they watched one another, Amanda recognized that making Matthew angry was not something she wanted to do. *What if he left her because she did something wrong?* She couldn't bear to be isolated in this place.

"I'm sorry, Matthew," she whispered again, fighting the anxiety that this situation had caused. Handing her the drink, he said, "Drink this, Amanda." Obeying, she gulped the liquid down, hoping that its contents would begin working quickly. Taking the empty glass from her, he set it aside on the table and pulled her into his arms, her back against his chest. His arm wrapped around her waist; his hand rested on her hip. "I'm sorry I snapped at you. Did I frighten you?" He felt her take an unsteady breath.

"A little," she admitted in a small voice. He was quiet for a few moments, then he said, "When you were down with the fever"—he began solemnly—"you were burning up, and it seemed that no matter how many times we soaked you in ice water, your temperature would spike right back up." Pausing, he then continued, "I could see in Molly's eyes that she wasn't sure you were going to make it, and that scared me. The thought of losing you." He squeezed her lightly with his arm. "We fought so hard to save you, Amanda. That's why I was so upset when I knew you were hurting. I don't want to lose you. Not to some stupid infection that could have been prevented, not to anything." Touched in a way that she couldn't put into words, Amanda twisted slightly in his arms, resting her cheek on his chest.

"I'm sorry I put you through that," she said sincerely.

"Don't apologize to me," he stated. "Apologize to yourself. You're hurting." Tears burned her eyes as she looked up at him.

"Yes"—dropping her gaze—"I was foolish. I deserve this pain."

"That's not what I mean, Amanda," he interrupted. "Is that why you didn't say anything to me? Because you feel you deserve this?"

"Partly," she admitted. "Every time I feel the pain, I remember my stupidity, and how close to death I truly came."

"Amanda," he began, and she looked up at him, her wide blue eyes meeting his.

"Thank you for taking care of me," she whispered, "and for saving my life." Taken aback, his throat tightened with emotion.

"You're welcome," he whispered back, kissing her softly on the lips. They sat quietly for several moments, when Matthew said, "Are you ready to take that walk?" Lifting her face, her smile lightened the shadows in her eyes.

"Yes!" she exclaimed softly. "I'm feeling better." Smiling, he sat up, pulling her with him, kissing her lightly on the nose.

"Good," he declared, "let's go."

Once outside, she shyly slipped her good hand in his, keeping herself close to him. He was so content to have her next to him, his happiness shining in his eyes.

He brought her to the center of the village, walking past the church and toward another large cabin. There was a sign that read "Women's Center." They stopped in front, and Amanda peeked in the windows, seeing several women in black looking back at her curiously. Instantly Amanda backed up, bumping into Matthew.

He smiled. "They're anxious to meet you. No one is allowed to interact with us until the three-day isolation is over." Amanda looked away from the building; pulling her hand, he walked in the opposite direction. "That's the building where the women spend most of their time. They do the laundry, sewing, quilting and a bunch of other domestic responsibilities. You'll see a mix of modern and old-fashioned conveniences. Pastor didn't think certain items would corrupt the village, but only make areas run smoother." They walked across the road to another cabin. *They all looked the same,* she thought, *how could they tell them apart?*

"This is the church hall," he stated. "This is where we have the village dinners every Sunday, and other special dinners. You know like weddings, baptisms and the like. We'll come here, together, this Sunday," he revealed, "to be announced to the village." Amanda swallowed the lump in her throat, nodding.

He brought her around, pointing out certain cabins of people he wanted her to meet. Then they stopped at a particular cabin; he looked at Amanda and smiled.

"This is my mother's cabin," he informed her. "I can't wait for you to meet her. She's really special to me." Amanda could see the devotion on his face and hear it in his voice.

"Matthew"—she hesitated—"I already met her." He looked at her in surprise.

"What?" he asked. Amanda looked down at their hands.

"Well, three days ago when you were called to your meeting with your pastor," she said quietly, looking back up at him, "she was with me for the day. She was the one that told me about the wedding."

His mouth opened to say something, then he closed it.

"She came to spend the day with you?" he asked slowly. Then seeming to regroup, he asked, "Did you like her, Amanda?"

"Yes." She smiled at his expectant look. "Very much. She was very kind to me." *And she gave me the hope I needed to survive this awful place,* her thoughts continued.

"Good." He smiled, and taking her hand, they began walking again. "I'm so glad."

CHAPTER 15

They walked around a bend in the road and came upon a large green pole barn. Amanda just stared at the building. It looked so strange to be set in the deep woods. Matthew stopped.

"This is where we do all of our work, so we make money to survive here. The men work here," he explained. She turned to him, a curious look on her face.

"What do you do in there?" she asked. He smiled.

"We build furniture," he stated simply. "You know, dining room sets, china cabinets and dressers. Then we sell them to large furniture companies." Amanda's mind began to spin as she looked back at the barn.

"You sell them to companies in the 'world'?" she asked, using his words. "Where I'm from?" *That means there are business records, receipts, proof of the village's existence*, she thought.

"Yes," he said, watching her carefully.

"And who does the public relations and the selling?" she asked.

He hesitated. Did he tell her too much?

"Our pastor does. He exchanges our furniture for money and other goods that we can use for our village."

"So, you don't see any of the money?" she asked.

"Why would any of us need money?" he asked. "Where are you going with this, Amanda?" He recognized the look on her face. She turned her back to him.

"Nowhere," she assured him. "I'm just trying to understand how things work here. If you don't have any money of your own, then how do all the different families shop for food and other items they need?"

"Well, that brings us to where we're going next," he said, tugging at her hand. They walked down the small road a little farther and came to another cabin. A large sign was nailed to the door, "Supplies & Rations."

"Every family is rationed out a certain amount of food and supplies. Depending on the size of family, the supplies are distributed accordingly." Amanda nodded.

"But what if you run out of something?" she asked innocently. He smiled at all of her questions, enjoying this exchange with her. This was the Amanda he had observed, and she was behaving so naturally; she probably didn't even realize it. For the first time since he had brought her here, the sad look was absent from her eyes.

"Well," he said, pulling her closer; his hands slid behind, resting on her lower back. She looked up at him, her eyes moving from his lips, and eventually up to his eyes. "We barter. Everyone here shares. This is a very tight community and we all stick together, for the most part. Any more questions?" She smiled.

"No," she said, her eyes falling to his lips again, "I guess not."

He smiled then lowered his lips, kissing her tenderly. Pulling away from her slowly, his eyes were intent on hers. Not speaking, their eyes stayed intimately connected. Without a word, he found her hand, and they began walking again back through the village.

"The school is over there," he said, pointing to the left of the village. "And, of course, the church," he added as they passed the white church. "That's where most of our time will be spent. He preaches at noon every day for the men, except Saturdays, and then it's eight a.m. on Sunday, for everyone." Amanda shivered when they passed, her hand tightening in Matthew's hand. He glanced at her from the corner of his eyes, but she was looking in the opposite direction.

"Now you've seen all of the village," he informed her. "I thought maybe you'd like to see our cabin in the daylight." He looked at her hopefully.

She smiled and nodded.

When they reached the cabin, he walked them right past it to the other side. There Amanda stood, and she stared in awe at the sight before her. The spectacular view he tried to tell her about the night before loomed before her. The green mountains and the valleys below her looked so beautiful mixed with the browns and several shades of oranges and reds. The colors weren't as magnificent as they were in New York, but the rest of the scene made up for the lack. The hills and mountains were as far as the eye could see. When she looked closer, she could see a river, winding in and out around the hills, filled with white specks that were large rocks. From where she stood, it looked like a small stream. The whole scene was magnificent, she thought.

Matthew was watching her expression and was pleased.

Squeezing her hand, he asked softly, "What do you think?" She was shaking her head as she turned to him.

"Matthew, it's beautiful," she stated, breathless. "I can't remember the last time that I've seen a more beautiful view."

"I love it here," he exclaimed.

"I don't know why, but it doesn't seem like we're in New York anymore." she remarked. When Matthew didn't respond, she turned to see him studying the view, but with a more serious expression.

"I can not tell you where we are, Amanda." he finally responded. "Do not ask again." Amanda flushed, looking away. *Another misstep with him,* she thought, a sinking feeling in her stomach. Unsure of what do now, she remained silent.

Thankfully, his tone was light when he reached for her hand, saying, "Let me take you to another place." He brought her into the woods on the other side of their cabin. Amanda was surprised to see a small worn path that twisted and turned amidst the trees. They walked for several minutes, and they came to a small clearing where the land seemed to disappear. Stepping to the left side of the edge of land, they began to descend down the rocky landscape.

"Matthew, where are we going?" she asked, her breathing labored from the most exercise her body was receiving since her fever. He looked over his shoulder.

"Do you need to rest?" he asked, concerned. She smiled and shook her head. "We're almost there," he assured her.

When they reached the bottom, they walked back into the woods. There didn't seem to be path, but Matthew knew where he was going. He pushed past a large hanging branch and stepped back to let Amanda by. She stepped into a small secluded spot. The large pine trees all draped their large branches, hanging low, creating an isolated area. The sun shining through the moving branches, caused by the light wind, created a sparkling effect. She turned and smiled at Matthew.

"This is nice," she said. On closer examination, she saw a small stool next to one of the tree's trunk, and a lantern was set on it. But what amazed her was the hole that was carved out of the trunk to make a secluded chair. "How neat!" she exclaimed excitedly. "Matthew, did you do this?"

"Yes," he admitted. "When I was a boy, this was my secret hideaway. My best friend's the only one who knows about it. I used to come here to think and read, or whatever. I spent a lot of time here after my father died." She turned back to him.

Her mood sobered as she remembered Katherine speaking of her husband and of what happened. Matthew became quiet.

"So," she began, "why are you showing me this private place?" He stepped toward her, touching her cheek softly.

"Because you're important to me," he said. "I don't want to scare you, but I do love you, Amanda. I've loved you from the first moment that I saw you and I knew you were made for me."

"Matthew," she started to say, her body tensing.

"No," he said, "you don't need to say anything. I just wanted to share this with you. Things will seem hard for you as you adjust and when you need to get away and think, you can come here." She searched his face. He was sharing a special part of himself with her, and she was overwhelmed.

"But let me warn you," he continued, his voice somber, "if you tried to escape from here, the electric fence is out this far, but camouflaged much better." Amanda stepped back from him as the warm moment was instantly replaced by the coldness of her imprisonment. She wrapped her arms around herself.

"I'm not going to, Matthew," she said soberly, turning away.

"Amanda," he began softly, "I don't want anything to happen to you. You mean too much to me." Keeping her back to him, he walked over to her, hugging her from behind. "Amanda?"

"It's all right," she said, turning in his arms to hug him, "I won't do anything stupid. I promise." Kissing the top of her head, he held her tightly.

"Thank you," he whispered.

Later that night, Matthew built a fire in the small fireplace. Amanda was snuggled into the corner of the sofa, covered with a blanket. He sat next to her, his arms rested behind his head. They both stared into the fire, deep in their own thoughts.

Amanda watched the flames dance around the logs. Memories of moments just like this at her home filled her mind. On many occasions, her family would be content to read in the den, with the fire blazing, all of them involved with their books. Every so often, her Dad would read a line from his book, and they would laugh or discuss it. So many moments that she took for granted . . . they all did! She blinked back the tears that threatened to fall.

It scared her, all these emotions. She felt so connected to Matthew, yet so torn with the sadness she felt for home, and fear for the unknown future here in this place. When she looked at Matthew, she knew she cared for him. Fear had sent her scrambling for something safe, and that had been Matthew. She cared for him now, that was all that mattered. He was going to keep her safe, and her hope now depended on him to bring her home.

She decided that she wasn't going to feel ashamed of her feelings for him anymore. He *was* her husband; no matter how much she tried to deny her feelings for him, they were still there. She was thrown into this awful situation, having no choice of what had befallen her.

"Amanda," he asked softly, interrupting her thoughts, "tell me about your parents." Tearing her eyes from the flames, she blinked at him in surprise. He turned his head toward her, a serious expression on his face. Her eyes searched his face.

"Why?" she asked slowly, confused by his request.

"I want to know about everything that is special to you," he said. She swallowed and looked back into the flames. She didn't know if she wanted to share her parents with him. "Please, Amanda?" he asked, sensing her reluctance. "Um," she started to say, "well, they're both great people and they're very important to me. I don't know what you want me to say." She fell silent.

"Who do you look like more? Your mother or father?" he asked softly. Amanda smiled unconsciously.

"Oh well, that's been a debate for years," she said. "I think that I look like my mom, but my dad insists that I look like him. It's kind of a joke with us."

"Are you closer to one more than the other?" he asked.

She shook her head. "Not really," she responded thoughtfully. "I'm closer to both, just in different ways. My dad and I are closer because we have a lot of the same interests, but my mom and I are closer when it comes to my feelings and emotions." She tried to explain the best she could. Thinking about her parents in this way made her feel a little confused inside. She thought she would feel sad, but she didn't. It felt really good to speak about them.

They fell silent again. Several moments later, he spoke again.

"This way of life is simple," he said softly, more to himself. Then he turned to her. "What did you think of our village?"

She hesitated as he jumped from one topic to another.

"I don't really know," she said, pausing. Then she continued, "I think that it's efficiently managed."

"I know that it doesn't come close to what you're used to out there," he said, "but I hope that you will learn to like being here."

Amanda stood, wrapped herself in the blanket, and walked over to the window. She looked out into the darkened night. The shadow of the woods surrounded them, and she could see the outlines of some of the cabins. *Learn to like it here*, she thought, *when hell freezes over!*

Walking over, he stood behind her.

"Amanda?" he whispered. She looked over her shoulder at him.

"I can learn to like being with you," she whispered then turned back to the window, "but I'll never learn to like it here."

He placed his hands on her waist, and he turned her to him.

"'That's a beginning," he whispered then slowly leaned down and kissed her tenderly on the lips.

CHAPTER 16

The morning the three-day isolation had ended, Amanda stood in the middle of the cabin that she had spent all her time in since her abduction. In her hands she gripped the black shawl tightly. *This was it.* Becoming close to Matthew had been so natural, and she had wanted every minute she spent with him. But now this is where the work would really begin. She had to become one of them. Katherine had told her. She would have to integrate herself with the "villagers" and learn to be one of them. *How was she going to do this?*

Matthew walked over to her, taking the shawl from her tightened grip and letting it fall to the floor. He took her hands, putting them between his, rubbing gently.

"Amanda?" he asked, smiling, searching her face. She was pale and so serious. Looking up to him, her eyes were wide with fear.

"Matthew," she said, finding it hard to swallow, "I can't do this."

"Amanda, you can," he said softly. "It'll be all right. I'm only going to work. You'll be in my mother's care and I'll be joining you again for dinner." She was shaking her head, not wanting him to leave her.

"Matthew, I don't want you to go," she said, her voice just above a whisper. He let go of her hands and took her face into his own hands. "I *need* you with me." He searched her face, concerned by her despairing tone.

"Amanda," he said, "I don't want to leave you but I have my responsibilities."

What if something happened to him? She would be left alone in this nightmare! What would happen to her then? Would she be married off to another member of the village; become another wife to someone?

Starting to tremble, she began to cry. "Let me come with you." She knew she never in her life felt such anxiety and fear.

Concern for the fear she expressed only increased his frustration. He was ordered back to work today, and if he did not fulfill his obligations, he knew that punishment would follow.

"Amanda, you can't," he spoke in a hushed tone, "you need to calm down, honey, please." Pulling her into his arms, he held her tight against him, hoping to calm her shaking.

"I can't be one of you," she cried into his shoulder. "I can't do this. Not without you!"

There was a quiet knock on the door, and then it opened without waiting for a response. It was Katherine, his mother. Looking over Amanda's head, a helpless expression was on his face. Watching Amanda cling to Matthew filled Katherine with an overwhelming sense of compassion. Walking toward the two of them, she drew on the time when she had been brought here twenty years ago. Remembering brought back the fear and the confusion so that now she could help Amanda get through this.

"Mom," he said quietly, eager for any help he could get.

"Hi, honey," she greeted her son. "I came to take Amanda with me." Amanda clung to Matthew, even tighter. "Amanda?"

Katherine touched her shoulder gently, feeling Amanda's shoulder shake with her sobs. She looked to her son's face and could see his eyes shining with tears.

"Amanda, let go of Matthew, child," she said gently.

"I can't do this," she cried, her voice muffled as she spoke, her face still buried in Matthew's shoulder. "I know what we talked about, but I can't."

"Yes, you can," she assured her. "You can and you will. You truly do not have a choice. Look at me, Amanda."

Amanda reluctantly lifted her tear-streaked face from Matthew and slowly turned to Katherine.

"I will help you through this," she said, her voice softer. "I will *not* let you do this alone." Amanda blinked tearfully, knowing that Katherine was being honest.

"I'm afraid," she admitted through her tears, looking back up at Matthew. "God, I'm so afraid." Matthew wrapped his arms tightly around her.

"Everything will be all right, Amanda," he whispered to her.

"Amanda," she said calmly, instinctively knowing her fear, "nothing is going to happen to Matthew. He *will* return this evening."

Matthew searched his mother's face as Amanda shook her head.

"But what if—," she cried, raising a shaky hand to swipe away her tears.

"Amanda," she said, "he'll come back to you. He's not going to leave you alone in the village." Matthew's eyes filled with understanding as his mother looked up at him and gently pulled Amanda apart from him.

"Amanda, nothing is going to happen to me," he declared. "I would never leave you alone here." She searched his face as he rubbed her arms affectionately. Though his assurances calmed her very little, she tried to stop shaking and was suddenly ashamed at her clinging behavior. She never clung, to anyone. Yet her fear was very real.

"Okay," she said, wiping the tears away with her hands. "I can do this?" she asked, looking from Matthew to Katherine. They both nodded.

"It's all right to be afraid, child," Katherine said softly. "It'll get easier." She held out her hands to Amanda, and Amanda slowly stepped out of Matthew's embrace to take her hands.

"Matthew needs to go to work," she said. "Let him go, knowing that you're fine." Amanda nodded and turned to her new husband. His concerned expression warmed her heart.

"I'm sorry, Matthew," she said, trying to smile, knowing she failed miserably.

He stepped over to her, and taking her face into his hands, he kissed her softly on the lips.

"Amanda," he said, "we're going to be fine."

"Okay," she said. The feelings that she had were so foreign to her that she wasn't quite sure how to handle them. She so badly wanted to cling to him, even now. He kissed her again, quickly, and then left the cabin. Amanda stepped toward the door, wanting to go after him, but Katherine held her back.

"Amanda, let him go," Katherine said softly, knowing how Amanda felt. "Let's just sit for a few minutes until you feel a little more in control." Leading her to the sofa, Amanda sat down.

She rested her face in her hands, her elbows resting on her knees.

"Who am I?" she mumbled into her hands. "I've never acted like this in my life! I don't even know who I am anymore."

Katherine sat down next to her and rested her hand gently on Amanda's back.

"Well, you've never been kidnapped before," she said softly.

"How am I going to do this?" she asked, looking up at Katherine. Katherine looked her directly in her eyes.

"One day at a time," she said firmly. "It's the only way you are going to survive this. Every day that you've made it through, is one day closer to freedom for you and my son."

Amanda closed her eyes and nodded.

"Amanda," Katherine continued, "pretend this is a play, a game, a school assignment. Whatever will work for you. You'll be playing a part, and you will need to guard your heart and your feelings. When you're alone with Matthew, then you can be yourself. The time that you spend with him, you will find the strength to make it through another day."

Amanda absorbed all that she said, knowing she was going to have to do this. Images of her parents flashed in front of her. She was told she would never see them again, but Katherine assured her she would if she became one of them. *A game. Pretend this is a game. Could she? If she played the game, she would go home.*

"Okay," she nodded, "let's do this."

Katherine smiled and stood up.

"Good, let's go!" she exclaimed, reaching her hand out to Amanda. Amanda looked at Katherine's hand, hesitating. Then slipping her hand in hers, she stood up.

This was it. This was her new life.

When they stepped out of the cabin, Katherine stopped and turned to Amanda.

"You will never visit this cabin again," she spoke softly to Amanda. Amanda turned her eyes from Katherine's and looked back at the cabin. Such a mix of emotions swept through her. Joy, for being able to be free from the prison she's known for weeks. Sadness, because it was the only safe place she had experienced here. Reluctance, because Matthew and her had become so close within the four walls of the small cabin—hating him, despising him, fighting him, then learning to depend on him. *She spent her wedding night here,* she thought, *it's so strange.*

Katherine took her hand and squeezed it. Amanda turned back to her.

"Will we live with you?" Amanda asked anxiously. Katherine smiled.

"Yes. For a while, but only a little while," she said. "Matthew will continue work on your cabin today. So it won't be long before you will have your own home. A home you will make special for Matthew and yourself." Amanda was quiet. "Amanda, I don't want to make you feel uncomfortable, but I watched the way Matthew and you were together. You both have become close?" Amanda blushed and looked away.

"Don't be embarrassed, child." Katherine assured her. "I am so pleased that you will not have such a difficult time as I did. As many women have. Matthew is truly a special man and I'm not just saying that because he's my son." She smiled as Amanda looked to her. "The way Matthew looks at you-" She turned away, tears filling her own eyes.

Amanda stopped and squeezed her hand.

"Katherine?" she asked gently. Katherine smiled through her tears.

"I'm all right," she said. "Seeing him with such love in his eyes reminds me of his father. I'm blessed by my child, but so blessed that you have been brought here." She grabbed Amanda's loose hand and held both of her hands in her own. "You were brought here for a reason and Matthew *chose* you for a reason. I want to remind you of the miracle you are in my life."

Amanda's own eyes filled with tears as compassion swelled in her heart.

"Now," Katherine seemed to collect her emotions and let go of Amanda's hands. "Let's introduce you to the women. Your formal introduction to the village will be in two days, on Sunday. But the women, you will meet now."

Amanda took a deep breath as Katherine led them to the Women's Center where Matthew had brought her only two days before.

Katherine opened the door and entered first then turned and smiled encouragingly to Amanda. She hesitated then stepped over the threshold, examining the room as she entered. On one side of the large cabin was a sitting area. There was a brown couch and two brown chairs placed opposite one another. A multicolored braided rug lay in the center with a coffee table placed in its center. The walls were the same raw wood of the cabin, and in the corner there was a fireplace, with warm flames blazing. Amanda turned her eyes to the other side and was amazed to see at least a dozen washing machines, and a dozen dryers on the farthest wall. There were a dozen ironing boards lined up, with irons placed on each board. Adjacent to the ironing boards were long tables where she saw several women had been folding piles of clothing. But now their eyes were settled on her.

"Mabel, Sarah, Mary . . . I want you to meet Rachel." Katherine smiled. Amanda started at the use of her newly appointed name. "Matthew's wife." The three women smiled and walked over to her. The seemingly oldest woman held out her hands to her, and Amanda hesitantly reached her hand out to her. The woman smiled warmly, her smile crinkling her eyes with wrinkles.

"Rachel," she greeted genuinely. "It's so nice to finally meet you. I'm Mabel. You *are* a beautiful girl!" Amanda couldn't help but smile at this woman. "Are you adjusting all right?" Amanda hesitated.

"She's doing just fine." Katherine smiled, answering for her.

"Hello, Rachel," greeted the next woman. She looked to be about thirty with blond hair pulled tightly back in a bun, and light brown eyes. "My name is Margaret. It's nice to meet you. Katherine, here, couldn't say enough about you." She smiled.

Amanda smiled and nodded.

"This here is Mary," Sarah introduced the next woman. She was a beautiful young woman about Amanda's age. She had her dark hair long and flowing down her back, and large dark eyes. Hers were eyes that Amanda noticed were not as warm as the other two women she had just met, but she was pleasant enough. "She's my daughter."

"Hello, Rachel," she said. "How nice to meet you."

"Thank you," Amanda said quietly.

Katherine took Amanda's hand again. "This is where we do our work. Let me take you into the next room, there's more women in there. Excuse us, ladies."

They stepped through a door that was toward the back of the cabin. Amanda was amazed when she stepped into another large room. The cabin was much larger than she had first thought. The room was bright with lights . . . electric lights! The first electric lights she had seen since her arrival here. She knew that they had electricity here, but she hadn't seen electric lights, only lanterns. She looked around the room and saw the room was full of sewing machines. There were women dressed in black at every table. Over to the right there were long tables with chairs, and there were several women sitting there, with needles in their hands, holding white material. It was alive with the sounds of the machines and the women talking amongst themselves.

Katherine clapped her hands and called out,

"Ladies?" The women looked up, a few at a time until there wasn't another machine running. "Ladies, I want to introduce our newest member to our village. This is my daughter-in-law, Rachel."

Many women came forward, smiling and introducing themselves; others just smiled and sat where they were. Amanda was overwhelmed by the genuine kindness that she felt from them all. So many women. Were they all kidnapped?

"Ah, Sarah, come," Amanda heard Katherine speak from behind her; turning, she watched Katherine take a young woman's hands into her own. She had curly brown hair that came to her shoulders, and she was smiling sweetly at Katherine. Katherine turned to Amanda.

"Rachel, I want you to meet Sarah," she said. "I think the two of you will be good friends." Sarah smiled shyly at Amanda; her wide green eyes met her own bright blue eyes, and there was an instant connection.

"It's nice to meet you, Sarah." Amanda smiled and shook her hand in a ladylike fashion.

"And you, Rachel," she said in a sweet, soft voice. "I've been anxiously waiting to meet you."

"You have?" she asked, looking at Katherine in confusion. Katherine nodded and smiled, knowing this relationship would be good for Amanda.

"Yes, you see," Sarah continued, "I'm Jimmy's wife. Jimmy and Matthew are best friends." Amanda stared at this beautiful young girl and knew she had found another true friend. "I hope we'll be friends"—pausing—"I know it's an awkward situation."

"Awkward," Amanda repeated softly, nodding her head. "Yes, that's one way of describing it."

"Rachel, Sarah has been here a little over six months," Katherine spoke softly. "She was the last woman to be abducted, before you."

Amanda searched Sarah's face.

"I thought the two of you would be able to help one another," Katherine whispered, "but as you know, Sarah, do not be caught talking about your old lives. It is severe punishment if you do." She was looking at Amanda as she spoke.

Amanda nodded, trying to understand the best she could.

"Good!" declared Katherine, clasping her hands together. "Sarah, you better return to your work." Sarah nodded and smiled.

"We'll talk soon," she said to Amanda.

"Yes, I'd like that," she said and watched her go back to her sewing machine. The other women had all returned to their places, and the room began to buzz again with work.

Katherine turned to Amanda. "Now that you've met most of the women, let me explain your duties. We all have a part to play in the village. Did Matthew explain any of what we do here?"

"Yes. He said that you make furniture and sell the items to larger companies," she said. Katherine nodded.

"Yes, that's right," she said. "The men make furniture and the women make clothes, quilts and linens. We also sell our products to earn part of our living here. But, as women, we have so many other responsibilities. Not only do we have to take care of our own cabins, things like laundry, cooking and cleaning, but also the village itself is our responsibility. There are four groups of women. Here"—she gestured toward the doorway—"let's go sit out in the other room, so that I can explain more, somewhere quiet."

They walked back into the sitting room. Once they were seated, Katherine continued.

"Now where was I?" she asked.

"Four groups," Amanda said.

"Oh yes." She smiled. "We're all divided into four groups. Each group will rotate on a monthly basis. The group in there is on what we call 'Production Duty.' They produce products to be sold. We have 'Cleaning Duty,' they clean all the community cabins, and the church. The 'Outdoor Duty' consists of gardening in the summer months and collecting kindling for fires for all the households and keeping the village neat. And the last group is 'Processing Duty,' but this duty is only assigned to the elder women of the village."

"What is it?" Amanda asked.

"It's the processing of the orders we receive for products, organizing payments and bookkeeping," she explained. "Only a few select women are chosen for this duty, and they are chosen by Pastor himself. For obvious reasons, of course."

"The men have their own sets of duties. Maintenance, building cabins, furniture making, security and such. There is a church service every day at noon for the men. After the services is lunch, at which time the men go home for lunch and dinner. The duties that we are assigned to, are only performed on every other day. On the opposite days women take care of the chores in our own cabins, and a little time to ourselves."

Stopping, she let Amanda absorb the information.

"It's so much, yet, it's not," she said quietly, sitting back.

"We really live quite a simple life here," she stated. "Simple, yet, controlled." The latter statement was spoken with slight sarcasm. Amanda gave her a small smile.

"You will be in the 'Production Duty' group to start off. Do you have any experience in sewing?"

"A little." She shrugged. "Just from what I learned in school."

"Well, do you remember Mabel?" Katherine asked. "You met her when we first came in?"

"Yes."

"She trains the new women of the village how to *produce*. So, she will teach you sewing and all of the other production work. You will start that today."

Amanda's heart began to race. "Where will you be?" she asked nervously. Katherine smiled and patted her hand.

"I'll be right with you," she assured her. "I'm not going to leave you." Amanda relaxed a little.

"Now let's find Mabel and get you accustomed to a machine." Katherine stood. Amanda stood with her then suddenly stopped. Without notice, the now-familiar tightness filled her chest, and her heartbeat sped up. Her hand went to her chest, and her face went pale.

Turning to her, Katherine noticed the change immediately.

"Rachel," she asked, coming to her side, touching her cheek, "what's wrong? What's happened?"

"I don't know," she whispered. "My chest, it hurts."

"All right, sit down," Katherine ordered. "You're just a little anxious about all of this. Try to take deep breaths and the pain should stop."

Amanda did as she was told, and slowly the pain began to subside. She turned to Katherine, who was watching her with concerned eyes.

"When will I be able to see Matthew?" she asked tearfully. Katherine smiled reassuringly at her, took her hand in her own, and lightly squeezed.

"I know this is scary for you," Katherine spoke softly. "The women didn't seem too bad now, did they?" Amanda shook her head. "Remember what I said. You need to take one day at a time. It will get easier, child."

Amanda lowered her head and began wringing her hands.

"I really wish I could see Matthew," she whispered. Katherine rested her hand lightly on Amanda's shoulder.

"You will," she assured her again. "When the workday ends, you will see him." Amanda nodded, having no choice but to accept what she was telling her. "Are you feeling better?"

Amanda lifted her head. "Yes," she said softly.

Katherine smiled. "Good. Let's get you working."

Hours later, Amanda got up from her seat at the sewing machine and stretched her sore back. They were done for the day, and Katherine stood a few feet away in conversation with Mabel. She had surprisingly caught on very quickly, much to Mabel's joy. Within the first hour on the machine, she was sewing arms on sleeves of men's shirts by herself.

She watched the other women close up their machines. They were smiling and teasing one another, and they seemed so happy. A few women smiled and said good night to her, and she returned the sentiments. She felt like she was outside of herself and was watching all of this unfold in front of her. *This is what she had to look forward to? This was her life now? How can this be?*

"It's strange, isn't it?" a soft voice whispered in her ear. She turned to see Sarah, the young girl she had met earlier, standing next to her. Amanda searched her face.

"What is?" she asked curiously.

"The lives we lead here." She smiled. "I'm sorry, you must forgive me, but I saw how you were studying everyone. I couldn't help but say something."

She looked over Amanda's shoulder. "I don't think that I'll ever get used to this way of living," Sarah said, lowering her voice to a whisper. "How can you take almost twenty years of living one way and be expected to live another and be contented?"

Amanda stared at Sarah. Here was someone who knew what she was going through. Someone who knew her fears, her hurts, her desire to be free. Sarah knew her feelings because she, too, was recently taken.

"I think you were right earlier," Amanda said softly.

"About what?"

"I think we'll be good friends." Amanda smiled.

Sarah smiled back. "Yes," she said. "I hope so."

"Okay, Rachel, we need to go home now." Katherine joined them.

"Yes, I need to go home, too," Sarah said. "May I walk with you?" she addressed Katherine.

"Yes, of course!" Katherine chuckled. "To be sure!"

CHAPTER 17

When they stepped out into the fresh air, Amanda was surprised at how the day had cooled off. Dusk was settling in, and she could see her breath as she exhaled. She breathed deeply the crisp air that was quickly filling with the scent of freshly lit fires from the cabins surrounding them.

Katherine noticed her wrapping her shawl tightly around her arms. "We need to get you a winter coat, Rachel," she said. "We'll do that tomorrow." Amanda just nodded.

They walked across the village and passed the church hall. Several cabins came into view. As they passed the third cabin, a small road twisted to the right.

"Well, this is me," Sarah said to Amanda. "Our cabin is right down here." She pointed in the direction of the road. "In case you ever need anything." She smiled, gave a small wave, and began walking down the road.

Katherine and Amanda continued walking.

"She's nice," Amanda said quietly.

"Yes, she is," Katherine said. "Jimmy and Sarah are a sweet couple."

"She seems so adjusted," Amanda said thoughtfully. They reached Katherine's cabin and went in.

"She is." Katherine continued the conversation as they settled themselves in the kitchen. "But make no mistake that she came to the village the same way you did. As many of us did. She has had time, that is all you need right now. You will see. It will get easier."

"Time," Amanda repeated. "But Katherine, I—"

The door opened, and Matthew stepped into the room. Amanda's face lit up. He was tired and dirty, but a beautiful sight in her eyes. When his eyes met hers, he smiled.

"Amanda," he greeted.

"Matthew," she whispered and quickly met him where he was. She hesitated in front of him, but when he opened his arms, she immediately stepped into his embrace. He kissed the top of her head as she clung to him.

Katherine watched the two of them together.

"How was your day?" he asked Amanda. She remained silent, just wanting to be held by him, and pretended that everything else didn't exist.

Matthew looked at his mother, concern in his eyes.

"How did her first day go, Mom?" he asked.

Katherine turned and put the bowl down that she'd been holding.

"She had a good day," she said, "but she had a hard time being away from you." Matthew nodded, his concern not easing.

"Amanda?" He gently pried her away from him, looking at her face. She was crying. "What is it, honey?"

She just shook her head, wiping hastily at her tears.

"Why don't the two of you go talk in your room," Katherine suggested softly. "I'll finish dinner." He nodded, his eyebrows together. "She needs to be with you. Go talk to her." Taking Amanda's hand, he led her out of the room.

Closing the door, he sat on his bed, pulling her toward him so that she stood between his legs.

"Amanda, what's wrong?" he asked. She avoided his gaze, not sure what was wrong with her, only that she was overwhelmed with emotion when she saw him standing in the doorway. Never in her life had she felt the feelings she was now experiencing. Dependency . . . anxiety . . . fear . . . love? She didn't know. "Why are you crying? Do your wrists pain you? Your hand?" She only shook her head. "Then what?"

"I don't know," she spoke softly. "I'm just happy to see you."

Matthew smiled and pulled her down, kissing her softly on the lips.

"I'm happy to see you," he said. "I thought about you all day. Was it difficult today?" he asked, his tone kind. She shook her head but then admitted,

"A little."

"Tell me about it," he said.

"The women were all very nice," she said. "They all seemed sincere." She paused. "I sewed today." She looked at him, a small smile playing on her lips. "Who would have thought that *I* would be sewing shirts when I was on the historical debating team, not two months ago?" Her eyes darkened, and her face dropped some.

Matthew lifted her chin gently with his fingertips.

"Hey, Amanda," he said, "it will get easier."

"I don't want to hear that anymore," she said softly. "It won't get easier because I *hate* it here! This is my existence now, Matthew? I get to sew clothes, clean and serve? This is the life that you brought me into?" She didn't raise her voice or become emotional; she was just stating how she felt.

Matthew sighed and looked away from her, his chest tightening, knowing he was still hurting her. Both silent, Amanda played with a button on his shirt.

"Amanda." He looked back to her. "I know I've said this before, it's a simple life here but it doesn't mean that we can't be happy. Together." Amanda searched his face. She so desperately wanted to plead with him to take her home, but she knew how he would react. He was not ready for such a request. Katherine had told her that it could take years. *Years . . . oh, how was she going to survive this?*

"I'm so scared when I'm not with you," she admitted softly. "I've never needed anyone. I always did things by myself"—she stepped back from him—"but I hate the feeling I have when you're not there. I feel so vulnerable!"

"Amanda, I know you're scared," he said, standing up in front of her, "but I will protect you. You'll not be harmed as long as you follow the rules and listen to me. I promise. I will keep you out of harm's way. I just need your help."

"I feel like I'm a soldier that was dropped behind the enemy's line and I'm provided with one source of protection and that's you. Then you tell me that I have to face the rest of the enemies, with no protection at all. I *hate* feeling vulnerable! I *hate* feeling helpless!" She began to pace. "How will you protect me if you're not with me?"

Matthew untucked his shirt and began to unbutton it. "I'm never far from you," he said, pulling his dirty shirt off. He walked to the dresser, reached in the drawer for a clean shirt as Amanda stared at his chest. She could almost feel her hands on his smooth skin, but she forced herself to turn away. "You may not see me, but I'm close." He pulled the black t-shirt over his head. "If you follow the rules, and do what's expected of you, then you won't need my protection."

"Do what's expected of me," she repeated quietly. She turned back to him. "I never asked for this. I never asked for you."

Matthew stared at her, a solemn expression on his face.

"Do you wish you never met me?" he asked quietly. She hesitated, wrapping her arms around herself.

"Yes. I mean, no. I don't know," she whispered. He walked over and took her shoulders gently in his hands.

"Amanda, you are the best thing in my life," he said. "I know I hurt you. Our tradition has hurt you, but the minute you were brought into my life, everything changed for me. You say that you're experiencing feelings that you never felt before. Well, so am I. I never felt the things that I feel for you. Is this what you expected out of life? I know it isn't. But here it is. You are alive and well. You're a strong person and you *can* make it through this."

"I am not strong," she whispered; her head was down.

"Amanda, look at me," he said. She slowly looked up; tears welled in her eyes. "Yes, you are. You are my wife and I will protect you with my life if I have to. Do you understand? You mean everything to me."

"How can you say that?" she asked, the tears trickling down her cheeks. "You've known me such a short time!"

"You forget that I watched you for months before you were brought here," he reminded her. "I admired who you were, before I met you. Spending the time with you, has only reinforced my admiration."

Amanda searched his face. He was being sincere, his feelings for her so evident on his face. She felt warmth spread from her head to her toes, resting her hands on his chest. *She wanted to go home but she never expected to care for Matthew.* She leaned in, resting her head on his chest.

"I'm so confused," she whispered. He wrapped her in his arms without words.

After several quiet moments, he spoke. "I'm going to help you through this," he whispered back. Amanda closed her eyes, feeling lost and alone in the madness that surrounded her.

The next day, the women did not have to work. So after breakfast, Katherine informed Amanda that she had a few chores she had to complete in her own cabin and encouraged Amanda to walk around the village on her own. Amanda didn't want to, but Katherine insisted.

Wrapped in a winter coat that Katherine had given her, she stepped out into the cool, frosty air. She shoved her hands in the pockets and looked to the right and to the left not knowing where to go. She decided to walk over toward the Women's Center. As she neared the Center, she came to the road that led to Sarah's cabin. Peering down the road, she couldn't see anything.

Should she visit her? Was it allowed? Deciding to take the chance, she slowly walked down the narrow road.

She walked around a bend of trees, and there sat a small cabin. It was sweetly situated, trees enclosing the cabin like a glove. There was a stone walk leading up to the large porch that extended the length of the front of the cabin. Two high-back rocking chairs sat side by side, a small table in the middle of them. Amanda stopped when she reached the walkway, listening to the silence around her. Deciding that it would be silly not to knock since she had walked all this way, she walked up onto the porch. She knocked lightly and waited. Several moments passed, and there was no answer.

Amanda turned to leave, when she heard humming. It was farther away but then got louder and louder. There was something familiar about the song that was being hummed. *Yes, it was Sarah.* Amanda recognized the voice, *but the song . . .* then a smile spread on her face as it dawned on her. It was a popular song that played on the radio about a year ago. Smiling, she walked down the steps, and around the back of the cabin. When she turned the corner, she saw Sarah loading some wood into her sack.

Amanda cleared her throat, allowing Sarah to know she was here. Startled, Sarah turned, her eyes settling on her. Her wide eyes soon became slits as she smiled her greeting.

"Rachel!" she exclaimed. Resting the sack of wood on the ground, she went to greet her. When she reached her, she took Amanda's hands into her own and squeezed them. Her cheeks were rosy from the weather and the exertion of her work. She looked directly in her eyes and smiled. "I'm so glad you came."

"Are you?" Amanda said, smiling in return. "Am I disturbing your chores?" Sarah rolled her eyes then smiled.

"No. Don't be silly," she declared. "I have the rest of my life to do my chores. Your hands are freezing. Come inside, I'll make you some tea!" She led Amanda by the hand into her home. Amanda noticed the coziness of her kitchen, all from the curtains to the matching dish towels. Sarah watched her observe the room. "Here, let me take your coat. Sit . . . sit."

Amanda handed Sarah her coat. "Please don't fuss over me. I didn't come to be a bother." Sarah just waved her hand at her.

"Stop. I'm so happy to have a guest. Well, one that isn't dull." She giggled and turned to put the kettle on the stove. Amanda smiled.

"I like the way you've decorated," she complimented Sarah, making small talk. Sarah smiled.

"Thank you," she said. "Trust me. I need to occupy myself with something. You will too, you'll see. Then we'll be sharing recipes. It'll be scary!"

Amanda said nothing. That seemed impossible at this particular moment. Sarah fiddled around the kitchen for a few more moments and then sat down across from her.

"Now," she said, her expression sobering. "How are you, *Amanda*?" she asked, using Amanda's real name. She looked from side to side then whispered, "You don't look like a Rachel!" Then she winked. Amanda giggled, and then she too sobered.

"How can I be?" she asked.

"It's hard, I know." Sarah admitted, softly. "I shouldn't even tease you. If I make a mistake and call you by your *sinful* name, I could get in trouble."

"Sarah? Well, that can't be your real name either, can it?" Sarah smiled and shook her head. "No, but I've been called it for six months, two weeks and four days. So, I'm kind of used to it."

"What is your real name?" Amanda asked. Sarah hesitated.

"Well," she began.

"Is it against the rules? You don't have to tell me," Amanda assured her.

"No, forgive me. It's not that. Everything is against the rules." She smiled, exasperated. "It's just been so long since I've used it. It feels strange. My real name is Elizabeth." Sarah sat back in her chair quietly. "Wow, it even sounds strange to me. Do you see what's happened to me?"

Amanda searched her face, seeing a sorrowful expression in Sarah's eyes. Turning away from Amanda, she stood to prepare the tea. A few moments later, she placed a steaming cup in front of Amanda.

"Thank you," she said quietly. "I'm sorry if I upset you."

Sarah quickly looked at Amanda.

"No, don't be silly!" she said, taking her seat again. "You haven't. It's so strange to be sitting across from someone that I can actually talk to about me. The real me."

Amanda leaned across the table, touching her hand gently.

"Can't you talk to Jimmy?" she asked. Sarah slowly shook her head.

"No," she spoke softly. "Jimmy. Well, Jimmy is a wonderful husband. But he is adamant about certain things and he expects certain behaviors. Talking about my past is not something he approves of. His belief is that life for me did not begin until I was taken by him and brought here."

Amanda stared at her.

"That can't be," she said. "That's ridiculous!"

"Rachel," she began, reverting back to her new name, "what isn't ridiculous about this place?"

Amanda just shook her head.

"Matthew's a special man, Rachel. He isn't like any of the other men. I even know that and I haven't been here a year yet. Jimmy and Matthew grew up together and Jimmy jokes that they were friends before they could even talk."

Sarah smiled. "He feels very protective of Matthew. Now don't misunderstand me. Physically, Matthew can handle himself. So much so, that he's part of the work crew that does the most strenuous labor here in the village. But he has a reputation for being nice, compassionate, understanding. A rarity among men . . . here, anyway. You couldn't have been stolen by a better man."

Amanda looked down at her hands encircling her warm cup. *Yes, Matthew was special,* she thought.

"You'll be able to talk about your life, I'm sure, with him," she declared. "But Jimmy and I, well, it's different. As crazy as this life seems, Amanda, I love him." Amanda could see this as she spoke of him, and the glow in her eyes would prove this to anyone. Amanda nodded.

"Sarah. Doesn't that sound strange? I couldn't have been stolen by a better person?" she asked exasperated. "I mean, is it so normal here?"

"Of course it's normal here," Sarah said solemnly. "Every day I lose more of who I was before I came here. You are losing the days even now as we speak. It's a hell that we'll never escape from." Amanda shook her head.

"No." she declared. "I cannot accept that—I won't accept that. I need to believe that I can go home." Tears filled Sarah's eyes.

"I understand what you're feeling because I've felt the same feelings. Day after day, you hope. You hope that someone will find you and expose this crazy place. You hope that you'll find a way to get out and then slowly you realize that you won't be found," Sarah said.

"But, Sarah!" Amanda exclaimed. "You can't lose hope. I know that you've been here a longer time than I, but you just *can't* lose hope, or you might as well consider yourself one of them. And you're not!"

Sarah nodded as the tears fell silently down her cheeks.

Looking up, she said, "There's nothing left to hope for. I have a good life. I have a husband who treats me well, and he loves me. But I *need* to be contented with what God has given me." Amanda shook her head again in disbelief.

"Sarah," she said, tears filling her own eyes now. Sarah smiled shakily through her tears.

"But I can remember my old life through you," she declared. "We can talk together, you and I. You'll do that with me, right? We'll have to make sure no one is around, but it'll be good to remember where I'm from."

"Sarah, God didn't give you this life! They did!" She waved passionately in the direction of the village. "Please don't give up!" Sarah smiled again.

"Don't be concerned for me, Rachel," she said. "I have to be resigned to make the best of the lot that I've been dealt. Please, let's talk about more cheerful things, shall we? Like, what are we going to do with these clothes? I've tried to add material to the waists of the skirts but then the other women thought . . ."

Sarah changed subjects, bringing them into another topic, and Amanda could only hear part of what she was saying. The sadness that she felt was overwhelming. She wanted to weep for the hopelessness that Sarah now carried with her. *Is this what she would be like six months from now? Is this the person she would become? God help her if she did.*

Sometime later, Amanda left, promising to come by the day after tomorrow, and walked back to Katherine's cabin. A note was left on the table that Katherine had left to do laundry and that they would have lunch when she returned. Amanda walked into the room that would be considered the living room and stood in the middle, thinking. She was so confused. *Would she lose more of herself every day?* If she had no reminder of who she was, she would probably sink into the abyss of her situation. *I don't want to disappear here*, she declared to herself. Katherine promised to help her escape and she couldn't forget this.

Amanda lay next to Matthew, listening to his breathing. His arm was wrapped around her waist, and her back was snuggled against his chest. She was restless, and sleep would not come.

Lifting his arm gently, she slid out of the bed. Reaching for her shawl, she wrapped it snugly around her shoulders and quietly slipped out of the room. As she stepped into the small living room, she noticed Katherine had kept a small candle burning. Walking passed it, she entered the kitchen. The cabinet door creaked as she opened it; finding a glass, she went to the faucet, filling her glass with water.

She looked out into the cold night at the other darkened cabins. The moon was bright, and the stars were shining their glory. Its brightness brought memories of the night she was retrieved from the shack and was led to the church. It seemed so long ago, yet it wasn't. *Could it be that it's only been a month since she was taken from her apartment in New York?* So much had happened. Setting the glass down softly on the table, she held her wrists up toward the window, examining the fresh scar tissue. She traced one scar gently with her fingertips. She had never thought about death before. Not before this. *How weak she had been.*

Her failed attempt to escape and then suicide. Her illness and fever that followed, and then her wedding. *Her wedding!* Holding up her left hand, she looked at the gold band shining on her finger, shaking her head. *Was she dreaming? Can all of this be true? Is human nature so changeable, or is it just her own weaknesses that have allowed this to be?*

Matthew was right about one thing. She was alive. As long as she was alive, there was hope that one day she would return home. Listening to Sarah had really frightened Amanda. Though she wasn't willing to accept that at the time of the conversation, it was fear that filled her. She stared out into the dark night, amazed at where she was. This wasn't a movie or some fictional story. This was her life. She was married, and she was now part of a cult or a utopian society. A society that she was being forced to be a part of, or she could be killed. A shiver ran through her.

She reached for her glass, taking another sip of her water.

The door was to the left of her. She could walk out that door and try her damnedest to escape, but she promised Matthew that she wouldn't do anything foolish again. She personally didn't think that her body could handle any more abuse. Katherine was right. The only way she was going to escape was with Matthew, and with a plan.

Matthew. Thinking of him brought warmth to her cheeks. *Is it possible to care for someone who has wronged you in the worst possible way? I guess it is,* she thought, *because I do care for him. He had become her closest friend. I have never been closer with another human being in my life,* she thought.

"Amanda?"

Amanda nearly jumped out of her skin. She turned to see Matthew leaning against the door frame that led into the living room. Her free hand had flew to her heart.

"Matthew!" she exclaimed in a whisper. "You scared me!"

"Are you okay?" he asked, pushing off the frame and walking over to her.

"I just couldn't sleep," she said. "How long have you been standing there?"

Standing before her, he replied, "Long enough."

She tried to search his face in the shadows.

"What were you thinking about?" he asked softly as he reached out and gently brushed a lock of hair from her eyes.

"Everything," she whispered, leaning into his hand. Her gesture meant more to him than any words she could have said at the moment. Awakening and finding her missing, he immediately thought she had tried to escape. He was more shocked than relieved when he found her standing in the kitchen. After finding her, he couldn't help but watch her. She looked so beautiful standing in the moonlight by the window. The silhouette of her beautiful body was outlined by the glow of the moon that cloaked the night.

"You seemed so sad," he said. She hesitated then turned to set her glass on the table.

"Sad?" she said. "Yes, I suppose that I am most of the time." Turning back to him, he pulled her gently into his arms, then she wrapped her arms around him.

"Most of the time?" he whispered, in her ear.

She was silent for a moment, then she spoke.

"I'm not when I'm with you," she admitted softly. "Which doesn't make any sense at all."

"Because I brought you here," he stated solemnly. Tears burned her eyes.

"Yes," she whispered. She tilted her head up so she could see his face. "How can that be?"

He searched her face, seeing the tears shining in her eyes.

"Because I love you," he said softly, "and I never meant to hurt you so much. I think that maybe"—he paused, then—"you know that." She reached up and rubbed the stubble that was beginning to show on his face, remaining silent. "*Do* you know that?" he asked. Her eyes slowly traveled up to meet his, his eyes earnestly seeking hers.

"Yes," she said. "I think," She pulled gently out of his arms, walking over to the sink; turning, she leaned her back against it, facing him. "I think that you only did what you were taught. I think that if you knew how devastating it is"—she struggled to keep her voice even—"to be ripped away from the only life you know. I don't think that you would have taken me."

He walked slowly over to her, taking her small face into his hands.

"I wouldn't have," he declared softly and with such passion. "I never would have hurt you the way that I have! It tears me up to know that I've hurt you so." He stepped back away and pulled a chair out to sit. "But if things would have been different then I never would have held you in my arms or touched your amazingly soft skin or seen how adorable you look when you sleep." Looking back at her, she saw the tears shining in his eyes, which was almost her undoing.

"Matthew," she said, coming to kneel before him. She took his hands in hers, wanting to say something but not knowing what. Searching his face, he looked adoringly at hers. "Matthew, I . . ."

He leaned down and pressed his lips on hers, her arms slowly encircling his neck. He gently pulled her up onto his lap as he continued to kiss her. After several moments, he broke off the kiss and stared into her eyes.

"Matthew?" she whispered.

"I don't know how all of this is going to work, Amanda," he whispered, "but it will, I promise." Amanda hesitated then nodded as she reached out to kiss him.

He picked her up and carried her back to bed. There, he made love to her so tenderly that it brought tears to her eyes once again. Soon after, they both fell asleep.

CHAPTER 18

O ver the next two months, Amanda began to adjust to her new life. She had been introduced to the village as a new member; Matthew and she had moved into their new cabin, and life was beginning to become more familiar to her in the village as the days went on.

A fast learner, the women loved to teach her new things. Sewing, knitting, quilting—Amanda really began to enjoy these things because it kept her mind occupied. Keeping her mind occupied seemed to be her means to sanity in such a strange place.

The church services were the only part of her new life that she could not adjust to. The pastor stood in front of his followers and taught them to obey God and him as one. A service would not go by that he wasn't yelling at them that God's punishment would soon be on them if they did not obey him, their leader. Amanda didn't like him from the first time she ever saw him, but now she was filled with dislike *and* fear. She seemed to be the only one that realized that this man was positively insane. With an insane person, anything could happen.

Her family never really belonged to a particular church. They went to church services faithfully on holidays, but never with any consistency. She didn't have much experience with godly teachings, but she just knew that this was wrong.

Daily interactions with the people of the village proved to her that they were decent and God-fearing individuals. Even the women that had been abducted seemed to have embraced this new way of simple living. Sarah included, maybe not as much as the others, but she was on her way. Amanda envied such choices. She had not been able to do this but she had been here only a short time. Her biggest fear *was* embracing this way of life and losing her desire to go home.

She had never run a household before, so she had to adjust to cooking *and* household chores. When they had moved into their own cabin, it was a little unnerving. Soon she found her niche, and their home began to run smoothly, finding that she actually liked their cabin and was trying to add her own little touches. After her required sewing work, she would work on making curtains, with the help of Sarah, for her own windows. Every day, Matthew would come home and notice something small that she had done. This pleased him immensely, he could never express how much because he knew how hard this was for her; and to see her trying made him love her even more.

The only time she forgot about going home and wanting to be free of this place was when she was with Matthew. He was her light in this darkness; he was her joy in the gloom. He had become her life. There was Katherine, and she had become closer to Sarah, but Matthew gave her the peace in her heart that she yearned for daily.

It was him she was waiting for now. She stood at the edge of the woods, by the path that led to his secret place, holding a basket filled with food that she had prepared for a picnic. It was Saturday, and there was no work done on this day. He did have a meeting with Pastor this morning but promised to meet her by noon. They agreed they would go spend the afternoon alone. She longed to be alone with him, with no distractions. Within the time that she had been here, she realized how well liked he was, and how dependent some people were on him. Several of the older members were especially fond of him, and he had so much compassion for all of them that he helped them whenever they asked.

He was late. Shifting her feet, she was tired of standing in one position. She looked toward the small road that led to the heart of the village and still no sign of Matthew. Squinting up at the sun, the warmth was intoxicating. It was a beautiful day! The air was still cool, but it was invigorating. Sighing, she decided to go ahead, knowing he would join her when he was done. Making her way along the path, she eventually came to the clearing; stepping aside, she continued her descent. When she reached the bottom, instead of finding her way to the trees, she turned and walked toward the river. Finding a rock as close to the water as she could, she sat down, leaned over, and allowed the water to rush over her hand. It was so cold it made her smile. She looked around at the trees, the rushing water blocking out all the other noises.

It was January, yet there wasn't any snow. This wasn't the first time that thought had entered her mind. *Where was she?* She looked back down at the water. What *river was this? Where did it lead to?* Realization swept over her. They couldn't have an electric fence over the river. That means . . . her mind started to spin. She looked down river and saw the water bend to the right and disappear about a quarter of a mile away. Rising to her feet, she leaned over to see how far around the bend was visible. It was rough water, not one to swim in. *If she had some sort of raft or canoe or . . .* She straightened. *What was she thinking? She had no experience with rafts or rivers, and she'd probably kill herself trying.*

Pushing the thought away, she sat back down, cupping the icy water in her hands, splashing some on her face. *It felt so good!* After a few more minutes, she stood again, picking up her basket. As she turned to go, her foot became caught between two rocks, and suddenly she lost her balance. Her basket dropped to the ground; her arms waved in the air as she tried to regain her footing. But in the end, she was lost. The cold water hit her body like a thousand icy needles. She didn't even have time to scream before she was taken under and swept away. The current pulled her under and refused to let her go. She bumped and scraped rock after rock under the water. Panic began to fill her as her chest ached from holding her breath. *She needed air!* Desperately she struggled and finally managed to break the hold of the current that held her so strongly. She crawled to the surface, gasping and crying, trying to grab hold of something to stop the river from taking her away. The trees around her were a big watery blur as the river tried to consume her for itself. She was pulled under several more times, smashing her head and limbs against the slimy rocks below the surface. As she reached the bend, she was finally able to grab a rotted tree limb hanging off the embankment. She struggled to pull herself up, her body weighing twice as much with her soaked black dress.

She pulled herself up, her arms shaking with strain; her skirt tore on the rocks littering the ground. When her body was completely out of the water, she lay the side of her face in the dirt, gasping as much air into her lungs as she could take. Only then did the pain from the river's abuse break through her shock, the exhaustion of her struggle against the current, and her brush with death. She began to cry and shake uncontrollably in the cold air.

Matthew followed the path down to the clearing and stopped, looking down below him. Amanda was probably in the secret place already. His meeting went longer than he had anticipated, but it was more disturbing than anything. His pastor seemed so much angrier lately, and critical. But he didn't want to think about him right now. He wanted to see his wife.

Turning to make his descent down the rocky path, something caught his eye. He turned back and walked to the edge, squinting to see what it was. Not quite sure, but it looked like the picnic basket Amanda had made last week. His heart began to beat quicker, his breathing seemed to stop. He scanned the river below him but saw nothing. Quickly he made his descent, stumbling and slipping on the rocky surface. When he finally made it to the bottom, he ran over to the place where he saw the basket. It was lying on its side, the contents spilled on the rocks. He looked around him, panicking. Cupping his hands around his mouth, he yelled, "Amanda!" He tried to yell above the water's roar. He ran along the edge of the river, stumbling over the rocks, yelling her name. "Amanda!" His eyes scanned the water and the embankment, looking for something. Anything.

He kept walking and yelling her name. Finally, after walking some distance, he saw some fabric. It was on a large rock set in the center of the river. Matthew hopped on several rocks and still had to lean way over to grab it. But he did. He held the wet piece of black material in his hands. It had to be from her dress; tears burned his eyes as he looked frantically around him.

"Oh God, Amanda, please be all right!" he croaked, his throat raw from yelling her name. He made his way back to the embankment and kept walking. "Amanda!" he yelled. As he turned the bend, he stopped dead in his tracks. He heard something! Walking a couple more steps, he stopped. Was that crying? He quickened his steps.

"Amanda!" he yelled. "Amanda, where are you?"

Amanda's sobs began to subside; she was beginning to feel numb with cold. She rolled over, struggling to sit up, yelling out as pain shot through her side, and she began to cry again. Then she heard something. *Was she imagining it? No, there it was again. It was his voice. Matthew!*

"Matthew!" she screamed, with the last of her strength. "Matthew, I'm here!"

He heard her. Running now, he came around the shrubs and trees, finding her. She was lying in the dirt, soaked from head to toe, her dress torn and tears mixed with dirt on her face.

"Oh my god!" he exclaimed, coming quickly to her side. He took her face in his hands and began kissing it all over. "I thought I lost you." She was crying again, this time with joy. He began to scoop her up, and she yelled in pain. "Honey, what's wrong? You're hurt. Where?"

"My side," she cried. "I think I broke something."

"All right," he said, kneeling next to her, trying to think of what to do. "All right, let's just sit here for a second."

He sat down on the ground, resting her head on his lap. She was shaking uncontrollably from being wet and exposed, when he came to the only conclusion.

"Amanda, I'm going to have to move you," he said to her. "You'll freeze to death out here. I know it will hurt, but I have to pick you up." She was so cold. "Do you understand?" She nodded.

He managed to stand up, and then with one quick swoop, he had her in his arms. She bit her lip, moaning at the excruciating pain.

"It hurts," she whispered.

"I know, baby," he spoke softly, "I know just hang on, okay? Please hang on." He tried to hold her tight enough to ease her shaking, yet not to hurt her.

It seemed like an eternity until Matthew walked out of the woods, their cabin finally in view.

"We need to get you out of these wet things," he said. "Then I'll go get the doctor."

Once inside, he set her on their bed. She was shaking so violently he quickened his pace. He unbuttoned her shirt, peeling it away from her shivering body. He clenched his jaw at the bruises and scrapes that covered her. Laying her back carefully, she cried out in pain. Tears filled her eyes even as she tried to be strong. He removed the skirt and wrapped her up tightly in the thick blankets that covered the bed. He went down on his knees, next to the bed, touching her cheek gently.

"Amanda," he said softly. "You're going to be okay. I'm going to get the doctor, all right? I won't be gone long, I promise." Her eyes were tightly squeezed, but she opened them slowly, turning to him.

Seeing the concern in his eyes, she whispered, "I'm okay"—then wincing in pain—"really."

He stood, leaned down, and kissed her forehead. Then he left.

Hours later, the doctor stepped out of their bedroom.

Matthew stopped his pacing; Katherine stood up.

"Well?" "Is she all right?" they asked in unison. The doctor held up his hand.

"She's all right. I gave her a tonic that will help her sleep," he explained. "She seems to be my only patient lately, other than Old James." He tried to lighten the mood, but Matthew and Katherine didn't crack a smile. "All right, you two. Rachel will be fine. She broke a couple of ribs, some serious bruises and scratches. Possibly a slight concussion, but she will recover completely. I wrapped her ribs tightly. She needs to keep them wrapped for at least six weeks. I've left a bottle of the tonic I gave her on the dresser. Matthew, son, breathe," he teased. "Why don't you go and see her. She'll be a little drowsy, but she shouldn't be asleep yet."

Matthew nodded, grateful to be by her side; leaving the doctor to talk to his mother, he slipped quietly into their bedroom. The candle was burning on the dresser, and as he walked toward the bed, he couldn't help notice how small she looked. She was wrapped snug in several blankets, her cheeks finally rosy with color.

She turned and watched him walk hesitantly to the bed. Smiling, she reached her hand out to him.

"Hi," she whispered. Smiling, he sat in the chair that the doctor had been using.

He took her hand in both of his. "Hi, yourself," he said softly. He searched her face and felt comforted at what he saw. "How are you feeling?"

Licking her lips, she said, "A little sore."

"Amanda, what happened?" he asked. She closed her eyes for a few seconds then opened them up again.

"I don't know," she whispered. "I was waiting for you . . . by the river . . . and . . . when I stood . . . I lost my balance . . . and I fell." He bent his head down and kissed her hand. When he looked up again he wore a serious expression.

"I found the basket," he said. "I thought"—refusing to finish, he clenched his jaw—"I'm sorry I was late."

"Matthew?" she whispered. When his eyes touched hers, she continued, "It wasn't your fault."

He nodded. "I know. But if I hadn't been late then you wouldn't have—"

"It was my own clumsiness," she interrupted.

He just held her hand quietly, rubbing it softly.

"We didn't get to have our picnic," she whispered, trying to smile.

"There will be other picnics."

She nodded, sadness reflecting in her eyes. He stared at her. *How much things have changed*, he thought. She, at one time, hated him, and now . . .

"You better stop or someone's going to think that you really care for me or something," he teased. Smiling, she closed her eyes as sleep called for her.

"Amanda," he said before she slept, "I love you."

She smiled again. "I know," she whispered then fell asleep.

Katherine opened the door quietly and looked in. She had talked to the doctor some more and then walked him out. Now her heart went out to both of them. Matthew sitting in the chair, his body leaning on the bed, asleep, and Amanda sleeping, her hand entwined in his.

She walked silently over to the bed, watching Amanda. How much could this girl take? She seemed to be really trying to accustom herself to the village. Did she jump in the river or fall? Was she possibly trying to escape, like the doctor had suggested? She didn't believe so. She and Matthew had grown much closer; it was obvious to anyone who spent any time around the two of them.

She rested her hand on her son's shoulder. He stirred then woke. He turned to his mother, then looked at Amanda, who still slept peacefully. Katherine motioned for him to leave the room with her, and he followed. Once they were seated in the living room, she told him the doctor's opinion.

"That's ridiculous!" Matthew proclaimed, his voice getting loud. "She wouldn't throw herself in the river to escape!"

Katherine remained seated, her hands folded on her lap.

"I know that, Matthew," she said quietly. "That's what I told the doctor. But if this *opinion* gets back to Pastor, you know that he won't be happy." Matthew stood and began pacing.

"He couldn't possibly believe such an opinion." he said.

"The doctor seemed to think," Katherine continued, "that this was what she was doing. He said something about her being on a 'course for destruction.'"

"Course for destruction?" asked Matthew. "What the hell is that?" Katherine's eyes flew to her son's face.

"Matthew, you will calm down," she said firmly. His face dropped.

"I'm sorry." He seethed, fighting back his frustration. "I'm just so . . . angry."

"I understand," she said, "but you need to be careful."

"He thinks that she's attempting to hurt herself. Some kind of way for her to deal with her abduction."

"That's absurd!" he declared passionately. "The doctor can't tell Pastor that." Katherine stood and came to her son's side.

"I spoke with him and asked him to seriously consider what this kind of report to Pastor would do to you and Amanda," she explained. "He understood my meaning, and promised to prayerfully consider what he was going to say."

"Prayerfully consider?" Matthew snorted in disgust.

"Matthew!" Katherine exclaimed in surprise. Never did she see him act disrespectful when it came to the ways of the village. What hope this gave her!

"I'm sorry, Mom," he again apologized, "but this is Amanda we're talking about. I won't let anything happen to her and I don't care what the doctor's opinion is!" Grabbing his coat, he stormed out of the cabin.

Katherine watched her son walk toward the small road. He ran his hand through his hair and then shoved his hands in his coat pockets. She put her hands up to her face; tears filled her eyes as a smile played on her lips. He was beginning to see things as they truly were, she thought. Matthew and Amanda would leave the village. She was sure of it now! It was time to begin preparation; she nodded to herself then turned to go check on Amanda.

The water pounded her down, suffocating her. She screamed, but the water filled her mouth, muffling her, and she began to choke and gasp.

"Amanda! Amanda, wake up!" Amanda was pulled from the watery nightmare, opening her eyes to see Matthew leaning over her.

"Amanda?" he whispered softly. Her eyes began to focus, and she looked up at him. "You were dreaming."

Nodding, she swallowed. "It was horrible," she whispered. "I was drowning."

He gently wiped the tears off her face. "You're all right. You're safe in bed," he said softly. She felt his warm body next to hers.

"What time is it?" she asked.

He smiled. "It's early, about three or four. How do you feel?" he asked. She searched his face in the shadows.

"All right," she said, knowing the pain was there beneath the throbbing in her side. "How are you?"

"I'm good," he said, reaching out and touching her cheek. "I'm worried about you."

"I'm so sorry," Amanda said.

Matthew tried to search her face in the darkness. "Sorry for what?" he asked softly.

"For everything," she said. "It was so stupid being so close to the river—"

"Stop, Amanda," he said. "There's nothing for you to be sorry about. It was an accident and I just want you to be well."

They were both silent for a few moments.

"Hey, I have an idea, if you're up to it," he said, trying to cheer her up.

"I am," she said, not caring what it was.

"Tomorrow, well, actually today, let's have that picnic we were supposed to have yesterday."

She smiled in the shadows.

He loved her smile. "We can have it right here in the cabin. I'll move the furniture and we'll put a blanket down on the floor."

"Yes," she whispered, looking up to him. He was propped up on one elbow, leaning over her. "That would be nice."

Lying back down, he gently rested his arm below her ribs. His head rested next to hers.

"Matthew, what about your duties?" she asked quietly. He was silent for a moment. "Matthew?"

"I've been released from work for tomorrow," he said, in a quiet tone. Something in his tone sent questions running through her mind.

"Is everything all right?" she asked, suddenly feeling anxious.

"Yes," he whispered and kissed her ear gently. "Don't worry. Get some rest, Amanda."

She lay quietly in his arms as she stared up at the ceiling. He wasn't telling her something, but eventually her fight against sleep was lost to her exhaustion.

CHAPTER 19

The following morning, Amanda awoke feeling very warm and cozy. The chill that had consumed her from the ice water had dissipated. Slowly opening her eyes, she blinked to adjust to the bright sunlight streaming through the windows. The dull pain in her chest was an instant reminder that she had fallen in the river yesterday. Pulling herself up, grimacing in pain, she refused to lie in bed and be helpless. Somehow she managed to stand up, slowly walk over to her closet, and pull out a clean dress with undergarments. With very slow movements, she slid out of her night gown and carefully dressed. She was just finishing the last button on her shirt when the door opened quietly.

Matthew peered around the corner.

"Amanda!" he gasped, searching her pale face. "What are you doing? You're supposed to be in bed."

"I can't, Matthew," she said quietly. "I can't stay in bed."

"Amanda, you're so pale." He walked to her side. Her long blond hair was tousled from sleep.

"I know," she said. "Please, Matthew, let me stay up."

Chuckling softly, he shook his head. "Like I could stop you once you've made up your mind." He smiled. "Can I help you with your hair?" Relieved, she smiled and nodded. He brushed her hair until it was so smooth it shined. "You're so beautiful."

He leaned down and kissed her cheek softly. Amanda blushed, bringing color to her cheeks. "You have company."

"I do?" she said, turning to him, her eyes alight.

"Yes. My mother is here and, of course, Sarah," he informed her. "Once they are gone, we'll have our picnic."

Surprise splashed across her face. "Oh, Matthew!" she exclaimed, smiling. "I forgot!"

He gently pulled her to him. "Yes, well, I didn't." He smiled; leaning down, he kissed her gently on the nose. Sobering, he said, "I almost lost you yesterday. It scared me."

She stared at him. "It scared me," she whispered. "I don't think that I'm going to go swimming ever again." She tried to lighten the mood. He wasn't amused.

"See that you don't," he said softly; taking her hand, he led her out of the room.

Within several moments, Katherine had her situated on a chair and covered with a blanket. Sarah sat on her right and Katherine on her left as Matthew watched their doting attention with a smile. He handed Amanda a cup of fresh coffee.

"Are you all right?" he asked, meeting her eyes. She smiled her gratitude for the coffee and nodded.

"I'm all right," she confirmed. Turning to her two friends, she added, "I'm really all right, ladies. Please don't fuss over me."

Matthew chuckled as they assured Amanda that she needed them to fuss over her. He couldn't disagree. Amanda's experience yesterday was too frightening for all of them, and she was still so pale.

"Well, ladies," Matthew intervened, "I'm going to step out for a minute and I'll return shortly." She looked up at him anxiously, and Katherine placed her hand on Amanda's. She turned to Katherine, who nodded to let him go, then turned back to Matthew.

"You won't be long?" she asked softly.

"No," he said, softly; leaning down, he kissed her lightly on the lips.

Amanda watched him leave, and an uneasiness filled her. She just knew something was going on that she wasn't aware of; pushing her anxiety back, she turned her attention to her friends.

"Rachel . . . ," Sarah exclaimed, "you must have been terrified!"

Amanda nodded. "More than you know."

"Of course she was terrified, Sarah!" Katherine said, exasperated. "She was pulled downriver!"

"Now tell us what happened, child," Katherine said quietly. "Matthew said the two of you were going to have a picnic. Now what were you thinking about? It's the middle of the winter!"

Amanda smiled.

"The weather has been mild," she explained patiently. "We wanted to spend the day outdoors. I wore extra layers so that I'd be warm and that's what made it more difficult to pull myself out of the water."

"How did you manage to get out?" Sarah asked.

"I almost didn't," she explained. "Just when I was able to get some air, the current pulled me back down again . . . I thought . . ." She stopped and looked down at her hands. "I truly thought that it was the end for me." Katherine squeezed her hand.

"Oh no." Katherine smiled. "You have much more to experience in this life." She looked into Katherine's eyes.

"But that's just it," Amanda said seriously. "I can't believe that two months ago I thought the only thing to do was to kill myself, and I knew I'd been wrong to do that. But yesterday could not have confirmed it more to me—I love my life. I'm not ready to die any time soon!" Katherine nodded, understanding.

"Listen," Sarah said somberly. "I went to the church this morning for work, before I found out what had happened to you, and the other women were talking." She stopped, not sure she should continue. Katherine and Amanda watched her, waiting. "They were saying that, it was believed that you tried . . . to escape." Katherine didn't react; Amanda just stared at her.

"I don't believe that, of course!" Sarah exclaimed. "I know you wouldn't have jumped into the river on purpose."

Amanda turned to Katherine.

"You know about this already, don't you?" she asked. Sighing, Katherine nodded.

"Not much gets past me here," Katherine said soberly. "It's the talk and news spreads rather quickly here."

"Matthew knows about what's being said, doesn't he?" Amanda asked. Katherine again nodded.

"Jimmy was outraged when I told him what I heard," Sarah declared. "He said it was ludicrous to think that you would try and escape."

"There are many villagers that have come to adore you, Amanda," Katherine informed her. "I don't believe that they will believe that you tried to escape." Amanda just shook her head sadly.

"But they're all women," she said quietly. "Women have no say in anything here." Katherine and Sarah remained silent for they knew Amanda spoke truthfully. "What about the pastor?" Amanda still refused to call him "her" pastor.

Katherine shook her head.

"I don't know what he knows or believes," she said. Sarah shook her head as well.

"I don't know either . . ."

"Where did Matthew go?" She directed her question at Katherine. Katherine remained silent. "Come, Katherine, tell me."

"A meeting was called at the church," she admitted quietly. Amanda bit her lip, color draining from her face.

"If . . . if it's determined that I tried to escape . . . I could . . . die," she said, just above a whisper. Both of the women exclaimed "No!" in unison.

"That won't happen, Amanda," assured Katherine. "Matthew will not let it happen!"

"Will Matthew be punished?" she asked nervously. "Please tell me that he won't be punished because of my clumsiness!"

Katherine hesitated. "I don't believe that it will come to that."

"I knew Matthew wasn't telling me something . . . ," Amanda whispered. "Oh God, this is awful!" She tried to stand up.

"Whoa!" Katherine stated firmly, pushing her gently back down. "You will not get up!"

"Katherine, please!" she cried. "I can't just sit here!"

"You can, and you will!" she ordered. "You can't do anything but wait. You can't go to the church, you'll be refused entry. You know that. Your ribs are broken, for glory's sake, Amanda."

Frustrated, she settled back in the chair.

What have I done? she thought to herself. The tears filled her eyes, knowing she couldn't handle it if they did something to Matthew.

"Sarah, let's give Rachel a rest, shall we? Why don't you go home for now, and you can visit again later when things calm down."

Sarah agreed and said her good-byes quickly. Once she left, Katherine seated herself next to Amanda.

"Rachel, look at me." Katherine's tone had an urgency attached to it. When Amanda's eyes met her own, she said, "Matthew is really close." Amanda didn't have to ask any questions. "He was furious last night, when he found out what the doctor believed. He left here determined to change some opinions. His attitude toward the village is changing. I'm so hopeful!"

Amanda searched her face. *Could her freedom be so close?*

"Katherine," she said, her eyes shining, "truly?"

Katherine nodded, smiling. "He's already viewing circumstances differently. I have already begun preparations."

Amanda looked at her hopefully. "Katherine, what-"

Katherine held up her hand. "No. I won't discuss them. The less you know the better."

"What if today goes bad?" she asked, suddenly concerned again. Katherine shook her head again.

"Everything will be fine," she explained. "I have faith that everything will work out."

Amanda nodded slowly, not convinced. After spending the next hour and a half on pins and needles, the pain in her chest had grown stronger and stronger as the minutes passed. She refused to take an herbal tonic because she wanted to stay awake for when Matthew returned.

Katherine had moved to the kitchen to prepare lunch as Amanda had become increasingly restless. Finally she couldn't take it anymore, so she threw the blanket off her and struggled to stand up. She bit her lip so hard, trying to hold back the pain; she tasted blood, but she stood. Pushing her hair out of her face, she walked toward the door. As she opened it, Katherine came into the room.

"Rachel!" she exclaimed. "Where do you think you're going?" Amanda held up her hand to Katherine.

"Don't," she declared firmly. "I need some air. I'm just going to walk around the outside of the cabin." Shaking her head, Katherine relented; leaning over, she took Amanda's shawl from the hook by the door.

"At least put this on," she said, not happy.

Amanda took the shawl and stepped out into the cool air. It felt good. She slowly walked over to the edge of the slope and stared down into the valley. Thoughts took her far away, so she didn't hear Matthew walk up behind her. So when he gently wrapped his arms around her hips, she jumped, jarring her ribs, causing her to cry out in pain.

"Amanda, I'm sorry!" he said. She stilled, waiting for the pain to subside, and when it did, she turned and struggled to give him a small smile.

"You . . . scared me," she gasped.

He wore a pained expression. "I hurt you," he said.

She rested the palm of her hand on his chest. "No, I'm all right," she said. "You just surprised me, that's all." Looking up at him, she searched his face. "What happened?"

He gently pulled her to him and stared down into her wide blue eyes. "So you heard," he said, and she nodded.

"Well, there's nothing to worry about," he said quietly. "This time, anyway." Tensing in his arms, she continued to watch him.

"What do you mean, this time?"

"We're being watched, Amanda," he disclosed. "We're being watched more closely than I had anticipated. We need to be careful not to have any more accidents." He saw the fear shining in her eyes as she stared at him silently and he, more than anything, wanted to erase it.

He smiled. "I think," he said, turning and leading her toward the cabin, "that it's time for our picnic."

"Matthew," she said, stopping and looking up at him. "Do you think that I was trying to escape?" she asked reluctantly. He shook his head, without hesitation.

"No," he said. "I don't." Relief washed over her, but not for long. "But sometimes it doesn't matter what I believe."

They continued to walk. *What kind of way of living was this*, she thought. *Now she would have to live every day in fear?* When they reached the door, he turned to her.

"Amanda, it's over. This situation. I want you to rest and feel better, all right?" he said softly. He bent down, kissing her softly on the lips. "Hey." He lifted her chin gently as she looked at him sadly. "You're very special to me and I would never let anything happen to you. Do you trust me?"

"Yes," she answered softly. He smiled.

"Let's go kick my mother out and have our picnic," he teased. She gave him a small smile and nodded her head.

Soon they were on their blanket, having their indoor picnic. Matthew had arranged the food, with Katherine's help. Katherine had smiled sweetly as she said her good-byes. At first, Amanda had a difficult time relaxing; thoughts of the days' happenings dwelled on her mind. But after some lighthearted banter and Matthew's teasing, she relaxed and began to enjoy this special treat. As he sat and she lay on his lap, Matthew talked to her softly in her ear, and they spoke warmly to one another. Watching him as he talked and laughed, she realized that she was truly happy when she was with him. It felt so good to feel happiness when she never thought she would feel the emotion again. The pain that she was suffering from paled in comparison to the joy she was experiencing. They talked for hours, and Amanda was quite content. He watched her too as she talked and giggled, loving her so much yet waiting for so long to see her happy. *This* was the girl he had watched and knew he would marry.

The day passed, absent of fear and with no interruptions. When the night came, they lay in bed together. Amanda closed her eyes; the pain was strong but she felt loved.

Hours later, when Matthew knew that she was asleep, he slipped quietly from bed. Pulling on jeans and a sweater, he carried his shoes through the cabin so as not to wake Amanda. Once on the porch, he pulled them on and walked out into the dark night. It only took minutes for him to reach his friend's house, and he knocked lightly on the door.

Several moments passed before Jimmy greeted him. His hair was tousled, and he was rubbing his eyes. "Hey, man," he yawned.

"Hey . . . can you talk?" Matthew asked, his tone quiet. Jimmy searched his friend's face in the shadows.

"Yeah, sure," he agreed, "Do you want to come in?" Matthew shook his head.

"No, I'd rather walk," he said. Jimmy nodded in agreement.

"Give me a minute to throw some clothes on, I'll be right out." Matthew walked down the steps and stood in the walkway, his hands shoved in his pockets. Not long after, Jimmy came out. "Ready?" Matthew nodded, and they walked toward the trees. They walked a good distance, Jimmy giving his friend sidelong glances, before Matthew spoke. Then finally he did.

"I'm confused," he admitted, stopping on the darkened pathway. "Jimmy, I went to that meeting today with such . . . anger, that I . . ." Frustrated, he ran his hand through his hair, walking a couple of steps away from his friend. "I mean, I was sitting across from men that I've respected my whole life, and yet, what I felt . . ." Unable to say it, he fell silent. Jimmy watched his friend, again wishing Matthew didn't feel things so much, thinking that sometimes it paid to be callous. Matthew looked up. "Pastor sat across from me, with a look in his eyes that I can't ever remember seeing. It was so strange . . . so hostile."

"Matthew, Rachel has been a thorn in his side since she arrived," Jimmy stated quietly. "I can't remember the last time a new bride has caused such commotion." Holding up his hand at Matthew's angry expression, he continued, "Now I'm just speaking the facts, and you know it. I like Rachel, Matt, I do, but you know it's true." Taking a step closer to his lifelong friend, he went on, "None of us had any idea that she was so strong-willed and that she would be such a challenge. We both know that Pastor likes order and likes everything around him to fall into place, without problems." Matthew nodded, crossing his arms in front of him.

"You think he's angry because of the disruptions?" Matthew asked, not believing this himself. Jimmy shrugged.

"I don't know," he said. "Maybe." Matthew shook his head.

"I don't," he said. "I think there's more to it." He started walking again, Jimmy falling into step with him. "Rachel hasn't been a problem since right before our wedding. She's adjusted fairly well, considering everything she did to herself." He looked over at his friend. "You've seen her, you've been around her. Don't you agree?" Jimmy nodded.

"I do," he said. "I think that she's doing well. Sarah has grown close with her, too. But"—pausing, then—"it doesn't matter what we think, you already know that." Matthew nodded in agreement.

"I know," he said quietly. They reached a clearing that opened to a small pond, deep within the woods. They both took a seat on the embankment, their usual place for private conversations. "Jimmy?"

"Hmm?" Jimmy replied as he threw a rock into the water. It made a small splash, the moonlight shining on the rippling water.

"Have you ever wondered what life is like outside of the village?" Matthew asked cautiously. Jimmy went still, staring at the water for several moments. Then he slowly turned to Matthew. His eyes were questioning.

"We've seen what life is like," Jimmy stated quietly, searching his friend's face. Matthew turned toward the water.

"I know we've seen it," he said, "but have you ever wondered what it would be like to live out there?" Jimmy watched Matthew, concern making an icy path up his spine.

"No, never," Jimmy declared, his eyes not leaving Matthew. Matthew lifted his eyes to the stars, a somber expression on his face. "Have you?"

Sighing, Matthew slowly brought his gaze down to the water, still not looking at his friend. "No"—pausing—"until now."

"That's a dangerous way of thinking," Jimmy said softly, a hint of steel behind his tone. Matthew turned to him, searched his face, then slowly nodded.

"I know," he responded, accepting his friend's reaction. It was dangerous, yet Matthew didn't like what he'd been seeing lately. It concerned him, and he didn't just have himself to think about anymore. He had Amanda. "I know the dangers"—then he picked up his own rock, throwing it into the water—"but the way we do things here, just doesn't seem right anymore." Fearful of losing his friend, Jimmy spoke up.

"It's not your place to judge what's right or wrong, Matthew," Jimmy declared hotly. "You're not an elder or a leader!" Rising to his feet, he looked down at Matthew. "I suggest that you stop thinking so much and control your wife!" With this, Matthew got to his feet, knowing now where his friend stood. Anger surged through him at his comment, but Matthew held his tongue. "For glory's sake, Matt, this is our home! You're playing with fire and I don't like it one bit!"

Matthew forced himself to relax and to appear casual. Shrugging his shoulders, he gave his friend a small smile. "Jimmy, relax. I'm just a little frustrated and I needed to vent. I'm not stupid!" Jimmy searched Matthew's face, doubtful, then slowly nodded, letting out a breath of relief.

"Don't scare me like that, man." Jimmy tried to smile but couldn't. "Talk like this . . . could get us both killed." Matthew nodded soberly, then stepped over to his friend and slapped his shoulder.

"Sorry, Jimmy," he stated. "I'll be more careful. I'm ready to go back, morning will be here soon." Agreeing, they both walked home in silence, both deep in their own thoughts.

When Jimmy crawled back into bed, Sarah had turned over and snuggled up against his cool body. Sensing he was upset, she blinked open her eyes, to see him staring up at the ceiling. "What is it, Jimmy?" He looked down at his wife, searching her eyes silently. Concerned, she propped herself on her elbow. "Jimmy? Are you unwell?" Closing his eyes, he pulled her close, holding her tightly.

"No, I'm well," he sighed then was quiet for a few moments, burying his face in her sweet fragrance, needing her love at this moment. Then he whispered, "I think I'm losing my best friend." Sarah stilled in his arms, lifting her head to look at him, her eyes wide and questioning. Their eyes held, with no words being spoken. Then suddenly he pulled her head down to his, capturing her lips in his own, kissing her in desperation. He needed to bury the hurt that was pounding at his heart.

CHAPTER 20

Amanda finished washing the morning dishes, looking out the window in front of her. The mountains and valleys below were so beautiful. The land was turning green and plush. The birds sang, and spring smells filled the air. Once again she thought of home as she picked up the hand towel and dried her hands.

It has been six months since her abduction, she thought sadly. No one had found her, pushing the painful thoughts back, the hurt never lessening. She walked into the bathroom and glanced in the mirror. The front of her long blond hair was pulled up, leaving the rest to flow down her back. She hadn't been feeling well lately. She ran the tips of her fingers over the dark circles under her eyes, thinking she may have the flu. Dizziness, nausea, and vomiting had plagued her for the last few days. Matthew had mentioned she looked tired lately, but for the most part, she was able to hide her symptoms from him. Fear being her motivation, since her ribs had healed, she had tried extra hard not to even have a hangnail. She knew that if Matthew knew she was unwell, he would make her see the doctor, who would then report to the pastor. Telling Matthew just wasn't an option.

Leaving the bathroom, she walked into their bedroom. She made the bed and began to gather the laundry that needed to be done for the day. Taking one of Matthew's shirts from the closet, she tossed it into the pile she had created on the bed. Suddenly stopping, she walked over and picked the shirt up. She smiled and slowly brought the shirt to her nose, closing her eyes;

she breathed in deeply his masculine scent, not believing how much she had grown to care for him.

"Rachel?" a woman's voice called out to her, interrupting her thoughts. "Rachel?"

Amanda walked out, holding Matthew's shirt in her hands.

"Hi, Sarah," Amanda greeted with a small smile. "I'm just gathering our clothes. I'll be right there."

She quickly threw the rest of the clothes into a canvas bag then threw the bag over her shoulder. She pinched her pale cheeks, trying to add some color to her complexion, not wanting any extra attention.

She rejoined Sarah, and they left for the Women's Center. Once outside, they fell into a companionable silence. Amanda closed her shawl tightly around her. The temperature was not cold, but she was cold in her bones. Whatever sickness she suffered from, she hoped she wasn't contagious.

Sarah glanced at Amanda out of the corner of her eyes.

"Rachel, are you okay?" she asked quietly, her tone natural.

Amanda looked at her quickly, then away again. *Damn.*

"Sure," she lied. "Why do you ask?" Sarah shrugged her shoulders.

"You don't look too well," she said, concern in her voice. Amanda was quiet.

"I'm just tired, I guess," she admitted softly. Sarah watched Amanda carefully, and she looked back at Sarah directly. "Truly." Sarah reluctantly nodded, and they continued on.

"I know what you're doing," Sarah said quietly, after a few moments had passed. Surprised, Amanda looked at her.

"What do you mean?" she asked her friend.

Sarah stopped and turned to her. They were halfway down the small road leading to the village. The trees rustled as a light wind blew, birds singing their melodies around them.

"You're not well," Sarah began, "and you're afraid to tell anyone."

Heat rising to her face, Amanda stopped and refused to look at her.

"No," Amanda lied. "That's not true."

"Amanda!" Sarah exclaimed. Amanda looked up at her, eyes wide. Sarah never called her by her real name outside of their cabins. "You're lying to me."

Frustration filled Amanda. "Fine!" she admitted. "I *have* been feeling low the past couple of days. Why do I want to make a big deal about that? Everyone feels under the weather sometimes." Sarah set her bag down on the ground, leaning in, and lifted her friend's chin.

"Let me see you," she demanded. Amanda looked up, and Sarah searched her face. "You're so pale. If it's not such a big deal, then you must have told Matthew, right?" Amanda closed her eyes and hesitated.

"Not exactly," she said quietly.

"Mmmm," Sarah said.

"Sarah," Amanda began, her voice breaking, "please don't tell anyone. Please. I don't want anyone to know."

Sarah searched Amanda's face, seeing how desperate she was to hide her sickness. "Amanda, no one is going to punish you for being ill," she said rationally.

Amanda shook her head. "That's right, because no one is going to know," she declared.

Sarah was quiet.

"Sarah, promise me that you'll keep it a secret?"

"I promise," she reluctantly agreed, "but I don't think that you're going to be able to hide it much longer. Matthew's going to notice, sooner or later."

Amanda nodded. "I'm hoping for later."

"If you're really ill, you need to see the doctor, Amanda. For everyone's sake," Sarah stated and picked up her bag.

"If I can work with broken ribs, then I can work feeling like this," Amanda declared.

"I don't think—"

"No, Sarah . . . please, I don't want to talk about it anymore." They continued on in silence.

Entering the Center, they greeted the other women. Amanda was thankful that her assigned laundry day was not with a large number of women. Amanda and Sarah started their laundry and then took their seats next to the window. Sarah was drawn into a conversation with another woman, Mary, about the Sunday dinner menu, so Amanda sat by the window, picking up her needlepoint.

It wasn't long before the room was filled with the scent of detergent, and Amanda fought the nauseous feeling this was creating. Vaguely hearing Sarah and Mary talking, bile began rising, and she struggled desperately not to get sick. *Laundry detergent? It never made her sick!* Moving so quickly she startled the other women, Amanda ran for the bathroom and, there, became violently ill. As she hung her head over the basin, tears streamed down her face; she was feeling miserable. Sarah knocked on the door quietly.

"Rachel? Are you okay?" she called. "Let me in."

"Leave me alone," she moaned. "Just leave me alone."

As she sat on the floor, she felt her stomach calming. Standing up, she splashed some water on her face and rinsed her mouth, pushing her hair back with her damp hands. There wasn't a mirror, but she knew she must look awful.

Slowly opening the door, she found the women in a group waiting for her to come out. She tried to smile but didn't quite manage. Mabel, one of the elder women of the village, came over to her, smiling from ear to ear.

"Rachel," she practically exclaimed, "how long have you known?" Amanda looked at Mabel as if she had three horns on her head. *What was she talking about?* She really wasn't in the mood to be teased. Walking away from Mabel, she returned to her seat. Mabel followed, Sarah on her heels.

"I don't know what your talking about," Amanda said flatly, not wanting to talk to anyone at this moment. Sarah took a seat next to her, an uneasy look on her face.

"You mean you don't know?" Mabel asked, surprised.

"Know what?" she asked, getting quickly annoyed. Mabel chuckled softly.

"I keep forgetting how young you are," she said. "Why, Amanda, you're with child!" Amanda stared at Mabel, not moving or breathing. *With child . . . with child . . . with child . . . no . . . no . . . NO! She couldn't be!*

"Oh, Rachel!" Sarah exclaimed, neither happily, nor in dismay. This was not good, Sarah knowing Amanda would not be happy. Amanda just shook her head.

"No, I can't be," she denied weakly, but deep down she knew. *The sickness, the tiredness, the dizziness . . . there had never been a fever. I'm pregnant? Oh my god!* Tears sprang to her eyes as she turned to Sarah who took her hand and squeezed.

"It's okay," she whispered. "Oh, Rachel."

The other women now came to her side and started congratulating her, but she wanted them to go away. Her chest tightened, and breathing became difficult. *This can not be happening.* She stood abruptly, pulling her hand away from Sarah and pushing past the women, running out the door. She heard Sarah call her name, but she didn't care.

This can't be happening. A baby. Here . . . in this place . . . it couldn't be true. How was she going to escape with a baby? How was she ever going to get home now? Sobs wracked her body violently as she ran.

She reached her cabin, running around to the back, hesitating only briefly before running down the now-familiar path; coming quickly to the clearing, she descended the rocky slope. Falling and slipping several times in her rush, she finally entered the woods to the secret place. Once inside, she threw herself down on the ground. *She needed to get out of here; she couldn't wait any longer! Matthew, oh God, Matthew!* Her heart ached for him. *How could she leave without him?* She weakly pushed herself up. *She loved him,* she realized; *oh God, she loved Matthew! What was she going to do? What was she thinking? Oh God, she just couldn't be pregnant* . . . she stood and began pacing; *what was she going to do?* Then she stopped; cradling her face, she began to sob.

Matthew swung the ax, splitting the log cleanly. He reached for another, placed it on the slab, and swung, splitting the wood. He was reaching for another when he heard Jimmy calling his name.

"Matthew!"

He looked over his shoulder to see Jimmy and Sarah walking toward him. His relationship with Jimmy had become strained ever since that night months ago. Though they worked together companionably, their conversation never strayed passed village activities. Matthew wiped the sweat that was dripping in his eyes, noticing the serious expression on Jimmy and the worried one on Sarah. He dropped the ax off to the side. *Amanda.*

"What is it?" he demanded. Sarah had tears in her eyes.

"Matthew, I went to get Rachel this morning, and she didn't look well. She said she was tired," she said, wringing her hands together. Matthew nodded in encouragement for her to continue.

"She told me she wasn't sleeping well," he said quietly, his eyes on Sarah.

"But when we went to do the laundry, she became so sick—"

"Sick? How? What do you mean?" he interrupted, stepping forward. "Where is she—"

"Listen to her, Matthew," Jimmy interjected. Sarah swallowed and continued.

"She was vomiting in the bathroom"—her voice soft—"and when she came out, Mabel offered her congratulations," she began and looked at Jimmy for reassurance. He nodded and squeezed her hand. She turned back to Matthew's confused expression. "She's with child, Matthew."

Stunned, Matthew stepped back, staring at the two of them. A child. Amanda was pregnant.

"Matthew," Sarah continued.

"Rachel's . . ." He looked up and met Jimmy's eyes as his friend watched him. "We're having a baby?" Where was Amanda? Fear washed over him. What had she done? "Where is she, Sarah?" His voice was just above a whisper.

"She was so distraught and upset that she ran away. She left her work and ran . . . I tried to stop her, but . . . she was so upset." Tears filled her eyes.

"What direction did she run in?" he asked, a somber expression on his face.

"Your cabin," she said, "but I went there and I couldn't find her."

"Thank you, Sarah," he said and began to run toward his cabin. *Lord, let her be safe*, he prayed.

Within the hour she heard footsteps falling and turned to see Matthew parting the tree branches, stepping into the small area. She turned back around, knowing he'd come for her. Her head throbbed, her body ached, and she was suddenly very tired. As he slowly walked over to her, he did a quick examine of her to see if she was injured. Her skirt was torn, the elbow was hanging open on her left sleeve revealing a bloody gash. Her face was smudged with dirt and tears, and she had her hands resting in her lap, looking so sad and defeated. It hurt him to see her so.

He sat down next to her, not saying a word, letting several minutes pass before he spoke. "Are you hurt?" he asked softly. She bit her bottom lip, shaking her head. "You really scared me." Turning her face away from his, fresh tears trickled down her cheeks. Again more silence.

"Amanda?" he asked gently. She loved to hear him call her by her real name. She turned to him, looking into his eyes, seeing the concern and worry in their depths.

"I want to leave," she said softly. "I was going to leave . . . but"—she sighed—"I can't. Not without you." He opened his arms and she slid into his embrace. He kissed the top of her head. She didn't want leave without him.

"I do love you, Amanda," he whispered.

"I love you, too," she whispered into his chest. Closing his eyes, he smiled, hearing those words for the first time. She loved him. He almost couldn't believe his ears.

"Could you say that one more time?" he teased softly in her ear.

"I love you," she said as he tightened his arms around her.

"That's what I thought you said." He smiled.

They were quiet again for a few moments.

"You know, don't you?" she finally asked.

Hesitating, he finally said, "Yes." She pulled back so she could see his face.

"Matthew, I'm not ready to have a baby," she said tearfully.

"I know," he said, "but we'll do this together. I'm going to be right here for you."

She moved out of his arms. "You don't understand," she said. "I wasn't ready to get married, but now I am. I wasn't ready to have a baby . . . and now . . . Oh my god . . . now I'm going to . . . I'm going to—" Her voice broke with a sob.

"Amanda." He reached for her, but she pushed even farther away from him. "Amanda?" She turned her tear-streaked face to his.

"I hate it here!" she cried passionately. "I've been trying . . . trying to do as you asked . . . fitting in . . . but . . . I . . . I hate it here *so* much!"

"Amanda," Matthew spoke her name softly as she shook her head at him.

"I miss my parents," she sobbed, struggling to her feet. "I miss my freedom"—he stood as she did—"and school . . . did you know that I was going to be in the Historical Foundation at my school?"

Matthew shook his head, not saying anything.

"Yep!" she cried, wiping her face with her sleeve, smearing the dirt and tears. "Yep! You may not know what that is but that was so important to me! And now . . . now I'll never know that experience . . . never fulfill *my* dreams!" She continued to cry, covering her face with her hands. Matthew stood, helplessly watching her. What could he say? He did all this to her. He took her dreams from her. Moments passed by, and her crying subsided. She wiped her face with her hands and looked at Matthew.

"A baby . . . Matthew," she said, just above a whisper. "I'm nineteen years old! I don't know the first thing about having a baby." Matthew took a step toward her and took her face in his hands. He searched her eyes.

"Amanda, we'll do this together," he said softly. "It's scary for me too. But there are a lot of mothers here . . . that can help. My mother will help us."

She put her hands over the top of his. "But I want *my* mother," she cried. Tears stung Matthew's eyes as he saw the misery in her own, his heart aching for her.

"Amanda."

"I can't have a baby here!" she declared, her voice hardening.

He held his breath, hearing what she was saying to him, and he wanted to take the hurt away from her. But, *leave?* He abruptly pulled back.

Dizziness overwhelmed her, and he had to reach out, grabbing her shoulders to steady her.

"You need to rest," he stated. "Let's go home."

"Matthew, *please?*" she begged weakly, but he shook his head.

"I can't talk about it right now, Amanda," he said firmly. She closed her eyes painfully. He touched her face gently, and she opened her eyes to meet his.

"We will talk, Amanda, just not now, okay?" he said gently. She searched his eyes then nodded.

"Okay," she whispered.

He took her hand, and they slowly made their way back to the cabin. Once they reached the clearing where their cabin sat, he turned to her.

"Amanda," he began, searching her dirty face, "this is my way of life. I can't just—" He stopped and looked toward the small road that led to their cabin. Loud voices were coming nearer. "What is this?" he asked aloud. He pulled Amanda snugly to his side and walked in the direction of the voices. Soon Pastor appeared with his two assistants, James and Steven, or "cronies" as he and Jimmy had labeled them years ago. "Matthew!" he said loudly. "I have reports that your wife has tried to escape." He looked irate, his face red, nostrils flaring.

"No, sir!" he declared righteously. "She was upset and wanted to be alone. I knew exactly where she was." Matthew had never spoken so haughtily to his pastor before. But now he had Amanda to protect, not just himself.

The pastor's eyes became slits. "All right, Matthew," he growled, believing Matthew was lying to him. "You both have left your duties unfinished. What do you have to say about that?" he asked. Matthew was silent, a watchful eye on the pastor and the two men by his side.

"We did," he finally said quietly. "But we will finish them now." The pastor nodded toward his men, and they came forward.

"Sir?" Matthew asked as he was grabbed by the men. "What are you doing?" Amanda cried out as they shoved her away.

"Matthew!" she screamed. The pastor walked up to Matthew and got right in his face.

"I warned you to have control over her," he hissed. "She has caused quite a commotion in the village and has left her duties unfulfilled, as you have. I warned you."

"You've been waiting haven't you?" Matthew asked incredulously. "All this time, you've been waiting for the smallest mistake!" The pastor backhanded Matthew viciously. Amanda attacked the pastor, screaming. He turned quickly and shoved her down to the ground. Matthew struggled to get to her, but the men held him, and the pastor turned back to Matthew.

"Do not question me, boy!" he growled. "I think you're forgetting yourself." He waved his hand, and his men dragged Matthew off.

"Matthew!" Amanda screamed from the ground. He tried to look back at her, but he was forced forward. The pastor was left standing over her.

"You . . . you little heathen." He reached down, yanking her up. "I knew I would have problems with you. Matthew's too blind to see you for what you are."

Amanda flinched away from him.

"Leave me alone!" she cried. He twisted her arm slightly, and she cried out in pain.

"I will teach you a lesson," he declared. "Come, child, and let me show you who the god is in this village." He roughly dragged her down the small road and through the center of the village. Amanda noticed the usually busy village was deserted. When they reached the church stairs, she began to struggle with him. She almost slipped out of his grasp, but he turned and slapped her hard across the face, stunning her, ending her struggle.

Fear coursed through her body, and she was shaking uncontrollably. He dragged her through the church, and once inside his office, he threw her on the floor. He locked the door behind him and then walked around to the other side of his desk, his breathing heavy from the exertion of dragging her. She came up on her knees and crossed her arms in front of her.

"Where's Matthew?" she demanded.

"Do not question me!" he yelled loudly, and she couldn't help flinching back.

He opened a drawer in his desk and placed a packet of papers in front of him. His breathing finally evening out, a sinister smile appeared.

"I wanted to share some information with you," he began, smoothly. "It seems that they have now officially withdrawn you from college. Your parents have packed up all of your belongings from your apartment."

The color drained from Amanda's face.

"Yes," he said, enjoying himself. "Your parents have hired a private investigator because the authorities have slowed down their investigation." Walking around the desk, he came to stand over her. "Get up." He grabbed her arm painfully, helping her stand. "You must be thinking there is some hope that they will find you and bring you home," he hissed into her ear. Fear rippled through her body, and she fought the nausea that plagued her. "Don't you?"

Amanda clenched her teeth. "Yes," she whispered, and he let go of her arm roughly.

"Yes, of course you do," he replied. "But let me burst your bubble. It just happens that the private investigator that they've hired . . . works for me." He started to laugh sadistically. Amanda's hand flew to her mouth, and twisting around, she vomited right on the floor. When she was done, her dry heaving turned to sobs. The pastor had returned to his seat and was sitting with his hands folded over his stomach. "Yes . . . yes . . . it is sad, isn't it?" he continued, amusement in his voice. He was truly enjoying this, she thought in disgust.

Amanda wiped her mouth with her sleeve, her sobs subsiding as she struggled to stand up, feeling so weak and horrified with what he had told her.

CHAPTER 21

"I did hear the good news!" he declared. "You have created another member of our village. How pleasing. Another soul to control." Amanda stared at him, biting her tongue. She never intended for him to see her child because she would either be free . . . or dead.

"Where's Matthew?" she asked again. The pastor smiled.

"You will see Matthew soon," he replied. "He's receiving his punishment for not being able to control you." Panic rose in her eyes.

"What are doing to him?"

"You should have been concerned with that before you made such a scene today." Standing back up, he walked to her side. "You see, I like a calm village. No commotion, just peaceful living. And when this peace is disturbed, well, the problem is taken care of. You, my dear, have been a disturbance and a problem since you arrived. I told Matthew we could find other uses for you. But he wanted you," He looked her up and down, lust in his eyes. "Not that I can say I blame him."

Anger rose up in her, and she looked up at him, a disgusted expression on her face.

"You call yourself a man of God?" she said to him, disdain in her voice. "You don't have one good quality in you. You're just a *snake!*" He backhanded her suddenly, splitting the skin below her eye and knocking her to the floor. Then he was on top of her, twisting her onto her back; he threw his large body on top of hers. Reaching under her clothes, he roughly touched her with his large hands. Sobbing, Amanda was shoving and scratching at him.

He tried to put his mouth on hers, but she wouldn't hold still. Somehow she managed to shove her knee between his legs. Groaning, he rolled off her, and she scrambled out from under him. Grabbing at her, he caught the hole in her sleeve with his fingers, and ripped it clean off her as she stood up and ran for the door.

Unlocking the door, she swung it open and slammed into Simon. The large man had been her guard when she was first abducted, and he caught her from falling back from their collision. Looking down at her bloody face and torn clothing, he looked over her head at his pastor.

"Please, Simon," she whimpered, thinking he was going to bring her back in the room. With a stunned expression, Simon looked at his pastor.

"Pastor, what are you doing?" he asked quietly. Within the brief moments it took Simon to assess the situation, the pastor had stood and was straightening his clothes.

"Simon, good man," he said in his authoritative voice that he liked to use when preaching his sermons. "She attacked me and you stopped her from getting away. Thank you. We can meet later, you and I." He tried to dismiss him, but Simon looked at Amanda, seeing clearly that she was the one being attacked.

"Rachel," he started to say.

"Don't speak to her!" the pastor yelled at Simon. "Let her go, and leave!" Simon's eyes did not leave Amanda's terrified eyes.

"Please, Simon, help me," she begged. Anger contorted his expression, and he looked at his pastor. Without saying a word to his pastor, he nudged Amanda gently by him. "Go to your cabin," he said gently then turned angrily back to his pastor.

Amanda didn't stay to see the confrontation but ran out of the church and toward the small road. Terrified that the pastor would send his men after her, she ran as fast as she could. She reached her cabin and slammed the door behind her, locking it, throwing herself in the corner by the window. Her body was shaking violently.

She wanted Matthew! Oh God, what have they done to him? Hours later she still sat in the corner, the sun was setting, and she had dozed lightly. She woke to a large thump at the door. Whimpering, she thought that it was the pastor returning to get her, but then there was only silence that followed. She slowly stood, crying out in pain as she straightened out of her uncomfortable position. Creeping to the door, she put her ear to the rough wood. Nothing. *Then what was that noise?* She unlocked the door slowly, and it was pushed open by the weight on the other side. Crying out, startled, she realized it was Matthew.

"Matthew!" she screamed. "Oh my god!" She reached to help him up, and he yelled out in pain. His face was pale and constricted with pain. Kneeling down next to him, she asked, "Matthew . . . Matthew what can I do . . . what happened . . . oh God . . . what did they do to you?" She was crying openly now.

Struggling to sit up, he answered, "Bed." He grunted in pain. "I just need to lie down." He struggled to stand with her help, and they walked to the bedroom. She could feel the dampness on the back of his shirt. *What did they do?*

"Matthew, you're all wet. Let's get this off," she said, reaching for his shirt.

"No!" he yelled, then softer, "No, Amanda, I just need to be alone." He lay down on his stomach, grunting. She stood next to him feeling helpless, tears streaming down her face; she started to leave the room, when she looked down at her sticky hands to see them covered in blood. Horrified, her eyes wide, she turned back to Matthew. His shirt was not wet with water . . . *it was blood!*

"Matthew, you're bleeding!" she cried. "What happened? Please, your scaring me!" She knelt down next to the bed so she could see his eyes. He shakily reached out and touched her battered face.

"Are you okay, Amanda?" he whispered as she leaned her face into his hand.

"Don't worry about me," she cried. "Please, Matthew, let me help you." He searched her face, hating how frightened she looked.

"Okay," he said quietly, wincing in pain. "Get some warm water . . . and a cloth . . . scissors . . ."

"Okay," she said, immediately standing up, retrieving the items he asked for. On her way back, water overflowed from the bowl, making a path on the floor, because she was shaking so badly. "Okay, Matthew."

Watching her made him feel worse. "Amanda." She met his eyes. "Calm down, hon. "She nodded, tears streaming down her face. *He was her life! If something happened to him* . . . "I need you to slowly cut up the back of my shirt."

He gasped when she lifted the material slightly to begin cutting. With the last cut, she gasped out loud. He was covered with at least twenty foot-long open wounds. Her hand went to her mouth, and she stepped back, swallowing the nauseousness that washed over her.

"Matthew," she gasped, trembling from head to toe. "Why? I don't understand."

"Obedience," he whispered painfully. The word slammed into Amanda, taking her breath away. *Obedience . . . her obedience . . . or lack of . . . this was her fault!*

"Matthew, I'm so sorry," she cried, "this was because of me."

"Amanda, stop," he said gently as he struggled to sit up.

"Don't move, Matthew," she said. He ignored her, sitting upright on the bed, turning to her; he took a good look at his battered wife, seeing her sleeve missing and her face bleeding. His eyes became slits.

"Amanda," he asked quietly, "what did *he* do to you?"

Amanda shook her head, tears shining in her eyes. "I don't want to talk about me," she cried, standing away from him, a pathetic sight, afraid to touch him. "Oh God, I . . . I'm so sorry, Matthew."

He searched her face and stared into her sad, abused eyes. I did this to her. Looking down, he pulled his ruined shirt off, tossing it to the floor. He opened his arms to her, and she hesitantly shook her head. "Look what I've caused. No, I can't," she whispered.

"Amanda, please," he said quietly, using words he knew she wouldn't refuse. "I need to hold you." She closed her eyes; how would he ever forgive her for what she did to him? Trembling, she stepped closer, then into his arms. Careful not to touch his back, she buried her face into his neck.

"I promise I'll do everything you say," she cried. "I won't do anything wrong ever again."

"Oh Amanda, stop," he soothed her. "Hey," He pulled her back slightly so he could look her in the eyes, taking a deep breath of his own, fighting against the pain that throbbed through him. "This isn't the first time that I've been through this. I will heal." She tearfully searched his eyes.

"Why did it happen before?" she asked softly, her brows together in confusion.

"When I was a boy," he began then clenched his jaw in pain. "Jimmy and I thought it would be funny to take people's laundry off their clotheslines, and switch them with other people's." He took a shaky breath.

"For that, you were whipped?" she asked.

"Lashes," he gasped as he moved slightly. "Ten lashes."

She shook her head. "For a childish prank . . . I just don't understand this place! What kind of godly people are they, that they can treat each other so cruelly?"

He lifted his hand to her cheek. "Amanda, every society has to have order," he said quietly. "This is our way."

Her bottom lip trembled, still not understanding. "I need you so much, Matthew. I couldn't bear it if . . ."

His eyes were intent. "Hey"—meeting her eyes—"nothing is going to happen to me," he reassured her firmly. "Just help me clean my back, okay?"

She nodded silently. Lying back down, she began cleaning his wounds. He grunted in pain as she touched him with the wet cloth, but soon the lacerations were clean and bandaged. After making him a herbal tonic, he was now sleeping peacefully on the bed.

Amanda walked into the bathroom, turned on the shower, and took her tattered clothing off. She went and stood in front of the mirror, her hands settling on her belly. *I have a baby in here*, she thought. Tears filled her eyes as she looked in the mirror at the horrible reflection that stood in front of it. The left side of her face had a stream of dried blood that had drained from the wound under her eye, which was already beginning to bruise. She had open cuts on her arms and legs from her tumble down the hill and not to mention the bruises the pastor bestowed on her from his attack. Still feeling his hands on her . . . touching her . . . she covered her face and sobbed quietly, not wanting to wake Matthew. He would have raped her if Simon hadn't shown up, she was sure of it. *She knew all along that he was insane.*

Stepping into the hot shower, she scrubbed furiously at her body, trying to rid the feel of his hands on her. *She felt so dirty.*

Finally clean and dressed, she climbed into the bed next to Matthew. She was so exhausted, battered, and bruised . . . she fell asleep.

"Amanda . . . Amanda!" She slowly pulled herself out of her exhausted slumber. Struggling to open her eyes, she focused her vision on Katherine's face. Blinking rapidly, she sat up.

"What's wrong?" Amanda asked, disoriented. "Is it Matthew? Where is he?"

"I'm right here," he said, stepping into sight, standing next to Katherine. Relief washed over Amanda as she tried to clear her thoughts.

"Amanda, are you all right?" Katherine asked, concern written on her face. "My glory, what has he done to you? Come, I need to take a look at you." She gently took Amanda's hands and pulled her to her feet. "Let's go in the bathroom. Matthew, you stay out here." Amanda looked over her shoulder at her husband.

"Matthew, are you well?" she asked. "Are you in pain?"

He shook his head sadly. "Amanda, don't worry about me. I'm worried about you." He followed them out of the bedroom, stopping at the bathroom door. His mother turned to him and put her hand on his chest.

"Give me a few minutes to check her over . . . then you may see her," Katherine said quietly. The concern on his mother's face made him worry more, and he stepped back and leaned against the wall.

He had woke quite early in the morning, just as the sun was rising. The pain on his back was excruciating, causing him to crawl out of bed for more herbs. When he had returned to the bed, Amanda's back was to him, and he could see her body moving with every breath that she took. He walked over to the other side of the bed so that he could see her face, and what he saw made him step back in shock. She had a large gash under her eye, the surrounding skin black and blue, beginning to swell. He pulled the covers back, slightly revealing her arms that were covered in bruises. He wanted to weep at what his pastor had done to his defenseless wife.

He gently reached over and touched her shoulder, trying to wake her. "Amanda?" he whispered. "Honey, wake up." But she continued to sleep, undisturbed. Anger washed over him, and he stepped back and began pacing the length of the room. What did Pastor do to her? If he touched her, in any way, he would . . . Matthew stopped suddenly in the middle of the room. He would what? What could he do? Realization washed over him as he finally understood the absolute control the pastor had on the villagers. Pastor had waited for another mistake on Amanda's part, and he sprung into action without hesitation. And Matthew wasn't there to protect her. Oh God! He covered his face with his hands.

It wasn't long after that his mother had rushed into their cabin, her face constricted in sorrow at what she might find. Discovering Matthew walking around had given her tremendous relief. Yet Katherine felt frightened when Matthew brought her to Amanda's bedside, and she immediately began to wake her up.

Once in the bathroom, Katherine closed the door quietly and turned to look at Amanda; she wanted to cry at the sight of her abuse. Her hand went over her mouth to cover the trembling of her lips.

"Amanda," she began, "tell me what happened." Amanda was fully awake by now and stepped back from Katherine. Shaking her head, she turned toward the mirror, gasping at the sight of the bruises, touching her face tenderly with her fingertips. *How ugly he'd made her face!* Tears welled in her eyes as Katherine came to stand behind her and looked at Amanda's reflection in the mirror.

"Can you tell me?" she asked softly. Amanda looked down.

"No," she whispered. Katherine closed her eyes, fearing the worst. "I want to forget it." she said, stepping away from Katherine.

"Amanda, let me check that you don't have any more injuries that may need treatment." Amanda wrapped her arms around herself.

"No," she whispered again, shame spilling from her soul. She didn't want anyone to see the bruises he'd put on her body or explain how he'd touched her. She shivered just from the awful memory.

"Would you rather Matthew checked you?" Amanda's eyes flew to Katherine's face.

"No!" she said, astonishment on her face. "I don't want to be checked. Leave me alone!"

Katherine stared at Amanda.

"Amanda, did he rape you?" she asked, just above a whisper. Amanda's tears overflowed as she bit her lip and shook her head. Silence filled the small room, and Amanda refused to meet Katherine's eyes, standing still, hugging herself.

"All right," Katherine said softly. "Why don't you get dressed. Here, I brought your clothes in." she said, handing Amanda fresh clothes. "When you're ready, come out. Matthew is anxious to see you." Katherine opened the door, looked at Amanda anxiously, then walked out, closing the door behind her.

Matthew searched his mother's face. "Well, is she all right?" he questioned her. Katherine put her fingers to her lips, signaling for him to be quiet, then motioned him into the other room. Matthew followed anxiously. "Mom, please tell me what's wrong."

"Matthew," she began softly, "I don't know what he did, but she has closed herself off and she won't talk to me about it. She did say that he didn't rape her. But I wonder. The bruises that she's wearing are . . ." Tears shined in his mother's eyes. "I just can't imagine what he did to inflict such damage."

Instantly anger shot through him; grunting, he turned and punched the wall behind him. The wood crackled and broke.

"Matthew!" his mother called. "Hurting yourself more will not resolve this situation."

He paced the room with abrupt movements. "You don't understand!" he declared to his mother painfully. "I promised to always be there to protect her! I failed. I wasn't there and he . . . he hurt her . . . ," he said, his voice choking with emotion. "God only knows what he did."

Katherine walked to her son, taking his arms into her hands. "Matthew. There was no way that you could have protected her against Pastor, and deep down you know that. In this village you have no authority, and you never will. He will do what he pleases and when he pleases. Suddenly you're ignorant to the rules that you have lived by your whole life?" Matthew pulled away and looked at his mother heatedly.

"No!" he said hotly. "I'm not. I've never been subjected to breaking any of the rules of the village, so how could I have known . . . how could I have seen . . . how . . ." He hesitated. Katherine's hopes soared. "How twisted it all is."

Katherine continued, "Do you think that what he did to her yesterday will be the end? Or you for that matter? Do you think that he won't continue to demand complete obedience from you? And"—she hesitated purposely—"from your child?"

Matthew's eyes flew to his mother's, anger flashing in their depths.

"That will not happen," he growled. Turning, he ran his hands through his hair.

"What will you do?" she asked him softly. When he was silent for several moments, she said, "How can you possibly stop it from happening?"

He turned back to her, determination hardened on his face.

"We'll leave," he said firmly. "I'll take my family, you included, and leave." Katherine swallowed then nodded tearfully.

They both turned as they heard the bathroom door open. Soon Amanda appeared around the corner. She was dressed, her hair left long as she tried to hide the swelling bruises on her face.

"Amanda!" Tenderness instantly replaced the anger that he had been consumed by only moments before. He met her across the room and rubbed his hands up and down on her arms. He searched her face and saw how she avoided his eyes. "Look at me, Amanda." She looked down and around, then, finally, she painstakingly forced herself to look at him.

Katherine slowly slipped out of the cabin. Preparations needed to be finalized, she thought as she hurried away.

Matthew saw her once-bright blue eyes dull with pain. His own eyes teared, and before he could speak, she did.

"Matthew, how's your back?" she asked. "Do your cuts hurt bad?"

He shook his head. "Amanda, how can you be concerned with me when you're hurt? I was so consumed with my own pain last night, that I didn't get a chance to help you."

"I didn't want your help," she revealed. "I was so scared last night. Your back . . . it was so . . . bloody." She pulled away from him. "I still can't understand how they could do that."

"Obedience is enforced here," he said quietly. "Consequences."

"It was all my fault," she said, her voice sad, shaking her head. Matthew just watched her, not caring about what happened to him. She was so pale and fragile, and she carried his child. *Pastor battered my wife*, he thought angrily, *and my child within her!*

"Amanda, it was not!" he stated heatedly. "Stop blaming yourself!"

She looked at him, her bruised face only partially hidden behind her hair. "It was my fault. I knew that I wasn't allowed to leave my work, and I did. I just wasn't thinking. And I—"

"It was my job to instill fear in you, to explain the consequences that could happen here," Matthew said, his voice quiet. "I didn't want to frighten you any more than you already were. I'm being blamed for not controlling you, Amanda. It wasn't because you ran out on your work."

"But you did explain—" she started to say.

"No," He shook his head, crossing his arms in front of him. "I was vague, and I was supposed to use more forceful methods to put you in your place." Amanda stilled, understanding him completely.

"I . . . see," she whispered, slowly sitting on the sofa.

"Amanda," Matthew began softly. She looked up at him slowly. Knowing by his tone that he was concerned for her, she wrapped her arms around herself again. "Your face."

She reached her hand up and touched her battered cheek. "I'm all right." Her voice was soft. Matthew shook his head as he knelt in front of her.

"What did he do to you?" His voice was as soft. She looked into his eyes, seeing his concern for her. But she couldn't tell him. She was struggling inwardly, yet she could not bring herself to talk about it. Tears trickling down her cheeks, she just shook her head. He covered his face with his hands, in despair.

"Matthew," she cried. "Please don't be angry with me."

He pulled his hands away. "Oh God," he declared. "I'm not mad at you! Come here." He pulled her into his arms. She hid her face into his chest, feeling safe and warm. He kissed the top of her head. "I'm so sorry I wasn't there to protect you." Amanda said nothing, just clung to him. Then he heard her small voice.

"I'm sorry I wasn't there to protect you."

Matthew maneuvered himself onto the sofa, scooping her into his arms. He sat down slowly, careful of his back wounds, and settled her onto his lap. They sat quietly in one another's arms.

"Matthew?" she asked.

"Hmm?"

"What happens now?" she asked in a small voice. "What will he do?" Matthew was silent. "Is . . . is the punishment over?" Her voice trembled, and he tightened his embrace. "Yes. This time," he replied.

CHAPTER 22

They sat together for another hour, when there was a knock on the door. Amanda instantly sat up, looking at the door in fear. Matthew rubbed her hair gently.

"It's all right, Amanda," he said. "I'll get it." He put her gently to his side and walked to the door, opening it to see Pastor and James in the doorway.

"Sir?" he asked, an undercurrent of anger seething in his voice. Pastor instantly noticed the change in Matthew. Amanda knew it was the pastor; overcome with fear, she hugged her knees to her chest.

"Matthew," Pastor said, "we're here for a meeting." They began to walk in, and Matthew stood firm where he was, blocking them from entering.

"About what?" Matthew demanded roughly. The pastor looked at him in shock. Matthew was outright challenging him.

"Matthew, do not question me. You will let me in, or I'll have you thrown in isolation," the pastor growled. Anger burned in Matthew's eyes, but he stepped aside and let them in. Matthew saw Amanda cowered into the sofa and quickly went to her side. He pulled her up and held her close to his side.

"Good, she's up," the pastor stated. "Then you will both hear what I have to say. You are both on probation. One, and I mean one more incident and you'll both spend a week in isolation. *This* punishment is nothing like the one you will receive next time." As he said this, his eyes fell viciously on Amanda. Matthew felt her shaking by his side.

"Be warned. You will return to work tomorrow." Nausea overwhelmed Amanda; stumbling from the room to the bathroom. The men watched her

flee. "And don't think that because she's with child that her load will change."
Matthew stared him straight in the eye.

"No, sir!" he said sarcastically. Again the pastor was taken back. They
left the cabin, and the pastor gave orders to James to have Matthew watched
carefully.

Matthew quickly went to the bathroom. Amanda was on her knees in
front of the toilet basin. One hand held back her hair, and the other held on
to the cold ceramic; she was sobbing. Matthew instantly knelt by her side.

"Oh, baby, it's okay!" he soothed, grabbing a towel and helping her wipe
her mouth and face. He stood and pulled her up. "Amanda." She continued
to sob uncontrollably, and Matthew felt helpless. He brought her into bed,
laying her down, and he lay down next to her, holding her close. "Please . . .
Amanda . . . it's all right . . . don't cry."

Her sobs began to subside, and she turned to face Matthew, burying her
face in his chest.

"Amanda, talk to me," he demanded softly. She took some shaky breaths
and pulled back so she could see him. Her bruised face still filled him with
remorse.

"I don't know what to say," she stated miserably. Then she whispered, "I
want to go home." Matthew pulled her close again.

"I'm sorry, Amanda," he said softly. "I'm so sorry."

"We'll get through this too," she said quietly. "Isn't that what you should
be saying to me?" Without warning, Amanda pushed away from him and sat
up. "What happens now, Matthew?" He slowly sat up, watching her.

"What do you mean?" he asked cautiously. Rising to her feet, she put her
hands on her cheeks. "Look at me," she cried. "I mean"—dropping her hands,
she began pacing the room—"what are we supposed to do? Begin the day
tomorrow the same way? Continue on as if nothing ever happened? Continue
on like you were never given lashes and I . . ." She stopped, shaking her head;
she wiped the tears away. "I can't do it. I won't do it." She abruptly turned and
walked out of the room. Matthew stood as quickly as he could and followed
her. He entered the living room area to see her walking out the door.

"Amanda!" he called to her; ignoring him, she kept walking. She entered
the wooded area, on to the path. She heard him behind her, but she quickened
her pace. Reaching the clearing, she stood at the edge of the land, looking
down at the drop off. Yesterday she ran here to be alone, to try and handle
her news of the baby; and now here she was, about to do the same thing.
Revolting memories of the pastor's large body on top of hers flashed before
her, and she closed her eyes, trembling.

Matthew stopped behind her. "Amanda," He touched her arm gently.

She shrugged off his touch. "I can't be here anymore, Matthew." Her voice just above a whisper, she said, "I'd rather die than stay another day here." And she took a step closer to the edge. Pebbles and dirt fell to the rocky ground below them, and Matthew grabbed her arm fiercely, pulling her back.

"Amanda!" he yelled at her; she gasped at his painful grip. "Stop it! Just stop it!" He pushed her back toward the pathway. She stumbled over her feet and fell on her side. Grimacing in pain, she shoved at his hands as he tried to help her up.

"Leave me alone!" she yelled at him. "Don't touch me!" Matthew straightened, his expression hardening, and he stepped back some. She stood shakily to her feet.

"Go back to the cabin, Amanda," Matthew said to her, his voice cold. He was speaking to her as he never had, and Amanda raised wide eyes to his, her lips parted to speak, but then she closed them when she saw his expression. "Go . . . now!" He took her arm roughly, turning her around and pushing her forward. Amanda choked back a sob, stumbling her way back to the cabin, her eyes blurred with tears. Hurt, confused, angry, and frightened, she made her way back.

Once inside the cabin, Amanda stood in the living room, looking around. There was nowhere for her to go. Matthew had followed, and she heard him close the door behind him. She crossed her arms in front of her, keeping her back to him. He had never behaved the way he just had, and she just didn't know what to expect from him.

Feeling defeated, she walked over to the chair and sat down. She followed Katherine's advice and did her best to fit in, but she knew that she could never belong here, even by pretending. The pastor had some sick attraction to her, and it frightened her more than anything. He would do whatever he could to destroy her, hurting Matthew in the process.

"Amanda, what were you thinking?" Matthew demanded, coming to kneel before her again. His anger had dissipated, his voice quiet. Confused, she searched his face, not answering him. *Was he angry with her?* He was so cold and rough only moments ago, and now . . . and now he wasn't. "After everything we've just gone through, you run again? You're just not thinking!" Standing up, he paced the room. "Pastor is not playing games with us, Amanda, don't you understand that?"

Hesitantly she nodded, knowing very well he was not.

"I know you're upset," he said, stopping to look at her, but keeping his distance. "You have every right to be, but . . ." He ran both his hands through his hair, sighing. "You have to think before you react—I can't protect you here. I thought I could, but what happened yesterday . . . this is life or death."

She looked up at him, fear shining in her eyes.

"You have to promise not to go anywhere," he continued, "for a while, anyway. He'll have you and I, both watched. I know the way things work."

Amanda looked down at her entwined hands that rested on her lap; an overwhelming wave of sadness washed over her. Matthew pulled her up by her hands. "Amanda, I'm sorry," he said, "for what happened to you." He lifted her chin so that she was eye to eye with him. "But I care for you too much for you to continue to put yourself in danger. You and our baby." His last sentence came as a whisper. Her eyes filled with fresh tears, and she nodded, knowing that he was right. *She just wasn't thinking rationally, but how could she under these circumstances?* The village was sucking the life out of her, and the urge to escape her suffocating fear was to run. Matthew had a shredded back, and she a bruised body to show for her spontaneous fleeing, and yet she did it again. *Thinking only of herself, not of her unborn child or . . . of Matthew,* she silently cursed to herself. She wiped away her tears with her fingers.

"You're right," she said softly. "I'm sorry, Matthew."

"Oh, baby," He leaned in and gently kissed her on the lips. "You scared the hell out of me, Amanda. You have to stop doing that!"

Her lips trembled beneath his. "I'm just so frightened," she admitted. "I'm so frightened, Matthew."

Pulling her toward him, he held her in his arms, and she wrapped her arms around him, burying her face in the crook of his neck. "I know, I know," he spoke softly to her. After a few moments, Amanda spoke again.

"Your pastor told me that the private investigator that my parents hired to find me works for him. Did you know that?" she cried. Matthew went still in her arms, and when he pulled away, his expression was closed. He moved away.

"No," he said, "I didn't know that." He walked to the window, moving the curtain slightly to look outside. "But it doesn't surprise me. There are a lot of people out there"—waving his hand in the direction of the trees—"that work for our village. People that even helped me to bring you here."

"It's hopeless," she sniffled. "I'll never be found." The despair he heard in her was heartbreaking.

He walked back to her, taking both her hands, searching her face.

"I told you that from the beginning," he said quietly. She nodded, looking up at him.

"But," she wept, "did you actually expect me to give up hope? To stop wanting my old life?" He reached over and brushed her hair out of her face.

"Part of me did," he admitted. "I thought that what we have together would ease the longing, but I knew that I couldn't erase your memories." He stepped away from her, walking into the kitchen. Hesitating, she slowly followed him. He was leaning his hands on the sink, his head lowered, his back to her.

"Matthew, I don't want you to think that your love doesn't mean anything to me," she said, walking over to him, touching his side. "It does. It's the only thing that's allowed me to survive this long. And . . . I *do* love you." He covered her hand with his.

"I know," he said softly, lifting his head to look out the window. She stood by his side silently for several minutes before he turned to speak to her.

"Amanda," he began, looking at her tenderly. "I love you more than I've loved anyone or anything in my life. I'd give my life for you," he said, and she believed him. "I want to take you away from here." Shock splashed across her face.

"What?" she asked, not believing what she'd just heard. His eyes met hers, and she noticed how sad they were.

"You heard me," he said. "I want to take you away from all of this."

She searched his face. "Matthew . . . really?" she asked desperately.

He nodded. "I don't know when or how, but I'll figure out a way," he said quietly. "I don't want you or my child to suffer at the hands of my pastor anymore."

Amanda woke up, sweat streaming down her face. She had a terrible dream that the pastor was chasing her. Sitting up, she turned to see Matthew still sleeping by her side. Reaching over, she touched his cheek tenderly, then pushing her damp hair out of her face, she slipped out of bed and walked slowly to the bathroom. A dull pain had started in her lower back, but she ignored it. She finished what she had to do then went to the kitchen to make herself an herbal tonic.

Emptying her glass, she walked back toward the bedroom. Halfway across the living room, a sharp pain ripped across her abdomen, nearly knocking her to her knees. She held her stomach, not knowing what was wrong, and didn't move for a few moments, the pain seeming to stop. Taking a deep breath, she slowly stood up and continued on. Just as she reached the doorway to her room, the pain lashed across her again. She grabbed on to the woodwork, doubling over.

"Oh God!" she cried out, tears stinging her eyes. She stumbled away from her room toward the bathroom. *What was wrong?*

"Amanda?" Matthew sleepily called out. "Are you all right?"

She didn't want him to see her like this!

"I'm . . . I'm all right," she strained to say. "I'll be—" Another excruciating pain ripped through her body. Then it happened. She felt a gush of warmth travel down her legs. Looking down, she saw her white nightgown was covered in blood. "Oh . . . God . . . ," she whimpered. But before she could react, another pain ripped into her body, and she couldn't help but cry out; this time the pain knocked her to her knees, and she collapsed onto the floor.

Matthew had heard her cry, and then the loud thump. Jumping out of bed, ignoring his own pain, he ran to the bathroom. Once in the doorway, he stood in shock. Amanda was lying on the floor, a puddle of blood around her, crying out in pain. Snapping out of it, he went to her side immediately.

"Amanda?" he asked anxiously. "What's wrong?"

She looked up at him, her face colorless. "Matthew," she whispered. "I think it's the baby."

Fear ran through him rapidly as he realized that she was miscarrying and she could bleed to death. He watched it happen to other women in the village.

"Okay," he said, trying to think. "We need to stop the bleeding, Amanda." He lifted her up, and she cried out from another pain.

"Oh . . . God . . . Matthew . . . it hurts so bad!" she cried. He carried her to their bed; throwing back the covers, he set her down gently.

"Hold up your arms," he ordered, and he pulled her bloody gown over her head. He bunched up the gown and placed it between her legs. Then he ran to grab towels from the bathroom. When he returned, the gown was drenched with blood. *So much blood!* He threw it onto the floor, replacing it with towels.

The pain kept coming and coming. Amanda was exhausted and in so much pain she wanted to die.

"Amanda . . . please . . . honey . . . hold on . . . ," he pleaded, scared. "I have towels to stop the blood,but I have to get the doctor!"

"No!" she screamed. "Please, don't leave me!"

Matthew looked at her helplessly.

"Amanda, I don't know what else to do," he said. He watched her cry out from another pain. "I won't let you die!"

He left the room, and the cabin, never running so fast in his life. He reached the doctor's cabin, and he nearly broke the door down by his pounding. The doctor opened his door to a frightful sight. Matthew stood before him, his eyes wide and panicked. His white long johns, chest, and arms were stained with blood.

"Matthew, son, what's happened?" the doctor gasped.

"Doc, it's Rachel," Matthew choked out, "the baby . . ." The doctor understood immediately.

"Yes, all right." The doctor turned, pulled his jacket off its hook, and grabbed his bag.

"Please, Doc, hurry!" he begged. The old doctor ran back with him, hoping he himself didn't have a heart attack.

When he saw Amanda, covered in blood and her skin so white, he went right to work. "Matthew, get wet clean towels right now," he ordered. "We need to clean her up so I can see what I'm doing." He walked over to Amanda, as she crumbled up in pain again. He touched Amanda's cheek gently with his rough palm,

"It's going to be all right, child. I'll take care of you." His words were kind.

She whispered in pain, "Help me." Then Amanda slowly slipped into unconsciousness, and Matthew witnessed this when he came back into the room.

"Amanda . . . No!" he called out to her, coming to her side.

"Matthew, she'll be all right," he said calmly. "The pain and loss of blood have become too much for her. It's better that she not be awake for this."

The doctor cleaned her up then turned to Matthew.

"You need to leave now," he ordered. "You'll not want to witness this."

"I want to stay with her!" he stated firmly. The doctor sighed.

"Fine, but sit up by her head and talk to her. Even though she's unconscious she still may be able to hear you. Don't look back at me. I can't take care of both of you."

Matthew agreed and placed a chair by her side. It was then he realized she was completely bare. He grabbed a blanket and began to cover her up, when he suddenly noticed the bruises on her body. Anger surged through him when his eyes fell on the bruises across her breasts; clenching his jaw, he covered her up gently.

He touched her cheek tenderly. "What did he do to you?" he whispered, struggling to control his emotions that threatened to rise up. He needed her to recover, then he would be angry.

Hours later, the blood had slowed down to a normal flow, and the doctor had delivered the tiny baby, discarding the tissue, and then cleaned her up. Together they changed the bedding and placed her on clean linens. Matthew put a clean fresh gown on her, and she lay under the covers, looking pale, weak, and small.

In the living room, the doctor and Matthew both sat in silence, trying to recover themselves. Finally Matthew spoke.

"Doc, don't tell me you're going to say she did this to herself," he declared hotly. The doctor shook his head sadly and rubbed his hands over his tired face.

"No," he said. "Her body wasn't ready to have this child. But"—he paused, looking at Matthew—"she will birth many children for you, my son. All in time." Matthew lowered his head. All he wanted was for Amanda to heal and recover. He didn't care if they ever had children!

"How are *you* feeling, Matthew?" the doctor asked quietly. He knew Matthew had been given twenty lashes; everyone did, knowing it was a traditional punishment for disobedience in the village. He also had witnessed Pastor dragging Rachel into the church and had a suspicion that Rachel's loss of the baby had nothing to do with her body's readiness. But he wouldn't share this information with Matthew.

"I'm fine," Matthew stated, his voice dull and flat.

"I have some ointment that will help with the burning," the doctor offered.

"No," he said sharply. "I don't want anything."

They were silent again. Soon the doctor stood and stretched his back, feeling as old as he was. "All right, Matthew," he said softly. "I will take my leave now." Matthew stood, walking him out. At the door, the doctor turned to Matthew and took his hand in his own.

"She'll be fine," he assured him. "I will return in the morning to check on her, but just stay by her side. If she wants a drink, give it to her but I doubt she'll want any food. What she has gone through is very painful, physically and mentally. Shall I send for your mother?"

"No," he said quietly. "I want to be alone with her right now. You can bring her with you in the morning." The doctor nodded and said his good-byes.

Matthew walked slowly toward the bedroom. He leaned against the doorframe and watched Amanda sleeping. The same thoughts bombarded his conscience. He did this to her. He brought her here, torturing her with his way of life. If they weren't here, she never would have lost the baby.

He pushed off the frame and walked slowly to the bedside. Leaning over, he gently lifted her limp hand into his own, rubbing her skin softly with his thumb. She looked so helpless. What have I done? Tears formed in his eyes, and he lowered himself to his knees next to the bed.

"Oh, Amanda," he whispered, bringing her small hand to his lips. "What have I done to you?" He rested his head on the bed, and suddenly he remembered the bruises he had seen on her body. What had happened to her? Matthew stood abruptly. His quick movement shook the bed, and Amanda stirred. Her eyes fluttered open.

"Matthew," she whispered hoarsely. His eyes flew to her face.

"I'm sorry I woke you," he said softly, kneeling back down. She turned her face to his, licking her dry lips.

"What time is it?" she asked softly.

"A little after three," he replied. "Are you in any pain?" She broke eye contact with him and looked away. "Amanda? I need to know, hon."

Then she turned back to him. "Only a little," she said softly.

"Would you like some water?" he asked, but she shook her head.

"No, thank you."

"Matthew?"

"Yeah?"

"It was the baby, wasn't it?" she asked sadly. Matthew hesitated.

"Yes," he whispered. "You had a miscarriage." Even in the shadows, Matthew could see the tears shine in her eyes. She was silent for a few moments.

"Isn't it strange," she said, "that the day after I found out that I was pregnant, I lose the baby?" Matthew remained silent. "Maybe God heard me when I said I wasn't ready to have a baby," she said quietly.

Matthew squeezed her hand, "That's not it at all!" he exclaimed. "God would never punish you, Amanda!"

She searched his face in the dark. "No?" she asked. "If he's not punishing me, then why am I here? Isn't being kidnapped, forced to be married and live here, where I don't belong, punishment? If I'm not being punished then you explain to me why I . . . why I . . ." She broke off, her voice shaking with tears. She grabbed the covers and turned her back to Matthew. Matthew reached out to touch her shoulder but then pulled back. She didn't want him to touch her, he was sure of it.

"Amanda," he spoke softly as he stood up. "God didn't do this to you. I did. My people did. I believed, I always believed that the way my people lived was the right way. I always did, until you. This isn't how God wants us to live. I've been so blind." He tipped his head up, looking at the ceiling. "No, God didn't do this to you, Amanda." He closed his eyes. "I'm so sorry, but it's me that you have to blame." Emotion overwhelmed him, and he left the room abruptly.

Amanda lay on her side, listening to him leave. She squeezed her eyes tightly, her heart aching. Her misery was complete, and a heaviness had fallen upon her. She just wanted all the hurt to go away.

CHAPTER 23

Matthew sat on his front porch steps and stared up at the stars. He, too, felt pretty low. He loved Amanda so much, and it was killing him to see her spirit dying in front of him. He needed to take her away from here. But how? Would Jimmy help? Could he trust telling anyone? Matthew shook his head, thinking to himself, knowing he couldn't involve anyone else. He wouldn't ever want to put anyone else in such danger. If they were caught, death was imminent. Matthew knew now that his pastor wouldn't hesitate to have him and Amanda erased from this life. If they were to escape on foot, could Amanda handle it? Her body was so weak from all the abuse she has endured since he brought her here that he questioned her strength. Especially now, after the miscarriage. Where would they go? If he brought her home, would he lose her for good? Would she learn to hate him, once she had her freedom? He ran his hand through his hair. He realized it didn't matter. It was a chance he had to take because he loved her too much to see her suffer any more. He would rather lose her to her old life than see her like this.

The night animals were moving about in the woods nearby; the tree frogs were calling to their mates. Matthew noticed how serene the night was around him, yet he was filled with so much turmoil. He sat there on his porch until the sun rose, deep in his own thoughts.

Not long after daybreak, his mother came hurrying toward him, the doctor trailing behind.

"My god, Matthew," She grabbed his extended hand. "What more can she take? How are you? Are you all right?"

Matthew shook his head and stood up. "No, Mom," he said sadly. "I'm watching Amanda's spirit die before me. I'm killing her by keeping her here."

"She lost the baby then?" she spoke softly. He nodded, fighting back his own tears. "We really didn't even have time to get used to the baby . . . and now she's . . . well, you can see for yourself." He stepped back and allowed his mother to walk in ahead of him, just as the doctor reached the steps.

"Morning, Matthew," he greeted. "How did she do during the night?"

Shaking his head, he said, "The best she could, I suppose." Nodding somberly, the doctor followed him in.

They walked to the bedroom, the door already opened, with Katherine standing quietly by the bed, watching Amanda sleep soundly. In the morning light, Katherine could see how pale she was, dark circles so prominent under her eyes, only adding color to the injury she had already sustained from the pastor. Reaching over, she rubbed Amanda's cheek gently with her fingertips. Maybe she waited too long, Katherine thought to herself. Maybe she should have pushed Matthew a little harder to realize he had to leave. Was it too late? Was Amanda's spirit truly crushed? Lord, please let her have at least a little fight left, she prayed. Sadly she turned, giving the doctor the room he needed, and joined Matthew in the other room.

She found him slouched in a chair, staring at nothing in particular. It hurt her to see her son so depressed. She sat down across from him. "Matthew?" she said his name, trying to get his attention. He slowly met her eyes. "I have to tell you something. Something important." He noticed the seriousness of her tone, but his expression remained impassive. "From the first moment you returned to the village with Amanda, I noticed a difference in you. For the first time, I saw a light in your eyes that you've been missing since your father died. I believe that you felt strongly for Amanda from the beginning." His attention caught by this, Matthew sat up and rested his elbows on his knees and nodded.

"I believe I did," he admitted softly.

"Then I began to notice that you started to actually see things for what they really were. You had never had a relationship with anyone from the outside world, so you never doubted the way we live here. You accepted this way of life to be the only way of life, but then," She moved from the chair to kneel in front of him. Taking his hands into her own, she looked up at her beloved child. He searched his mother's face, her face glowing with love for him. "Then you brought Amanda here, and I knew that God had answered my prayers. She has been my miracle! She's *your* saving grace!"

Matthew's eyebrows came together in confusion.

"I don't understand," he began. Shaking her head, she put a finger to her lips, silencing him as the doctor stepped out of the bedroom. They both looked up at him. Sighing tiredly, he said, "She'll recover physically much quicker than emotionally, I'm afraid"—rubbing a hand through his white hair—"I've seen this before. It'll pass, in time." His voice was compassionate. Matthew stood up and shook his hand.

"Thank you, Doc," he said, "for everything." Nodding sadly, the doctor left the cabin. Returning to his seat, his eyes settled on his mother.

Continuing, she said, "From the time that you were a baby, I prayed for a way out of the village. Your father and I were very close to leaving, but then the accident changed everything. After his death, I continued to pray. But a different prayer. Not one for me, but for you. I prayed for a way out for you. There's so much to see, so much to experience, Matthew! The world is full of sinners, yes, but we're all sinners here too. The only perfect, sinless person was Christ, and you know that! I know what the world has to offer you and now Amanda had made this all a possibility. Without her in your life, you would never have seen the truth about the ways of the village, and I am so thankful for that." Pausing, she brought her hands to her mouth, then down again. "I have been planning, Matthew."

"Planning for what?" he asked, overwhelmed by all that she was telling him.

"For the day that you will leave," she said quietly. Matthew searched her face, confused.

"Mom, what are you talking about? How did you know that I would ever think about leaving?" he asked.

She smiled up at him. "A mother knows her son," was all she said, standing up and walking to the other side of the room. "I have money. I have supplies, and I have a way out for you and Amanda."

"Mom, you're scaring me," Matthew said impatiently, standing and walking over to her. "What are you saying? You have a way for Amanda and me to leave? That, in itself, is too much for me to comprehend. But you expect me to leave . . . *without you?*"

Katherine nodded, a small smile on her face.

"Matthew, my life is here now. This is all that I have known for the past twenty-three years. I've lived here longer than I have out there and I wouldn't know the first thing about living out there anymore."

"But what makes you think that I'm going to know how to live?" he asked, taking his mother's hands in his own. "We can learn together."

"If your father were alive things would have been so different," she spoke softly, her eyes shining with unshed tears. "The world has nothing to offer me anymore." Matthew shook his head vehemently.

"I don't believe that!" he stated. "What about me? I need you!"

"I have loved like I will never love again," she continued in her soft tone. "I desire nothing more out of life than the simplicity that I have come to accept. My hopes and dreams are for your future, Matthew. Yours and your children."

"But, Mom, even you know that the teachings and the rules here are absurd!" he exclaimed. "I know that you do."

"Yes, I do," she said, "but they are harmless to me. I do my duties and I do them well. I love the Lord, regardless of how angry Pastor can preach. I read my Bible, and I know my god. I will live my life here, and I will die here. And when I do, I will be buried beside my husband, your father."

"Mom," he began, "you're not being rational!" His own eyes were tearing. "I can't leave you, I just can't. You have to come, Mom, I won't go without you!"

"I'm desperate for you to see the real world," she exclaimed passionately, her fists coming to rest on her chest. "To discover the possibilities and to experience what the world has to offer. The wonders of the world are endless!"

Matthew shook his head at her silently. "You said that your hopes are for my future and my children?" Continuing, when she nodded, he said, "What about your grandchildren, Mom? Don't you want to be there for them at least?"

"Son, my life will be complete, knowing that you are free from this place, and safe. But especially that you and Amanda truly love each other." Matthew turned and ran his hand through his hair. "I know that you will love your children as I have loved you."

"Amanda's special," he spoke softly, "but when freedom is granted, will our love survive?" He turned back. "What if she doesn't love me? She won't need me *out* there. What if she decides that she never wants to see me again? I'm the one that kidnapped her in the first place!"

"She would never decide that," a soft whisper came from the bedroom doorway. Katherine and Matthew turned in surprise to see Amanda leaning against the doorframe.

"Amanda, you shouldn't be out of bed." Matthew hurried toward her, but she held up her hand, stopping him midway.

"I do love you," she said softly. "I'll always love you!"

His heart melted, and he took her into his arms, holding her close.

"You see, my son," Katherine spoke from behind him. "What the two of you have is very special. Amanda would not desert you."

He walked Amanda to the sofa and helped her to sit. She had wrapped herself in the quilt that had covered the bed. Her face was pale and still bruised, but Matthew loved her with all his heart. He sat down next to her, taking her hand in his own.

"Is this really going to happen?" Amanda asked both of them. Matthew hesitated, looking down at their hands that were entwined. Katherine sat down in a chair across from them.

"Yes, Amanda," she said quietly. "If Matthew agrees, of course. I have everything ready." They both turned to Matthew.

Matthew looked up at his wife's battered face and then silently turned to his mother's sweet expectant face and sighed.

"I know we need to leave," he began quietly. "I can't watch as my wife is abused and I'm helpless to stop it, but I don't want to leave you, Mom."

"But, Matthew, this is what I want," she explained softly. Amanda felt the struggle that was being fought within him, and she knew that she couldn't persuade him one way or the other. It had to be his decision because there could be no regrets.

He turned to Amanda, meeting her eyes. Surprised as he was, with the abuse she had endured and the miscarriage, he saw a small glimmer of hope. Nothing in this world could make him take that hope from her.

"All right," he consented. "We'll go."

Amanda walked into the cabin, a bunch of wildflowers in her hand and a basket of berries. Entering the kitchen, she placed them on the table and set the berries in the sink to wash them. She reached above her and took a small glass vase off the shelf and filled it with water then set the flowers in it, placing it in the center of the table. Smiling, she returned to the sink.

It had been two months since the miscarriage. Surprisingly, Amanda still carried a sadness in her heart; though she hadn't been ready for a baby, losing it was even worse. Last week the doctor had examined her, looking for signs of infection and scar tissue. He gave her a good report that she wouldn't have any problems having other children, and Amanda's spirit soared. Amanda couldn't understand herself anymore, and she just stopped trying to understand her feelings and behaviors. After suffering such a loss, she now longed to have a baby. Not just any baby, Matthew's baby.

Bending down below her to another cabinet, she took out a colander and placed it in the sink. She turned the water on, humming a hymn, and dumped the berries in the colander. After they were washed, she wiped her wet hands on a dish towel that hung on a nail by the sink. She then took out the ingredients she needed to make muffins. Matthew loved her berry muffins, and he was working hard over at the furniture shop. She mixed the ingredients and put them in the warm oven. After washing her hands again, she turned to leave the kitchen. Deciding to work outside while the muffins cooked, she walked to the door, her eyes falling on the brown crate. Averting her eyes, she walked out onto the porch, picked up her broom, and began sweeping.

The brown crate. In the crate, two backpacks held clothing, nonperishable food, and some personal items—mostly Matthew's that he wanted to bring with him when they left the village. Amanda had put some things that were special to her too. A shawl that Katherine had made for her, a trinket box Sarah had given her, and a few of Matthew's baby clothes Katherine had given her for their next baby. When the crate was removed, it would be the sign that it was time to go. The crate would be loaded onto the delivery truck that would bring furniture and goods into the city.

Matthew and Amanda would wait until dark, then they would slip into the truck and hide in a bureau that was just big enough for the two of them. In appearances, the bureau was the same as the others that were made. But Matthew had crafted this particular one himself, making an inside lock so that the doors could not be opened by someone on the outside once they were locked inside. When they reached the city, they would then leave the truck and slip away. This was the plan that had been made for them, and it was reviewed several times, always in secrecy.

Amanda stopped sweeping and looked up, her eyes scanning the valley. *It was so beautiful here*, she thought. If only they weren't part of the village, this would be a perfect home. She would miss seeing the valley and how the seasons transformed it. Sighing, she finished sweeping then returned to the kitchen. Removing the muffins, she allowed them to cool then placed them in the basket, covering them with a red checkered cloth.

She left the cabin and walked down her small road. Before she reached the village, she turned and walked into the woods. Matthew had shown her a shortcut to the other end of the village. She was so thankful not to have to walk through the village; though surprisingly enough, after Amanda's and Matthew's punishment, life went on like the abuse had never happened. They both continued to go to work and church services, the villagers behaving the same as they always have. Even the Doc or Simon, who had saved her that dreadful day, treated her and Matthew as if nothing out of the ordinary had happened.

It was very difficult for Amanda to face the pastor again. She feared him even more than before, which she didn't think possible. Matthew never allowed her to come within ten feet of him, making sure that he would never touch her again. But he watched her, she knew. She had caught him a few times, and the look in his eyes made her shiver. She still hadn't been able to talk about the attack to Matthew, and she didn't know if she would ever be able to share such humiliation.

It angered Amanda at first, this chosen ignorance. But then she realized that it would have been harder if everyone had treated them differently. So Matthew and Amanda resumed their life. Amanda accepted that knowing she was going home gave her the strength and the will to continue this life.

She began to hum again as she walked on the path. To think that she was going to see her parents again soon was nearly enough for Amanda to burst, though she realized that she had to keep her excitement smothered and for herself alone. Admittedly, she has mixed feelings about leaving—she would miss Katherine, who still refused to leave, and Sarah and Jimmy, along with some of the other women she had come to know. She would miss the secret place Matthew had made for himself, and the beautiful view outside their cabin. But home . . . the yearning for home was so much more powerful.

Stepping out from the trees, the furniture shop loomed before her. She entered the building, nodding her head at the men that she passed. She saw Matthew working on a chair in the far corner. He was carving an intricate design, concentrating intently, not realizing she was there. Smiling, she was instantly filled with warm feelings as she watched him. She walked slowly toward him, and he caught a glimpse of her as she did.

Looking up, he smiled. "Hey, you!" he greeted her warmly. "What brings you here?" He stuck out his hand, and she slipped her hand into his; pulling her gently toward him, he kissed her tenderly on the lips. When they parted, Amanda couldn't help feeling disappointed. He must have seen this, because he chuckled. "Now don't make me leave my work now because you know I will." She blushed slightly and smiled.

"I brought you some berry muffins," she said softly. "I thought you could take a break."

He smiled. "Sure, I can," he said. "Let's go outside." He grabbed a cloth from the workbench and wiped his hands, dusting himself off. He stopped and said something to Jimmy. Jimmy smiled, nodded his greeting to Amanda, then turned back to his work.

They stepped out into the sunlight, Matthew taking her hand, leading her over to a fallen tree they used as a bench. He straddled the log, letting go of Amanda's hand as she settled herself. She placed the basket before him, and he smiled as he reached in and grabbed a muffin.

"Mmm," he said as he bit into the still-warm muffin. Smiling, she let him finish his treat, looking around at the trees that surrounded them, breathing in the fresh summer air. "How are you?" Matthew asked as he finished his second helping.

She turned to her husband. "I'm good," she replied honestly. "It's so beautiful today."

"Yes," he said. He reached over and touched her cheek gently. "Amanda?" She lifted her eyes to him; the affection he saw there was nearly his undoing. "You know how much I love you, right?"

She smiled and nodded. "Yes," she whispered.

"I need to tell you something." Swallowing, he wiped his mouth with a napkin. "I found out today we're still being watched," he said quietly. Her smile disappeared.

"Still?" she asked, the color draining from her face.

"Yes," he said, hating the information he had to share. "Jimmy overheard James, Pastor's assistant, asking questions. Questions about us." Amanda looked away.

"Oh, Matthew," she said, shaking her head, "I can't . . ."

"Shhhh," he said gently putting his fingers to her lips. "Amanda, we're still leaving." The last word was a whisper. "I'm telling you only because we're going to have to be extra careful, okay?" She took a deep shaky breath and tried to smile. Relief couldn't come close to describing what she felt at that moment. "I expected as much. This is all part of our probation and I should have known it would last this long."

He pulled her into his arms so that her back rested against his chest. Wrapping his arms around her, he squeezed her gently.

"Did you think I was going back on my promise?" he asked softly in her ear, his warm breath sending shivers through her.

She shook her head. "I didn't think that you would, just that," she began, "something would happen to *make* you break your promise. I'm just so nervous that it won't happen, and I'm a little scared if it does." She admitted to him.

"But you want this, Amanda?" he asked quietly. "This is what you've wanted, right?"

"Yes." She didn't hesitate. "But . . ." She tried to gather her thoughts.

"What is it?"

She leaned her head back against his chest.

"I'm so different," she finally admitted softly. "I'm not the same person I was before . . . well, before I came here."

Matthew was silent as she turned in his arms so that she could look at him.

"My god, Matthew, I'm married!" She smiled at him. He smiled in return and touched her cheek softly with two of his fingers.

"Yes," he said, "you are."

Her smile faltered slightly, and a sadness filled her eyes.

"I'll never be the same person I was," she said quietly. "I can never go back." She looked away. "I wonder though. Do you think that I'll still be interested in the things that I was before I came here?" she asked, looking back up at him. He, too, had turned serious.

"I do," he said. "I think that I forced you to grow in ways that you probably would have taken years to do. I think"—he hesitated, looked away, then back again—"that I scarred and hurt you, but you are still the same person, Amanda." Searching his face, she weighed his words in her mind. *She was scarred and hurt, devastated and confused, but did he do this to her?* In truth, partly, but only out of ignorance. She could not hold him responsible for what has happened to her. Maybe she was blinded by her love for Matthew, but she wouldn't blame him.

"Matthew," she whispered; he looked down into her shining eyes. "You didn't do this to me. You didn't know any better." He looked away, clenching his jaw.

"Amanda," he started to say, his voice gruff, "I'm almost twenty-four years old. I've been out there." He waved his hand toward the trees. "I see how the world works out there, and I saw how the world works here. I chose to ignore the village's way. I chose to—"

"No!" she interrupted. "You were taught to choose that way." She lifted her hand and touched his cheek. "You accepted the only way of life you were taught and I will not accept anything else, do you understand? You are just as much of a victim as I am. I love you, Matthew. Please know that I don't blame you!"

She threw her arms around his neck before he could respond. He slowly wrapped his arms around her waist. "Oh, Amanda," he whispered, closing his eyes tightly. "I love you too." She truly loved him, almost as much as he loved her. She pulled back and smiled up at him tearfully.

"Now have another muffin, or I'll think that you don't like my baking." she teased him. He chuckled and watched his wife in amazement as she reached into the basket and handed him a muffin with the sweetest smile on her face.

"What do you mean?" he exclaimed. "I love your baking! I tell you that all the time."

"No, not all the time."

"I do too!"

"No, you don't."

"Yes, I do," he exclaimed, reaching to her side and tickling her.

"Matthew!" She laughed, and they continued laughing and teasing one another until he had to return to work.

CHAPTER 24

I t would be another month before they could leave, but the day finally came. It was a hot, humid day in August. Amanda came home from the Women's Center, her shirt drenched, her hair damp. It had been a long day over the sewing machines, and all she wanted to do was wash up and change her clothes. She was already unbuttoning her blouse as she entered her cabin.

She came to an abrupt stop when she saw Matthew standing in the living area, waiting. He was looking at her, her damp hair, her shirt unbuttoned, the light perspiration on her chest, and the slight swell of her breasts—and he never wanted her more than right that minute.

"Matthew!" she exclaimed, startled, and then smiled. She quickly closed her shirt, only slightly embarrassed. He smiled and met her across the room, taking her hands and gently removing them from her shirt.

"I liked it just the way it was," he teased and slowly opened her shirt to where it was but going a step farther by undoing the rest of the buttons.

"Matthew," she whispered, a small smile playing on her lips. He traced his finger down the opening of her shirt and leaned down and kissed her tenderly on the lips. Fire burned in Amanda's abdomen; moaning, she stepped closer to him. He slipped his arm around the small of her back and pulled her against him. Deepening the kiss, she clung to him passionately. Moments later, Matthew was leading her into their bedroom. After undressing her all the way, he pushed her gently to the bed so she fell back softly. He quickly undressed and lay down next to her, pulling her into his arms. He looked lovingly into her eyes and kissed her again.

"God, Amanda, I need you," he whispered.

"I need you too," she whispered in return.

They both clung to each other tenderly, passionately, and desperately during their lovemaking. Their desires sated, Matthew was lying over her, planting small kisses on her face, whispering sweet words to her. It was only after Amanda's mind began to function again that she realized he was home early.

"Matthew, why—" she began as he kissed her mouth, stopping her words.

"It's tonight," he said softly, continuing his kisses.

"What's to—" Amanda's body stiffened as realization set in.

"Tonight?" she gasped. Matthew stopped kissing her and looked down into her eyes, his mood serious.

"Yes. It's tonight. The crate has already been loaded." He rolled over and lay on his back, one arm behind his head. She turned to her side, laying her hand on his chest.

"It's really happening," she said, multiple feelings shooting through her. "I can't believe it."

Matthew said nothing as he watched Amanda's reaction. He watched the different emotions play in her eyes, still silent, even when her eyes met his.

"Katherine?" she said softly.

"Will be here for dinner, and we will finalize everything," he said quietly, his expression unreadable.

"Dinner?" she exclaimed. "Then she'll be here any minute! Look at me!" She scrambled from the bed and hurried into the bathroom. Moments later, Matthew heard the shower running, and he stared up at the ceiling. Several emotions ran through him, and he didn't know which one to deal with first.

His mother had found him this morning as he was walking to the furniture shop. She had stepped out of the trees, as he traveled along the path. "Matthew." She had come from around a tree, motioning for him to follow her. Initially startled, he then followed. Walking about a quarter of a mile into the woods, Katherine had stopped and turned to her son. She searched his face, soaking in his strong features, crystal blue eyes, and rugged appearance. He watched his mother look at him, and suddenly, deep in his gut, he knew why she was here.

"Mom?" he said, forcing himself to start the beginning of the end of his life here.

She nodded, seeing the understanding in his eyes. "It's time." Matthew looked around them, in all directions, before he brought his eyes back to his mother.

"What's the plan?" he asked quietly, a terrible sadness filling him. His mother gave him a watery smile and reached up, cupping his face with her small hand.

"All will be well, you'll see," she said softly, her own heart breaking. Matthew clenched his jaw and pulled his mother roughly into his arms, holding her close, tears burning the backs of his eyes. How was he going to do this?

"When did life get so complicated?" he whispered to her. She softly rubbed the back of his hair.

"When we realize that life isn't so simple," she replied, pulling back, taking her son's face in her hands. "As you know, the truck is being loaded today. You're bureau needs to be on it. I was able to get a hold of the inventory sheet, and the furniture order form." She shook her head. "Don't ask. I slipped the piece in with a special order for Williamson's. Of course, we both know that they didn't order it, but you'll be long gone before that mistake is noticed." She let go of him and reached down into her skirt pocket, pulling out an envelope. She opened his hand and placed the envelope in it. "There should be enough money in here to sustain you for a little while. When it's gone, you'll be on your own." He folded the envelope and stuck it in his back pocket, taking her hands into his own.

"Mom, I can't do this without you!" he declared softly. "Please come with us."

She gave him a reassuring smile. "Yes, you can. You're going to have your own family now. Your responsibility is to Amanda, to yourself, and to my future grandchildren. This is my wish, Matthew." Unable to hold back his tears, they streamed down his cheeks, knowing her decision was final. He hugged her again for only a few more moments before she gently pushed him away.

"Go to work," she said, "before they wonder where you are. Be sure that you act no different than you normally would. I will be by for dinner tonight, and we will go over everything one more time." He nodded, wiping his face on his sleeve.

"Mom—" he began again, but she shook her head and pointed in the direction that they came.

"Go, Matthew, I will see you tonight." Reluctantly he turned and walked to work, not looking back. Katherine watched him walk away and then tilted her head slightly toward the sky. "He's just like you, John," she whispered to her deceased husband. "Now he'll have the chance that was stolen from us. Watch over your baby." She slowly walked back to the village.

The water from the shower shut off, bringing Matthew's thoughts back to the present. "You're going home, Amanda," he whispered to the empty room. Then he, too, went into the bathroom to wash up.

Two hours later, Katherine was standing at the door. Matthew held her hands again, tears in his eyes, and she was smiling through her own tears.

"Well, this is it," she said softly. "You have the money I gave you, and the maps?" He nodded.

"Mom, please come with us?" he pleaded one more time. She shook her head.

"No, son," she said. "This is your time." She paused. "Now remember to keep an open mind. You'll see things that will make you want to judge the way we judge things here. You can't do that out there and oh, there's so much to see, Matthew!" Her eyes shone with the excitement that she felt for him. "Your father would be so proud of you, and the man that you've become."

Tears trickled down Matthew's face.

"I'm coming back for you," he said firmly. "When we're settled, I'm coming back for you and I don't care what you say." Katherine only smiled sadly. She pulled her son's face down and kissed both of his cheeks.

"I will always love you, and I will always be with you, as will the Lord. The Lord will guide you through this, and He will be your strength," she spoke softly to both of them. Setting her eyes on Amanda, she smiled, reaching out her hand, and Amanda grasped it, her own face wet with tears.

"Stand by your husband, Amanda," she spoke softly. "Things will be difficult when you return to your old life with a husband. Remember the love that you both share and how strong that bond is. Never let it be broken." Amanda nodded, crying. Letting go of Amanda's hand, she touched her tearstained cheek. "You're a strong and courageous young woman. Not just anyone could have survived what you have these past nine months. I am proud of you, and I know that you'll be a wonderful mother to my grandchildren."

Then she turned to leave.

"Mom, wait!" Matthew called, but she turned back holding up her hand.

"No," she spoke softly but firmly. "The longer I stay the harder it will become to let go. I love you, Matthew, with all my heart. Don't forget me, and all that I've taught you. You're a wonderful son, and you've always made me proud of you. Good-bye." She kissed her hand and blew him a kiss, then the door closed behind her. Matthew took a step toward the door and stopped. His back became rigid, his jaw clenched, he turned and abruptly walked into their bedroom.

Amanda watched helplessly as he tried to deal with his pain, and she felt even worse because she was the cause. She put her face in her hands and sobbed. *This was terrible,* she thought, *it wasn't supposed to be like this! Going home was supposed to be a happy occasion, but her heart felt like it was breaking all over again!*

The sun was beginning to set as Amanda watched from the front porch steps, her chin resting in her hands. Her eyes were dry; her head and heart ached. She knew the sunset was a spectacular show of pink and orange rays shining behind the clouds, but she felt numb inside. Behind her the door creaked open, and Matthew stepped out, coming to sit down next to her. She kept her eyes forward, unsure of how he felt.

"We should get ready to go," he said quietly. Amanda didn't move nor speak for a few moments. Her world seemed so confusing, and painful.

"Matthew," she began, her voice shaking with emotion. "I was thinking . . . I was thinking of how much you mean to me and I don't know how I could live"—she swallowed—"without you, but if you want to stay, I'd understand and—"

"No, Amanda," he interrupted her. He stood, taking her arms in his hands, and pulled her up with him. "My life is with you—we're in this together, you and me. I won't stay here or send you away." She nodded tearfully as he pulled her into his arms. "You're everything to me, Amanda."

"And you to me," she said. "I'm so scared."

"I am too," he said quietly, "but everything is going to be all right." Holding her hand, he led her back into the cabin. Amanda straightened things around the cabin, restless and anxious. The tension in the small cabin was thick, both Amanda and Matthew deep in their own thoughts that they hardly spoke. They both went to bed, knowing it would be several hours until they would walk through the woods, but neither of them slept. Finally it was time; they took care of last-minute needs, and within minutes, they were walking in the woods along the path that led to the furniture shop. It was a dark night, but Matthew was confident in his footing. They scanned the area before stepping out of the woods. Matthew led her carefully to the truck and helped her up then jumped up next to her. The bureau was located in the middle, the crate next to it; Matthew helped load it himself. He opened the door and helped Amanda slip in. She sat down in the tight compartment, and Matthew stepped in next to her. He situated himself and slowly turned the lock from the inside. Amanda's heart was beating so loudly she could barely hear anything else. They were both silent, their breathing the only sound in the closed space.

Amanda's eyes began to adjust, and she reached out and grabbed Matthew's hand, squeezing it tightly. He understood her fear and squeezed her hand back, trying to reassure her. Talking was too much of a risk, a risk neither of them was going to make.

Neither one of them slept that night, and when dawn finally decided to come, Amanda and Matthew were in pain from their uncomfortable confinement. The delivery crew arrived right on time, and they both held their breath as they double-checked the truckload. Matthew knew the men—Jeremiah, Phillip, and Paul, having worked with them since he was a boy. They were good, hardworking men, but very loyal to the pastor. If Matthew and Amanda were caught, the men would not hesitate to turn them in. They sat stiff with fear and apprehension as they listened to them exchange lighthearted banter, the laughing, and then finally, the engine starting, and then the truck was moving. It was then that they began to breathe again. Amanda looked at Matthew, tears of joy shining in her eyes. *She was going home!*

He gave her a small smile, took her hand, and brought it to his lips, kissing it softly. This was it; there was no turning back now.

CHAPTER 25

A little more than two hours later, Amanda could hear the sounds of civilization. Other vehicles could be heard, and people talking to one another, and before long, the truck stopped. Amanda looked to Matthew, who had his fingers to his lips, telling her to be quiet. The delivery men left the vehicle and were talking amongst themselves. They couldn't hear what they were saying, but Matthew knew the routine. He had made this run more than a dozen times in his life. They left early, always arriving before the factory was open, giving them the excuse to visit the coffee shop across the street. In thirty minutes, they would return and begin unloading the truck.

Laughter and talking among the men began to fade as they walked away from the truck. Matthew struggled to stand, his face contorting in pain from being stuck in one position for so long. He slowly turned the key and opened the door quietly. He could see the three men crossing the street. He needed to get Amanda and himself off the truck and behind the building before the men were seated at the coffee counter. The large window in the shop always gave a clear view of the truck.

He stepped out and turned to take Amanda's hand. She bit on her lip as pain shot through her own limbs, but stepped out with him. He quickly lifted the crate, removed the backpacks, and set the crate back in its original position. He jumped over the side of the truck that was facing an alley and turned to lift Amanda down. Taking her hand, they ran as fast as they could down the alley to the back of the furniture factory. The backside of the property was shadowed by a large wooded hill. Matthew led them in this direction, running through the brush, using his arm to shield them from the branches that tried to block the way. Up they went, breathing hard and struggling, their energy almost gone, fear being their only driving force. When they reached the top, slightly over the hill, they stopped, both dropping to the ground. Unable to speak to one another, they both were lying on their backs, gasping for air.

Several minutes later, Matthew turned his head to Amanda.

"Are you all right?" he asked hoarsely. Still trying to regain her normal breathing, she nodded. He reached for her hand and squeezed it. "We'll wait. We'll wait until they make the delivery, then we'll go back down. We don't want to take the chance of them taking an unplanned tour of the city, seeing us on the street."

Amanda looked up at the sky, the trees blowing in the wind, the sunlight sparkling through. The sky was a brilliant blue, the clouds white as snow, and they were running for their lives . . . literally. It seemed so surreal, the beauty of the day and the seriousness of their situation. She felt Matthew's hand holding her own and felt safe.

"Should we change now?" she asked quietly, finally being able to talk. Katherine had managed to find "worldly" clothes for the two of them. Though they had asked how, she had refused to tell them. She informed them that they would stand out in their black attire, and she had been right. He sat up, turning on to his knees, and crawled to the top of the hill. The truck was still parked where it was, a sign that they were still at the coffee shop.

"Yes," he agreed. They both opened up the backpacks and pulled out jeans, plain white t-shirts, and sneakers. Amanda hadn't worn jeans for over nine months. She smiled as she held them in her hand.

"What are you smiling at?" he asked, looking down at his own clothes.

"I miss jeans." She smiled. "It's been so long."

"I've never worn anything other than our black clothes," he said, somewhat to himself. Amanda watched her husband as he began to unbutton his shirt and remove it, his chest shining with perspiration. As he pulled the white t-shirt on over his head, he caught her watching him, not missing the adoring look in her eyes. He smiled.

"Amanda," he teased, "are you going to get changed?" Her cheeks flushed slightly, and she nodded. She stood up and began unbuttoning her own clothes.

Several minutes later, they were dressed and the black clothes shoved into their bags. Amanda couldn't help but admire Matthew in the clothes. He was looking over the hill, when she came up behind him, hugging his waist.

"You look wonderful in these clothes," she said softly. "It's so nice to see you in 'normal' clothes." He turned in her arms, holding her close and looking down into her face, their blue eyes connecting. He searched her face, his eyes caressing her with tenderness.

"There's so much I don't know about," he began softly, hating to admit to ignorance in anything. "About how to live out here. I spent a lot of time out here but only when I was observing you. And even then, we restricted ourselves as much as possible from 'worldly' things." She smiled up at him.

"I'll show you," she said softly. "But now you have to stop referring to everything as 'worldly'. Out here, it's all normal."

His brows came together in dismay. "Right," he said and stepped slowly out of their embrace. "Normal." Turning, he looked over the hill again, Amanda watching him. "They're unloading the truck. It won't be long now." He pulled the map that Katherine had made for them out of his bag. "And according to this map, the bus station is two blocks . . . that way." He pointed to the east, turning to her, seeing her watching him. He knew why. This was going to be so difficult for him, just as it was for her to live his way of life. How could he express that to her, knowing what she had suffered? She stepped toward him again.

"Matthew, are you scared?" she asked him. He looked away, into the dense woods, searching for something, yet nothing. He slowly turned back to her, knowing she was waiting for an answer.

"No more than you were," he said. She was caught by surprise. *That's what he was feeling,* she thought, *that he had no right to be afraid after what she experienced.*

"There's a difference, Matthew," she said softly. "There's no restriction here, no confinement. The freedom is exhilarating!" She sat down on the ground, hugging her knees. "But I have to admit, I'm a little scared myself." He slowly joined her on the ground.

"Why?" he asked. "This is what you've waited for."

She nodded, agreeing with him. "But remember when I said that I was different?" He nodded, remembering the conversation outside the furniture shop. "Well, what if everyone thinks I act different, even strange for that matter? I mean, when I first came to the village, I thought everything was strange about it. Then I had to live there. What if I've picked up strange behaviors, too, not even realizing it?"

"Well," Matthew began, "you'll have to stop walking into rooms backward." His eyes were lit with humor. She laughed at him, slapping him lightly.

"That's not funny!" She smiled, and he chuckled.

"I don't think that you have anything to be afraid of," he said, becoming serious. "I think that you'll pick up, right where you left off." He picked up a stick and began to peel it. "And your family will be so happy to have you back."

"Yes, they will," she agreed readily, "but they'll have to be happy to have both of us because you're my husband, and I won't accept anything less."

"They won't be pleased to see me," he said solemnly. "I'm the one who took you in the first place."

"I don't care if they are pleased or not," she said haughtily, facing him. "You're my husband!"

Matthew nodded, but he knew that no one was going to be happy to see him. He even had to face the possibility of being arrested. Her family would make it difficult for her, and he knew there was going to be a lot of pressure put on Amanda. He couldn't—no, wouldn't—stand by and watch her suffer because of him. He had already decided that he would leave and disappear before causing her any more pain. Standing up, he looked over the hill.

"They're gone," he said, turning to her. "We'd better go."

They were both filled with anxiety and nervousness; picking up their bags, they began to walk down the hill.

Amanda stared out into the darkness, flashes of headlights reflecting in the bus window. *North Carolina. That's where she had been these nine months,* she thought, shaking her head at no one in particular, feeling so strange. They were going to be in New York in five more hours, and she was completely unprepared for what would happen when she showed up on her parents' doorsteps. She was so excited to see them tears of joy burned in her eyes. So much has happened to her that she didn't know how or where she would begin to tell them or even if she wanted to share her experience in the village. *Maybe she wouldn't,* she thought as she turned to Matthew, who was sleeping in the seat next to her. People wouldn't understand, she knew that already, that she loved Matthew. His hand was draped on her leg as he slept, and she reached down and covered his hand with her own. He was her life, and he'd been her salvation in that place, and it didn't matter who was to blame. She couldn't undo her love for him, and she didn't want to.

Turning back to the dark night, anxious thoughts plagued her conscience, knowing the village knew that they had escaped by now. The pastor would have confronted Katherine first, then Sarah and Jimmy. She said a silent prayer for her friends, knowing the pastor's wrath would be enormous, at such a betrayal. They knew where she lived because they had observed her life. *They knew where to find them; would they come after them? Would they be that bold?* She feared they would but prayed that they wouldn't.

She stifled a yawn, clearly exhausted, pure excitement only had kept her awake this long. Sleep was calling her, and moments later, she rested her head on Matthew's shoulder and fell asleep.

The cab pulled up in front of her parents' house. Amanda could only stare at the beautiful sight. The familiar flower boxes on the windows filled with her mother's favorite flower, impatiens. The sprinkler was spraying the lawn, watering the dry grass that comes at the end of summer. The air was filled with fresh cut grass and buzzing bees. Time seemed to stand still for her. There were several times when she thought that she would never set eyes on this place again. She clumsily opened the door and stepped out of the vehicle, her legs shaky. Matthew paid the driver and slid out after her. He touched her lower back with his hand, letting her know that he was there.

Assuming that both her parents were at home, seeing both their cars in the driveway, she couldn't move for the longest time. Then taking a shaky breath, she walked up the front walkway, holding Matthew's hand tightly at her side. Hesitating at the door, she looked up at Matthew. He smiled encouragingly and nodded his head.

"Matthew," she whispered.

"I know," he whispered back, "I love you, too." She smiled then reached for the doorknob. Tears filled her eyes as the familiar scent of home washed over her.

"Mom! Dad!" she called, her voice tremulous. "I'm home!"

Amanda heard glass break from the other room, and then her mother appeared slowly around the corner. When she saw Amanda standing in the foyer, a sob broke out of her throat, and her hands went up to cover her mouth.

"Dear God!" she cried. "Max!" she screamed. "Max, it's Amanda! Oh my god! It's Amanda!" she sobbed as she met Amanda across the floor.

"Mommy." They clung to each other, crying and laughing.

"Diane, what are you   ," asked Amanda's father as he came down the front staircase. He saw his wife holding the most beautiful sight in the world.

"Amanda!" he gasped. "My god, it is you!"

Amanda looked up, tears streaming down her face.

"Hi, Daddy," she said quietly.

He nearly slid the rest of the way down the stairs; he was in such a hurry. He embraced his wife and daughter and cried shamelessly with them. They touched Amanda's hair, her face, her shoulders, making sure she was real, that she was truly home.

Matthew had stepped outside, allowing them the privacy of Amanda's homecoming. Tears burned his eyes at the raw emotion that was being displayed. He again was dumbfounded with realization of the effect the village's traditions had on families. He should have known! He should have opened his eyes, instead of his blind devotion to his people! Angry with himself and everything he represented, Matthew shoved his hands in his jeans pockets and paced the front walk.

It was several moments later when Amanda pulled back from her parents' embrace. She wiped away her tears, looking adoringly at them.

"I never thought I would see either one of you again," she whispered.

"Amanda, what happened—"

"How did you—," they both began speaking at once. Amanda shook her head, holding up her hand.

"I . . . I will tell you everything," she promised soberly. "But first there's someone that I want you to meet." They watched her, confusion written all over their faces. Amanda stepped outside then returned with a young man at her side. Matthew wore a serious expression and nodded at both of her parents.

"Mom, Dad, I want you to meet Matthew . . . my husband."

Amanda rubbed her face, frustrated. The room was filled with commotion—detectives and police officers all loomed before her. The detective, Sergeant Stevens, had asked her to repeat her story several times, and she was tired. It was early evening, and it had been a long two days. All she wanted to do was lie down next to Matthew. She looked up and moved her head so that she could see him. He was sitting across the room, being questioned by another group of men. He looked up and caught her eye. Though he didn't smile, he winked reassuringly, comforting her.

Her parents sat on either side of her, showing their support. Their reaction to introducing Matthew as her husband was one of shock and anger. Especially when they learned that he was one of the men that had originally abducted her. Yet Amanda stood her ground and wouldn't allow them to attack Matthew. It had taken a few minutes to calm themselves, but they were so happy to have her home, deciding they could talk about it later. In turn, this meant ignoring Matthew as much as they could, not withholding angry glares at every opportunity.

The authorities were called, her father insisted, explaining how hard the city officials worked to find her. He pulled out a scrapbook of all the flyers, missing persons articles, and photographs they had used to try and find her. He even held a video in his hand of news reporters allowing them to plead for her abductors to bring her home, her parents pleading, and interviews with her friends from school.

Amanda looked at these items and felt cold, feeling as if they were talking about someone else. She should have felt grateful that they had worked so hard to bring her home; it's what she had hoped so desperately for, but all she could do was hand these items back to her parents, feeling empty.

It had now been hours, and she had explained to them exactly what happened the night she was taken. The men being in the apartment, the shack, the praying at the church. Then her details turned to just telling them about the village and the disturbing traditions and ways of life. She didn't tell them all that had happened to her—the suicide attempt, her wedding, the river, the abuse she suffered from the pastor, or her miscarriage. *What would come of her telling them all of these things? To make them feel sorry for her? To hurt her parents for not being able to protect her? No, she couldn't and wouldn't do that.*

"Amanda, I know this is hard for you. But I really need to make sure I have all these details correct," Sergeant Stevens said. Amanda nodded.

"I understand," she said quietly.

"The night you were abducted," the detective continued, "you said there were two men in dark clothing in your apartment." She nodded. "Okay, what do you remember after that?"

"I woke up in the cabin or shack," she said, remembering it vividly. She was again repeating the same information over again when she noticed movement on the other side of the room. She looked passed the sergeant and watched in horror as an officer began handcuffing Matthew, reading him his rights. She struggled to stand up; as she did, her parents tried to hold her down.

"No!" she screamed. The room became silent, and everyone turned to watch and see what would unfold. "*What are you doing?*"

"Honey, it's for the best," her mother tried to tell her.

"He kidnapped you, Amanda," her father said, struggling to hold her down. She screamed and hurled her fists.

"Let me go!" Finally receiving as much as abuse as they were willing to take, they let her go. She ran to Matthew and threw her arms around him, crying. Matthew kissed the top of her head.

"Amanda, it's all right." He tried to soothe her quietly.

"No!" she sobbed as she looked up at him, tears pouring down her face. "No, I won't let them take you!" She reached out and shoved at the officers standing around him. "*Get away from him! Leave him alone!*" she growled tearfully.

"Amanda, no!" Matthew yelled. She stopped, looking up at him. "No, baby," he said more quietly. She searched his face desperately. "Listen to me. They need to do this." She was shaking her head tearfully.

"Amanda, honey, let them go," her father said next to her. She turned angrily to him and put up her hand, stopping him from coming closer.

"No!" she said loudly. "You did this, didn't you? You knew, you knew this would happen. *How could you?*" she accused him. She grasped Matthew's shirt. "I won't let them, Matthew."

"Amanda, please listen to me," Matthew said quietly. They looked at one another as though the room full of people did not exist, Amanda's sobs was the only sound in the room. "This is what's right. I'm guilty, hon. Now calm down. Stop crying, Amanda," he said softly, his eyes tenderly taking in every beautiful feature before him. She took deep breaths, trying to stop crying, her chest shuddering. "Now, kiss me before I go." She shook her head.

"Matthew, no, you're not guilty. I won't let them—" "Amanda, you can't stop them," he said, wishing he could hold her in his arms.

"But I'm not pressing charges!" she yelled, turning angrily to the people surrounding her, her eyes meeting her father's. "Daddy, do something! They can't take him, I'm not pressing charges."

Her father who could conquer the world and chase away the monsters in her dreams was speechless. He looked helpless and small at that moment. The sergeant intervened and came to her side.

CHAPTER 26

"Amanda, we just need to bring him down for more questioning," he said in a soothing tone. "We won't press any charges until the morning."

"No!" Amanda snarled. "You won't press any charges. Because I'm not pressing them. He's my husband! You can't take him. I'm an adult and no one in this room can override me! If you don't let him go, I'll change my story and will go to every newspaper in this country, if I have to. And I'll tell them that I went on my own free will, that I ran away to get married, and now you're holding my husband, who's innocent!"

"Amanda," Matthew began. But then she moved so quickly that she startled the men around her. She grabbed the tape recorder that the sergeant had left on the table and quickly ripped out the tape.

"Amanda, don't do that!" The sergeant wasn't as calm as he was a few minutes ago. "That's police property."

"You have no proof that I was kidnapped," Amanda said calmly and ripped the ribbon from the tape, tearing it. The sergeant sighed and rubbed his hands over his tired face.

"I really wish you hadn't done that," he said. "All right, everyone out, and go home. Except you, Mike. Uncuff him and wait outside for me." Amanda began to breathe normally, walking to her husband, standing in front of him. The officer uncuffed him, and Matthew's hands went around his wife and hugged her tightly; she buried her face into his neck. The room cleared out slowly, and her parents watched Amanda with Matthew. When everyone had gone, he spoke to Amanda.

"We don't need you to press charges against Matthew," he said to her. "He broke the law. He committed a felony in the law's eyes, whether you see it that way or not." Amanda pulled away from Matthew and turned to the detective.

"I don't know what you're talking about," she said quietly. "I ran away, to be with Matthew. There's no felony here." Matthew couldn't believe what she was doing. The sergeant again rubbed his face and turned to her parents.

"Max, Diane, I don't know what you want me to do here," he said. Max, Amanda's father, back to normal, joined them in their small circle.

"Amanda, there was a room full of witnesses that heard your story tonight. The destruction of the tape will not be enough to free Matthew," he said compassionately to his daughter. Amanda's courage began to crumble, but she straightened her back and looked directly at both of the men in front of her.

"I *will* do what I said," she said. "I'll go nationwide and tell them that you're all lying. I'll have the public on my side and I'll turn this whole situation into a fiasco."

Everyone stared at her, dumbfounded.

"Amanda," her mother finally spoke up, coming to stand next to her husband. "Honey, why are you doing this? *He* kidnapped you. *He* took you away from *us*, all this time?"

"*He* is my husband!" She began to raise her voice again. "*I love him!*"

"Honey, you're just confused," her mother said softly. "You couldn't possibly know what love is, living under such duress."

Amanda's eyes hardened as they met her mother's eyes.

"Don't tell me that I couldn't possibly know what love is," she stated hotly. "You have no idea who I am. Do *not* presume to know how I feel!" Shocked by her daughter's words, her mother opened her mouth and closed it without a word being spoken. Matthew was just as shocked at Amanda's behavior, not believing how hostile she was treating her parents.

"All right, let's all calm down here." The sergeant tried again. "Let's sit down and talk rationally." After hesitating, Amanda then nodded, and she and Matthew sat down on the loveseat across from her parents. Once they were all seated, the sergeant continued, "Now maybe we can work out some kind of deal." He addressed Amanda directly. "Maybe, if Matthew gives us as much information as he can and helps to lead us to this . . . village . . . then we can let him walk free."

Max and Diane shifted uncomfortably in their seats. The sergeant turned to them. "Will you agree with this?" he asked. "Your daughter has the same strong will as the two of you. A fight in her that I don't know if we're all willing to challenge." Diane turned to Amanda, exasperated.

"Don't you see what he's done?" she exclaimed, giving Matthew a disgusted look. "He's brainwashed you into thinking that you love him. That's what cults do." Amanda clenched her jaw and turned to the sergeant.

"I have your word," she said, "that you won't arrest Matthew as long as he cooperates?" The detective nodded. She stood up and walked over to a desk in the hallway; taking a piece of paper and pen from the drawer, she brought it back to the detective. "I would appreciate that in writing. But wait." She left the room as the detective stared at the paper in surprise, bringing back the officer named Mike. "A witness," she explained to everyone. "Daddy, you're a notary. Could you please find your stamp and notarize this please?" Her father hesitated then stood up to leave the room.

"Maxwell, what are you doing?" Diane asked in surprise. "Notarizing that paper won't mean a damn thing and you know it! You're going along with this?" He looked at his wife and then at his long-lost daughter, nodded, and then walked away. Moments later, he returned, and the paper was written and notarized.

The sergeant shook his head. "A family of lawyers," was all he said.

"Matthew, would you cooperate with them? Would you be willing to help the authorities to capture and arrest the pastor?" Matthew had been listening and watching all that had been taking place around him. During this time, he was thinking about what he would do. Amanda had fought for him as he was about to go to jail; she had attacked the officers like a vicious momma bear protecting her young—all for him. She truly did love him; how could he let her down? He would be setting his friends free, his mother. The only thing that pricked his conscience was that he knew that freedom may not be what they want. He knew that the traditions would continue, and other women would be taken—women like Amanda. The thought of putting another woman through the pain that she had suffered was inconceivable. He slowly nodded then turned to the detective.

"Yes, I agree to cooperate," he said. Amanda smiled and kissed him quickly on the lips. Then she turned a serious look to her mother.

"What do you know about cults?" she asked her mother, with instant heat in her voice. "Have you ever lived in one?"

Her mother was taken aback by Amanda's attack.

"Of course not, Amanda," she said. "You know that I haven't. I've read about them."

"Well, until you experience firsthand on how things work there, then don't talk to me about brainwashing!" she said. "None of you have any idea what I've been through. Yes, Matthew had a part in taking me, but he was raised believing that it was right, that it was normal. For the people in the village, it is normal! If I didn't have Matthew in there, I would have killed myself a long time ago!" Her parents gasped. "Look!" She shoved her wrists out at them. Her mother's hand flew to her mouth, mortified by the scars she saw on her daughter's wrists. "It's not like I didn't try. Matthew took care of me. I could have been taken by a different man, a man that didn't care about my feelings or me at all. But Matthew took me, and he loves me!" Emotion shook in her voice. Matthew rested his hand on her leg, reassuring her. She relaxed some, sitting back slightly, grasping his hand.

"All right," Sergeant Stevens said. "Matthew, why don't you tell us everything that you can about your village." Matthew nodded, then he began to explain Amanda's abduction, the observation, and where they brought her. He talked about the village rituals and marriages and their way of life. He even brought up the business transactions that took place, giving very detailed information about the monetary exchange, paperwork, and the bookkeeping. The last thing he mentioned was the involvement of the Tanner's private investigator. The sergeant wrote things down quickly, seeing his tape was destroyed; he was anxious to follow these leads.

When Matthew was done, he was emotionally exhausted. Amanda held his hand as her parents looked on helplessly.

"I can't believe this," Max said quietly from his side of the room. "I can't believe that *you*"—he pointed accusingly at Matthew—"that *you* kidnap my daughter, but then have the audacity to *marry* her!"

Amanda shook her head sadly. "Didn't you listen to anything that was just said?" she asked quietly, her energy spent.

"How do we know that the marriage is legal?" her mother questioned, not willing to accept it. "Is this man an official pastor? How do we know he's not some escaped mental patient, pretending to be a pastor or minister?" Matthew shook his head slowly.

"No. He's a registered minister," he said quietly. "You'll find our marriage license is legal as well."

"I'm going to believe *you*?" she accused. He just shrugged his shoulders, not seeming to care if she did or not. Tears filled Amanda's eyes. *They were being impossible!* Maybe she would too, if she was in their shoes, but it was just too much. She got to her feet, pulling Matthew up with her.

"I'm tired," she said quietly. "Actually I'm exhausted and so is Matthew. We haven't slept in over forty-eight hours and we need to sleep." Without letting her parents say a word, she turned to the detective. "Sergeant Stevens, would you mind giving us a ride to the Holiday Inn over on Route 5?"

"Amanda?" her father asked, surprised, standing.

"That's not necessary," her mother interjected as she too bounced to her feet. Amanda ignored them both, awaiting the sergeant's reply. He hesitated, looking at the Tanners then back to Amanda, nodding.

"Sure," he said, "it's on my way back to the precinct." He glanced at Max and Diane. "Listen, this is probably for the best. A lot has happened here tonight. Why don't we all get some rest and resume this in the morning. This is a very emotional time for all of you, and you all need to think about how you want this to end." Gathering up his written information, he walked to the door. He turned back around to Max and Diane. "I will swing by and pick Amanda and Matthew up in the morning, and we'll meet again." Amanda and Matthew followed quietly, scooping up their backpacks that they had left by the door.

"Amanda!" her father called. She looked over her shoulder, seeing her father struggling with his feelings and her mother crying. It broke her heart to see them like this, when this was her only wish, to be with them, when she was in the village. But it would break her heart even more if they couldn't accept Matthew. "Don't go," he said, his voice breaking. Tears filled her eyes.

"I'm sorry, Daddy," she said, "but you've given us no other choice." With that, they walked out of her house.

Amanda and Matthew were silent as they rode in the back of the unmarked police car. Sergeant Stevens glanced at them often in the rearview mirror. Amanda sat close to Matthew, their arms entwined, both looking out their own windows, deep in their own thoughts.

He pulled up in front of the hotel and got out of the vehicle. He walked over and opened Amanda's door for her. She scooted out, her bag in her right hand, Matthew holding her left. Turning to the sergeant, she looked up at him, sorrow in her wide blue eyes. Compassion filled him as he tried to understand the struggle she was facing inwardly. She straightened her back and put out her hand.

"Thank you, Sergeant," she said, clear and strong. Oh yes, he thought, this was Max's daughter all right. He gave her a small smile.

"You're welcome," he said, shaking her hand. Matthew put out his hand as well. The sergeant looked at him directly.

"You're a lucky man, Matthew," he said. "We were ready to drag you off to jail, and throw away the key." Matthew nodded.

"Thank you for the ride, sir," was all he said. They walked through the automatic doors and checked in at the front desk. Within twenty minutes, they were using their key card and entering their room. The pain that Amanda was enduring was apparent in her whole demeanor, and he himself was overwhelmed with a dozen different emotions. Amanda threw her bag on the bed closest to the door.

"I need a shower," she said quietly. "Why don't you rest, and I'll be right out. Are you hungry? We could order room service." Matthew shook his head.

"No," he said. "Amanda, what you did back there . . ." She just shook her head.

"I'm so disappointed in them," she admitted softly. "I never expected them to be so obstinate"—She paused, rubbing her forehead—"I don't know what I expected."

Matthew walked over to her and rested his hands on her arms, rubbing lightly.

"How else could they react, Amanda?" he asked. "I did take you, remember? If I were them, I'd have me tarred and feathered." She looked up at him, confused.

"You knew this would happen. You knew they'd arrest you?" she asked, surprised. He was silent for a moment, then he answered, "I knew that it was a possibility. It was something I knew I'd have to face," he admitted. "Amanda, I know that out here I broke the law. You informed me of that plenty of times, if I remember correctly." She flushed. "How did you think that I'd be received?"

She just shook her head and stepped away. "I don't know what I was thinking," she said then turned back to him. "You were willing to leave the village, knowing that you may have been arrested. Why?" she asked, still confused. He sighed and ran his hand through his hair then looked up at her, pain in his eyes.

"Because I love you, Amanda," he said softly. "I was holding you in my own type of prison, and I couldn't sit by and watch your spirit die. It was. I saw it happening before my eyes. You mean too much to me"—he turned, frustrated—"and they were *never* going to touch you again!" Tears filled her eyes.

"Oh, Matthew," she cried, stepping into his arms. "This is such a mess!" He held her close to him. Yes, he thought, it was.

"Amanda, go wash up," he suggested. "You'll feel better." He pulled her away from him gently, and she nodded tearfully.

Moments later, Amanda was standing under the hot water, letting the powerful spray beat on her face, feeling so lost and torn. She loved Matthew, and she loved her parents. She was home at last and things couldn't be more confusing. Her heart ached, as well as her mind and body, and she felt like she was under a whole new set of challenges. And she was tired, tired of it all. She sat down on the shower floor and just cried—cried for herself, her parents, and for Matthew.

Matthew stood outside the door of the bathroom, his forehead and his fingertips pressed lightly on it. He squeezed his eyes shut as he listened to her cry. It hurt him so much to know how much pain she was in, and he felt so helpless, wanting to stop all the hurt that he'd caused her. He pushed away from the door, his jaw clenched, and walked to the bed furthest from the door and sat down, feeling the pressure weigh on him.

When Amanda came out of the bathroom, she found him on the bed, his elbows resting on his knees, his face resting, covered by his hands. He looked up at her, soaking in every inch of her that was dressed in her nightgown that she had brought from the village; her hair was damp and hanging down her back. Her eyes were red and puffy, but she was such a sweet sight when she smiled shakily at him.

"Hi," she spoke softly.

"Hi yourself," he said, just above a whisper. She came and stood in front of him; he sighed as he wrapped his hands around her waist, pulling her close to him. He rested his head on her belly and closed his eyes. He wanted to tell her how sorry he was and how much it hurt him to see her like this, but it wouldn't change anything. She knew he was sorry, but the reality was he did this to her. She rested her hands on his head, running a few fingers through his brown hair. He pulled back gently and slowly stood up. Leaning down, he gently kissed her on the lips. Closing her eyes, she allowed herself to be drawn into him. When he pulled away, her lips were puffy, and her blue eyes were watching him. "Let me wash up," he said huskily, and he walked into the bathroom.

While he showered, Amanda pulled back the covers on the bed and slid beneath the cool, crisp sheets. She stared up at the textured white ceiling, her eyes following the circle patterns. Just one touch from him, and she felt like she was on fire. When she was with him, it was so easy to forget about the pain and hurt that surrounded her. He kissed her, and it felt like they were the only two people in the whole universe. *That was how it had been in the village, and it was proving to be the same out here,* she thought. Within minutes, he was showered and came out wearing a white towel. He walked to the other side of the bed and slid in next to her; she moved next to him, and he propped himself on his elbow. Leaning over her head, he turned the light off, and the room was pitched into darkness; a small stream of light from the streetlights shone in through the part in the thick curtains hanging on the window. Their eyes adjusted as they looked at one another tenderly.

"Amanda," he started to say, but she put her fingers on his lips.

"Shhhh," she whispered, "Just touch me . . . please, Matthew."

He leaned down and engulfed her with his kiss. Clinging to each other, their love sealed their souls together. Their lovemaking was passionate and intense; the tumultuous feelings that they were both feeling seemed to entangle themselves within one another. As they rose to the peak of their passion, Matthew's eyes connected with Amanda's, and together they leaped over the edge. Only moments later, their breathing labored, Matthew lay lightly on Amanda. He looked up at her, his eyes shining with tears.

"Amanda, I love you with all that I am," he whispered. Tears filled her eyes and overflowed, her heart filled with the warmth that only he could give.

"I love you more than you'll ever know," she whispered. He rolled over and pulled her close to him, and that's how they slept, entwined in each others arms.

Dawn came quickly, and Amanda's eyes fluttered open when she felt the sunlight on her face. She turned her head to see Matthew standing in front of the window. He wore his blue jeans, his hands shoved in the pockets, shirtless. She watched him for a long time, before he turned to her, smiling when he saw her awake. Her hair was tousled from sleep, her cheeks pink from the warmth of the bed.

"Good morning," he greeted her softly, wanting to crawl back in bed and make love to her again, but he restrained himself. She smiled sleepily at him.

"Good morning," she said. "Have you been up long?" He shook his head.

"No," he said then nodded his head toward the table that held the coffee pot, a small smile playing on his lips. "I tried to figure that thing out, but I think we should just buy some coffee." Pushing her hair out of her eyes, Amanda chuckled softly.

"All right." She sat up, holding the sheet over her bare breasts. "I'll wash up, and we'll go downstairs." Nodding, he forced himself to turn away from his beautiful wife.

True to her word, she was ready within minutes, dressed in the clothes she had worn the day before, and they walked hand in hand down to the coffee shop that was located on the first floor of the hotel. After ordering some breakfast, Matthew reached for Amanda's hands, holding them in his own, searching her face.

"We need to talk about all of this," he said quietly. She looked down.

"I know," she said softly. Looking up at him, her eyes instantly filled with sadness. "Maybe it would be best if you and I left. We could move to . . . somewhere . . . just you and me." Matthew shook his head.

"No," he said. "You need to work this out with your parents or you'll never be completely happy."

"I'm completely happy when I'm with you," she declared. Matthew's eyes connected with hers.

"I'm happy when I'm with you too and, though I'd like to have you all to myself, that's not possible. You have your family back, honey, this is what you've waited for. I wouldn't be able to live with myself if, one day, you started to resent me because of all of this!" He waved his hand in the air, and when she shook her head, he spoke again. "No, Amanda, you will. We need to do this right." Looking down at their hands, she was silent for what seemed like an eternity to him, but then she looked up at him.

"You're right," she admitted. "I need to resolve this one way or another. But let's get one thing straight." He smiled at her tenacious tone; his little fighter was back. "If they don't accept you, Matthew, then we're leaving. What are you smiling at? I'm being serious here!" Her eyebrows came together in annoyance.

"I'm sorry." He smiled. "You look so beautiful when you're angry."

"Matthew, stop," she smiled, then slowly sobered up. The waitress served their breakfast and refilled their coffee cups. When she walked away, Matthew spoke.

"How would you like your parents to handle this?" he asked softly, and she shook her head.

"I don't know," she admitted again. "I guess I'm asking a lot. I think they should just be happy that I'm home. Take me for what I am."

"All right," he conceded, "but you're not the same girl you were before you came to live at the village"—he skirted the whole kidnapping issue—"you've grown up a lot, Amanda, no thanks to me. Everything that you've been through," He looked down now, then slowly back up. "Do you think that maybe that's been a shock to them too?"

"I suppose it has," she said. "I'm not my daddy's little girl anymore." She was twisting her wedding ring unconsciously.

"I think that if you give your parents some room to accept all that has happened to you . . . the changes . . . me . . . that they'll come around. It's obvious that they love you and their anger toward me, is justified, Amanda." She nodded slowly.

"I know," she said, her voice cracking. "But I love you and I want them to see you as I do." Matthew smiled affectionately at her.

"I know," he said softly. "But that takes time. I had to grow on you too, remember?" She looked up at his teasing eyes.

"That was different," she said, with a small sad smile.

"Yes, I know," he said soberly. "When we go there today, let them feel what they're feeling. Don't try and force me on them. It won't do any of us any good and it will just make things worse." Amanda searched her husband's face.

"How do you know so much?" she asked wearily. He smiled.

"I don't," he said, "but I'm on the outside looking in and I can see more than you."

"All right," she agreed, "I'll try what you said." He smiled and brought her hands to his mouth and kissed them.

CHAPTER 27

Hours later they sat across from Amanda's parents, along with Sergeant Stevens. Arriving had been a quiet affair, with Max and Diane both looking as if neither of them had slept. After offering everyone something to drink, they decided to get down to business.

Max cleared his throat.

"I did a lot of thinking last night, Amanda, Matthew." He forced himself to nod at him. "And I guess I have some questions."

"All right," Amanda said. Amanda and Matthew sat in the same spot they had sat in the night before, again holding hands.

"Okay," he began. "Matthew, why of all the girls on that college campus, did you choose my daughter?" Matthew cleared his throat.

"Well," he said. "My pastor actually has people posing as students that evaluated particular students. We give somewhat of a description of the type of woman, with particular qualities, that we're looking for and these people find them." Matthew was honest and surprisingly spoke with confidence, not going unnoticed with Max. He noticed this confidence in him, and it both irritated him and, surprisingly, pleased him. Matthew turned and looked at Amanda, a certain sadness filling his tone. "I was given three choices," he said softly, "and I chose Amanda." Max rubbed his face, looking frustrated.

"Did you know this, Amanda?" he asked. Amanda looked up at her father.

"Yes, Daddy," she said quietly. "Matthew told me everything."

Her mother was shaking her head. "I don't understand. How can you want to be married to him after everything he's done to you?" she asked, confusion replacing the anger of the previous night.

"There are so many things that you'll never understand about me now," Amanda said softly. "I'm not the same person I was, you must know that by now. But what happened in there, what I went through . . . what we went through," she said, looking at Matthew then turning back to her mother, "not knowing, you'll never understand."

"Well, then tell us," she pleaded with her daughter. "Tell us something that will help make us understand!"

Amanda just shook her head sadly. "Telling you won't make you understand," she said quietly.

"Excuse me, I don't mean to interrupt, but, Matthew, how many of these people are out there?" the sergeant asked, all business.

"The pastor has people everywhere, sir," he explained. "For whatever purpose he needs fulfilled, the people are there to help him. I'm not sure how many and where."

"This is truly amazing," the sergeant said. "This is a bigger cult than Waco, it's an organization! I'm going to need to get the FBI involved. What about the people that work on the college campus, can you help me with them?"

"Yes, sir," Matthew said quietly. "I'll tell you all that I know. But Pastor was quite good at limiting our knowledge to just what we needed to at the moment."

"With the information that we have now," he said, "we have a case against this man you call 'Pastor,' and not so much on you." The detective's mind was reeling. "Can you find the village?" Matthew hesitated. He could, but this was too much, wasn't it? He didn't want them to go barging in and destroy all the villagers' lives. They were his family. The detective watched his expression close up. "We'll talk about that later." He stood up and opened his cell phone, walking out of the room. The room was silent now that he had left. Matthew turned to see Max and Diane looking at him, but the hostility was gone from their eyes, replaced by something he couldn't read.

"Matthew, I need to know what your intentions are, now that you've married my daughter," her father stated, looking at him directly. Matthew didn't back down.

"Well, sir, I plan on taking care of my wife like I have for these past ten months," he stated, "but I have to admit, that there's a lot that I don't know about living out here. My exposure to this way of life has been limited."

"I'll show you everything," Amanda stated lovingly to Matthew. He smiled at her. Max watched how his daughter looked at this young man before him. The love she had in her eyes and the way she glowed when she was near him couldn't be denied. But what if she was brainwashed? What if she is confused? Time was the only answer. Time. So much time, this man, sitting in front of him, stole from his family. He loved his daughter, but his daughter loved this man. He was so torn between what was right and securing his daughter's affections.

"How do you plan on supporting her?" he asked. "You do know that it's not a community effort to survive here, correct?" The sarcasm was evident. Matthew chose to ignore it, but Amanda sighed loudly.

"Daddy," she began, but Matthew squeezed her leg, letting her know that everything was under control.

"I do realize that," Matthew stated. "I'm a good carpenter. I've been making furniture since I was twelve years old. I'm sure that there are companies that would hire someone like me. Our village sold to a lot of the top furniture stores, nationwide."

"You don't need to work for those companies, you're too good," Amanda piped in, then turned to her father. "He could start his own business, with a little help in the right direction. Daddy, his work's excellent."

"I see," he said. He turned to look at his wife, and she shook her head then turned to Matthew.

"If you love my daughter so much, couldn't you consider separating? Have some time apart, let Amanda try to regain part of her life here that she lost?" she asked sincerely. "If you truly love each other, then you can stay married. But if you realize that it wasn't meant to be, you can divorce and quietly go on with your lives."

Matthew and Amanda just stared at Diane. Matthew, knowing how much he loved Amanda, felt as if someone had punched him in the stomach. Amanda felt the familiar tightness return to her chest at the thought of not being with him.

"Absolutely not!" Amanda said. "My god, Mom! Would you want to be away from Daddy?"

"No, honey," she said calmly. "But we weren't married under circumstances like the two of you." Amanda looked at both of her parents as if they were a dragon with two heads. She then turned to look at Matthew; he was searching her eyes, the hurt obvious in his eyes, and she was sure hers reflected the same. She then turned back to her parents.

"There is no way in *hell* that we're going to separate," Amanda said firmly.

"Matthew?" Diane asked him directly. Matthew hesitated, looking from Amanda to Diane.

"I love Amanda with all my heart, Mrs. Tanner," he said. "Being away from her would be . . . unbearable." His eyes on his wife, he added, "But I love her enough, and I trust our love enough, to let her have some time away from me." The confidence in him amazed Max. A man in his circumstances had nothing to be confident about. Amanda looked at him wide-eyed, tears burning her eyes.

"Matthew, I don't want to be away from you," she said, just above a whisper.

He took her hand and brought it to his mouth and kissed her hand softly.

"Maybe it's for the best," he said softly. "Maybe it would be better for you to readjust without me." She was shaking her head, her tears now falling down her cheeks.

"No, Matthew," she cried. "I don't want to be away from you."

Max thought it would be a good idea to jump in.

"Amanda, we can rent an apartment for Matthew," he stated, running with his wife's idea. "He can spend his time trying to start up this business of his. I have some contacts that would be willing to help out, I'm sure." Amanda refused to look at her father. Matthew knew what they were doing now; they were trying to sell the idea to her. But it didn't matter; he loved her, and he was willing to do whatever it took to prove that to them and to Amanda. Amanda shook her head at Matthew, then back at her parents.

"No. I won't do it." She sat back and crossed her arms. Diane scooted to the edge of her seat.

"Just think about it," her mother said softly. "All I'm asking is for a little time on your own. To prove to your father and I, and to yourselves, that this is real. What you have for one another . . . that these feelings"—she swallowed—"you have, are real." By Amanda's and Matthew's expression, Max wasn't encouraged.

"I can't believe I'm going to say this. But you and Matthew can stay here as long as you want, regardless of what you decide. I'll do all that I can to accept this marriage. I thought I lost my daughter for good—I can't ignore the fact that she's been returned to us, however different," he said, looking affectionately at Amanda. Turning to Matthew, he said, "I can't promise to be friends at this point, but I'll try my best. You're welcome to stay with our family, and to make it your temporary home if you choose to."

"I appreciate that, sir . . . ma'am," he said to Amanda's parents, truly grateful.

"Oh, Daddy!" Amanda exclaimed tearfully. "Thank you, thank you." She hurried across the room to hug him. "Thank you, so much." She turned and hugged her mother. "Thank you, Mom." Each parent held her close, trying not to let her go again.

"Think about what I said, all right, Amanda," her mother whispered softly, "just think about it." Amanda didn't comment but pulled away and turned to Matthew. He got to his feet, smiling at her, and she stepped into his arms and hugged him.

"I love you," she said softly, her face burying into his chest.

"I love you, too," he said, kissing the top of her head.

Later that night, Matthew lay in bed, staring at the ceiling in Amanda's bedroom, in her parents' house. Diane's request wouldn't leave his thoughts. He couldn't help thinking that maybe she was right, and his heart ached just thinking about not having Amanda by his side. But he did *force* her to marry him. Did she feel she *needed* him, or did she actually *love* him? Confusing emotions ran through him.

He didn't want Amanda to be with him because she was confused by her emotions. She was dragged into his world and forced to live a certain way, but he loved her too much for her to be with him, if she wasn't sure why. Surviving his way of life together just wasn't a good-enough reason to be together. His beliefs didn't include divorce, his vows were forever, but he chose his bride, she didn't choose him. He needed to know, he needed to know that she loved him, for him, not out of necessity—loved him not out of some obligation or for protection. She didn't need any protection from anyone out here, knowing she was very confident in her old lifestyle. He witnessed this firsthand these last couple of days when she had taken control of situations and had made decisions for them.

He looked down; Amanda's head lay on his shoulder, her hand rested on his chest. She was sleeping. She was so beautiful; he clenched his jaw and looked away. God, he didn't want to let her go! But his decision was made. There wouldn't be a person in her life that would accept him, if they didn't know for certain that she was with him for the right reasons.

He gently rolled her over, covering her face with gentle kisses. She stirred from sleep and smiled warmly at him.

"Matthew," she whispered softly, reaching her hand up and touching his face. He leaned down and kissed her softly, pulling her close to him. He then made love to his wife, the woman he loved more than himself, showing her without words how much she meant to him. Afterward, when she snuggled up next to him, it was tears that fell from his eyes. When morning came, he arose before the first light, dressed, and sat down in the chair in her room adjacent to the bed. He watched her sleep for the longest time, tears burning the back of his eyes. This would truly be the hardest thing he ever had to do.

Amanda had the sweetest dream. She dreamt of them being near a cottage, somewhere in the country. She was walking in a field of wildflowers, Matthew holding her hand, such a feeling of peace and contentment surrounding her. She had turned to Matthew, and he was smiling . . . turning over, she felt the mattress next to her and realized he wasn't there. Blinking open her eyes, she slowly sat up, sleepily looking around, her eyes finally resting on him sitting in the chair. He had his right elbow resting on the arm of the chair, his chin rested in his hand; he was wearing a serious expression.

"Matthew, are you all right?" she asked groggily. His throat was so tight that he almost couldn't speak and almost couldn't go through with his decision. He clenched his jaw and steeled himself against the pain he would feel, knowing he needed to do this, for both of them.

"I'm leaving," he said quietly, but in a rough voice. Her eyebrows came together in confusion. Rubbing her eyes, she swung her legs off the side of the bed.

"Matthew, what are you talking about?" she asked softly, not believing what she just heard. Her heart began to pound, her throat dry.

"Your mother was right," he said. "We need some time apart."

Shaking her head, tears instantly springing to her eyes.

"No, we don't," she declared. "She just wants to get rid of you. I won't let—"

"This isn't your decision. It's mine," he said, his voice cold. "I'm going." He stood up, throwing his backpack over his shoulder, and stepped toward the door. Panic filled her. She moved quickly, standing, blocking his way, and taking hold of his arms.

"No, wait!" she cried earnestly. "Please, Matthew. Please don't go."

He looked down into her face, tears falling from her eyes. His heart was breaking right there, in Amanda's childhood bedroom.

"Amanda, I can't stay," he said. "I need to know that you love me for me. I forced you to marry me, you need time to figure out what you want."

"No, Matthew," she cried. "I want you, I don't need time!" she cried. He moved his arms so he could take her face into his hands.

"Amanda . . . God," His voice was hoarse and restrained. "I love you so much." He kissed her tenderly, tasting her tears that had fallen on her lips. "But I need to know." When he pulled back, he forced himself to look away from the pain in her eyes.

"Matthew, I need you, *please*," she pleaded, now sobbing. He pulled her off him and set her back, reaching for the doorknob. "Where will you go? Do you have any money?" She tried to calm down, knowing now that he wouldn't back down from his decision. "We used most of it already." He turned back.

"I'll be all right," he said. "Don't worry about me."

"Don't worry about you?" she exclaimed, wiping her face with the back of her hand. "You've never lived out here. I don't understand how—"

"Amanda, I'm a grown man, not a child," he stated brusquely. "I'll make my way on my own."

"When will I see you again?" she cried. "Matthew, please . . ."

He shook his head.

"I'll return at Christmas," he informed her. "Then you can tell me what you've decided." Her eyes widened.

"Christmas? That's over four months away!" she exclaimed. "Please, Matthew don't leave me!" She tried one last time. He opened the door and turned one last time; taking her face in one hand, he kissed her hard on the lips. When he pulled away, he said his last words.

"I'll come back for you. I love you, Amanda!"

Amanda watched him walk away from her down the stairs, hearing the front door close quietly behind him. Hurrying to her window, she was surprised to see a cab waiting for him out front. She pressed her fingers to the window, tears falling down her face. "I love you," she whispered as he got in and closed the door; she watched the cab drive away, leaving her heart shattered into a thousand pieces.

"And how long have the nightmares been going on?" she asked. Amanda looked up at the psychologist.

"They started the night after Matthew left," she admitted softly then turned away as Marty, the psychologist, observed her. She was wearing a white cotton tank top, grey gym shorts, and white Keds. Her blond hair was pulled back in a sloppy bun. She was a beautiful young woman, the doctor thought to herself. There was so much hurt and pain beneath the surface, the dark circles under her eyes only being a small sign.

"Can you tell me about them?" she asked.

"No," Amanda said, not looking at her.

"All right," she said softly. "Last week, we talked about your suicide attempt. You contracted a fever?" Amanda fidgeted in her seat, then looked up, meeting Marty's eyes.

"Yes," she said quietly.

"And when you woke up, you found out that Matthew had nursed you the whole time you were ill?" she asked. Amanda nodded her head.

"Tell me about your feelings for Matthew at this time," Marty requested. "You had been gone"—she looked down at her notebook, then back up—"about two weeks at that time?"

Amanda nodded but was silent for several minutes; Marty patiently waited.

"I was angry with him," she finally said quietly. "I was grateful he took care of me but I was confused." She stood and paced the doctor's office. "I was so scared, but I wasn't afraid of him anymore."

"Go on."

"I was angry with him for doing this to me, you know?" she exclaimed suddenly, her eyes shining. Marty nodded. "But he was so gentle and kind to me." Her voice softened. "I was torn. I wanted to hate him. I really did, but I . . . couldn't. Even then, I couldn't hate him." She sat back down, looking back up at Marty. "I was drawn to him."

"Amanda, it's quite normal to be drawn to someone who's being kind to you, especially when you're a prisoner in a hostile environment," Marty said softly. "There was nothing wrong with how you felt."

Amanda shook her head tearfully.

"It was all wrong," Amanda said. "I shouldn't have been there. I mean, why me?" Marty just shook her head, having no words to say. "We were married two days later, but you have to understand something." She looked desperately at Marty. "I *wanted* to be with him. I *needed* to be with him."

"He was a comfort to you in a terrifying situation," Marty said. "Anyone would have felt the same feelings." Amanda shook her head and covered her face with her hands.

"You don't understand," she said. "We had to . . . well, we had to *prove* that we . . . that we . . . consummated the marriage." She spitted the words out.

"I understand," Marty said softly. Amanda looked up at her, tears on her blushing cheeks.

"No"—she shook her head—"you *don't* understand," she exclaimed, in a harsh whisper. "I *wanted* to be with him because I was attracted to him.

When we . . . we . . . were together . . . it was . . . wonderful." Her last word was a soft whisper.

"Why is that so awful?" Marty asked. "What was wrong with being attracted to him? There's nothing wrong with enjoying being with a man." Amanda shook her head,

"I hardly knew him," she said softly, slumping back in her seat. "He kidnapped me for God's sake and the next thing you know, I'm sleeping him and liking it!"

"Taking into consideration everything you've told me, you didn't have a choice to be with him," Marty explained. "Didn't you say that the women were forced if they didn't comply?" Amanda slowly nodded.

"Yes, they are, but—"

"So your wedding night with Matthew could have been horrible," Marty said quietly, "yet it wasn't." Amanda looked away, biting her lip.

"No, it wasn't," she whispered.

"Did you know that in Bible times it was common practice to publicly consummate a marriage? In some villages, the whole town waited outside the tent to see the sheet covered with the virgin's blood," Marty said. Amanda looked at her, saw that she was serious, and shook her head. "In some primitive cultures, even in this present day, this ritual is not uncommon. There's nothing for you to be ashamed of."

"Maybe," Amanda admitted, not quite believing her.

"But being drawn to kindness and being attracted to someone, does not necessarily mean that you love the person," Marty explained softly.

Amanda's eyes snapped to Marty's.

"I know that," she said sharply. "I didn't love him then. I slowly fell in love with Matthew, and I know what love is. I didn't before I met him, but I do now! I know what I feel in here," she said as she put her hand over her heart. Anger surged through her, and she shifted in her seat. "I don't like doing this. I don't like dissecting everything that happened to me in there!"

"I know that it must be difficult, Amanda," Marty began, "but it's important that you work through your feelings."

"Work through my feelings?" she repeated. "No, this is just making me relive things that I don't want to relive. Look, Doctor, I know that my mother hired you, and that she thinks this is what I need, but it's not. I'm not suppressing anything and I know how I feel." She stood up. "I've talked to you for four weeks and I still love Matthew, I'll love Matthew no matter what happened in there, and I'll always love him. We're wasting each other's time." Marty stood up as well.

"I'm sorry you feel that way, Amanda," she said quietly. "Though you think that I am, I'm not trying to convince you *out* of love with Matthew. I'm just trying to help you work through what *did* happen in there. You've been through a lot, and I think that talking about it will help you and Matthew."

Amanda hesitated at the door.

"I don't think it will," she said softly.

"Why not give it one more week, and then if you've felt like you've had enough, then we'll end our sessions," Marty suggested.

"All right," Amanda agreed. "One more."

CHAPTER 28

Amanda stepped from the office building, squinting as her eyes tried to adjust to the sun. Lifting her hand, shielding her eyes, she looked to where she parked her car. Spotting the vehicle, she walked slowly toward it.

It had been over a month since Matthew had left her that dreadful morning. After keeping to her bed for several days, she had no choice but to get up and try and figure her life out. Though she had not stopped thinking of him constantly, she began to try to make up for lost time. At first, she felt that she couldn't do anything without him, but with her parents' gentle support and encouragement, she took small steps to regain part of her life.

For her first outing, her mother insisted on bringing her to the local spa. It felt good to enjoy such worldly pleasures again. She had her hair cut several inches so that it now settled in the center of her back, her body massaged, her nails done, and a wonderful facial. After spending the day there, they had had a nice lunch and did some shopping. Her mother had spent a small fortune on new clothes for Amanda, and she *did* appreciate all that her mother was doing, but the ache in her heart was constant.

Lunches with her father, long walks in the woods, and drives into the countryside—all of these wonderfully soothing activities, yet sadness still shined in her eyes. Her color was back, but sleepless nights were keeping the dark circles from dissipating.

She reached her car, a silver BMW her father had purchased for her when she began college two years ago. She opened the door and slid in. Turning the car on, she rolled the windows down to let the heat escape. The days were still exceptionally warm, while the nights had grown colder, changing the color of the leaves. She rested her hands on the steering wheel, and then slowly her head followed. It was hard to imagine that next month would mark the anniversary of the day she was abducted. A whole year of her life from her friends and family, and she was now a stranger to them. And to herself. With Matthew she felt whole, and she so desperately wanted to see him. She squeezed her eyes tight, his face so vivid in her mind. His wonderful smile, his gentle touch.

She sat up quickly. He promised to return for Christmas, and he would come back; she knew he would. He had to. She started the car and drove out of the parking lot. She pulled out into traffic, her mind drifting when her phone rang, startling her. A ghost of a smile touched her lips as she pushed the button, keeping her eyes on the road, and listened to the monitor.

"Yes?" she called into the speaker phone.

"Amanda?" her mother asked. "Are you on your way home?"

Amanda sighed. Her parents have been supportive and encouraging, and at times . . . overbearing.

"Yes, I am."

"Good . . . good," she exclaimed. "You'll never believe who came to visit you. He's here right now." *Matthew, oh my god, can it be?* Almost as if reading her thoughts, her mother's voice became more gentle. "It's Jared, honey. He heard you were home."

Amanda stopped breathing. *Jared. She hadn't thought of him in so long,* she realized guiltily. *Jared.*

"Honey?"

"I'll be there shortly," she stated and hung the phone up.

Turmoil filled her as she remembered the last time they had seen each other. She couldn't forget that night, but she struggled to remember her feelings. Color rose to her cheeks as she remembered the kisses they'd exchanged. *Oh God, how was she going to face him?* Then a horrible thought filled her. *Did her mother call him? Did she tell him to come over? No, no, she never told her parents about their relationship. She hadn't had time. But did he?* Her hands gripped the steering wheel tightly, her knuckles turning white. *She didn't want to see him, did she?*

Several minutes later, she pulled into her driveway, alongside Jared's black Cherokee Jeep. Trying to steady herself, she slipped out of her car. She entered the house through the side door, being too much of a coward to go through the front entrance. The side door brought her into the kitchen to see her mother pouring lemonade into two glasses; she looked up and smiled at her when she walked in.

"Hi, honey," she said. "Isn't it wonderful that Jared came? He's back at school, but decided to drive here for a few days."

Amanda came forward, setting her keys down; she leaned her hip on the center island. "Mom, how did he know I was home?" she asked quietly, searching her mother's face. Her mother met her eyes, understanding the question perfectly.

"Really, Amanda." She put the glass pitcher back into the refrigerator; turning back around, she placed her hands on her hips, exasperated. "All you have to do is turn on the television. The news programs are constantly reporting your return home." Amanda blinked. *She was right, of course. How did she expect to hide from her past, when they were plastering her life all over the country?* When she had first seen herself on TV, she was stunned, hurt, and humiliated. Her father had to gently explain to her that the story about her abduction went no farther than her sudden return home. The FBI wouldn't allow anymore information about the village or where she'd been to be leaked out before their investigation was over. Yet it still angered her to be talked about on national television when these people didn't know the first thing about her.

Amanda nodded and looked anxiously toward the hallway. Her mom stepped toward her, taking her shoulders and turning her to face her.

"He's so anxious to see you," she said softly. "He called when you first came home, but your father told him that you needed some time, and he's been very patient. Amanda?" Amanda looked up and met her mother's eyes. "He was devastated when you disappeared. Heartbroken. It was so obvious that he cared for you."

Amanda nodded, not speaking. *Yes, he cared for her.*

"He worked with the police endlessly," she continued. "He sat for hours giving the description of the men that ran into you that night, comparing sketches, doing everything that he could to help."

Tears burned the back of Amanda's eyes. So much happened here, at home, when she had been abducted. When she had been crying in desperation for help in the cabin, so many people were doing everything they could to find her. Her mother let go of her and reached for the glasses, handing them to Amanda.

"Here," she said gently. "He's in your father's study. I thought the two of you could use some privacy to talk without your old mother eavesdropping," she teased lightly. Sighing, Amanda took the glasses and walked down the hall to the study. The door was open, and she stepped in hesitantly. Instantly the familiar scents assaulted her senses as they always did—the sweet smell of the leather furniture, her father's cologne. Even the books had an odor all of their own; old and new volumes lined every wall, placed on mahogany shelves. She had so many childhood memories in this room—from sitting on her father's lap as he read her nighttime stories, to taking naps on the leather sofa as he worked at his desk, to doing her homework with him reading next to her, answering any questions that she had. The room comforted her, her mother knew that. She was trying to help Amanda when Amanda thought she was trying to hurt her. Feeling ashamed, she stepped farther into the room, and there he was. His back was to her as she looked at him. A white t-shirt stretched over his broad back, and he wore khaki cargo shorts, with his familiar battered sandals. His black hair was slightly longer than it had been when she had last seen him, and he seemed a little thinner.

The jingling of ice from the glasses of lemonade she held caused him to turn. When he did, their eyes met. He was just as handsome as ever, she thought; a beautiful tan covered him from head to toe, from the adventures that she was sure he had this past summer. She noticed a wariness in his expressive eyes, not the typical confidence she remembered so well.

"Amanda," he breathed out, trying to get a grip on himself as he slowly stepped toward her. She looked so beautiful, yet so frail. She was thinner but appearing the same. She was smiling now, but the smile didn't reach her sad blue eyes. Stopping about a foot away from her, reaching out, taking the glasses and setting them on the end table near them, he turned back to her.

"Jared." She smiled sweetly, but he could feel her anxiety from where he stood. He reached out and gently touched her cheek.

"Oh God, Amanda," he gasped, ignoring the tension this caused; he gathered her into his arms fiercely. Holding her tightly, he buried his face in the fresh scented curve of her neck, the small strands that fell from her sloppy bun tickling his face. She hugged him back, emotions scorching her mind and soul. He was warm and secure, and memories of their friendship rushed over her, the history they had, the budding romance that was stolen from them. Squeezing back the tears that wanted to fall, she was happy to see him, no matter what confusion she felt. She had missed him, yearned for him, in the crucial moments of her ordeal. *How could she forget that?*

When he pulled back, he cupped her face in his hands.

"God, Amanda, you look good," he said, his voice soft.

"You do too," she said, her voice matching his own as he searched her face silently. He could feel the change, the wall that was up, and though he expected it, the hurt still pierced him.

"Can we sit a while?" he asked. She smiled and nodded.

"I'd like that," she said sincerely. They both sat on the leather sofa, turning inward so that they could see each other better. Silent, they weren't sure where to start or what to say. After a few awkward moments, Jared spoke.

"Have you been in touch with Shelby?" he asked, smiling.

"No," Amanda answered quietly. She refused to admit that she didn't want to see anyone. Anyone, except Matthew, that is.

"She's doing well," he answered cheerfully. "She's decided to give school another chance." She looked at him; her eyebrows came together in confusion.

"Give school another chance?" she asked. "What do you mean?"

"Oh, you didn't know?" he asked, surprised. "I thought that your parents would have told you." By the look on her face, she was ignorant of what went on. "After what happened"—he hesitated—"well, she kind of couldn't stay at school anymore, some sort of emotional breakdown. Her parents came and helped her pack up, and she left. Just like that. I didn't even know she'd left until I ran into Jake."

Amanda's eyes had widened as he told her.

"An emotional breakdown?" she asked. "Why?"

"She blamed herself for what happened to you," he explained softly. "She felt like if she hadn't gone out that night, nothing bad would have happened."

Amanda shook her head, saddened.

"That's ridiculous," she said sullenly, admitting to herself that at one time she had believed that. That was before she found out the truth of her abduction.

Jared reached for her hand, taking it gently into his own.

"She isn't the only one to blame herself," he whispered. She looked up at him, seeing the tears shine in his eyes. "If I had stayed with you . . . we both noticed those weird bastards. I should have stayed." She squeezed his hand and shook her head, her own eyes filling, deciding it wouldn't be wise to tell him that one of those "weird bastards" was now her husband. "You weren't comfortable being alone and we both knew that."

"It's not your fault, Jared," she said sadly. "Please don't blame yourself. If it didn't happen that night, it would have happened at a different time. Not you or Shelby could have prevented it."

Searching her face, his confusion was written on his own.

"What do you mean?" he asked as she looked down at their hands.

"I was chosen by these people," she said quietly then looked up at him. "They had watched me for months and I didn't know." His eyes widened in disbelief. "They would have found a way."

"How? I don't understand!" he gasped. She shook her head, biting her bottom lip.

"It's just what they do," she said, knowing she didn't have the strength to explain what had happened to her. "I can't."

He squeezed her hand. "It's okay, Amanda," he said. "You don't have to talk about it."

She nodded, trying to rein in her emotions.

He saw the painful anguish in her eyes, and it hurt him so much just trying to imagine what she'd been through.

"Are you all right?" he asked. "I mean, now that you're back?"

She looked up at him. "I am," she said. "I'm a little confused. My life came to an abrupt halt and now . . . I don't . . . know." Her thoughts were hesitant and broken.

"What about your goals?" he asked gently. "Your passion for history?"

Amanda just shook her head. "I don't know," she said sadly. "I don't know who I am anymore."

"Maybe in time," he began, but sadness echoed in him as well.

They were quiet for a few moments; he played with her fingers, his eyes on the gold band that she wore.

"Your mom explained to me that"—he swallowed, almost not able to say the words—"you're married."

Amanda's throat closed, and her chest tightened. *How could she talk about this with him?* She nodded, unable to speak.

"Oh, Amanda, it's all right," he whispered, seeing her tears. He wanted to gather her in his arms again, but he didn't know if she would let him. Instead he reached over and gently wiped her tears away.

"I didn't come here to hurt you," he whispered. "But I still"—he hesitated—"care about you. I've missed you terribly."

"I've missed you," she cried. "It's just that so much has happened. I don't know." She stopped and shook her head.

"It must be awkward to be home now, huh?" he asked. She looked up into his eyes, and he was stunned by the misery he saw. In the years that he had known Amanda, he never saw her truly unhappy.

"Awkward doesn't even begin to describe what I feel," she admitted softly. "I feel so . . . out of place here."

"What would make you happy again, Amanda?" he asked softly.

Instead of admitting to Jared that all she needed was Matthew to come back, she just shook her head.

"I've got an idea," he said brightly. "Why don't you come back to school with me!" She looked up, surprise splashed across her face.

She started to shake her head.

"Wait, before you say no, listen," he continued, getting to his feet. "You could just come for a week. I have my own place this year, and you can stay with me." He hesitated. "I'll sleep on the sofa. There are so many people that would love to see you."

"They would love to ask me questions!" she accused. "Questions that I can't, no, won't answer. No, Jared, I couldn't."

"Amanda, people care about you there," he said seriously.

"No!" she exclaimed, much sharper than she had intended. He was surprised but said nothing. She got to her feet as well. "You don't know what it's like to be back. People treating me like I'm going to break or looking at me like I'm some freak or whispering about me as I walk by. It's awful, just plain awful." She began to pace. "When I was there, all I could think about was getting home. Being home with everyone but things aren't the same anymore! They never will be, and I hate that! I hate what's happened to me and everyone around me!"

"Amanda," Jared began.

"No!" she interrupted, holding up her hand, stopping him from speaking. "I'm not the same person that you knew before. I'm not *her* anymore. I want to be, *oh God*, do I want to be, but I just don't know how to be." Her voice lowered to a whisper as she looked up at him, her voice filled with anguish. "You don't know how angry I am that I kept you away for so long. I was so selfish that I refused to share my life with anyone and you stood by me anyway, just being a friend. I'm so angry that I waited and now it's too late! I'm angry because we never had the chance to know." She choked on a sob. He took a step toward her, and she put her hand back up. "No . . . Jared . . . no."

"Amanda, it's not too late," he began. "We could try and pick up where we left off. We could—" Her harsh laugh cut him off. She was shaking her head.

"You don't understand," she stated grimly. "It's too late because I love someone else. I love my husband."

Jared stood still, his features frozen, his breath hitched.

"I'm sorry," she whispered, her features melting in despair before him. She sunk to the sofa again and put her face in her hands and cried. Her words cut into him like a knife. When he heard she was married, he knew the circumstances of their marriage were bizarre, so he didn't believe—no, he didn't *want* to believe that she would remain in the marriage. He cared for her, and even if she did love another, he would always care for her. He kneeled down in front of her.

"Amanda, please don't cry," he whispered. She slowly looked up from her hands. Tears streaked her face, her eyes swollen and her nose pink.

"When I was first taken," she began softly, "I would think of you. My heart ached because I knew what we would never have." His eyes were shining with his own tears. "I didn't recognize the ache for what it was, but I must have known then, that my old life was over. Stolen from me, never to be returned."

"Amanda," he said softly, "you just feel that way. Things will fall back into place. Sooner or later."

She looked at him sadly.

"It's not *'things'* that are so different," she whispered. "It's *here* that is." She rested her hand over her heart. "It's *here*."

He slowly nodded, with the knowledge that he might have lost the only girl he had ever cared about. But he refused to accept it. He stood up slowly, sighing. Shoving his hands into his short pockets, he walked to the other side of the room.

She watched him, her heart aching, as he reached for a book from the shelf. Taking it down, he began flipping through it. Before her abduction, they had been good friends. Their chance at a relationship had come and gone, but she would always care for him. He closed the book, not really seeing any of the words, putting it back in its place, turning to her. Walking over to her, he stuck his hand out. She looked at his hand hesitantly then slowly slipped her hand into his, and he gently pulled her to her feet.

"Amanda," he began softly, "I don't want to leave."

She nodded tearfully, biting on her bottom lip.

"I planned on staying for a few days," he began. "If you don't want me to, I will leave, but God," He pulled her hand to his lips and kissed it. "I don't want to!"

"Don't go," she said. "I don't want you to leave."

He pulled her into his arms once again and held her close. When he pulled away, she saw his eyes shining with tears.

"Jared, I've hurt you," she whispered. "I'm so sorry." He shook his head.

"No, Amanda," he said, "I didn't know if I'd ever see you again. I still care for you, I can't deny that. But I'm standing here, with you in my arms, and I'm so happy that you're alive and well. I just want to be with you, spend time with you. I know that you said there's no hope for us, but I need to be near you right now. Can you understand that?"

"I do understand. I feel the same way, I just"—she hesitated—"I don't want you to think . . . I mean . . ."

"As friends, okay?" he insisted, wanting so much more. "I won't pressure you." Relieved, she gave him a shaky smile.

"As friends."

CHAPTER 29

The attic door creaked open, and she walked up the narrow stairs into the warm, dusty room. It was a typical attic; old furniture, paintings, and boxes of clothes that weren't used scattered along the floor. Two small round windows placed on either side of the house allowed sunlight to stream into the dim room. Dust particles lingered almost motionless in the air, locked in the sun rays that shone through the white lattice that decorated the windows. Amanda smiled, remembering coming up here as a little girl and looking through the old items that her parents had saved since their own childhood. Life was so much simpler back then, so much clearer.

She turned a small corner and came to what she'd been looking for. She looked down at the large brown box for several moments before she knelt to open it and slowly took the lid off, setting it gently aside. As she set the lid on the floor, she noticed her mother's handwriting, written in black marker were the words *Amanda's College Memories*.

Amanda sat down on the floor and crossed her legs under her. Papers were on the top; she sifted through them, smiling as she recognized the graded exams, term papers, and old assignments. She found her books and her backpack. Holding the worn blue bag up to her nose, she inhaled the familiar scent. Setting aside the bag, she reached into the box, finding a packet of photographs. Opening the envelope, she began looking at the photos. They were of a hiking trip a bunch of her friends and her had decided to take a year and a half ago. They portrayed groups of her friends laughing and having fun, Amanda and Shelby hugging—evidence of their good friendship.

Tears burned behind Amanda's eyes; she remembered that day so well, like it was yesterday. She continued to flip through, stopping when she came to a photo of Jared holding her. He was standing behind her, his arms wrapped around her waist, her back to him, and she was laughing, looking into the camera. She could almost hear their voices . . . and her heart constricted. Jared and Amanda hadn't had the chance to become intimately involved, but as Amanda thought back, they acted like a couple. She suddenly realized that all of their friends had accepted them as such, except for her. Memories rushed back, times they had spent together. He never pressured her into more, never asked for more than she'd given. Not until that fateful night. She'd known they were meant to be together, but for her own reasons, she had made them wait. And now . . .

Was she so selfish, so self-involved not to notice life happening around her? Was she so wrong to accept and enjoy the life she'd been living, without fear and bitterness to this unfair world? She didn't think so then, but oh, how naive she'd been in these photos! What could have prepared her for what she had endured this past year? Amanda had spent countless hours studying the history of the world-famous historical figures, wars, and the world tragedies. Nothing and no one could have prepared her for her loss of innocence, not just loss of purity of her body, but of her mind and soul. She was a completely different young woman than she was in the memories in this box, even if her loved ones didn't know this, or weren't willing to accept it. Life no longer looked the same to her, nor was it the same. She had respect for the taste of pure fear, a taste that she'd never experienced before. Now she no longer felt understood, relatable.

With one hand she wiped at her damp cheeks and put the photos aside. She found notebooks and more papers that she shuffled through. When she reached the last book, her hand froze. Without seeing it, she knew what it was. It wrenched her heart because she knew that it was the center of her world a year ago, and she was so afraid to look at it again, fearing that it would mean nothing to her. She took her hand out of the box, empty. Her thesis for her entry into the Foundation Committee. *Was it only a year ago that she sat in Mrs. Williams office, being handed the exciting assignment?* It seemed a lifetime ago.

"Amanda?" her father called. "Are you up here?" he asked, his voice getting closer as he climbed the stairs.

"Yeah," she replied. He rounded the corner to see his little girl sitting on the floor, in tears, surrounded by books and papers.

"Honey, what are you doing?" he asked softly, squatting down to her level. She gave him a shaky smile.

"I don't know," she admitted, looking down. "I'm scared, Daddy." She looked back up at him, fresh tears spilling to her cheeks. He reached out and touched her hair.

"What are you scared of?" he asked.

"Of not knowing who I am," she said softly. Reaching in the pile, she found a photo of herself, laughing, showing it to him. "I'm not her anymore. I feel so"—swallowing, she looked back at the picture—"lost."

Her father studied the photo, and it was pure will that he was able to hold back his own tears. When he looked back to Amanda, he cleared his face of his own emotional turmoil that he was dealing with. He'd been mourning the loss of his little girl since she returned—married, angry, scarred, and bruised inside and out. Still not having shared any details, she just gave the vague descriptions that she had given the police. She walked around with her sad blue eyes, trying to show everyone that she was all right. He sat down next to her.

"No, you're not her anymore," he agreed softly. "She was a child just beginning to see the world. I've always said you were a light into this world in everything you touch."

She shook her head sadly, looking down.

"I still believe that you're that light," he continued seriously. "Some bad people tried to extinguish that light, but they lost." She looked up. "They lost and you won. Even though they may have dimmed that light, it's not gone. Every day that you've been free, the light gets stronger, and it will continue to get stronger. Don't let them win now, not now that you're free." She nodded, wiping her tears.

"It's hard," she whispered. "I miss Matthew so much."

He gathered her into his arms, holding his baby close to his heart.

"I know, love," he whispered, "I know you do."

She pulled away slightly, to peer up at him. "Daddy, he will come back, won't he?" she asked, her heart in her eyes.

"Yes," he said, "he will. He loves you too much not to."

Amanda smiled against her father's shoulder. *Yes, Matthew loved her.* She held on to that knowledge desperately.

"I know when he comes back, you'll like him once you get to know him." Her voice was small and hopeful.

"If I don't like him, I already respect him," he said quietly. "His decision not only proves his confidence in you and your feelings, but it was a gift to us. A gift of time."

"Yes," she whispered, pushing aside the hurt his absence caused.

"I came up here to see if you wanted to go to camp this weekend?" he asked. "Your mother and I thought that it would be nice to bring Jared with us. Some quiet R&R on the lake, what do you think?" She hesitated, not sure if she wanted to have Jared so close, but he had honored his word and hadn't pressured her in the last couple of days.

"I'd like that," she agreed. "I'd like that a lot."

He hugged her for a few more moments. Then he helped her put the piles around her back into the box. When they were finished, he took her hand, and they walked back down the steps. The light turned off, the forgotten thesis still sat untouched at the bottom of the box.

"Look what I brought you." Her mother smiled, carrying in a steaming cup of coffee. Amanda blinked open her eyes and smiled. She sat up sleepily, pushing the quilt away from her.

"Mmm," she said as she took the cup from her. She cupped it with both of her hands, warming them.

"Did Daddy start the fire yet?" she asked. Her mom sat down on the edge of her bed, her arms wrapped around herself.

"Yes," she said, "but it's still chilly down there."

Amanda leaned back on the wall that the bed was against, taking a sip of the coffee.

"This is good. Thanks, Mom," she said, and her mom smiled.

"No problem," she said. "Finish it up, then get dressed and come join us for breakfast. Daddy's attempting an omelet again," she whispered, her voice laced with humor. "I tried to convince him to wait for you to make them, but he insisted."

Amanda laughed, knowing exactly what the outcome was going to be. *A mess!*

"Okay."

Her mother left, and Amanda sipped her coffee as she looked around the room. It was quite small, her room. Enough room for a bed and a small dresser, but it was her room. She had spent so many summers and weekends in this room. There were faded photos and magazine cutouts from her childhood still plastered on the wall. She didn't have the heart to remove them, not wanting to forget her silly phases.

They had arrived two days ago, and for the most part, it had been exactly like she had hoped—relaxing and quiet. The atmosphere was peaceful, a lot of teasing and light conversations. Amanda took another sip of coffee, but she couldn't miss the concerned looks that her parents exchanged with one another. Nor could she deny the frustration they were feeling for lack of knowledge of what had happened to her in the village. Sometimes it seemed, at rare moments, the tension was so thick you could actually cut it with a knife. There were even moments when she had caught Jared and her father in deep conversation, but they would quickly change the conversation to include her when she joined them. Amanda frowned as she looked into her cup. It's not that she couldn't understand their feelings, but she didn't want them to be hurt. If they knew everything that had happened, it *would* hurt. That and many other emotions, and she didn't want to do that to them. She sighed and finished her coffee.

Once she was dressed in jeans and a warm gray wool sweater, she walked downstairs. The smell of the fire and breakfast cooking was delicious. "Good morning." She smiled when she entered the kitchen. Her father was at the small stove, wearing her mother's pink apron. He smiled as she stood on her toes to kiss his cheek.

"Good morning, love!" he greeted. "Did you sleep well?"

"Yes," she said. She joined Jared and her mother at the table and accepted a refill of coffee from her. Jared smiled at her over the rim of his coffee cup.

"Your father and I thought we could all take the boat out today," she said. "Jared volunteered to help Daddy pull it out of the water, before we leave."

"A last trip through the lake?" she asked. "Yes, that would be nice."

"We'll just pile a bunch of warm blankets and bring a couple of thermos full of hot chocolate, and some lunch and we'll make a day of it," her father piped in as he put a plate in front of Amanda.

"Yes, let's do it," she agreed. Staring in dismay at the pile on her plate that was supposed to be an omelet, she missed the meaningful glance her parents exchanged.

After breakfast, they got to work. Amanda and her mother worked in the kitchen, preparing sandwiches and snacks, while Jared and her father gathered the blankets and were preparing the boat for use. Soon the work was finished, and they boarded the boat.

Amanda smiled; her face turned into the cool, crisp wind that hit her cheeks. She breathed in deeply, savoring every moment. She was wrapped in a warm quilt and sat across from Jared. When she opened her eyes, she found him looking at her. She would have to be blind to miss the affection that shined in his eyes. Looking away, she felt slightly uncomfortable.

It was nice having him there with her and her parents. Amanda appreciated his company, but more because there didn't seem to be time to corner her, wanting answers. This made her very happy, but she couldn't help feeling like she was giving him the wrong idea. The ache she felt for Matthew was not getting better, but worse. She missed him so much that sometimes she felt like she couldn't breathe. *Where was he? Was he safe? Did he miss her? Did he ache for her like she did for him?* She blinked her eyes and turned her face back toward the wind. About an hour later, her father slowed the boat down and put it in auto drive. Her mother took a thermos out and began to hand out cups of cocoa. Everyone was quiet, involved in their own thoughts. Though she hoped she imagined it, she felt that underlying tension again. She tried to ignore it, but as she began to observe the others, she realized that their behavior seemed odd. They avoided her eye contact, and more than once, she saw Jared clenching his jaw. Knowing him so well, she knew that it was something he did when he was nervous. She straightened her back, her chest tight, and waited.

It wasn't long before her father sat down next to her, clearing his throat.

"Amanda," he began, hesitating as she looked up at him, her expression unreadable, "we had other reasons for bringing you out here. Before you say anything, I know how despicable our behavior may seem, and that you might feel like we tricked you, but hopefully, you'll understand." Amanda's heart was pounding so loudly that she was having a hard time hearing him speak. Her throat dry, she asked, "What do you mean?" She searched his eyes, noticing the tension. She glanced at her mother, who was looking down at her folded hands, and then to Jared, who watched her tentatively.

He cleared his throat again. "We brought you out here because we need some answers," her father started to say. "We haven't wanted to push you away. But your mother and I, and after talking to Jared some, we need you to talk to us."

Amanda closed her eyes then slowly reopened them.

"I see," was all she said, feeling her body begin to tighten with tension. All three of them looked at her, searching her face, concerned about her quiet tone.

"Amanda, honey," her mother began gently. "We can't imagine what you have suffered, but waiting home, not knowing if you were alive or"—she couldn't bring herself to finish the sentence—"was very difficult. You need to work through your hurts and anguish, but holding them inside won't help you. It's not helping us either."

"We're having a difficult time too, Amanda," her father stated. "We know so little of what happened to you in there. When you came home with Matthew, you threw in our faces that you tried to kill yourself." He hesitated, his voice full of emotion. "We've noticed the horrible scars on your wrists, but know nothing about what caused you to want to take your own life. Can you understand our feelings?" Amanda glanced at all their faces and then looked down at her own hands.

She didn't want to do this. She didn't want to do this.

Without looking up. "You planned this boating trip," she accused, not asking, but stating. "Is this your own form of kidnapping?" She looked up into the shocked faces of her loved ones, knowing how hurtful the comment would be. *But dammit, she didn't want to tell them of her nightmare! Not here, not now!*

"Amanda," Jared spoke softly, "that's not fair."

She looked back down, knowing he was right.

"I don't want to talk about the village," she said softly, her hands beginning to shake. "You don't want to hear what happened." She wrapped her arms around herself; suddenly the beautiful autumn day became ice-cold. Jared left his seat to kneel before her, taking her shaking hands into his own, and began to rub them, trying to comfort her.

"Amanda, it would bring us out of the horrible darkness that you've allowed our imaginations to fall into," her mother spoke softly. "You don't need to share everything with us. Just . . . something."

Her mother's voice sounded so desperate that Amanda began to yield. Her nightmare in the village belonged to her, and she struggled not to share it, knowing the damage it was going to cause. But she didn't want her parents to suffer because of her silence.

She looked into Jared's face; his love for her showed clearly in his eyes, and she felt a sickening feeling inside. She slowly pulled her hands out of his.

"Jared," she said weakly, "you shouldn't be here." Her eyes were filled with tears. "I shouldn't have allowed you to come."

He searched her face, confused. "Why, Amanda?" he asked, taking his seat again.

"I just didn't want to lose our friendship, that's why I . . . ," she began, "but I know how you feel about me, and it was wrong to let you come." She was shaking her head. Leaning over, he rested his elbows on his legs.

"Amanda," he said, "I chose to come here, knowing how you felt. I can't change what I feel, but *I* chose to be here."

Amanda rubbed her face with her hands.

"Oh God!" she declared. "How could you corner me like this?" she asked, turning to her parents accusingly. "How could you do this to me?"

Her mother sadly shook her head.

"Amanda, we didn't see any other way," her father spoke gently. "We've tried to talk other times, but you wouldn't let us. I know you're hurt, but please talk to us."

She was in a boat, in the middle of the lake, and she was trapped. She knew this feeling very well. A rage began to build in her, and it scared her. She spent the last year being controlled in every aspect, and now she was being forced into a situation that she didn't want to be in. The rage was quickly replaced with anxiety, and she stood up suddenly, startling the others. She tossed her quilt aside and began to move about the boat.

"Amanda, please sit, honey," her father asked. "There isn't anywhere to go."

"Amanda," Jared said, coming over to her, "come and sit down."

She looked up at him, a wildness in her eyes that he had never seen before. Putting her hands out, she pushed him back with all her might. He lost his balance due to the rocking of the boat and fell at her parents' feet.

"Amanda!" her mother yelled. "Please calm down!"

Amanda barely noticed her father helping Jared up.

"Something's wrong with her," Jared spoke quietly to Max.

Suddenly she felt her air supply stop; she struggled to breathe, but she couldn't. Her hands went to her throat, and she gasped.

"Amanda!" She could hear her father calling her name as he rushed to her side. She looked up at him, her eyes wide, her hands clasping his flannel shirt. Her breaths were coming too short, not satisfying her lungs. "Amanda, try and relax, you just need to calm down, honey, please!" Her body writhed, self-preservation overwhelmed her, and then she felt the darkness. It was slow as her chest heaved, but soon she couldn't see her father anymore, and she welcomed the dark.

"Maxwell!" Diane screamed, rushing to his side. *"Do something!"*

Max held Amanda in his arms as she lay unconscious. Her face was pale, her breaths coming in short gasps, but she was still breathing.

Jared scrambled to the controls, removing the auto drive; he swung the boat around, and at full speed, he headed in the direction that they had come from. He looked over his shoulder and watched Amanda's parents sitting on the boat floor with their daughter in their arms. Diane was crying; Max's face was like stone, gray and rigid. Amanda was wrapped tightly in his arms.

Jared turned back around, clenching his jaw. Why did this happen to them? Oh, Amanda, what did they do to you?

CHAPTER 30

There weren't any dreams, just a blackness that Amanda floated in peacefully. When she awoke, it was simply blinking her eyes open, and she was back among the conscious. Her eyes focused on the ceiling of the cabin, knowing she wasn't in her bedroom, but in the family room. The only light in the dark room was the fire blazing in the fireplace on the back wall. She turned her head to see Jared in the rocking chair. His head was resting on the back, his eyes closed. Her mother was curled on the love seat, asleep. Thoughts of the day played in her mind. She couldn't begin to explain what had happened. She had panicked; she knew that, she thought, propping herself up on one elbow, scanning the room. Her father sat on the floor in front of the fire, his arms wrapped around his legs as he stared into the flames. "Daddy?" she whispered. He instantly turned.

"Amanda," he said softly, rising to his feet, coming to her side; he sat down on the edge of the sofa and pulled her into his arms. "You scared the hell out of me!"

She hugged him back. "What happened?" she asked, talking into his shoulder. He pulled her back gently.

"You had an anxiety attack," he said. "How do you feel?"

"I think I'm fine," she said. "Daddy, I'm sorry."

"Sorry for what?" he asked, searching her face. He reached over, lightly brushing some hair away from her face.

"I'm sorry if I'm hurting you," she whispered.

"Oh, honey," her father began, "your mother and I love you so much. It's horrible to know that you're hurting and not knowing the reason why. *We* are the ones that need to apologize. We should never have put you in such an awkward position this afternoon." He stopped, his eyes meeting hers. "We were completely insensitive."

"Oh Daddy," she said, her voice somber. "I know you want me to tell you things, but you really don't want to know. I don't want to hurt you."

"It can't possibly hurt us more than it has you, and you lived through it. But what do *you* want to do?"

She looked toward the fire that created flickering shadows on her face. Her heart ached, and she was so confused. "I want all of *this* to go away," she whispered, turning back to her father.

He nodded his head, and they both became quiet. Amanda looked down at the scars on her wrists.

"All right," she whispered. His eyes darted to her face as she slowly looked up and met his eyes.

"All right, what?" he asked, his voice tight.

"What do you want to know?" she asked. Hesitating, his mouth opened to move then closed again. Then sighing, he reached out, touching her hair lightly.

"We have a lot of questions," he said. "But let's wait until morning. You need your rest, and I know that your mom and Jared would like to be awake." Amanda frowned as she looked toward the fireplace. He noticed. "What's wrong, honey?"

She glimpsed over at Jared, sleeping in the chair.

"Daddy, I don't want Jared to—" she whispered hesitantly, looking at her father. "I care for Jared, Daddy, but as a friend. I *love* Matthew. No one seems to understand this. I don't feel right sharing . . . sharing what happened, with him."

"Amanda, we understand more than you think. All of us," he spoke quietly. "But maybe Jared needs to hear what has caused the change in you. Your change of heart toward him. It may be the closure he needs to move on."

Amanda shook her head. "I don't know if I can." It was going to be hard enough to share with her parents, let alone Jared.

"Can you give it a chance?" he asked. "We'll see how you feel in the morning." After a few moments, she reluctantly nodded.

Her father then woke up her mother and Jared. After several minutes of assuring them that she was fine and that she'd forgiven them for what they had tried to do, the three of them shuffled off to bed.

Amanda was still wrapped in her blankets, but she sat up, staring into the fire. *It was so strange being back with her family,* she thought; *it seemed so unreal.* Thoughts of the cabin that Matthew and her had shared came to mind. There were several moments that she did just this, but she was there, in the village, when the two of them had been together, in their cabin, alone, sharing intimacy and conversation. *It had been wonderful.* There was never a day that she didn't long to be home, but she cherished her time with Matthew and grew to love him more every day. They had made their cabin a home, and it surprised Amanda that she missed it. Her homemade curtains and Matthew's beautiful furniture that he'd made himself. But especially the spectacular view of the valley below them. She remembered staring out the window every morning with a cup of coffee in her hands and was always in awe of the beauty that God had created. She couldn't help compare their cabin with this one. Her parents liked the best of the best. It was filled with the best furniture, linens, and art decor. You didn't feel like you were camping in this cabin, but it gave her parents pleasure to be able to get away and still have the same luxuries they would have at home. Amanda used to feel the same way, before she'd been ripped from her sheltered and secure world. Now such luxuries were just that, luxuries. After living such a simple life for all the months she was in the village, the life her parents lived seemed so extravagant.

Of course, the peacefulness that she experienced at the cabin in the village was eventually shattered the minute they left and had to complete their duties. *At least she had been with Matthew,* she thought, tears forming in her eyes. She missed him desperately. He made her feel safe and loved, like no one else ever could. She longed to feel his arms wrapped around her, to hear his heart beating in his chest as she rested her head on him.

Amanda wiped the tears away with her hands. She missed Katherine, Sarah, and Jimmy. She hoped they didn't suffer terribly at Pastor's hands when their escape was discovered. But the sick feeling that dwelled in her gut, whenever she thought of them, convinced her they most likely had. This filled her with incredible guilt. It seemed like everyone around her was hurt because of her, and her chest ached with the inner turmoil that surged through her.

She stood up, the blanket wrapped around her, and stepped outside. Once on the porch, she stepped forward and leaned against the railing. The night was so cold she could see her breath. The stars shone brilliantly on the lake, the reflection bright and beautiful. She smelled the air, the trees, and the water and sighed with the pleasure of the scent. She had many childhood memories, and she'd always been happy here. The emptiness that lingered in her heart, the loneliness that filled her, wouldn't disappear. The happiness that had once filled her seemed so foreign to her now, and this caused great sadness to settle over her. *Would she ever be normal again? Could life ever be like it was before?* There were moments when she wanted this, and then she would realize that Matthew wouldn't be part of her life if she were to have that particular desire realized. The thought of him not being a part of her life was a sharp suffocating pain in her heart and mind.

She started when she heard the door behind her, turning to see Jared in the doorway.

"Hey!" he said softly, closing the door behind him.

"Hey," she replied, turning back around. He joined her on the railing, leaning his hips against it.

"I couldn't get back to sleep," he said softly. "I see you couldn't either."

She gave him a small smile. "No," she said. It didn't escape her notice, how close he was standing to her.

"You know what I was thinking about today?" he asked.

"What?" she asked.

"When we got back to shore, with you," he spoke quietly, looking out toward the lake, "after what you had said to me on the boat, all I could think about was the night I walked you home. The night that, well, the night you were taken." She hugged the blanket tighter around her shoulders.

"What about it?" she asked softly, not really wanting to know.

He sighed, pushed away from the railing, and walked to the steps.

"I waited a long time to kiss you," he said, walking down a couple of steps then sitting on the top stair.

Amanda sucked in her breath, her head bowed.

"I know," she admitted. "Jared, I'm—"

"No, don't, Amanda," he interrupted her gently. "Don't apologize. I was as much to blame for that. I was so afraid of pushing you away that I didn't." She walked over to him and sat with her friend on the stairs.

"Jared," she began.

"That night, you spoke about your purity vow to me, remember?" he asked, not really wanting a response. They both had that night burned into their memories. "That was one of the reasons I didn't want to scare you. Pretty much everyone knew about your vow." He smiled at her surprised expression. "When a beautiful girl doesn't seem to want to date, people talk. Even Shelby stuck up for you on more than one occasion. She really respected your choice and I almost think she regretted her . . . well, her choices. Anyone who got

to know you, respected you. It was so sweet that you thought I didn't know."
He smiled at her, and she actually blushed and looked down.

"I didn't know how much talk I caused." She shrugged, with a small smile.

He smiled. "I know that. You have to understand, that most girls are
generous with their affections." He smiled sheepishly, trying not to use the
wrong words. "I was always curious"—he paused then looked at her—"when
did you decide to make that vow?"

She smiled as she played with the edge of the blanket.

"Well," she said, "I was actually here, at camp. When I was twelve, I
met this girl whose family was renting a cabin down the way." She pointed
in the direction of the road. "Her name was Anya. I'll never forget her. We
became really good friends that summer." She smiled, her eyes toward the
lake as memories played in her mind. "We would ride our bikes together, play
games, swim, listen to music. Silly stuff that girls do at that age. One day we
were in the fishing boat that belonged to the cabin she was staying in, and
we were pretending to be . . ." She stopped and could feel her cheeks stain
with warmth. "Well, that doesn't matter," she said, pulling her hair behind
her ear, in a nervous habit that took his breath away. It dawned on him that
he'd forgotten that adorable habit.

"Tell me," he breathed.

"No, you'll laugh." She smiled. He chuckled softly, shaking his head.

"I promise, I won't," he said grinning.

"All right," she continued. "We were lying on the floor of the boat,
pretending to be princesses, tied up by a wicked witch, that was jealous of
our unfailing beauty. We were floating to our doom, waiting for our prince to
come rescue us." Smiling, she placed her hands over her face. "I can't believe
I just told you that!"

"I think that's sweet," he assured her.

"Anyway," she continued, "we started talking about what our prince would
look like. She was convinced that her prince was much better looking than
my prince. We were giggling and having fun, and then her mood changed.
She began to tell me a story. A story about a princess named Eileen. Eileen
had lived in a beautiful castle up on the hill high above the kingdom. She
was sixteen years old and the most beautiful maiden in the whole kingdom.
One day she met a prince while shopping in the marketplace." She said,
her mood sobering, "He was a very handsome prince and had the nicest
things to say. He made Princess Eileen feel very special." Amanda let out a
shuddering breath, the memory so vivid. "The prince convinced her to do
things that were not proper, things that she knew she shouldn't do, but her

prince threatened to leave the kingdom forever, if she didn't. Anya continued the story, but the more she spoke the shakier her voice became. I'd sat up at this time, and asked her if she was okay, and she said she was, then continued her story. Princess Eileen loved the prince so much that she couldn't bear it if he left, so she did what he wanted. And after she did, she realized that he wasn't a prince after all. He was an evil wizard in disguise. An evil wizard that had made the princess with child, and then he did the unthinkable. He left the kingdom for another land, and new princesses. But before he left, he bestowed a curse on Princess Eileen. When the time came for the child to be born, the princess breathed her last breath, and died before she could see her newborn child."

Jared sucked in his breath. Amanda looked at him, tears in her eyes.

"She was crying by this time, and I was kind of scared," she admitted. "Here we were, in the middle of the lake, and she was acting so . . . different. But her story was so heartbreaking that I knew that there was more to it. I didn't say anything, I just waited." Amanda paused. "Then Anya sat up, wiped her tears away and looked at me, and said, 'Eileen was my mother.'" She looked out toward the lake again. "It broke my heart to see her so sad. Then she explained to me that her parents were really her grandparents. Eileen had died while giving birth to her. She was sixteen years old."

"My god, Amanda," he said quietly. "How sad."

Amanda was quiet for several moments.

"Yes, it was sad," she said. "Anya told me that she would never allow a prince to talk her into anything. Then she explained to me that she had learned about this vow, that teenagers have been making. A promise that a girl would wait until the prince would walk her into the beautiful white cathedral, and marry her, before she gave herself to him. She then asked me to take the vow with her." Amanda smiled at Jared. "I was so moved by the story, that if she had asked me to jump off the nearest bridge, I would have."

He smiled at her.

"I made the vow with her," Amanda said softly. "At first because I felt so bad for her. But then later, when I was alone, I really thought about it. At twelve, you pretty much know enough of what happens between men and women. It scared me to think of myself in such a place and I was quite determined"—she smiled—"in my own naive way, that I could protect myself from all the evil wizards in the world. Obviously, as I matured, I realized men, in general, were not evil; only ignorance was." She was quiet, the familiar sadness slipping into her face again. "And now—well, now I know that there really *are* evil men."

He reached over and grasped her hand, squeezing it gently.

"So, there you have it." She tried to smile.

"Are you still friends?" he asked quietly. "You and Anya?"

"Well, I'd like to believe that we're still friends"—she gave a slight smile—"since she had such a profound affect on my life. She moved to Florida with her grandparents soon after that summer. We wrote to each other, but as the years passed, we kind of lost touch." She paused thoughtfully. "It's funny because I don't believe I've ever told anyone that story, beside my parents."

"Then I'm honored," he said sincerely, his eyes intent on her face.

Amanda looked nervously away. He held her hand, and she didn't pull away, realizing that she didn't want to. Confusion swept through her. After just being able to talk, about something other than her abduction, it allowed her to relax in a way she hadn't since she'd come home. They both fell silent, the night sounds filling the void. Insects chirped, the water slapping against the rocks, and the wind blew through the branches, sending more lifeless leaves sprinkling to the ground.

"Amanda?" Jared said her name softly, almost a whisper.

She swallowed, trying not to feel anything for him. Talking to him with such ease, her guard down, and laughing caused such a scattering of her senses. *She loved Matthew, remember that,* she screamed to herself. But before Matthew, there had been Jared.

"I said I waited a long time to kiss you," he began softly. "Please, look at me." She bit her lower lip and then slowly lifted her eyes to his face. "But I fell in love with you way before I found the courage to ask you about us that night. When we kissed, I knew you were the one for me. I knew that I'd marry you someday."

He searched her face, tears shining in both of their eyes.

"I know you felt what I felt that night, Amanda," he declared huskily. "I could see it in your beautiful blue eyes, and I felt it when your body touched my own."

She pulled her hand away from him, covering her ears.

"Please don't do this!" she exclaimed, standing to her feet; she began walking toward the lake briskly. *She could not do this. Not now. Please not now,* she silently begged, *oh God, this couldn't be happening.*

He caught up to her as her bare feet touched the ice-cold sand. Grabbing her arm, he pulled her around.

"Amanda, please, don't run away from me," he said, his voice filled with emotion. "I don't know how to let you go."

Her tears spilled from her eyes. "Jared, please, I'm married now," she cried.

"Because you were forced to!" he exclaimed passionately. "Can you stand here and tell me that you didn't feel anything that long-ago night? That if you weren't taken, that you and I wouldn't be planning our wedding right now?" She searched his handsome tormented face, images of Matthew competing with his own.

"I don't . . . know," she cried hoarsely. "Jared, I don't—"

He bent down and pressed his lips to hers. Immediately Amanda struggled to push him away, her hands pressed against his chest as she whimpered for him to stop. But then, slowly, the memory of his lips on her own, the last night they had together, burst forth from deep within. Her lips softened and yielded to his own as he wrapped his arms around her, bringing her into his desperate world. Passion surged through Amanda, and she struggled not to be drowned in the depths of his own need. The blanket slid from her shoulders, and Jared pressed her hips into his own; he deepened the kiss, slowly slipping his hand under her shirt to touch her bare waist. Skin on skin contact brought reality crashing back into Amanda's world. She broke the kiss and wrenched herself from his embrace.

"Amanda," he gasped, reaching for her again.

"No!" she yelled, holding her hand out in front of her. A sob racked her body as she realized what she'd done. "Oh God!" Turning, she ran back toward the camp.

"Amanda, wait!" he called after her, catching her arm again. "Please wait!"

"No, let me go!" she sobbed. "Please leave me alone."

"Amanda, you felt it too!" he declared. "What we had is not over, don't you see? It's not over!"

She shoved at his hand angrily. "No!" she stated hotly through her tears. "It is over, Jared!"

"Amanda, how can—," he began, his voice filled with hurt. Much of her anger left her, leaving sorrow in its place. She wiped at her tears.

"I'm still attracted to you, Jared," she said, her admission leaving a sour taste in her mouth. "I can only explain that because of being pulled apart before we ever had a chance. But like I told you when you first came to see me, our chance is over. It's gone!"

"No!" He shook his head vehemently. "I don't believe it. I won't believe it! I love you, Amanda, and you're . . . *mine!*"

She shook her head sadly. "No," she spoke softly, "I'm not yours, not anymore. I belong to someone else now."

"He made you marry him!" he declared, grasping a last bit of hope. "You would have married me willingly. You still can!"

She took a step closer to him, wanting to soothe his pain but knowing she couldn't.

"Maybe I would have married you willingly," she said, "but too much has happened, Jared. My life was hell this past year, and yes, I was forced to marry Matthew, but I *do* love him." She clasped her fist over her heart. "Desperately and completely." Reaching up, she touched Jared's cheek tenderly then whispered, "I'm so sorry." Then she turned and hurried inside.

He sat down on the steps and stared out at the sparkling lake, tears running down his cheeks. She was gone, he had lost her, and his life would never be the same again.

When morning came, Amanda was gone.

CHAPTER 31

A manda stepped out of her car, closing the door gently.
"What do you think?" asked the woman. She walked toward
Amanda, her hand extended. "How are you, Amanda?" she asked as Amanda
shook her hand.

"I'm well," she answered. The cold wind began to blow at them, biting
their skin.

"Well, let's go in and look around before the weather gets the best of us,"
the woman said. Amanda walked behind her. Mrs. Mackey was a pleasant
woman in her midfifties, Amanda estimated, and attractive. She wore a long
black wool coat over her gray business suit. Her graying hair was swept up in
a bun, a blue scarf wrapped around her neck. Amanda shoved her hands into
her own silver parka, protecting them against the cold, and looked around
at the property before her.

It had been another sleepless night that brought Amanda down this dirt
road. The small cottage was happily situated on a small incline about thirty feet
from the one-lane road. Off to the left side was an area enclosed by trellises;
brown ivy vines covered them entirely. On the other side, large maple trees
lined the property. Behind the cottage, thirty acres expanded in continuous
trees and fields. She had noted the For Sale sign that night a few weeks ago
and drove back during daylight, wanting to see the property. When she had
walked the land, she had fallen in love. She recognized the flower gardens had
overgrown from lack of care, knowing she could bring them back, thanks to
her training in the village. The enclosed trellis had two stone benches facing

one another on a large marble slab, where weeds and plants had created their own tangled world. But Amanda could see the property at its finest.

She had called Mrs. Mackey, the realtor, who shared the information and the price of the property with her. Both meeting her satisfaction, she asked to see it. Now here she was. Mrs. Mackey had unlocked the door and stepped aside to let Amanda walk through. Mrs. Mackey began her presentation, Amanda only hearing segments. She looked at the small cottage with affection. The rooms were not too large, nor too small, and they needed painting, some cosmetic work, but no major work seemed to be required. *It was perfect!* Months ago, the last night she had spent with Matthew, she had a wonderful dream. She dreamt that she was near a cottage. A cottage just like this one.

According to Mrs. Mackey, a man had this built for his aging mother who he had brought over from England. To ease her homesickness, he had this replica of an English cottage, with its resembling gardens, built. His mother had lived here happily for ten more years before she had passed away. The son couldn't bear to keep it so decided to sell. She said there were several potential buyers over the years, but they seemed to all withdraw their interest for one reason or another. Amanda believed that this cottage was waiting for her, and she knew they would be happy here, Matthew and her. It was only three quarters of an hour from her parents' home and was set back from the bustle of the city. Mrs. Mackey was still talking when Amanda turned to her, smiling.

"Now this kitchen has all the functioning appliances—," she was saying, when Amanda interrupted her,

"I'll take it," Amanda declared. Mrs. Mackey smiled.

"You will?" she asked. Amanda nodded, her eyes shining with excitement. "Wonderful! Let's go back to my office, and we'll discuss the details."

"Actually," Amanda piped in, "why don't we meet at my parents' office? They'll be expecting us."

"All right, then," she agreed, shaking Amanda's hand eagerly, anticipating her commission. Amanda gave her directions, got in her car, and backed out of the driveway. As she drove away from the house, she smiled. *It was home!*

It had been over a month ago that Amanda had run away from camp. How silly that sounds, but that was exactly what she'd done. She had left at dawn, completely distraught, her emotions frayed. She had walked into the small town and called for a taxi, who then had brought her to the nearest city, where she had caught a bus back home. Once there, she had gathered some of her belongings and checked in at the hotel that Matthew and her had stayed in on her first night home. She asked for the same room, and luckily, it was available. Once settled, she crawled onto the bed they had shared and cried. She cried until the tears seemed to dry up, then completely exhausted, she slept.

Awakening the following day, she knew that she had to contact her parents. She knew by that time they would be home and frantic with worry because she had left a short note saying she was fine but needed time alone. The last thing she wanted to do was discuss her abrupt departure from camp. After showering, she had thrown on some clothes and sat down next to the phone. She hadn't known what she would say. *How could she explain her confusion and sudden panic?*

Instead of calling them that day, she had avoided contact with anyone. She was so ashamed of her behavior with Jared, overwhelmed with guilt for her attraction to him and how she hurt him. The loneliness that had surrounded her was unbearable, but she didn't feel like she could reach out to anyone. No one understood her anymore. She felt so disconnected from everyone . . . everyone except Matthew.

Three days had passed, and she only felt worse each day. Picking up the phone, she had finally called Marty, the therapist her mother insisted she see. Marty had come to her room, where they talked for hours and hours. She comforted Amanda, held her while she cried, and assured her that all the feelings that she was dealing with were normal after such a traumatic experience. After their intense meeting, Amanda allowed Marty to call her parents and let them know where she was.

They had arrived within the hour to collect her. Thankfully, Marty had sat with her parents, in the hotel room, to explain how their pressure for details was harmful to her. The best way for Amanda to heal and be able to take steps to recovering her independence was to let her be—listen to her, be there for her, but never pressure her for their own purposes.

Her parents were truly repentant, revealing their own insecurities on how to handle Amanda now that she was home. Once Marty felt they were all at a better place, she had left them. Amanda agreed to go home, but in her heart, she knew it was only going to be for a short duration.

Then she'd found her cottage. She made her parents aware of her intentions the same day she drove over there to see it in the daylight. Knowing she was of age, she decided to claim her inheritance that her grandmother had left her in a trust. She would live off the trust until she decided where her life was going, promising her parents that she would then reinvest the money that she didn't use. She knew it was very difficult for them to sit back and allow her to make the decisions that she was making. But they knew that changes needed to be made and were willing to go to great lengths to do that.

Amanda pulled her car over in front of the law office. *This was it.* She was finally doing something that felt so right. When she walked in the doors, she could hardly contain her excitement. Soon she would be a homeowner, and she was determined to make it a home for when Matthew returned to her.

Amanda lifted the paint can, pouring the thick white liquid into the rolling pan. Once it was filled, she stood up and looked at the work she had completed. This was the third room she had painted, and the cottage was coming along very well. She rolled the roller in the paint and turned to continue her work on the wall.

"Okay, honey," her father called, walking into the room. "That was the last box." She looked over her shoulder at him and smiled.

"Thanks, Daddy!" she said. Her father rested his hands on his hips and looked around the room.

"You're doing a great job, Amanda," he declared then turned his searching eyes on her. She looked quite adorable, wearing a blue painter's jumper that had paint smears and drops spattered on it. Her hair was pulled up in a ponytail, with a white bandana covering the top of her head.

"Thanks." She accepted the compliment cheerfully. He smiled at the paint that decorated her nose and her left cheek. She set the roller back down.

"You know," he said, "this is the happiest I've seen you in a long time." She only smiled and pushed away a stray piece of hair with the back of her hand. "Are you sure that you're going to be all right here alone?" He tried not to sound concerned, but he knew he failed.

"Yes," she stated confidently. "Two weeks from now, Matthew will be home. Then, I won't be alone anymore."

"Yes," he said quietly. "I have to admit something to you, Amanda." She looked up at his serious tone. "I truly expected you to realize that you didn't love Matthew—that you were only confused or just infatuated."

She looked down at her paint-spattered hands, then back up.

"I know you did. So did Mom," she said, with no malice. "But I do love him, Daddy."

"I've finally begun to accept that," he admitted. "However he is to blame for hurting our family, he must have done something very right to have won your heart." Looking up at her father, smiling, she said, "Yes, Daddy, he's done a lot right."

"All right, love." He leaned over and gently brushed her cheek with a kiss. "Be safe. And call me if you need me. You have my cell phone number?"

"Yes." She chuckled. "It's on the list of all the emergency numbers that *you* placed on the wall by the phone!" she said and walked him to the door.

"That's right." He smiled. Kissing her cheek tenderly, he stepped outside.

She waved as his car pulled away, the tires making a crunching sound on the snow-covered road.

Walking back in, she continued to paint her living room. After about an hour, she stood up and stretched her back. She walked into the kitchen, opened up the refrigerator, and took out a can of soda then reached into a box near the table, searching for a glass. After finding one, she rinsed it out with water then poured her soda in the glass. She walked back into the living room and switched on her stereo, admitting that she did feel a little anxious, and tried to shrug off her tension.

She walked to the window and looked out into her yard; the late afternoon sun was casting an orange glow over the white snow that had fallen recently. It was so beautiful. "There's nothing to be afraid of," she mumbled aloud.

"You're right," a male voice spoke softly from behind her. Gasping, Amanda turned to see Matthew standing in the doorway. Dropping her glass on the floor, she was frozen in place, not hearing the soda making a fizzing noise as it crawled across the wood floor. *He looked so wonderful!* His brown hair had been cut into a more popular style, shorter on the sides, slightly longer on top; he wore a pair of jeans with a navy turtleneck sweater. His blue eyes twinkled with amusement, his hands resting on the wood casing of the door. Tears formed in her eyes. *Could it be?*

"Matthew," she whispered. He absorbed everything about her. The dark circles under her eyes, her beautiful expressive eyes that were now watching him in disbelief. His beautiful angel covered in paint. He couldn't help but smile.

"Hi, baby," he said softly, stepping into the room; he extended his hand. A sob escaped her lips; her hand flew to her mouth as she looked at his hand, still unable to move. *She couldn't believe he was here!* All the hurt and loneliness poured from her soul as she stood before her husband. "Amanda." He came closer and stood before her as she shook her head, crying. He opened his arms, and she threw herself against him, wrapping her arms around him. Burying her face into his shoulder, she breathed in his scent. So familiar, and so . . . *Matthew.* He held her tightly to him, tears shining in his eyes. They stood in one another's embrace for several minutes, Amanda's crying slowly subsiding.

He tenderly kissed the top of her head then leaned back so he could look in her eyes. Her face was wet with tears, her nose pink.

"I thought you'd be happy to see me," he teased gently. She reached her hand up and touched his face affectionately.

"Oh, Matthew!" she whispered. "I've missed you so much!"

"And I you," he whispered huskily, bending his head until his lips touched hers. Searing passion broke through the dam caused by separation, their souls, their bodies as one, on fire for each other. The gentle lovemaking they had always known was replaced by a wild urgency of unfulfilled desires. From the center of the living room, they staggered into the bedroom door. Matthew had pressed her tightly to the door, her arms pinned by his own above her head as he crushed her with his demanding kiss. She couldn't get enough of him and was desperate to have more. With the handle jarred, the door flew open; they stumbled around boxes to the bed. Amanda felt the bed on the back of her knees, but he held her up, kissing her lips, her face. He pulled the sleeve off her shoulder, his lips tasting her, but he wanted more. Reaching in front, he tore open the front of the jumper, buttons flying in a clatter to the floor. Sliding out of the outfit just as eagerly as he wanted it off, she then reached for his sweater, quickly pulling it over his head. He shed his jeans and then lowered her to the bed more gently than he had wanted. Matthew caressed, his hands demanding; Amanda tasted his skin that burned beneath her lips. Trembling with need, they were suddenly, almost violently, joined together, their souls connected, their love sustained, their union complete once more.

Much later, Amanda rested her head on his chest, her hand lying on his stomach. His left arm was wrapped around her, his hand resting on her hip, his other, bent, supporting his head. "How did you know where I was?" she asked softly. The room was darkening as the late afternoon began to turn into early evening.

"I called your father last night," he admitted. "I wanted to feel things out."

"Last night," she repeated. "He spent the whole morning helping me move, and he never said a word."

"That would be my fault," he said quietly. "I wanted to surprise you." He paused a moment. "But to say that I was surprised, would be an understatement, when I found out that my wife had gone and bought herself a cottage outside of town." Amanda smiled and rubbed her cheek against his chest.

"I wanted to surprise *you*."

"You've been busy, haven't you?" he asked affectionately.

"Mmm," she said. Then she remembered what he had said moments before. She propped herself up on her elbow, her eyes full of questions. "What do you mean, you wanted to 'feel' things out?"

He averted his gaze slightly and squirmed a little.

"Well, I wasn't sure," he began, his voice strained. "I wanted to know if—"

He stopped and slowly brought his gaze back to hers. Her eyes were bright with tears. "Oh, Amanda, don't cry, honey."

"You thought that I would decide that I didn't love you?" she asked, her voice just above a whisper.

"No, not at first," he admitted, "but then . . ." He reached his hand behind her head, playing with her hair.

"But then?" she asked. His eyes met hers; a sadness that mirrored her own was evident in their depths.

"But then, I didn't know," he said.

"How could you doubt me?" she accused him softly. "Do you think me so weak?"

"Weak?" he asked surprised. "No, not weak." Looking out into the darkened night through the window next to the bed, he continued, "Vulnerable, yes."

"I was a mess when you brought me home," she said. "Then you left me"—tears trickled down her cheeks—"and I needed you!"

He looked back at her, pain visible in his eyes.

"No, Amanda," he said, "you needed time to be with your family."

She shook her head and rested it back on his chest.

"No," she denied. He pulled her back up, her teary eyes meeting his.

"Don't you see how we would have always been judged?" he asked her softly. "That we would've never been accepted?"

"No," she said. "Matthew—" "*I* needed to know, Amanda," he said firmly. She looked at him, surprise in her eyes.

"But why?" she asked. Shaking his head, he gently set her aside. He sat up and found his jeans on the floor. She watched silently as he slipped them on, stood up, and walked out of the bedroom. Standing, and again searching through another box, she found some fresh clothes. Putting on some underclothes, jeans, and a sweatshirt, she ran her fingers through her hair as she stepped from the room, not understanding why he walked away. It scared her to think that four months apart could make them strangers.

She found Matthew in the kitchen, standing in front of the large window, his back to her, his arms crossed against his chest. She walked around the table, hesitating a couple feet away. "I've upset you," she said softly.

He sighed, shaking his head, but stayed where he was.

"No, you didn't," he said quietly. She dug her hands into her jean pockets, waiting. Moments later, he turned to her slowly, his eyes meeting her anxious stare. "I needed to know that I didn't somehow brainwash you. I needed to know that what we had in the village, we could have out here."

"Brainwash me?" she asked. "Matthew, that's ridicul—"

"No, Amanda, it's not," he stated, his tone hard. "I spent my whole life living in there," he said, pointing out the window. "I thought everything in there was normal. Then I met you and I realized it wasn't. When I brought you home, I realized that my whole life I'd been deceived. If I was brainwashed into believing that our way of life was right, how do you know that I didn't brainwash you into loving me?"

"Because you didn't convince me to love you," she said softly. "I fell in love with you, Matthew because . . . God, for so many reasons." She took a step closer to him. "Brainwashing is changing the way someone thinks, not what you feel in your heart."

He so desperately wanted to pull her into his arms, but he held back.

"Have you had doubts, Amanda?" he asked softly. "While I was gone?"

"No!" she stated, without hesitation. "Not once, not about you."

"Then what kind of doubts?"

"Doubts about me, who I am, my sanity." She tried to smile, trying to make light of it. He looked pained.

"I did that to you," he said solemnly. "I've really messed up your life."

Amanda silently searched his face. *He was punishing himself,* she thought, *but it wasn't the first time he had done this.* For some reason he seemed even more discouraged, yet she couldn't deny that he did affect her life in a negative way at one time. She wouldn't insult him.

"Matthew," she said softly. "I did a lot of soul-searching while you were away." She walked to the other side of the room, opened a drawer, shuffled through it, and then walked back over to them. The only light in the room was the moon shining through the window and its glare on the snow. She placed a small glass jar on the table, dropped a votive candle into the center of the jar, then with a flick of her fingers, used a lighter and lit the candle. A warm glow instantly filled the room. She smiled up at him sheepishly. "I kind of got used to the whole candle thing." She returned to stand in front of him. "I realized a lot about myself. I was a very selfish person—"

"Amanda, no you—," he tried to interrupt, but she held up her hand.

"Let me finish," she said quietly. "I *was* selfish, and I *was* self-centered. My intent was not to hurt anyone, but I know I have." Jared's image came to mind. "I was given everything as a child, all the comforts life could give, and then some. I never needed to ask for anything, yet I was determined to prove myself. To prove that I could be something, that I could make something of myself without any help. To do that, I had a one-track mind and it didn't include anyone but myself."

"I'm not denying that I didn't care for people. I'm not a mean person, that's not what I'm trying to say," she said softly. "But I was always so self-involved in my own little world that I had created, that I was oblivious to life around me. To the people around me." She paused, looking up at him. "Then it was all taken away."

"Amanda—," he began.

"But I'm beginning to believe that my life really began, when I met you," she said softly, looking at him, her eyes shining in the candlelight.

"I don't understand," he said, looking confused.

"It wasn't until my sheltered life was ripped from me did I really, truly, begin to appreciate it," she said. "Matthew, why keep reliving the obvious? We both know why you did what you did and we also know who's really to blame, don't we?"

Matthew looked away.

"I've tried to figure out why everything happened to me," she admitted. "I don't know. But I won't try and figure out how I could love you with everything that I am!" He looked back at her, his heart in his eyes, still hesitating. "That's just the way that it is. I do love you, Matthew, you mean everything to me." She stepped closer and rested her palms on his chest, staring up at him adoringly. "I'll always love you," she whispered.

Finally reaching for her, he grasped her tightly in his arms, burying his face in her hair. "Oh, Amanda, I love you so much!" he said, his voice hoarse with emotion. She held him, her heart expanding with the joy of being in his arms again. When he pulled back, he looked down at her. "Amanda, I have to admit something to you."

She smiled at him. "What?" she asked, touching his cheek tenderly.

"*I'm* really messed up," he admitted quietly, his eyes still filled with torment. "These last few months, I recognized just how much."

"We'll help each other," she said seriously, "Together we'll try to figure out where to go from here."

He nodded, kissing her forehead. "I've been back to the village," he said quietly. Startled, she pulled slightly away, to look up at him.

"What?" she asked, her eyes wide.

"You heard me," he said. "I've been working with the FBI. Part of my penance." He gave her a humorless smile. "I showed them where it's located." He stepped back from her.

"Matthew, I thought—" she began but stopped at his disgusted expression.

"What?" he asked sharply. "That I would never betray my people?" He laughed harshly. "Well, it turns out, I'm a coward."

"You are not!" She raised her voice to him. "You're the most courageous man alive!" A moment of tenderness crossed his face as his eyes rested on her own, but it quickly disappeared.

"They arrested a couple of the students that helped me find you," he admitted quietly, sliding his hands into his pockets. "They confessed that they were paid one thousand dollars a piece to help and keep silent." He paused and ran his hand through his hair. "I had no idea that kind of money was involved."

"A thousand dollars . . . for a life," Amanda said softly.

"The FBI found an employment agency that was hired by the village to find and hire these people. They've found out so much, Amanda. So much that I never knew about. Things that I know no one else knows about in there."

"What things, Matthew?" she asked.

"Illegal and shameful actions," was all he said. He backed up against the wall and slid down to the floor. "So much money." Reaching up, he extended his hand. She quickly slipped her hand into his and joined him on the floor. "Amanda, my people, my family—we've been so deceived."

"Oh, Matthew," she whispered, wanting to erase the haunted look that settled on his face. "You were born trusting him. How could you have known?"

"I don't know," he said, "but I would still be in there if it hadn't been for you."

Amanda swallowed. "Is that a good or bad thing?" she asked. He brought her hand to his lips and kissed her lightly.

"Don't be ridiculous," he said. "You're the best thing that's ever happened to me." He looked down, her hand still enclosed in his; he rubbed his thumb over her skin. Deep in his thoughts, she waited. After several silent minutes had passed, he continued. "The FBI set up a huge operation, not far from the village," he began again quietly. "Not far from the electric fences. They're monitoring the activity coming, going and within. You remember Sergeant Stevens?" She nodded. "Well, he's working close with the FBI, and kind of helped me out, explaining things that I didn't understand. He was able to show me some of the video footage from the village." He took a shuddering breath. "There's been no sign of my mother."

"Matthew, I'm sure she's fine," Amanda assured him, hoping desperately that she was right. He nodded, wanting to believe her, yet he hadn't been able to shed the dreadful feeling he carried with him since that day.

"The fact that you won't press charges against me," he said, "is stopping them from going in and arresting Pastor. Right now they're waiting."

"But if he's doing illegal activities—" she began.

"Yes, they know that, and could arrest him for only those crimes," he explained patiently. "But they want him for kidnapping too, and they believe that he'll carry on our, I mean, the tradition. And when he acts, they'll catch him." He hesitated. "And when he's arrested, the FBI will then destroy the village and the only way of life that my people have known." The guilt he was carrying was killing him.

"Don't you think that it's best that way?" she asked softly. "They, too, would realize how deceitful Pastor really is."

"There are times when I believe that," he agreed, "but most of them prefer to have the simple life. They won't want, nor will they be able to live out in this society. It's *them* that I am concerned with. Where will they go? What will they do? I have you, and you have your family. But who will they have?"

"I don't know," she said. "Maybe the women's families?" Matthew shook his head. "No," he said. "Maybe the younger women, but most of the women that have been there have put that way of life behind them. Most won't want to return. Not all the women came from loving families, like you."

Amanda looked down again at their hands. "Why do you feel so responsible to them?" she whispered. He looked at her in surprise.

"Because this is my fault," he said, exasperated. "It's my fault that they'll lose everything."

"No, it's not," she said. "It's the pastor's fault."

"Yes," he acknowledged, "but I'm the one that has drawn attention to the village. What right did I have to assume anything about what they would want?"

"But there may be many people there that want out but are too afraid of the pastor to risk it," she countered, refusing to allow him to accept such a responsibility. He searched her face. "What you did was right. They might not think that it's what they want, but it's what's right because what he's teaching is wrong."

"I know it's the right thing to do, out here," he said softly, "but I belonged in there. I believed what we did was right and so do the rest of the villagers. They won't understand." Amanda was quiet. He seemed to have dwelled on this for a long time, and one conversation with her was not going to change his mind. His healing would happen in time, like her own.

"Why don't I make us some dinner," she suggested. "Are you hungry?"

His eyes met hers, and a slow smiled crept on his face.

"Yeah, I guess I am," he said. She smiled and started to stand. "Amanda." He grabbed her hand, becoming serious. "I'm sorry if I hurt you when I left."

She sat back down, cupping his face in her hands.

"Promise"—her throat tightened—"to never leave me again."

He leaned forward, tenderly kissing her.

"I promise," he whispered, his own voice full of emotion.

CHAPTER 32

E ndless conversation, total seclusion, and love filled the next couple of weeks for Amanda and Matthew. Eventually their private time had to come to an end. It was Christmas Eve, and they had promised to spend the weekend with her parents.

Amanda groaned as the sunlight pierced her sleepy world. She pulled the warm comforter over her head, and Matthew chuckled huskily, wrapping his arm around her waist, pulling her close, her back resting against his chest.

"Good morning, my love," he whispered and kissed her temple.

"Good morning," she whispered back, not as sweetly. Matthew smiled against her hair.

"Are we grumpy this morning?" he asked softly.

"No," she admitted wistfully. "I just wish we could stay in bed all day."

He chuckled again.

"Again?" he asked.

She giggled this time. "Okay, okay, again," she admitted. "I've grown quite fond of our all-day bed retreats."

He squeezed her closely. "As I have," he whispered softly, "but, alas, your parents are expecting us. So, we must part ourselves with our comfortable bed and get up for Christmas."

She sighed loudly. "I suppose you're right," she said after a few moments. She turned in his arms, smiling, tilting her face upward, her sleepy eyes meeting his own. "I love you, Matthew."

His expression sobered, his eyes caressing her face affectionately.

"I love you," he replied tenderly; bending his head, he kissed her lips softly. Then pretending to growl, he rolled away from her, sitting up. "Arghhhh! Nice try, Mrs. Ryan, but we're getting up!"

Amanda giggled and pulled the covers over her head.

"Get over here!" he laughed, jumping back under the covers.

"Do you have all the presents?" Amanda called from the front door of their cottage. Matthew looked over his shoulder, his arms full of gifts, on his way to the car, an open trunk waiting for him.

"Yeah," he called. "I sure hope so," he muttered under his breath.

Amanda giggled on her way down the walkway.

"I heard that!" she laughed. Matthew just smiled in her direction. He watched his wife as she put their bags in the backseat then turned to him, giving him a glorious smile. She wore her silver parka, her cheeks rosy from the cold, crisp morning air. Her hair was left down, a beautiful cascade of blond hair, her bright blue eyes radiating her joy. He also remembered those rosy cheeks this morning as she lay beneath him while they made love. God, he loved her!

He slammed the trunk closed and walked over to the driver seat.

"Everything locked up?" he asked as they both slid into their seats.

"Yep!" she said. As they drove from their cottage, Amanda gave him a sidelong glance. "What were you thinking about back there when you were loading the presents? You looked so serious."

"Oh, not much," he said quietly, giving her a small smile. "Just about how much I love you."

She grasped his free hand, squeezing it gently, smiling. "Oh," she said. "I thought maybe, you were, I don't know, tense about going to my parents. You haven't seen them since, well, since before."

His expression sobered, and he kept his eyes on the road.

"No," he admitted. "I'm not tense. I actually have seen your father a few times."

Startled, Amanda looked at him. "What?"

He glanced at her, then back to the road, squeezing her hand.

"Don't be upset, Amanda," he said softly. "He was concerned about how the investigation was going." Amanda swallowed. *My father had talked to Matthew . . . seen him . . . and he never said anything.*

During the last couple of weeks, Matthew had shared how he had managed to survive in the past four months, admitting to her that he was just as devastated that morning when he'd left her, that he had the cab drop him off at the hotel they stayed at together. For two days he, also, stayed in bed. Depressed and heartbroken, several times he was so tempted to go to Amanda but forced himself not to. There he stayed and tried to figure out what he could do to make a living. Feeling frustrated, he called the police station, looking for Sergeant Stevens. Meanwhile, Sergeant Stevens had heard of Matthew's departure from the Tanner family.

He was concerned for Matthew, now knowing his past and lack of knowledge about the world. He hadn't forgotten his crimes; neither did he want to lose contact with the young man during the investigation, so he invited him into his own home, assuring him that his wife would love having him as a guest. Reluctantly, yet partially relieved, he had accepted the sergeant's hospitality. It was the sergeant that began to help him adjust to this "world." Matthew began to trust him, and it was difficult to hold back information on the village when he and his family were being so kind. So that's when he compromised his friends and family, while praying he was doing the right thing.

The sergeant found him a carpenter position with a small company that creates unique furniture pieces. The owner, Mr. Simons, was a gruff but kind man. He paid a decent wage and was fair, accepting Matthew, not treating him any different than the next employee, even though he knew about his past. Matthew respected him, and Mr. Simons was impressed with Matthew's ability and experience with wood. It didn't take long for Simons to trust him with difficult pieces and high-paying clients. Matthew began to save his money. Mrs. Stevens took the time to show him how to bank his money, use a checking account, and all the other paper functions that come with handling money. He acquired a driver's license; though he knew how to drive, he'd never been tested. Mrs. Stevens helped him shop for clothes and personal belongings, patiently answering all of his questions.

Matthew had grown fond of the Stevens. There were many a night that he ached for his own mother, wondering about her fate, and then about his wife, and how she was doing. The constant ache he carried with him. But the generosity that the Stevens had shown him made such a difficult time at least bearable.

Living this new life was a constant challenge to him and a way of life so opposite to everything he'd ever been taught. He kept his Bible close at hand, relying on his faith to help him through his confusion and turmoil. The Stevens brought Matthew to church with them. He was inspired by the awesome cathedral they attended, spending more time examining the artists' work than listening to the sermon. But eventually he began to listen to the kind words of the man of God, so different than what he'd been used to. Realizing there were no harsh accusations, no punishing threats.

The months had passed slowly, and the investigation helped keep him distracted and confused. All the anxieties and fears that he fought succumbing to vanished when he stepped into the cottage two weeks ago.

Matthew turned and glanced at Amanda. She had turned her head and was looking out the passenger window. He tugged at her hand.

"Amanda," he began. She turned to look at him, her blues eyes, which had been shining, now appeared sad.

"Matthew, you don't know," she started to say, "how hard it was being without you. My father knew how hard it was for me, and he never said anything."

Matthew slipped his hand from hers, resting both his hands on the steering wheel. "That's because I asked him not to say anything to you," he admitted quietly.

Amanda's jaw dropped as she stared at him. "What?" she asked. "Why would you—" He squeezed the wheel, his knuckles whitening.

"You don't think that I wanted him to tell you?" he interrupted, looking at her and then back at the road. "I was hurting too! I wanted to see you. But I knew—I knew if you found out where I was, that you would've tried to find me. And then we would've never known if . . . we wouldn't have had the time to see . . . to prove to everyone . . . that you really loved me."

Amanda tried to understand, sitting quietly for a few moments.

"How many times did you see him?" she asked softly, searching his profile.

"Twice," he said. "Sergeant Stevens arranged a couple of meetings, and I *am* part of the investigation."

"I see," she said, looking away, then back again. "And how was he to you? He wasn't rude, was he?" she asked, her tone softening.

"No, he wasn't," he admitted. "To tell you the truth, I'm a little curious on how I'm going to be treated today." Amanda leaned her head on his shoulder.

"Don't worry," she declared. "My parents know how much I love you, and my other relatives, well, they're going to be curious. My mother promised to keep the gathering small and I am excited to see my family again."

Matthew kissed the top of her head. "I know you are," he said.

"Matthew!" her father called. "Amanda!" he greeted, joining them on the walkway. "Merry Christmas!" He hugged them both. When he stepped back, Matthew couldn't keep the surprised expression off his face, and Amanda giggled at him.

"Merry Christmas, Daddy!" She kissed him on the cheek. "We just have a few more things in the car," she said, tossing her head back in the direction of the driveway.

"Well, let me help you," he said. "Matthew, why don't you set those on the porch and help me." Matthew took a deep breath. Here we go, he thought.

Amanda cast a nervous glance at her father's retreating back but smiled at her husband.

"Go," she said. "It'll be fine." He nodded, then set his load down. He stopped in front of Amanda, kissing her lightly on the lips, his eyes twinkling with humor.

"If I'm not back in twenty minutes," he teased, "send out a search party."

"Matthew." She giggled again and walked inside.

Matthew joined Maxwell at the car. He looked in the trunk, knowing there was only one present left and that this was not just a helping hand. Maxwell was leaning his hip against the back of the car, his arms crossed. Matthew stopped a couple feet from him, his hands shoved into the pockets of his khaki slacks.

He cleared his throat. "Sir?"

"I just wanted to speak to you alone, before the night begins," he said. "Amanda looks wonderful." Matthew looked toward the house; the front door was closed.

"Yes, sir," he said, his voice full of emotion. "She is wonderful!"

"I want to welcome you properly to the family, Matthew," he declared, straightening, holding out his hand. Matthew searched his smiling face then, hesitantly, shook his hand.

"Thank you, sir." He smiled back. Maxwell took the present out of the car, tossed it to Matthew, then closed the trunk.

"You're my son-in-law. Call me Max," he stated cheerfully. "You know, Matthew," he said as they walked toward the house, "this whole situation couldn't be much more bizarre, and well, my wife . . ."

"You don't have to explain, Mr.—uh, Max," Matthew interjected. "I know it's going to take time." Max nodded, smiled, and slapped Matthew's shoulder good-naturedly.

"She'll come around, don't worry," he said, and they walked into the house.

The festivities began soon after they arrived. Aunts, uncles, cousins, and friends poured through the door. Holiday greetings could be heard throughout the house. Curiosity was an understatement about Matthew and Amanda's relationship.

Other than a few rude comments, everyone was polite. Amanda was so happy to see everyone but was completely exhausted by the end of the evening.

It was close to eleven o'clock when the last guest finally left. Amanda was lying on the couch, her head resting on Matthew's lap. The fire was burning low, reflecting pretty colors on the Christmas decorations hanging from the tree. Max sat in his leather chair, next to the fire, holding a drink in his hand. Diane was sitting in the adjacent chair.

"It was a nice party," Diane said. "Everyone seemed to behave themselves." Diane was reserved with Matthew, when he had walked in with her husband earlier. But as the night progressed, she'd watched Amanda with Matthew. Someone would have to be blind not to see the love they have for one another. And laughter. Diane couldn't think of one time since Amanda's return that she laughed. It seemed tonight that's all she did. The laughter was always when Matthew was directly involved. It brought tears to her eyes to see how happy Matthew made her, the happiest she had seen her daughter in a long time. He'd done as she had asked, giving Amanda time to readjust. She had to admit she believed that Amanda would come to her senses and end her relationship with him. The two of them were committed to one another, anyone could see that. For this, she would accept him.

"Can we exchange some presents now?" Amanda sat up, her face lit with excitement. Everyone laughed.

"What?" Amanda asked, pretending ignorance.

"Oh, Amanda!" her mother laughed. "In that, you haven't changed!"

"You're right!" she agreed, smiling. "So can we?"

"Yes, of course!" her mother agreed. "But remember the rules . . . just one!"

Matthew watched the closeness of Amanda's family. His family now. He fought the sadness that he felt, longing to see his mother, and realized how awful it must have been for Amanda to be away from her loved ones. He forced himself to smile as Amanda scurried off the couch, over to the tree, moving several boxes until she came to a small one. Then she got to her feet.

"Mom, Dad, I hope you don't mind, but I'd like to give Matthew his present from me," she said softly.

"Not at all, honey," they both said. Matthew sat up, a little surprised. The Christmas they had spent in the village consisted of no present exchange. The pastor didn't allow such materialism. Matthew smiled at Amanda's beautiful face.

"What did you do?" he asked.

"You'll see," she teased, handing him the box. He moved it around in his hands. "Open it."

Chuckling, he did. Lifting the lid, his hands went still as he stared at the gift. Amanda watched and waited. He lifted shining eyes to meet her own.

"Amanda," he said, slowly lifting out the gold watch.

"Oh, Amanda!" her mother explained. "It's beautiful!"

"Very nice!" her father chimed in. Matthew met Amanda's eyes again. "Thank you," he said.

She smiled. "Do you like it?" she asked. "There's an inscription on the inside of the band. Here"—turning it over for him—"look." Matthew read, *To my one and only true love.* His eyes shining, he slipped his hand behind her head, pulling her gently in for a kiss.

"Thank you," he repeated as he released her. She nodded, tears shining in her own eyes now. "I love you," he whispered.

"I love you, too," she whispered back. Turning away, she saw her parents watching the two of them intently. Blushing slightly, she reached back under the tree for another wrapped gift.

"Mom, Dad, this present is kind of special. I wanted to give this to you tonight," she said, her tone becoming serious. She looked at Matthew anxiously, and he nodded his head in encouragement. "I thought about this for a long time, before I knew this would be the perfect present for the two of you." She handed the gift to her mother hesitantly.

Her mother accepted the gift, looking at her husband questioningly as he shrugged his shoulders. She slowly unwrapped the paper and found in her hands a flower-covered book, with the word "journal" on the cover. Confused, she looked up at Amanda.

"I don't understand," she began. Amanda smiled, swallowing the lump that had formed in her throat. She looked from her father to her mother.

"I know how important it is for you to know of my experience in the village," Amanda began. Diane's hand flew to her mouth, tears forming in her eyes; her lips trembled. "I didn't know how to tell you so I wrote it down."

"Oh, Amanda," her father began, becoming emotional. Amanda was kneeling on the floor; Matthew reached over and rested his hands on her shoulders. She reached her hands up and touched his.

"Amanda, I don't know what to say," her mother began. Amanda smiled through unshed tears.

"Please don't say anything," she said. "You may not like the gift much after you read it, but"—her voice changed, becoming abrupt—"don't look to Matthew to blame. You'll be upset when you read some of the things I wrote.

But you have to know that my love for Matthew won't change and what I went through, was not his fault!" Her parents both nodded, speechless.

They exchanged a few more presents, and then her parents retired for the night. Matthew snuggled to Amanda closely on the sofa, the house became quiet, and they both watched the flames dance in the fireplace.

"I think that went well," Matthew said softly.

"Mmm," Amanda murmured. "Do you think they were tired or do you think they're reading the journal?"

"I think they're reading," he said.

"Me too." She sighed. Her back was resting against his chest; she turned so that she could see his face. "Did I do the right thing?"

He searched her face. "Yes," he answered after a few moments. "I think it's better that they know. I just wish, I don't know." He looked toward the fire.

"What, Matthew?" she asked. He slowly turned his eyes back to her.

"I guess I just wish that it wasn't me that caused all of those painful things," he said soberly.

"Matthew, it wasn't your fault, we've been over this," she said, not unkindly.

"It will always be my fault, Amanda," he stated and looked away again.

She rested her cheek against his chest. "If you didn't do what you did, then we would never have met," she declared. Pausing for a long moment, she then continued, "You're my soul mate, Matthew. We were destined to be together."

He wrapped his arms around her tightly. "Oh, Amanda!" he declared softly. "I don't deserve you!"

Closing her eyes, she savored his warm protective embrace.

"We deserve each other, Matthew," she whispered. He loosened his arms and pulled her back slightly so she could see his face.

"I have something for you," he said softly. "I wanted to wait until we were alone to give it to you." Amanda slowly sat up as he stood up and left the room. She hugged herself, missing his warmth. He walked back into the room, a small box in his hand. He knelt down before her and held out his hand.

Her eyes rapidly searched his face. "Matthew?"

"We never had the chance to do this right," he said softly. "I want to make things right." He opened up the small box and held it open for her. Amanda gasped at the beautiful diamond ring that was nestled in the velvet folds of the box.

"Matthew!" she exclaimed.

"Amanda," he began, "will you marry me, again?" he asked, his eyes shining with emotion. Shocked, Amanda looked up from the ring to Matthew's beautiful eyes, and she burst into tears, covering her face with her hands.

Flustered, Matthew snapped the box closed and joined her on the sofa, gathering her into his arms. "Amanda, I'm sorry," he consoled her softly. "I thought that you'd be happy."

She lifted her tear-streamed face, shaking her head. "I am . . . happy!" she cried. "I just . . . never expected . . ." She buried her face on his chest. Matthew smiled and held her close.

After a few moments, she began to calm down. When she sheepishly pulled away, she smiled.

"Should I assume that you accept?" he teased softly.

Wiping her face with her hands. "Yes," she said. "Yes, I'll marry you again." She touched his face with her hand. "I love you, Matthew," she whispered.

"I love you, too," he whispered back.

CHAPTER 33

The next morning, Amanda was awakened by Christmas music drifting into her childhood room. Rolling over, she felt Matthew begin to stir from his sleep. She propped herself up on her elbows. He blinked open his eyes, seeing his smiling wife.

"Good morning," she greeted. He turned to his side, facing her.

"Good morning," he greeted hoarsely, his voice not yet ready for use. "Is that music I hear?" he asked, scowling.

Amanda chuckled. "Yes. The Tanner tradition." She twisted her body and snuggled her back up against his chest. He wrapped his arm around her waist as she held her hand up, staring at the shining diamond that decorated her hand.

"It's funny," she said softly. "I didn't think I needed this."

"Needed what?"

"The ring, a wedding," she said, "because I'm just happy being your wife. I didn't think about how it happened anymore, just that we're married. But now . . ."

He tightened his arm around her, holding her closer.

"But now?" he asked softly.

"But now I realized that I really did want this!" she admitted. "I want the diamond and the dress. I want to write invitations and plan the wedding and especially, I want my Dad to walk me down the aisle."

She gently pulled away from him and sat up. "Do you think that's shallow?" she asked softly, her eyebrows coming together.

Matthew smiled and rubbed her arm softly.

"No," he assured, "I don't." She gave him a small smile, then a serious expression covered her face. "What is it?"

She looked up at him. "I don't know," she whispered. "I'm so happy and that makes me scared sometimes."

He sat up. "Scared?" he asked, confused. "But why?"

"I'm scared because I feel like this is a dream and I might wake up, that something terrible will be there," she said, just above a whisper. She gave him a shaky smile. "I know it must sound silly." He cupped her face gently in between his hands.

"Amanda, your nightmare is over," he whispered. "I plan on spending the rest of my life trying to make up all that I've done to you! It's all right to be happy."

"Matthew—" she started to say, her hands covering his.

"No, shhhh," he said and kissed her softly on the lips. "No more talk about this. We're getting up and going to have breakfast with your parents. We need to tell them our plans. All right?"

Smiling, she replied, "All right."

They both washed up, dressed, and then hand-in-hand descended the stairs. Both of her parents were in the kitchen. Her mother was still in her bathrobe, sitting at the breakfast counter, a hot cup of coffee in her hands. Her father was in a sweatshirt and sweatpants, leaning against the counter, his arms crossed over his chest. They both smiled.

"Good morning!" her mom said. She seemed tired and her cheerfulness a little strained. "Merry Christmas."

"Thanks, Mom, and to you too." She kissed her cheek then hugged and kissed her father. "That coffee smells wonderful!"

"Sit, Matthew, relax," her father said. Matthew did, trying to decipher the mood that they were in. Amanda set about fixing Matthew and herself some coffee. She walked over and placed a mug in front of Matthew. He smiled his thanks and took a sip, almost choking when Diane gasped, startling him.

"Amanda!" she exclaimed. "What in the world?" She stood up and rounded the counter, playfully snatching up her hand. Amanda grinned from ear to ear. "My god, it's beautiful!" Her eyes flew to her husband's, then she looked at Matthew. Maxwell pushed himself from the counter and walked over to his daughter, taking a look at the ring. Amanda looked up at both of her parents.

"Matthew asked me to marry him again," she announced. "We're going to have a proper wedding." Shocked, both pairs of eyes fell on Matthew. He cleared his throat and stood up; the room was silent until the realization set in. Then Maxwell smiled and met Matthew across the room.

"You continue to surprise me!" he declared, shaking Matthew's hand, his eyes shining. "That's some ring!" Amanda's mother hugged her daughter, tears shining in her eyes. Then she walked over to Matthew; he hesitated, but she reached out and hugged him.

"Congratulations!" she whispered tearfully. "And thank you." When she pulled away, Matthew was so surprised by her affection that he just stood there speechless. He glanced up at Maxwell, and Maxwell winked.

"You've done good!"

Diane turned back to Amanda. "Have you decided on a date?" she asked. Amanda looked at Matthew and smiled.

"No," she said. "We want to plan the wedding with the two of you."

Diane's hands flew to her mouth, covering her wide grin.

"Oh, this is," she began, "this is so wonderful!"

"Well, kids, I do believe that you just gave your mother the best Christmas gift possible!" Maxwell laughed, taking a sip of his coffee. "Does that mean I can take back the gifts that I bought you?" he teased his wife. They all laughed.

"Don't even think about it, Maxwell!" Diane smiled.

"All right, wife!" he said. "My stomach is demanding food!"

"All right, all right," she said. "You boys go in the other room. Amanda will make breakfast, while I pretend to help."

"Come on, Matthew," Max said. "Bring your coffee, and we'll go and lounge in the other room."

Matthew smiled and kissed his wife on the cheek.

After they left the room, Amanda turned to see her mother take the journal that she'd given her from her robe pocket. She placed it on the counter and looked up at Amanda. Amanda nodded and quietly sat down.

"You read everything," she stated. Her mother's mood had sobered and she nodded.

"Yes. Your father and I both did," she said quietly. When Amanda's eyes met hers, she saw the tears that trickled down her cheek. "Amanda, what you went through—," she began. Amanda reached over and rested her hand on her mother's.

"Mom," she said, "don't. I'm happy. Truly."

"I don't know what to say," Diane admitted. "After reading this"—she picked up the book—"I felt such anger and hatred for Matthew and . . . his people. Yet, after everything that happened, you love him."

"Mom, I wish I could explain everything so that it made sense, so that you would understand," Amanda said, resting her chin in the palm of her hand. "But I can't."

"You must have been so scared!" her mother exclaimed painfully. "The hardest thing for me to accept was that your father and I were helpless to protect our baby!"

Amanda's eyes was stung with tears as she nodded. She took a deep breath.

"Mom, I wrote this for you to know what I went through. I don't like thinking about it. And I don't want to talk about it, okay? I'm trying to move on, and leave that nightmare behind me. Please, just be happy for Matthew and I. I love him so much!"

"Amanda, a miscarriage. Losing a baby is a traumatic experience, honey," she whispered. "You needed me and I wasn't there." Amanda stood and hugged her mother.

"You were there in my heart, Mom," Amanda said softly. Diane hugged her back, and they were quiet for a few moments, then she pulled back and wiped the tears from her cheeks, giving Amanda a shaky smile.

"This is truly insane!" She smiled. "But I won't stand in your way. You have my blessing, Amanda. Not that you need it. Matthew has proven himself to be a mature young man, and I see how he's trying."

"Thank you, Mom," she whispered, hugging her again. "That means so much to me."

"How will we ever get through this?" her mother asked softly. Amanda squeezed her eyes closed.

"One day at a time, Mom, one day at a time."

CHAPTER 34

Amanda pulled open the car door.

"Amanda, wait!" Matthew called, from the front door. "You forgot your book!"

Amanda shook her head and walked back up the walkway.

"I don't know what is wrong with me this morning," she smiled. He stood in the doorway, holding her book and a travel mug in the other hand. Her eyes lit with surprise as he handed both to her. "Coffee! You are wonderful, my husband! I love you." She kissed him tenderly. "Thank you."

"You're welcome." He smiled. "Have a great day at school."

"Of course I will." She smiled, turning to walk away. "Oh, will you be working late?"

"Not too late," he said. "I *do* have half a wedding to pay for," he teased. "My wife deserves the best."

She laughed. "I already have the best!" she called over her shoulder. "I'll see you tonight." Then she got in her car, waving to Matthew as she drove away.

Amanda turned onto the main highway. She smiled as she sipped her coffee; looking at the clock, she realized she was running a little late for class. It was May, and the semester would be ending soon, much to her dismay.

Soon after Christmas, she decided that she did want to go back to school. Her father suggested taking a couple of courses at the local community college. So she enrolled for the second semester. She had been terrified to go the first day. Having so much anxiety, she had been very tempted to not go. But Matthew, who had returned to work at Mr. Simons's woodshop, switched to the afternoon shift and went to the college with her. Holding her hand, he walked her to class. When the class ended, he was waiting outside the door. She struggled with fear every day, though she tried not to mention it to Matthew because she didn't want to hurt him. But she had a habit of looking over her shoulder, for fear of being taken. Panic attacks had become more frequent, but it was something she needed to accept, knowing only time would take that fear from her.

A nice distraction was the wedding planning. Amanda and Matthew had both settled on an October wedding. Every Sunday they would go to Amanda's parents for dinner to talk about wedding arrangements. Her mother was completely absorbed in the event, and Amanda didn't mind. There was so much to do and organize that she was thankful for her mother's help, though decisions were not made unless Matthew and Amanda agreed. Matthew had insisted that he was going to pay for at least half of the wedding's expenses. Even when Diane threw large monetary figures at him, assuring him that they could pay for the wedding, he had remained stubborn. Diane had to relent but respected him all the more. There were times when Amanda was completely exasperated with all the details, and she just wanted to call the whole thing off. *They were already married anyway,* she thought. But Matthew would tease her and remind her how much she did want this wedding.

Matthew was doing well at the woodshop. By March, Matthew had moved from an assistant to Mr. Simons's manager. He gave Matthew the authority to approve or disapprove finished pieces of furniture. Before, he was able to help Mr. Simons's with high-paying customers. Now he was handling the most influential people on his own, allowing his commissions to go higher. With his new position, he was paid very well.

Life was sometimes hard for both of them. They both had good days and bad days. Matthew still remained involved with the investigation of the village. There were several weekends when he had to go to North Carolina, to the FBI encampment. Each time, he would come home a little more depressed. He still had no knowledge of his mother and had incredible guilt for believing he was a turncoat. Sometimes it would take days for him to cheer up, but he always did. The worst news of all was that his pastor had disappeared. The FBI had been monitoring the village for months with video and photographs. His pastor was on the earlier tapings, but recently, in the last two months, there wasn't any recording of his presence. The FBI felt that he was going to strike again. Matthew knew that his pastor never did any of the abductions himself, but he couldn't shake the uneasiness that his absence stirred within him.

With this knowledge, things could be tense in their small cottage. The emotional strain could be felt, but their love for one another only grew as the days went on. Matthew's sadness and Amanda's fears melted away when they came together as one, where their only focus was on each other.

Amanda stifled a yawn. She had stayed up late the night before, studying for an exam. She barely made it out of bed; she was so tired. Within a few moments, she was turning into the college parking lot. She shut off the ignition and reached for her backpack on the passenger seat. As she lifted it up, she noticed a cassette tape underneath. Reaching over, she picked it up with her free hand, turning it over, trying to identify it. Not recognizing it, she shrugged her shoulders and threw it back on the seat. Gathering her things, she hurried to class.

An hour later, she was back in the car. She turned the ignition and noticed the tape again. Opening the clear casing, she stuck the tape in the tape player. Throwing the car in reverse, she began to back up.

"Hi, Rachel," An eerily familiar voice played. Amanda slammed on the brakes in the middle of the parking lot. Ice-cold fear slid down her spine; her chest tightened, restricting her breathing. "Did you think that I would forget about you so easily?" the tape continued. "I know where you are, and I'm watching you so get ready to come home." The tape ended with his sinister laughing. Amanda slammed her fist against the tape player, pounding until the tape came out. Shaking and crying, she pulled the car over into an empty parking spot.

She needed to find Matthew! Digging in her backpack, she frantically searched for her cell phone. *Where is the damn thing!* Her hands shook furiously; she struggled to keep her thoughts straight. *Matthew, Matthew, Matthew . . .*

Terrified, she looked around her, hit the button on her door, locking herself in. *Where's my phone?* She threw her backpack onto the seat, backing the car up, her tires screeching as she pulled away. *She'll just drive to the shop. Yes, that's what she'll do*, she said to herself.

"Where do you think you're going?" the disgustingly smooth voice asked. Amanda screamed when she saw the pastor's face in the rearview mirror. He was in the backseat. As she struggled to keep the car controlled, she realized that he was holding a large hunting knife to her throat.

"Now calm yourself, honey. You don't want to cause an accident do you?" he asked, a sickly smile on his face. A sob escaped Amanda's lips as she tried to drive straight. Laughing at her, he said, "Yes, you should be crying because you've been a very naughty girl, haven't you? You know that you have, don't you?" He pressed the knife against her throat; a stinging sensation burned across her throat. "And naughty girls must be punished. Now I want you to head out of the city. Turn right here . . . there you go. Did you actually think that you and Matthew would live happily ever after, without me?" He smiled again. "You silly, silly girl. But don't worry. After I'm done with you, I'll be taking care of him."

"Why . . . why are you doing this?" she cried out. His smile disappeared, and an angry scowl crossed his face.

"Because no one . . . no one betrays me!" he hissed in her ear.

They drove a little over ten miles out of the city before he had her turn off the highway to a one-lane road. Once they left the highway, he took the knife away from her neck. Amanda glanced nervously in the rearview mirror; a thin red line stained her neck. *Oh, Matthew,* she cried silently. It wasn't long before the road came to an end, and there loomed an old abandoned cement factory. The large building was gray and foreboding. Biting her lower lip, she fought the hysteria that fought to be unleashed.

"Drive over there!" he ordered, pointing to the left side of the building. She hesitated with the accelerator as they hit large bumps in the parking lot. "Move, girl!" he yelled. They rounded the corner of the building, where there sat a red van. Amanda cringed inwardly. *Can this really be happening? Why is this happening?* "Stop here!"

He got out of the car and swung open the driver's side door. She involuntarily flinched from him as he reached for her. Growling at her, he wrapped his hand around her arm, squeezing it until she cried out in pain.

"Ow!" she cried, tears streaming down her face. "Please . . . please let me go!" she pleaded. "Haven't you done enough?"

He grabbed a fistful of hair and yanked her around to the back of the red van as she screamed out in pain. "You shut your mouth!" He yanked open the back door of the red van, and Amanda saw a makeshift bed with dark grey wool blankets covering it. Toward the front of the van was a red and white cooler, and a pile of white nylon rope. Fear and panic swelled up into her throat as he began to shove her in, and she began to fight for her life. Throwing her heel back, she kicked his shin, taking him by surprise; he grunted in pain. But he didn't let go, even as she twisted and scratched at him. He forcefully picked her up and threw her in the van. She landed on her hip and elbow, with a painful thud on the metal floor. "You little witch!" he growled as he jumped in after her. She whimpered and tried to scramble away, but he grabbed her leg with his vicelike grip. Reaching over, he picked up the rope with his free hand. It took him only moments to tie her wrists together, but her feet were still free. He lifted her body up and dropped her on the bed, and, forcing her arms over her head, he hooked the rope around her wrists over a peg, pinning her arms upward. Though confined, she kicked and fought him as he struggled to tie her feet. Frustrated, he reached out and smacked her face with the back of his hand. Stunned, Amanda instantly felt the skin on her cheekbone split. Feeling the familiar sting, she knew it was the same spot he had split months ago. Her vision became slightly blurry and her body limp. She felt him tie her up and hook her feet on a similar peg at the bottom of the bed.

He moved up toward her face. They were both out of breath.

"You've always been a wildcat!" he declared. "But I will tame you!" His eyes slowly roamed down Amanda's body. Her chest heaved up and down as she struggled to catch her breath; her shirt had been pulled up slightly during their struggle, revealing part of her abdomen. Bitter bile burned in the back of her throat as she fought the disgust she felt as his eyes trailed down her. *Please, no, God, NO*, she screamed silently. His hand reached out and touched her stomach. "Mmm." Amanda bit her lip, squeezing her eyes closed. "Well well well." His tone made Amanda's eyes open. "It looks like Matthew's been very busy. Expecting again, Amanda?" he asked. He didn't miss the surprise in Amanda's eyes. "Oh, you didn't know? I keep forgetting how naive you are." He took his hand away and grabbed her chin roughly. "You're safe right now," he said, his nasty-smelling breath filling her nostrils, "but I will have a taste of you before long. Our time will come!" Pushing away from her, he hopped out of the van, slamming the doors closed behind him. Within minutes, she heard him get into the driver's seat.

As the vehicle began moving, Amanda cried softly. Amanda had thought she was pregnant again, but she hadn't been sure. To say that she was shocked that the pastor knew would have been an understatement! Her crying turned to heart-wrenching sobs as she realized that Matthew didn't know about the baby. He might never know.

CHAPTER 35

M atthew turned the sander off and set it down and removed his protective goggles. Looking around him, he watched the other employees work. They were all concentrating intently on their furniture pieces. He could have sworn someone had called his name. Shrugging his shoulders, he tried to shake the uneasiness that had settled over him. He reached for the sander again, and as he lifted his arm, his watch fell off his wrist and hit the floor with a clang. Matthew froze. Normally his watch falling off wouldn't have been a big deal. Except that he never wore this watch. It was the watch that Amanda had given him for a Christmas gift. This particular watch had a secure latch that had to have a large amount of pressure placed on it in order for it to unsnap. He hadn't even bumped his wrist and knew that nothing he did had made that watch fall off.

He bent down and picked it up. Something was wrong. He examined the watch, finding nothing broken. Something was wrong! He put his machinery down, threw down his goggles, and practically ran out of the building. Without giving any notice, he got in his car and swung it around, driving in the direction of the cottage. Praying, just praying that Amanda was there, cooking dinner, and that he was overreacting. Please, Lord, let me be overreacting!

The tires screeched as he slammed the brakes in the driveway. Her car wasn't here. Maybe she stopped at her parents' house, he tried to assure himself. Yes, and she probably left him a message. He looked at the clock on the dashboard. Five thirty. Right now she was probably having dinner with them. He'd forgotten that he told her he was working late, and that's where she was. He breathed a sigh of relief. While he was here, he would go in and check the messages. Shaking his head, a smile played on his lips on his way into the cottage. Amanda was going to get a good laugh out of this one.

He walked in and hit the button on the answering machine that sat in the hallway on a small table. As he listened, he walked to the refrigerator for a bottled water. There were two messages from caterers returning Amanda's call; as the last message began, he took a sip of his drink.

"Hello, Matthew." The smooth voice of Pastor resounded through the empty house. Matthew spit his water out of his mouth. "I just wanted to assure you that your wife is doing fine. She decided to take a ride with me and I'll take real good care of her." His laughter echoed over the machine. "Don't worry, I'll be coming back for you too. One at a time, you know." Click.

Fear flooded his soul as he picked up the phone and dialed.

"Police Department."

"Sergeant Stevens . . . hurry, man!" he demanded, his hand shaking as he held the receiver.

Amanda stirred, blinking her eyes until they focused on the ceiling of the van. Her arms ached from being held over her head. It was dark, and the van was still moving. Matthew would know she was gone, as well as her parents. *Her poor parents,* she thought bitterly, *to have to go through this again. Except this time,* she feared, *she didn't think she would see them again.* Tears burned her eyes as she turned her head toward the side of the van and tried to wish herself away from this dreadful nightmare. Eventually she dozed off again.

She hadn't been sleeping long, when she realized the van had stopped. Still sleepy, the back doors flew open, startling her.

"Rise and shine, Princess!" he growled. "Your castle awaits you!" He climbed in and untied her hands and feet. Her limbs were numb from lack of circulation and movement. Stepping back out of the van, he grabbed her ankle, dragging her until he could get a solid grip on her. Picking her up, he threw her over his shoulder and then began walking into the dark night.

Amanda blinked, trying to focus as her head hung upside down. The familiar scent of the night air, the sound of his footsteps on the blanket of pine needles, triggered recognition in Amanda's confused mind. *He brought her back,* she screamed inside. *The village . . . she was back . . . God . . . No!* Finding strength where she thought she had none, she began to kick and scream in his arms.

"No!" she screamed as she pounded on his back with her fists. He cursed as he stumbled, losing his balance, losing his grip, causing her to tumble to the ground. "Where do you think you're going?"

She was crying as she tried to stand but couldn't. Frustrated with her uncooperative body, she screamed at him.

"Leave me alone!" she sobbed. He stopped, threw his head back, and laughed. A cold and vicious sound. She struggled to crawl away as he walked over to her patiently, standing over her, smiling sadistically, his arms crossed against his chest, then he bent over and picked her up. It was then that she saw the shadow of the cabin over his shoulder and knew what awaited her. *It was all happening again! Why was she being punished,* she cried to herself. "Oh God, no . . . please . . ."

He dropped her down on the cold, damp floor then turned to walk out. As he closed the door, she started to scream.

"No!" she screamed. "Please . . . Pastor . . . please, no! Don't leave me here . . . please!" She scrambled to the door and kicked it with all that she had. But he was gone. She heard the van's engine roar to life and watched helplessly as he turned around and drove away. The only sound that could be heard in the dark night was her choking sobs. She fell against the wall and slid down against the wood. She was all alone . . . miles from the village . . . miles from anyone. She wiped her eyes with her arm. *She was going to die,* she thought, her crying subsiding. A strange peace began to cover her, knowing this was the last night she was going to live.

Struggling to stand, she leaned against the wood, peering out through a crack in the wall. The night was clear, and the stars were bright. She didn't know why this was happening. Why had this lot fallen on her again, she didn't know, but she knew her time had come. Her hand went involuntarily to her abdomen, realizing her baby wouldn't have a chance, this knowledge cutting into her like a knife.

Matthew. Oh, how she loved him. She tried to remember back to the night that he'd come to get her from this very cabin, over a year ago. She'd been so frightened. *Not unlike tonight,* she thought sadly. "Oh, Matthew," she said softly, "know that I love you." She repeated this over and over again as she found the familiar corner to curl up in. Hours dragged by, and she slipped unconscious to an exhausted sleep. When morning came, she was shaking with cold, her arms tightly wrapped around her. Tears would not fall anymore; her heart lay heavy in her chest. She waited and waited until her nerves were strung tight. Out of the silence of the trees, she began to hear voices and footsteps. Fear rose up in her; though she knew death was near, she was still afraid of her dreadful fate.

Someone pounded on the wooden door, terrifying Amanda.

"Anyone in there?" It was a male voice. "Amanda Ryan, are you in there?" The voice sounded unfamiliar. *Was it a trick?*

"Yes," she croaked, trying to use her voice. "Yes, it's me . . . please . . . it's me!" She scrambled to her feet and stood shaking in the corner. At once the forest came alive with commotion; many voices and movement filled the area. Within minutes, the door was removed from the cabin, and a man in jeans and a black padded vest with the letters FBI printed across it appeared in its place.

"Amanda?" the agent asked kindly, "are you all right?"

Hesitating, Amanda choked out, "Yes."

"You're safe now. We're here to take you home," he said. Unable to move, she began to cry. The agent walked over, scooping her up into his arms, carrying her out of the cabin, the bright sunlight assaulting her senses so she hid her face in the agent's shoulder. Once he was a decent distance from the cabin, he set her gently down on the roof of a car. "Are you sure you're not hurt?"

"No," she whispered. "I'm not."

"Amanda!" She heard her name called out and scanned the crowd of people, looking for him. "Amanda?" Then she saw the most beautiful sight in the whole world. Matthew was hurrying toward her, his face pale with concern. She slid from the car and threw herself into his arms. They clung together furiously, Amanda sobbing in his arms. "Oh, Amanda! I was so scared . . . I thought that I . . . I couldn't bear it if . . . oh God, I love you!"

"I love you," she cried, refusing to let go of him.

"You were never alone, Amanda," Matthew spoke quietly to her, aware of only her, shutting out all that was going on around them. "The FBI followed the van the whole way. They waited until he brought you here and they got him, Amanda. They arrested him! It's over. It's all over!" He pulled her back so he could see her battered face. "Oh, baby, I'm so sorry," he whispered, tears shining in his eyes.

"Matthew, please take me home," she pleaded softly. "I just want to go home." And that's exactly what they did.

CHAPTER 36

"May I have this dance?" Matthew asked, interrupting Amanda and Maxwell as they were leaving the dance floor. Amanda smiled lovingly at her husband.

"You're the only one that I would allow to take my daughter from me," Maxwell teased. Matthew laughed, wrapping his arms around her, and swung her around. Amanda giggled in delight. "Hey hey hey . . . take it easy there! That's my grandson you're swinging around in there!"

Matthew smiled sheepishly then placed his hand tenderly on Amanda's swollen belly. He looked up at her, then back at his father-in-law.

"Yes, sir." Then he took his wife's hand and led her out to the dance floor. He pulled her close and whispered in her ear, "I love you, Amanda Leslie Ryan! You and my sweet baby."

"I love you," she whispered back and laid her head on his shoulder. "Matthew?"

"Hmm?"

"Are you happy?" she asked shyly. He shifted to look in her face.

"Are you crazy?" he asked. "This is my second wedding with the only beautiful woman in the world. I couldn't be happier!"

She smiled and nodded, resting her head back on his shoulder.

After a few moments of swaying to the music, she said,

"I wish Katherine could have been with us," she said softly. The tensing in his shoulders was so slight that she would have missed it if she didn't know him so well.

"I do, too," he said quietly. Then after a few moments, he added, "But in a way she is. I think she's watching us from heaven, with my father." She looked up at him, her eyes shining.

During Amanda's rescue operation and the arrest of the pastor, the village had been closed down. Villagers had scrambled, shocked and panicked, some surrendering peacefully, others escaped on foot, knowing the mountains better than the FBI agents. The cabins and the grounds had been searched thoroughly, all evidence that could be collected was. It was during this search that Katherine Ryan's whereabouts were finally discovered.

It was on a beautiful sunny afternoon; Matthew and Amanda's life had finally returned to a somewhat normal pace. They were in the garden, when Sergeant Stevens's car pulled into their driveway. Amanda was the first to notice him walking toward them, his face grim. She stood up, knowing something was wrong, and brushed the dirt off her jeans. Turning, she called to Matthew. He squinted at her, then beyond to the sergeant. Amanda watched him tense, then slowly let the hoe he was working with fall to the ground. When the sergeant was close enough, he nodded his greeting.

"Amanda, Matthew," he said. Amanda gave him a small smile.

"How are you, Sergeant?" she asked, her voice quiet. The somber look he gave her sent chills down her back.

"Sergeant," Matthew greeted him, holding his hand out. Sergeant Stevens shook his hand, nodding again. Then he shoved his hands into his pant pockets.

"I'm sure you both know that this isn't a social call," he began, then looked toward the house. "Maybe we should go inside."

"Sergeant, what is it?" Matthew asked. "Something's wrong, isn't it? Just tell us." The sergeant nodded, pressing his lips together.

"Right," he said. "I received a call today from the FBI. During their search, they found the village graveyard." This was what he hated most about his job. Bad news. Matthew crossed his arms in front of him, tensing. Amanda came to his side, and they both looked up at him. Letting out a deep breath, he continued, "I'm afraid we found your mother, Matthew. I'm really sorry." Amanda gasped.

Matthew's body went rigid, and his eyes moved beyond the sergeant. "I see."

"She was apparently buried next to your father," he continued. "According to the villagers that have been cooperating, her death occurred soon after the two of you left." Matthew nodded, his jaw clenched, and closed his eyes briefly. Rubbing his face, he looked down to see Amanda watching him, tears trickling down her cheeks.

"Any word on Jimmy and Sarah?" Matthew asked, his voice strained. The sergeant shook his head.

"Unfortunately, no," he said. "They were tracked ten miles into the mountain, but after that the search was called off." Matthew nodded again.

"Thanks for coming by, Sergeant," Matthew said and then walked toward the house as they watched. Amanda wiped her tears away.

"I'm sorry, Amanda," he said, turning back to her.

Nodding, she said, "Thank you for coming by yourself. I'm going to go see if he's all right. Excuse me." Amanda jogged up to the house, where she found him in their room, sitting on the bed, his back to her. His elbows rested on his knees, and he had his face covered. "Matthew," she said his name softly. When he didn't respond, she walked slowly to his side. Sitting down next to him, she placed her hand gently on his back. It was only then that he cried. She held on to him that afternoon, crying for Katherine and for Matthew. It was a devastating blow for both of them.

Matthew took Amanda's face in his hands.

"Hey, no sadness," he said softly. "Not today. This is supposed to be a happy day!"

She smiled affectionately at him. "Matthew," she said, "I wanted to thank you."

He looked down at her, confused. "For what?" he asked.

"For choosing me," she said. He searched her eyes; pain and love were reflected in their depths.

"Amanda—," he began. She leaned up and kissed him gently on the lips.

"No." She smiled. "We were destined to be together, Matthew."

He leaned down and kissed her ever so softly. "I love you, Amanda," he whispered again.

"I love you, Matthew." Amanda smiled and laid her head back on his shoulder.

She was truly happy.

CPSIA information can be obtained
at www.ICGtesting.com
Printed in the USA
FFOW02n1511110917
39834FF